JENNIFER SNOW

A Sweet
Alaskan
Fall

HQN

ISBN-13: 978-1-335-08130-8
A Sweet Alaskan Fall
Copyright © 2020 by Jennifer Snow

A Wild River Retreat
First published in July 2020.
This edition published in September 2020.
Copyright © 2020 by Jennifer Snow

Recycling programs for this product may not exist in your area.

This edition published by arrangement with Harlequin Books S.A.

For questions and comments about the quality of this book, please contact us at CustomerService@Harlequin.com.

HQN
22 Adelaide St. West, 40th Floor
Toronto, Ontario M5H 4E3, Canada
www.Harlequin.com

Printed in U.S.A.

CONTENTS

To all the Adrenaline Junkees
who'd rather soar through the air than keep their
feet safely on the ground—I see you, I envy you,
I am definitely *not* you. :)

A Sweet
Alaskan
Fall

PROLOGUE

10 years earlier...

SHE'D DONE SOMETHING TERRIBLE.

Fear wrapped around her heart the minute Montana Banks opened her eyes and only tightened its grip as she scanned the familiar surroundings of her bedroom. How'd she get here? She had no idea. Hours of her life had disappeared.

She shut her eyes tight, clenching her fists at her sides. *Remember... Come on, remember!*

The last memory that flashed in her mind was driving into the parking lot of the grocery store. A familiar song played on the radio. She felt good. Happy. The sun had been shining, and the mountain air blowing in through the open windows was warm and mild. She parked the car and glanced in the rearview mirror...

"Kaia!" She sat up straight in bed. "Kaia!" She looked around the room but she was alone. Where was the baby? Where had she left her little girl?

Footsteps sounded down the hall and drew closer, then the bedroom door opened and Tank entered. Montana jumped out of bed, dizziness and nausea hitting her like an ocean wave. She swayed off-balance, the room swimming around her, the floor wavy beneath her feet.

The feel of Tank's arms around her as her legs gave out

from beneath her didn't provide the comfort and security she was desperate for. "Kaia… I left Kaia…"

"Hey. Relax," he said, soothingly, but there was fear and pain and unease in his voice.

It terrified her. Struggling to focus, to rebalance herself, she gripped his arms and stared up at him. "I left her in the car. In the parking lot." How long? Outside it was now dark. The clock numbers blurred. What day was it? Where was Kaia?

Tank held her close, but his sigh was deep, resolute. "I know. She's okay. We found her."

Before it was too late. Before something terrible had happened to her baby girl. Her precious baby girl.

A sob escaped her, and her tears quickly left a large pool on Tank's shirt. She'd done the unforgivable. She could have lost Kaia. This wasn't the first time her injury had caused her to black out. To not remember. She wasn't getting better since her fall out of the sky, she was getting worse. She couldn't keep pretending to be okay. Or that she wasn't a danger to her daughter.

"I'm not okay," she whispered.

"I know." Tank sighed, holding her tight.

And they both knew what that meant.

CHAPTER ONE

Present day...

"HELLO, I AM Montana Banks. And I am addicted to BASE jumping."

Obviously not what they'd expected her to say. Eighteen pairs of eyes stared at her with varying degrees of judgment.

Safe space, my ass.

"Um...okay. Well, welcome, Montana," Jane, the director of the addiction's support group, said in the awkward silence. "I'm not entirely sure you're in the right place." She gestured to the manual on her lap as though searching for the rules. Or a reason to ask Montana to leave.

"This is a group for people addicted to things they shouldn't do, right?" Montana asked.

Jane glanced around the room. "Not things we *shouldn't* do. More like things we are trying not to do, things that negatively impact our lives or the people around us."

"Well, I'm in the right place, then," Montana said. Whether she'd come back next week was still up for debate. It had taken three months of living in Wild River, Alaska, for her to get enough courage to walk into the addictions support group, and this reception was precisely why. No one was going to take her challenges seriously. Not when her issue seemed a lot less serious than everyone else's.

Unfortunately, there was no group to support extreme

athletes with brain injuries that prevented them from fulfilling their life passion.

As different as the demons of everyone in this room were, they all shared the same storm cloud over their heads every day. One no one else saw. One they constantly battled against to find a ray of sunshine. Montana wasn't so different.

For her, that ray of light was Kaia, her ten-year-old daughter. Staring at the picture of the two of them on her cell phone, Montana released a deep breath. Moving to Wild River had been the right thing to do. She'd let her injury keep her from her daughter long enough. No matter how hard living in the small ski-resort town got, she would not abandon the little girl again.

But maybe the group wasn't the right place for her. She gathered her things. "It's okay. I'll leave."

"No, please stay," Jane said, her warm, welcoming nature returning. "Everyone, meet Montana."

"Hi, Montana!" the group said in unison.

"Why don't you tell us about yourself?" Jane said. She checked her watch.

Everyone was given the floor for ten minutes and pressure to sum up thirty-four years of life made Montana's heart race. Where to start? With the BASE-jumping injury ten years ago that derailed her future? Or further back to the incident that rocked her existence?

"I'm new to Wild River," she said. "I have a daughter here, and I am trying to reintegrate back into her life."

Nods. They all understood that. Alienation from family members and the struggle to find a way home again was a common thread in the group.

"I've started a new career with an amazing business partner, and I've made a lot of new friends here in town." Settling in had been disturbingly simple. Her new apartment was cheap and close to everything in town, and her landlord had no problem with her not signing their usual one-year lease, instead allowing her to pay month by month. Her new job at SnowTrek Tours launching a new legalized BASE-jumping location in Wild River had gone a lot smoother than she ever could have predicted, thanks to the local mayor who was an extreme junkie himself. She'd made friends—including Cassie, her ex-boyfriend's new girlfriend and the owner of SnowTrek Tours. And she was coparenting like a superstar with Kaia's father, Tank. Life was…simple. And easy.

Unfortunately *simple* and *easy* weren't enough for her.

"But every morning when I wake up, the first thing on my mind is jumping off a cliff." Wide eyes made her add quickly "With a parachute." A wingsuit actually, but she knew they didn't care about the details. "And the persistent temptation doesn't go away. It used to be a big part of my life. It was everything, actually. An adrenaline rush like no other, it was highly addictive." She'd started skydiving at age thirteen with her grandmother, then BASE jumping at eighteen when she was barely old enough to sign a waiver. She'd traveled all over the world with other extreme athletes and had soared over the most breathtaking scenery. She was among the top jumpers in the world and had even done a short stint in jail for an illegal jump off a city building…until the accident changed everything.

She cleared her throat and continued. "But I know it's not the right path for me anymore." Her unpredictable brain with its rare form of transient global amnesia and impaired judgment couldn't be relied on for a safe jump anymore. "What's that saying? *Those who can't, teach*? Well, that's where I am."

With her BASE-jumping fundamentals course booked solid all month long at the cost of $3000 a week, SnowTrek

Tours no longer had to worry about the competition, North Mountain Sports Company, opening their big new chain store and claiming some of SnowTrek's usual adventure-tour clients. Cassie's business was thriving in the larger store's shadow, and Montana was happy that she'd been able to help Tank's girlfriend and the woman who'd been her daughter's primary role model in Montana's absence all these years. But she couldn't deny the ache in her chest whenever she stood at the top of Snowcrest Peak, staring down into the breathtaking valley, knowing she'd never be able to soar over it again. It was too much of a risk when she wasn't sure what triggered her random bouts of amnesia, and if one were to happen midjump, it could be devastatingly dangerous.

"Thank you for sharing that," Jane said. "So, what do you do to help get you past the tougher days? The challenging times when you're tempted to give in?"

I see my dead sister, and she talks sense into me.

"I'm still figuring that part out," Montana said, taking a seat quickly before she could verbalize the thought and have them think she was even crazier than they did already.

Half an hour later, the meeting wrapped up, and she collected her things to head back to the office. The next day was the first day of her BASE-training program. The four-day course would teach wannabe jumpers the fundamentals, while keeping them safely on the ground. It was the best place to start with the new venture. Fall was only two months away, and winter would shut them down until spring, so Montana would have at least a year before the advanced courses started and she'd have to actually watch other people jump. Cassie thought her idea to use their first few months in operation to introduce athletes to jumping, hooking them early for their first jump next year, was a brilliant way to build their business. Montana accepted the compliment and didn't reveal that she just wasn't yet ready to see other people doing what she loved.

She tied her hair into a ponytail, laced her running shoes tighter and set off at a fast pace through town toward Main Street.

Breathe in. Breathe out. Exercise was supposed to help with the pent-up energy she had inside, but five miles a day and an hour of weight training barely took the edge off. The mountain air and the breathtaking view of the wilderness just made the itch stronger. Her parents had thought moving back to Denver was the best thing for her. They hadn't been supportive of her decision to come to Alaska, hesitant to believe she was well enough to live completely on her own, a million miles away from them. And some days, she wanted to agree with them, but after reconnecting with Kaia, she couldn't leave her. Skype chats and phone calls and letters may have worked in the past, but now that she was there, actually spending time with her daughter, she didn't want to lose that closeness they were forming.

Kaia was almost eleven now. She was growing so fast. Montana had spent years trying to get well enough to be in her life without putting her safety at risk. She wouldn't live another day without knowing Kaia and being there for her in whatever capacity she needed.

Even if it meant struggling every day to face her own limitations and eventually learn to accept them.

Ten minutes later she opened the door to SnowTrek Tours.

"No, I'm sorry, that course is full until May of next year," Cassie said, the landline phone pinned between her shoulder and ear, while she typed on her laptop. Several other lines were lighting up, and she shot Montana a desperate look through a veil of short blond hair falling across her face.

Dropping her things onto her desk, Montana picked up the phone and hit one of the lines. "Thank you for calling SnowTrek Tours. Can you hold for just a moment?" Twice more she repeated the action, then returned to the first caller. "Hello, sorry about the wait. How can I help you?"

"Hey, I'm calling about the Fundamentals of BASE course." Who wasn't? She'd been right about her prediction that legalizing the sport in Wild River would have SnowTrek Tours turning adventure-seekers away. But even *she* hadn't known how much things would have exploded for the small, local company.

The site wasn't even officially open yet, and they were booked solid for tour groups with professional, experienced jumpers in the spring, her advanced courses were already full and the Fundamentals course was even more popular.

Who knew there were so many adrenaline junkies in the world?

She was happy that things were going well, but being surrounded 24/7 by talk of the sport she loved and couldn't do was making her crazy. But at least she was involved somehow. It was the next best thing, and she couldn't complain. For nine years in Denver, she'd gone completely insane, holed up in the city, being treated like a child by her overprotective parents.

Baby steps.

She was living on her own and hadn't burned the place down yet.

She answered the third call. "SnowTrek Tours. How may I help you?"

"Well, you could start by going to dinner with me Saturday night."

Montana felt her face flush at the sound of Lance's voice. In the last three months, she'd been out with the local snowboarding god three times—two dinners and a coffee date.

But he'd been away for three weeks and had obviously been so busy he'd forgotten to text. She wasn't that woman—the one who couldn't take a hint. Clearly, he just wasn't that into her. Yet, here he was calling again. "I'm sorry, who is this?"

He laughed. "I deserve that."

"Yes, you do," she said.

"I'm sorry I was MIA. New York was insane. Back-to-back meetings and promotional events…"

Dates with countless groupies, casual hookups with no strings attached… She knew the lifestyle. She'd once been a professional athlete, traveling the world, meeting new people, getting involved temporarily, then moving on. Hell, Kaia had been the result of that lifestyle. For her, at least. Tank, on the other hand, had been in love with her back then, but Montana hadn't had a real connection with anyone, not allowing anyone in her life to get too close in a very long time. Not even her daughter's father.

Maybe more than just her brain was broken.

"And I left my cell in a taxi," Lance was saying. "That's why I'm calling you at work."

Lost cell phone. Not exactly the most creative excuse. "It's fine. I get it." It *was* fine. She *did* get it. They'd had three dates. They weren't exclusively seeing one another.

"So, is that a yes to dinner?"

Montana hesitated. She liked Lance, and she wasn't ready for a relationship, which made him the perfect man for her right now. But on the other hand, she wasn't interested in a fling either—not exactly the right example she wanted to set for her daughter. Therefore, that left a semi-casual thing that could potentially turn into more and leave her with a broken heart. The guy was a major player. He'd ghosted her for three weeks and would no doubt do it again.

But what was her Saturday-night alternative?

Hanging out at The Drunk Tank, the local bar she'd previously owned with her ex, with two couples very much in love? Or Netflix and take-out, while trying to drown out the sound of her next-door neighbor's attempt at learning to play guitar?

"Seven o'clock?" she said.

"I'll pick you up."

Montana disconnected the call and stared at it.

"Going out with Lance again?" Cassie asked, ending her own call.

"Yeah." She paused. "I know, I'm a sucker, you can say it." Hadn't she gone on about the fact that if the guy said he was going to call and didn't call, it was a clear sign to move on? Hadn't she claimed she was done with Lance? Several times now.

Cassie laughed. "I'm the last person on the planet to lecture you on giving second and third and fourth chances."

Cassie did get it. For years, she'd played the same cat-and-mouse game with Montana's ex, Tank. The two had finally gotten together, and Montana liked to think she'd played a part in Tank's eye-opening. Cassie was too amazing to find fault with. She was a successful career woman, the partner Tank needed in his life and a wonderful role model to Montana's daughter. Whoever said women couldn't build one another up and celebrate successes was wrong. The two of them were proof of it.

"He's just exciting, and I desperately crave excitement." Lance's adventurous, no-fear attitude was a reflection of her own, but she worried part of his waning interest in her was because she was no longer the extreme athlete she used to be.

Hell, she was a disappointment to herself.

"Just be careful fraternizing with the enemy," Cassie said, pulling up the window blinds and nodding at the chain store across the street.

Lance was the new poster boy for North Mountain Sports Company. Images of him and his new line of snowboards decorated their exterior windows, therefore Montana was careful what she revealed to him regarding the BASE-jump site and SnowTrek Tours' future business plans.

She bit her lip. "You don't think that's why he's dating me, do you?"

Cassie shook her head. "Oh, my God—no! That's not what I meant. I was totally kidding. He's dating you because he'd be an idiot not to. Look at you! I'd hate you if you weren't also the best business partner and co-mom I could ask for."

Montana nodded. They *were* amazing business partners and co-moms to Kaia. They were enough alike to agree on most things, and Montana was desperate to believe that they were different enough to both add value to the little girl's life.

Unfortunately, some days she questioned whether that was true or if Cassie could handle both just fine without her.

EDDIE SPRINTED FROM his truck to the entrance of the Alaska Department of Public Safety building in Anchorage. He yanked the door open and hurried down the hall toward the auditorium, his wet shoes squeaking against the tiled floor as he scanned the packed room for his family. All the chairs were occupied, and it was standing room only. He spotted them in the front row on the left and apologized his way through the crowd.

"You're late," his sister Katherine hissed as he took the saved seat next to her.

"Just got off shift an hour ago and had to turn on the lights to make it here in time." He hadn't even had time to shower and change out of his uniform for the ceremony honoring his mother's career on the force, but he'd made it.

"You still on rotating shifts?"

"Yes."

"Bored stupid yet?"

"As a matter of fact, things have been busy." Not that he was happy about the recent string of break-ins in town, but during his six months as a state trooper he'd only dealt with domestic-dispute calls, bar fights and busting teenagers for graffiti. He wasn't proving himself or moving up the ranks quickly within the force with those kinds of calls.

"Any leads on the break-ins?" Katherine asked as she dialed their middle sibling's cell.

"Not yet. It's odd. Nothing stolen. Just enough broken glass to be an annoyance to the store owner. Captain thinks it's vandals."

"There's more to it," Katherine said.

"Well, if you say so. I guess the head of the department must be mistaken." His oldest sister was a homicide detective. She'd seen the worst and was trained to think the worst. It made her good at her job. Terrible at relationships. She once pepper-sprayed a blind date who was simply reaching into his pocket for his inhaler when her intense questioning spurred an asthma attack. Unfortunately, her gut was almost always right. About pretty much everything.

She tucked her shoulder-length blond hair behind her ear as the call continued to ring. "Look, I'm telling you. Keep looking into it."

Leslie's face appeared on Katherine's phone screen, a view of sand, surf and palm trees in the background behind her, ending their conversation. His sisters could pass for twins, they were so much alike. On the outside, at least— same blond hair, same blue eyes, same tall, sturdy build. In comparison, as the baby of the family, Eddie looked like he was adopted, with his dark hair and brown eyes. As a kid, he often wondered, but as he got older, he recognized the features he shared with his father.

"Hey. Has the ceremony started?" Leslie asked.

"Not yet," Katherine said.

"Where are you?" Eddie leaned closer. Looked like the beach on Santa Monica Pier, but all of those West Coast beaches looked alike to him.

"Can't say." Leslie was jogging. He could tell by the way her ponytail swung back and forth and her breathing was controlled and steady. His sister was a firm believer in not wasting a second of time. If she had to be on a FaceTime call to see their mother presented with a State Trooper Hall of Fame award, she'd work out while doing it.

"Who are you protecting these days?" he asked.

"Can't say."

Eddie grinned. "Can we guess?"

"Nope."

They did anyway. It was game they loved to play with her. Once a state trooper herself, Leslie had quickly opted for the more lucrative profession of private-security detail to the rich and famous in California, refusing to admit that the sudden death of her fiancé had anything to do with the drastic life change.

"Is it Cameron Diaz?" Katherine said. She always started with her favorite actress.

"No," Leslie said.

"Dwayne Johnson?" Eddie asked. He always started with the most unlikely.

"Why the hell would The Rock need private-security detail on a beach?" Leslie's annoyance at this game never grew old.

"So, you're on a beach," he said.

"It's California, Eddie. It's one big beach. And I'm off duty."

"Dating anyone?" Katherine asked.

"Next question." Leslie was as tight-lipped about her personal life as she was about her job. She'd moved to LA two years ago and had only been home once. She took her NDAs seriously and revealed nothing to them. It was fun irritating her with questions, though.

"Are you coming home for Gran's nuptials?" Katherine asked.

Leslie rolled her eyes. "It's her third marriage. Why is she having a big wedding?"

"She likes the attention," Katherine said.

"When you get to be my age, you need to pull these kinds of stunts to get your grandkids to come back from their famous clients to visit once in a while," their grandmother suddenly chimed in. She had a unique ability to pop up when you least expected her, whenever she knew you were talking about her. In his rush to his seat, Eddie hadn't noticed her and her fiancé, Melvin, seated on the other side of Katherine. He smiled warmly at them now as his grandmother leaned over to join in on the call.

"Hi, Gran," Leslie said, lighting up at the sight of the older woman. "You know I'll be at your wedding...again." Their grandmother had practically raised Leslie, after their mother and her youngest daughter had had a falling out when she was fifteen and Leslie had gone to live with the matriarch of the family.

They'd all thought it was teenage rebellion, but the stubborn streak in the Sanders family ran deep. Neither woman would apologize, so Leslie stayed with Gran, and Mom pretended she was okay with it. It had been tough not having their sister at home, but the peace in the household with Leslie gone had been appreciated.

Having Leslie on FaceTime for this important milestone in their mother's life but live in person for Gran's wedding was just another way the two women continued to hurt one another, but…at least their sister had agreed to appear on the cell-phone screen.

"I didn't book a photographer for the wedding," Gran said. "Was hoping you'd do it."

Leslie looked uncomfortable as she shook her head. "I'm not really doing much photography these days."

"You'll think about it?" Ultimately, his grandmother would get her way as usual, and she knew it. No one liked saying no to her.

As predicted, Leslie nodded. "I'll think about it, but no promises."

"You look tired. You sleeping?" Gran asked her.

"Yes, I am."

"*With* someone?" their grandmother asked.

Eddie hid his grin. There was no question where their joy of razzing one another came from.

"Is the ceremony starting yet?" Leslie asked, checking her Fitbit on her wrist.

No one would tell their mom that Leslie had scheduled her run around the event.

"Any minute now," Katherine said. Sensing Leslie had had enough family bonding and was ready to disconnect, she turned the phone toward the stage.

"Have you gone for your tux fitting yet?" Gran asked him.

"I'll do it next week, I promise." He'd completely forgotten and, well, part of him still wasn't convinced his grandmother was going to go through with it. She was eighty years old and divorced twice already. She really did pull stunts like this for attention from all of them.

"Young man, if you show up to my wedding to give me away in your dirty uniform, smelling like the night before's heat…"

"Oh, don't worry, Gran," Katherine interrupted. "Eddie's not getting any heat. He's still patrolling the ski resort."

He sighed. Being around female members of his family always made him desperate for an escape. Sure, it had taken him several attempts to pass the police entrance exam, his dyslexia making the written component challenging. And sure, out of the three siblings, he had the least dangerous job. But the lack of respect from his very female-dominated family drove him crazy.

"I'll get the tux, and if you're lucky, I'll even get a haircut," he told his grandmother with a wink. He wasn't sure what the rush was. The wedding wasn't until November. Plenty of time.

"Do you have a date yet?" Gran asked. "I need to confirm final numbers with the event organizers."

As if one extra person either way would make a huge difference. She was just trying to get his relationship status out of him. Unlike Leslie, if Eddie was seeing someone, he'd be shouting it from the rooftops, not trying to keep it a secret. His dating life was also something he struggled with. Growing up and living in the small town of Wild River, everyone knew everyone. He'd dated just about every single woman in town. Once.

It was hard to find a spark with women he'd known his entire life, and he wasn't like some of the other guys who could hook up with tourists for a few nights. Therefore, his Facebook status would say *Relationship nonexistent*, if that option existed. He'd give anything just to be able to change it to *It's complicated*. "Nope. No date yet," he said.

"Shh. Ceremony is starting," Katherine said.

They all turned their attention to the front of the auditorium, and a silence fell over the room as the ceremony began.

His mother sat on the stage dressed in her uniform, her

medals and badges of honor proudly displayed as the head of the State Troopers of Alaska talked about her many accomplishments over her forty-year career.

His mother has been the second female state trooper in Alaska. Graduating from the academy top of her class in the sixties, she was a trailblazer for all women in the force. His sisters owed their own careers to the work their mother had put in.

Growing up without their father, who'd died of cancer when Eddie was ten, meant his mother held double duty as both parents. She worked long hours on the job, but she was always there for her kids. She may have missed birthdays or Christmases or softball games, but she was there in the ways that really mattered, raising her kids to be respectful, considerate people who gave back to their community. Her pride in her family had made them *want* to be people she could be proud of.

On the cell-phone screen, even Leslie's face beamed with unconcealed admiration as their mother was inducted in the State Trooper Hall of Fame and handed her plaque commemorating the event.

His mother was a true hero. One who had no trouble giving him shit.

"Why are you still in uniform?" she asked first thing, when she joined them after the ceremony.

"Hey, look! Leslie's on FaceTime!" Deflect. It was a defense mechanism they all employed with their tough-as-nails, take-no-shit mother. If she was focused on someone else, she left you alone.

And it worked.

She took the phone from Katherine, but Eddie couldn't listen to the strained conversation, quickly announcing his exit. "I'm out. Got to get back to Wild River before my evening shift."

Katherine checked her watch. "That's hours from now." She glared at him.

He shrugged. "Traffic might be bad."

His grandmother looked disappointed. "I thought you were joining us for lunch." She looped her arm through Mel's, and the older man's expression screamed *Don't leave me alone with the three of them*. But Eddie could only handle the women in his family in small doses.

"Next time." Eddie hugged his grandmother tight and shook Mel's hand. Then he hugged his mother quickly while she was still distracted by Leslie.

Unfortunately, she wasn't going to let him sneak off.

"Hey, hold up," she said, and Eddie sighed, slowing his pace.

His mother said goodbye to her youngest daughter and fell into step with him as he walked across the parking lot. "Have you heard anything about your transfer yet?"

"How do you know about that?"

His mother pointed to the badges on her uniform. "I'm retired, Eddie, not dead. I still have my finger on the pulse of things around here."

As long as she wasn't using that pulse/finger thing to pull strings to secure his transfer. He'd applied to the Alaska Bureau of Alcohol and Drug Enforcement division without telling his mother and sisters precisely for that reason... and to avoid their disappointed expressions if he didn't get the promotion.

But it had been weeks since his last written exam and physical, and still no word. "Not yet."

"When did you first apply?"

"Two months ago."

"It's taking longer than usual, but give it another few days. Keep me posted." She touched his shoulder.

A simple, casual gesture to most people. In his family,

that gesture meant *Don't get your hopes up*. He wasn't even sure if his mother realized it was her tell when she didn't have faith in them for something. She'd done it since he was a kid. When he wanted to play football but didn't make the team. When he wanted to ask Carla Spicer to the winter formal and she said no. When he'd failed his written driver's-permit test twice. Each time, his mother's shoulder touch had predicted the outcome. Or was it the negative energy he associated with it that became a self-fulfilling prophecy?

He hoped this time its predictive powers and ability to upset his karmic balance were wrong.

"Will do. Enjoy lunch." He hugged her again. "Congrats, Mom. I'm proud of you." He waved to the rest of his family as he headed toward his car.

Someday, he hoped his mother would finally have a reason to say those words to him.

CHAPTER TWO

SHE HAD FANTASIES about destroying that guitar.

Groaning, Montana rolled to her side and glanced at the time on her alarm clock. 7:34 a.m. There had to be some tenant agreement that forbade tenants from making unreasonable amounts of noise before a decent hour.

She wouldn't mind so much if Eddie could actually play, but he'd been torturing "Twinkle, Twinkle, Little Star" for six weeks now. It couldn't be that hard.

The wailing strings stopped, and Montana released a sigh, getting comfy between her blankets again. She'd been up well past midnight going over the course schedule for the first training group. Teaching was new for her, and she wanted to instill confidence in the beginner jumpers. Most of them knew who she was or at least had heard about her own jumping career—and its tragic end—so there was a lot on the line.

She took several deep, calming breaths as her eyes grew heavy and the lids closed. She was in that blissful middle ground between awake and slumber when the torture from next door resumed.

Tossing the bedsheets aside, she sat up and threw her legs over the side of the bed. She slid her feet into slippers, grabbed a cardigan sweater from the back of her chair and left her apartment.

In the hall, she knocked on Eddie's apartment door.

Footsteps, then the door opened. Eddie stood there in

his state-trooper pants and shirt, fully unbuttoned. Unlike his music, his abs were something Montana could appreciate, and she took a long moment to do so. After all, if he didn't want his body admired, why answer the door with it on display?

Toned, sculpted, tanned, smooth—the strong-looking chest gave way to one of the hottest six-packs she'd ever seen. Eddie had a surprisingly amazing body, hidden behind clothes that hardly did it justice. At about six feet tall, he had just the right balance of height and muscle ratio.

But his guitar playing sucked, and that's why she was there.

He smiled as he leaned against the door. "What's up, Danger?"

How many times had she asked him not to call her that? "Eddie, it's early, and some of us are trying to sleep."

"The guitar keeping you awake?"

"Yes."

"Sorry. I'm still on rotating shifts. Just got home, and I have trouble unwinding."

She raised an eyebrow. Unwinding from sleeping in his patrol car and chasing raccoons away from garbage bins in the back alley? They shared an apartment wall; she'd heard him complain about the lack of activity that life as a state trooper in a ski-resort town afforded him.

"Actually, I'm behind on the homework my guitar teacher assigned this week."

"You're taking lessons?" Was he shitting her? If he was serious, he should definitely ask for his money back.

"Yeah. My teacher says I'm a natural."

Right. "Okay. Well, if you could maybe wait until eight or eight thirty…"

"Sure. No problem. Sorry to wake you," he said, grinning as he ran a hand along his stomach.

Her gaze followed it, and she quickly averted her eyes. She'd filed her complaint; time to leave. "Okay..." She turned to go but the smell of something delicious reached her, and she leaned past him to sniff inside his apartment. "Are you cooking something?"

"A breakfast quiche—an old family recipe."

She blinked. She could never tell if he was serious or not. Dry humor or lack of humor, she'd yet to figure out. "Really?"

"No. The women in my family would rather dive in front of bullets than stand at a stove. It's just something I threw together from the leftover ham and veggies I'd made for dinner the other night."

"You cook?" Her mouth watered and her stomach growled the longer she stood there.

"Yeah. I did two years of culinary school before I went into the academy."

"Why?" Seemed like vastly different career options.

"Because I couldn't get into the academy, and I love to eat, so I figured it wouldn't be wasted time either way."

"Smart."

His smile was wide and arguably sexy. "Thank you. I thought so."

"I learn something new about you every day," she said, finding it oddly true. When she'd first met Eddie, he'd seemed like a one-dimensional, straight-laced, annoying guy who seemed to be keeping an eye on her. But in the last three months, she'd had no real choice other than to get to know him, and he was actually growing on her. Not the guitar-playing obviously, but other qualities like the way he always made sure he removed his laundry from the shared machines down the hall in the building so others didn't need to wait, or how he left extra quarters on top of the machine in case someone needed one, or how he opened doors and held elevators, or helped the elderly lady down the hall with her grocery shopping every Wednesday evening.

"I'm like an onion. So many layers." He paused.

Had she missed something? Was that a joke?

"And I cook with onions. See what I did there?" He waited. "Nope. Nothing. Okay, never mind. Would you like to come in for breakfast?"

Tempting. She wasn't exactly a great cook. Her idea of breakfast usually consisted of microwave popcorn or dry cereal. But, she was more tired than hungry, and so far she'd managed to keep her interaction with Eddie to tolerable-neighbor status. There was just something about being friends with a police officer that made her uneasy. He was the definition of good and she was...well, not good all the time, and he was always keeping an eye on her. Since she'd gotten lost in the woods months before and he'd helped the search and rescue crew find her, he'd been even more protective, it seemed. Letting him feed her was probably not the best idea. "Um...no, but thank you."

"Okay. No guitar before eight or eight thirty. Got it," he called, and she could feel his eyes on her as she went back to her apartment.

Two minutes later, she climbed back in bed and set her alarm for eight thirty. Unfortunately, now her stomach still grumbled and the recurring image behind her closed lids of Eddie's abs reminded her how long it had been since she'd had a naked male body in her bed.

So long, she actually couldn't remember the last time. Things with Lance were heating up. There had been a lengthy make-out session at the end of their last date, but she was holding back a little, and obviously her lack of sex was messing with her mind because in her half slumber state, she couldn't erase Eddie's body from her imagination as she drifted back to sleep.

An indeterminable amount of time later, the sound of a blender next door made her jump. "Oh, my God, Eddie!" She grabbed a pillow and covered her ears.

The noise continued. And continued. What the hell was he blending? Body parts? She banged on their shared wall.

"Sorry, Montana! All done," he called through the wall.

She needed to move.

"He's cute."

Not now. Her sister's ghost had the worst timing. "Well then, go haunt *him*."

"I don't haunt you. I visit."

"No, you appear as a result of my overactive brain cells because of the injury to my left temporal lobe when I'm overly stressed." Montana's therapist and her doctor had both confirmed that her sister's apparition was a side effect from the damage done to her brain. Unfortunately, they weren't able to get her to stop appearing.

"Exactly. I'm here when you need me." Dani jumped up onto the dresser, swinging her legs, the way she did when they were kids.

Of course, Dani *was* still a teenager. Apparently, spirits don't age.

But the most unsettling part of it all was that she was still in her swimsuit from the day she drowned. In Montana's mind, the clothes you die in were the clothes you stayed in for eternity. Definitely something to think about when getting dressed in the morning.

"What I need is sleep," Montana said.

Dani didn't take the hint. "What's your hang-up with Eddie, anyway? He seems nice enough."

Nice, sure. Her type, absolutely not. "He's a cop, and he thinks I'm trouble. Therefore, I'm under constant surveillance, living next door to him."

"It could be worse."

"Really? How? Eddie is so straitlaced and obedient."

"*You're* supposed to be that way too now, remember?" Dani had moved on to the lecture component of that day's visit sooner than usual.

"I know. I'm trying. But do you have any idea how hard it is to constantly fight every adrenalinecentric cell in my body?" Every part of Montana's being craved excitement and adventure and challenges. Living a nice, quiet, simple life was hell on earth for her. But for Kaia's sake, she was desperately trying to be happy with the life she was living now. No BASE jumping. No breaking the law. No jumping into casual flings.

Basically no living, as far as Montana was concerned.

"Yes!" Dani said. "I do know, and maybe *I* should have tried a little harder. If I had, I might have seen my seventeenth birthday."

If Montana was the wild one, her sister had been the reckless one. A division-one athlete, Dani had excelled at every sport—soccer, volleyball, basketball. But she was a champion diver, headed straight to the Olympics on the US swim team. So much promise, but she just couldn't stay away from anything sharp or on fire. Dani was drawn to danger.

And alcohol and illegal drugs…

"I'm doing my best," Montana said.

"I saw the motorcycle," Dani said, shooting her a look.

In death, Dani had finally recognized consequences for her actions, and now she was on a mission to prevent Montana from doing anything remotely dangerous.

"I needed something." Driving at warp speed down the highway didn't exactly scratch the itch, but it helped. Also, the motorcycle's vibration was appreciated in her ten-year celibacy.

"You're at least wearing a helmet, right?" Dani asked.

"Of course…sometimes." When Kaia was around, or the local authorities.

"Look, Mon, I love seeing you, but I'd rather if *you* don't visit *me* anytime soon, okay? So, be careful."

Montana got out of bed now that more sleep was out of the question. "I will. But now, you need to go away. Kaia will be here soon."

"I love Kaia! Let me stay. She won't see me."

"No, but I will, and I don't want my ten-year-old daughter or her dad to think I'm a lunatic." Montana headed toward the bedroom door.

Dani appeared in front of it, blocking her escape. "Fine. But think about what I said about Eddie."

"I'm dating Lance, remember?" Sort of. How closely was her sister monitoring her, anyway?

Her sister's ghost shivered. "Shit. Someone just walked over my grave."

"Not funny!"

"I know. It's creepy as shit. But it happens every time you talk about Lance, so I think it's a sign that you should break up with him." She rubbed her thin arms.

"No."

"Look, I don't make these spirit rules."

A knock on Montana's apartment door, and Dani was gone.

Montana turned in a circle, looking for her. Satisfied that she was once again alone, she shook it off and opened the door to Tank and Kaia. "Hey! My favorite person! And you're early." She hugged Kaia and stepped back to let them enter, hoping they couldn't sense her disruptive morning mood.

"Hey, Mom," Kaia said with a smile.

Damn. Hearing her daughter call her *Mom* would never get old. Kaia had a magical way of grounding her. Keeping her from tipping over the edge. Being near Kaia gave Montana a clear, definitive purpose, and she clung to that like a safety net. Whenever she got too antsy or started to question her life in Wild River, seeing Kaia reminded her what was important.

"Yeah, sorry for the early drop-off, but I have to get to the station. Is someone else here?" Tank asked, looking around. Her already-tiny apartment always seemed to shrink with Tank in it. At six foot five and two hundred and seventy pounds of solid muscle, her ex was big and scary on the outside, but squishy and lovable on the inside. They had always been great friends, and he was an amazing father. The way he'd welcomed her back into their lives and made the transition as easy as possible for her was something she'd always be grateful for. But the pressure of not disappointing him or Kaia did weigh heavily.

"Um...no. No one else is here."

"Oh, I thought I heard you talking."

"The TV was on before," she said. If she said she was talking to herself, he'd rethink letting Kaia spend the day with her.

His concerned look was one she hated but luckily had occurred less lately. She was proving that she was okay being on her own and that she could handle day-to-day stuff without anyone's help. Her memory loss hadn't created a cause for concern in months. And all joking aside, her lack of culinary skills actually put everyone's mind at ease.

"Okay." Tank nodded. He turned to Kaia. "Well, do you want to tell your mom your exciting news?"

Kaia shot him a look. Her dark eyebrows meeting in the middle. Obviously she hadn't. "Sure..." she said reluctantly.

Montana looked back and forth between them. "What's up?"

"I'm going to summer camp at Camp Willow." Kaia

looked nervous as she twisted a strand of long, dark hair around her finger.

"Wow! That's fantastic!" Montana studied her. "I thought you were excited?"

"I am. It's just… I leave in a few days." She paused. "For a month."

Montana's eyes widened. "Camp is a full month?"

"Yes, but Kaia's been going to camp every summer," Tank said. "Usually just for two weeks, but this is a great opportunity. Camp Willow is on the shores of Kenai Lake." He looked at Montana expectantly.

Had her ex forgotten she wasn't exactly up on Alaska geography? Was Kenai Lake an hour away or eight? Would she be able to visit Kaia, or was she actually going to have to survive a full four weeks—the entire month of August— without seeing her? "Right. Yes, of course," Montana said.

"You have no idea where that is, do you?" Tank asked.

"Of course I do. It's near…the water."

Kaia looked worried as she tucked her long dark hair under a baseball hat. "Are you sure you're okay with this, Mom? I don't have to go…"

"Yes, you do! You love the outdoors and camping and learning new survival skills. Of course you're going." She hugged her daughter again.

"You'll be okay without me?" Her daughter's muffled words made her feel even worse. She was the parent. Kaia shouldn't be worried about taking care of her.

"Absolutely," she said confidently. "And I have a surprise for you." She reached behind a chair for the new motorcycle helmet she'd bought her daughter. Bright blue with orange flames on the side. Kaia was going to love it.

"That better not be what I think it is," Tank muttered, his height allowing him a glimpse of the gift.

Montana paused before revealing the surprise. "What do you think it is?"

Tank shook his head. "No motorcycle rides for Kaia."

Buzzkill. Montana rehid the helmet. "Of course not!" She turned to Kaia. "Your surprise is coming in the mail... next week...once I order something."

Kaia frowned at Tank. "Come on, Dad! I have a dirt bike."

"Not the same thing." Tank's tone was firm. Final.

"It kinda is." Montana slammed her lips shut at Tank's intense glare. "Nope. Not at all the same thing. Your dad and I are on the same page here."

Kaia cocked her head to the side and raised an eyebrow.

"Page adjacent," Montana said. "Or even a few pages back. But definitely same book. A book on good parenting."

Kaia's exasperation was obvious. "Fine. It's really annoying that you two get along so well."

Tank laughed. "So, what's the plan for today?"

"I thought I'd take you up to the new jump site," Montana told Kaia. "If that's okay?" She looked at Tank.

If he was worried that Montana was taking Kaia out into the backwoods where she'd been lost for two days only months before, he hid it well. "Yeah, that's cool. Just be careful," he said, checking his watch. "I better get going." He kissed the top of Kaia's head. "I'll see you later."

"Bye, Dad," Kaia said.

"Hey, I'm just going to walk your dad out. Be back in a sec," Montana said, closing the apartment door behind her and Tank before turning to him. "You're seriously okay with her going to camp for that long?" she whispered.

"No, but you've met our daughter. If you want to take on this battle, I'll support you, then say *I told you so* when Kaia goes to camp, anyway."

Damn, he was so right in his assessment on exactly how that would play out. "Why is she so headstrong?"

Tank put his hands on his hips. "Seriously?"

"I just don't know what I'm going to do with myself for an entire month without her." It was definitely selfish, but she needed Kaia. She hoped to eventually get to the point where her daughter needed her more than Montana needed her daughter, but she wasn't sure that would ever happen.

"What are you talking about? You've got the jump site opening soon, and your training sessions start next week. Not to mention a certain someone occupying your evenings..."

Her eyes narrowed. There seemed to be zero girl code in these mountains. Instead, everyone was just one big friendly family, who knew everything about everyone. "Cassie told you about Lance?"

He nodded. "All I'm going to say is, you can do better. But as for Kaia and camp, be careful not to let her know this is bothering you. She was nervous about telling you, and I think if she senses you're not entirely cool with it, she won't go."

"Copy." She'd never hold her daughter back from doing anything.

"Great. Have fun today," Tank said with a wave, heading down the hallway. "Remember, no motorcycle!"

WHY HAD HE worked so hard just to play Candy Crush on his phone eight hours a day? Three attempts at the police entrance exam, followed by working his butt off at the academy and graduating third in his class, and now he was a human barricade.

Eddie sat on the wooden gate at the entrance of the newly constructed trail leading to the BASE-jumping site on the side of Suncrest Peak and rolled the sleeves of his shirt.

It had to be eighty degrees out there in the midmorning sun. The tree cover had been cut back to allow ATVs to safely navigate the trail, and he was cooking in the dead, late-July heat.

"All units in the area of South West Street and Main, please report to a break and enter at Gary's Convenience…"

The police scanner next to him hadn't stopped with calls all day. Unfortunately, the crimes were happening everywhere *but* Wild River.

His sister might be a jerk sometimes, but she wasn't wrong in her assessment. Living in a quiet, popular, touristy resort town was not going to give him the career he wanted. He wasn't looking for danger, but he struggled to feel like a real officer when his job most days consisted of keeping graffiti off the highway bridges and sweating his balls off, making sure no unauthorized hikers stumbled past this barricade. He'd gone into this career to make a difference. His sisters were either saving lives or solving murders. He ached to do something as important as they did.

Closing down level 134 on Candy Crush, Eddie checked his email on his phone.

Still nothing from the narcotics division. Apparently hitting Refresh a thousand times a day didn't make an acceptance email pop up. There had been nothing in his mailbox that morning, either, and he assumed they might call if his application was approved, but so far the phone wasn't ringing.

Hearing voices down the path, he tucked his phone away. First contact with other actual human beings in three hours. He stood up, seeing Montana and Kaia approach on the trail.

Had it gotten even hotter out here? Eddie unbuttoned the top button on his shirt and ran a sweaty hand through his hair, then smoothed it back in place.

He hadn't seen Montana out here in a few days. Not that seeing her out here had anything to do with why he'd accepted this post.

They were neighbors, and that hadn't made a difference in her noticing his existence. Not that he wanted her to, but damn, he was intrigued by her, and unless she was yelling at him to stop playing guitar, she barely even spoke to him.

Lance Baker was her type, and he was no Lance Baker.

Though, her eyes had lingered a really long time on his bare torso earlier that morning. Physically, at least, he met her standards, but she liked bad boys, and he was far from that description.

"What's up, Danger?" Watching her cheeks flush while her jaw tightened was the very reason he kept calling her that. *Annoyed but Hiding a Secret Amusement Montana* was by far the most beautiful Montana.

However, every version of her had him feeling emotions he hadn't in a long time. She was crazy sexy with her athletic build and supermodel height, but it was her striking features, the high cheekbones and brilliant eyes, that mesmerized him. Her zest for life radiated from her like a magnetic pull to a flame that he knew would engulf him if he got too close.

"I wanted to take Kaia up to the jump-site training grounds, now that the trail is done," she said, readjusting her backpack.

"I'll have to accompany you."

"Sure you can leave your post?"

"I can when the trouble's already up there," he said with a grin.

Montana looked away.

Kaia looked back and forth between them. "Are you two having a moment right now?"

He wished. He waited for Montana to answer the little

girl because, frankly, he had no idea. He'd never been great at academics or women. How many times had he missed a possible connection because he hadn't picked up on the social cues of flirting?

He liked to think his personality and semigood looks would eventually help him in the relationship department, but his focus was on his career anyway—until he saw Montana. Then he'd wished his entire career wasn't based on encouraging people to behave.

"No. We are not having a moment," she eventually told Kaia.

Eddie shook his head. "Not at all."

"Okay, sure… Should we go, then?" Kaia asked.

"Definitely."

Eddie moved the barricade aside and allowed them to move past, then fell in behind them on the trail. It took every ounce of strength to keep his gaze from landing on Montana's sexy ass in her bright red, body-hugging yoga pants. She seemed to own a pair in every color. Other than the few times he'd seen her in jeans, she seemed to live in the tight workout gear, and he had zero complaints. Before she'd moved in next door, he'd been the only person under forty who lived in the building. She definitely made the place more attractive.

"What do you know about *moments*, anyway?" Montana asked her daughter as they climbed the trail.

"Mom, I'm almost eleven."

Eddie hid a grin. Kaia had always been mature for her age. Growing up in Wild River with Tank, the little girl was independent and smart. She ran her own wilderness-safety course for young children and helped out at the search and rescue station with her dad. She could practically run the bar herself if Tank allowed her to stay past eight o'clock, and everyone in town loved her.

"So, you've had these moments?" Montana asked.

"Of course," Kaia said as if it should be obvious.

So much for Tank's belief that his daughter was a tomboy who wasn't into boys.

"But you haven't acted on these moments yet, have you?" Montana asked.

It warmed him to see the two of them together. He'd known Tank and Kaia for a long time, and he'd been hesitant to think Montana's reappearance in their lives would do anything but upset the dynamic that had been working so well for them. But he was happy to have been proven wrong.

Montana was a fantastic mother. A strong, confident role model for Kaia, like his own mother had been for him. She was letting things happen naturally. Not expecting too much from Tank and Kaia...or herself.

He'd love to tell her he'd been wrong in his initial assessment of her, but they'd have to have a real conversation for that to happen, and so far, their bickering and bantering was as deep as it got.

"Well, not yet," Kaia was saying, "but there is one guy at school I like."

"Well, I think now might be the perfect time to have a discussion about what happens when a boy and a girl like one another."

Eddie slowed his pace. What?

"You mean the sex talk?" Kaia asked.

"Yes," Montana said, glancing back at him.

Oh, hell no. "Okay, you win. I'm out. Have fun but please be careful," Eddie said, turning to head back down the trail. He was not staying for that conversation. It had been awkward enough when he'd had to sit through his own talk with *his* mother.

But Montana's easy laugh floating on the wind behind

him told him he'd just been set up. He shook his head as he continued back down the path toward the barricade.

Well played, Danger.

FOUR HOURS LATER, Montana parked her motorcycle in the hospital lot with thirty seconds to spare. Pulling off her helmet, she headed inside, eager for the blast of air conditioning awaiting her through the doors. The protective gear she wore while riding may be necessary, but damn, it was hot.

Her doctor and Cassie's best friend, Erika Sheraton, looked at her watch as she entered. "You're late."

"Nuh-uh. I have—" Montana checked her watch as she removed her leather jacket "—six seconds before our appointment."

"On time is the same as late."

"Bullshit. And besides, if I got here early, *you'd* just make *me* wait," she said with a grin.

Erika sighed. "Fine." She nodded toward Montana's helmet, her thick, dark brown, messy bun bobbing on top of her head. "Is there any point in rehashing the dangers of driving a motorcycle?"

"Nope." That conversation had already turned girls' night the previous weekend into a heated debate. Erika had argued that motorcycles were a hazard. Montana had argued that the big, jacked-up trucks on the roads were the real hazards to anything smaller than them, and Cassie had naturally remained neutral, arguing both sides and playing devil's advocate until Montana and Erika had regrouped to turn their criticism on Cassie's inability to pick a side.

Of course, it was all in fun. Mostly. No amount of arguing would change anyone's viewpoint on the subject. They just agreed to disagree. Luckily, it was one of the few points of contention between the three of them. When Montana had first arrived in Wild River, Erika had been worried that she'd come back to steal Tank from Cassie, then when she realized that wasn't the case, she'd been worried that Montana would steal Cassie from her.

Montana had successfully proven that she wasn't in town to steal anyone. She just wanted to integrate into all of their lives, and by supporting her as a friend and her new doctor, Erika had helped her do that.

"Okay, come in, then," Erika said.

They headed down the hall to a treatment room, and Montana hopped up onto the examination table as Erika closed the door behind them.

"How are you feeling on the adjusted dosage we started you on last visit?" Erika asked.

A lower dose of her memory-enhancement medication. She was hoping to eventually wean off it altogether. "Fine. A few headaches the first week, but they've gotten better." They happened every time she changed her meds. Nothing to worry about.

"Any new episodes?"

"No." The last amnesia episode had happened months ago when she'd been hiking the trail to the jump site. It was similar to a blackout where, without warning, she'd instantly forget where she was or what she was doing. The episodes were temporary but scary as hell, and the last one resulted in search and rescue having to find her.

"Good." Erika checked her vision with her light. "Appetite okay?"

"I don't know if I'd say it's okay. I'm eating everything in sight lately." Luckily her five foot eight frame could accommodate the extra ten pounds she'd gained since arriving in town.

"Pregnant?"

"That would require sex, and I think my daughter might have a better understanding of that these days than I do."

Erika's eyes widened. "Kaia's having sex? Does Tank know?"

"No! Oh, my God, no! She's not." She shivered at the thought. "At least, I don't think so..." She shook her head. "No. She's only ten, and she's super open with us. She would tell us."

Erika raised an eyebrow. "If you say so." She coughed.

"Let's get back to more pleasant topics, shall we? Like my brain injury."

"Are you still having the hallucinations?"

"My sister? She's still visiting."

Erika nodded, wrapping a blood-pressure cuff around Montana's arm. "Are there particular times or situations when she appears?"

"Mostly when I'm stressed."

"Does she provide comfort?"

"She might if I didn't feel crazy talking to someone only I can see."

"You're not crazy." Erika pumped the blood-pressure machine. "Blood pressure's good, even after talking about Kaia's sex life and your dead sister. Impressive."

"Do you believe in ghosts?" Montana asked.

"No."

"Neither do I. Therefore, I'm crazy."

"Your sister had an accident, right?" Erika jotted notes in Montana's file and sat on the edge of her desk.

"She drowned when she was sixteen. I was fourteen." That summer had changed everything. She and her sister had been so close. Only two years apart, they did everything together. They were kindred spirits, always looking for the next adventure. They'd shared everything and kept no secrets from one another...except the biggest one of all—that Dani had fallen in with a group of older girls, who liked to get high and drunk after school, and instead of attending swim practice, she was spending more and more time with them. Montana hadn't known until their parents went away for a weekend and Dani invited her new friends over for a pool party. She hadn't wanted to hear Montana's opinion when they'd gotten into their parents' liquor cabinet.

"You were there when she died?"

"Sort of…" Montana had left the backyard party to hide out in her room. She was angry with Dani and was debating calling their parents when she'd heard the other girls screaming in the backyard.

Whenever she thought about that day, the image of her sister floating facedown in the pool always appeared in her memory as clear as the day it happened.

"Maybe it's some sort of repressed guilt you might be feeling," Erika said, "over the fact that she died so young?"

"Maybe."

"What does she say? What do you two talk about?"

"Lately, she just has an opinion on my love life."

Erika cocked her head to the side. "Tell me you're not still seeing Lance."

"Can I have *Doctor* Erika right now, please?" Her *friend* Erika had far too much to say about her choice in men already. Seems no one thought Lance was the right one for her. But while she appreciated everyone's concern, both Erika and Cassie were so in love with their significant others right now, they couldn't quite grasp the concept of casual dating.

Which was all she was doing with Lance.

"What about Eddie?"

Heat rose up her neck. Why did everyone keep bringing up the hot-but-unexciting cop? "What *about* Eddie?"

"Has he gotten the nerve to ask you out yet?"

Are you two having a moment?

He's cute.

Oh, sure, the voices reappeared at the mention of Eddie. She would not think of it as a sign. She didn't believe in signs.

She didn't believe in spirits, either, but she had regular conversations with one.

"Eddie's not interested in me. I think Eddie is afraid of me," she said.

"That's true. But trust me, he's also very interested in you. I'm sure he'd like to handcuff you for more than one reason, if you catch my drift..."

Montana lifted Erika's stethoscope and spoke into it. "Paging *Doctor* Erika."

"Fine. Sorry. Back to your broken brain. I do have some news about the trial program I mentioned."

"Another new drug?"

"Yes, but this one is already blowing the doors off the medication you're currently on. Early trials were very successful in regaining memory functioning, and it has helped several patients who were reporting auditory hallucinations."

"So, I'll still see my sister, she'll just be mute?" That might work.

Erika laughed. "No, they are currently testing its effect on visual hallucinations as well. I'll know more in a few months."

Montana nodded. "Okay."

Erika took a step closer. "But you are doing really well. Your last scan showed no change."

No change. Not better. Not worse.

When she'd first started different treatments after her injury, there had been significant improvements with each new drug, each new therapy... But things had leveled off in the last few years. Doctors claimed this was as good as it got. Unfortunately, the current status still resulted in hallucinations, confusion and memory blackouts sometimes.

The current status wasn't good enough to get jumping clearance.

"There's no need to switch things up or try something new," Erika said in her silence.

Just say yes. Agree to the new drug once it's approved. "Can I think about it?" she asked instead.

"Of course."

For years she'd been searching for a way to stop the hallucinations from happening, but now, faced with a real possibility that they could, Montana wasn't so sure she was ready to say goodbye to her sister again.

CHAPTER THREE

Seeing Tank's truck pull into the school parking lot a few days later, where yellow buses waited to take local, school-aged kids to various summer camps, Montana climbed off her motorcycle and walked toward them.

"Hey, Mom!" Kaia said, climbing out of the back seat with an oversize duffel bag almost as big as she was.

"Want some help with that?" she asked.

"Nah, I got it. Thanks," Kaia said, pulling her baseball cap lower over her eyes.

"Hi, Montana," Cassie said, getting out of the passenger side. "Wow! Look at all the kids. So excited! I still remember meeting here every summer, so stoked about going to camp."

Montana nodded and forced a smile. She'd never gone to summer camps. Her parents took Dani and her on adventures all over the world. Money hadn't been an issue for their family, so they'd spent months traveling the globe. Exciting, exotic locations. Days spent hiking and rock climbing and deep-sea diving. They'd gotten a better education when their heads weren't in a book, and it been an amazing childhood—until her sister drowned and her parents did a one-eighty. Their protective gene, which had formerly been lacking, had kicked in full force, and Montana wasn't allowed to do anything even remotely dangerous anymore.

Of course, that had only made her rebel. She'd started skydiving with her grandmother as soon as she was able.

Then BASE jumping—the most extreme and dangerous of sports—became her life passion.

"And you're sure this is a good idea?" Montana whispered to Tank as Cassie led the way to the Camp Willow buses. "A whole month away?"

Tank raised an eyebrow at her. "I told you. I barely had any say in this. She saved the money herself, researched the camp and all of its offerings, registered. All I did was sign the permission slip. And you agreed this was a good idea, too, remember?"

Reluctantly.

"She's going to have an amazing time. She will learn so much. I went to this camp every summer, and I started going a lot younger than Kaia. She'll be fine," Cassie said, falling into step next to them, but even *she* seemed to be trying to convince herself the closer they came to actually saying goodbye to Kaia.

A group of tweens and teens boarded the bus, and Montana frowned. "Are those boys going to Camp Willow, too?"

Kaia's cheeks reddened, and she stared at the ground. "Yes."

Tank surveyed the groups of kids. "But they must have separate camps—"

"Okay, don't get upset," Kaia said quickly.

"It's a co-ed camp?" Tank's eyes widened as his voice rose.

Cassie shot a look at Kaia. "You didn't tell him that part?"

Tank turned to Cassie. "You knew?"

Cassie shrugged. "I thought it was common knowledge."

"No!" Tank said. "I guess I assumed incorrectly that it was like all the other camps she's been to."

"Those were *Girl Guide* camps, Dad," Kaia said with an eye roll.

Parenting miscommunication. With the three of them weighing in on every decision, it was bound to happen.

"Dad, relax. They have separate cabins for boys and girls," Kaia said in an effort to defuse the situation.

Tank was tense as he nodded. Veins appeared in his neck, and his biceps twitched. "They better be separated by a lake or mountain or something."

"Dad, be cool about this," Kaia pleaded.

Would Tank still let Kaia go? Montana completely supported him if he decided to change his mind right now. Unfortunately, she still didn't feel like she'd earned the right to pull rank and forbid Kaia to go, even in light of this new development.

Cassie touched Tank's arm and nodded her head to the side. "Parent group meeting?"

"We'll be back. Do not get on that bus," Tank told Kaia.

Kaia folded her arms across her chest. An annoyed look on her tiny features said if she didn't get to go to camp that month, they were all in for a really shitty August.

"Okay, so we failed to do the research on this camp," Cassie said.

It made Montana feel the tiniest bit better to know her ex was capable of a parenting fail. He always seemed to do everything right, but she would have readily continued to feel inadequate to know that they weren't sending their daughter off to something she wasn't prepared for.

"But Kaia did. And she feels ready for this," Cassie said.

"So, you think we should let her go?" Tank asked her.

Montana fought the tinge of jealousy she felt over him wanting Cassie's opinion first, but she had to get used to the fact that, while she may be the biological mom, Kaia lived with Cassie, and Cassie had been Kaia's primary female role model for most of her life. She couldn't—and didn't want to—replace that.

"Yes," Cassie said. "We need to show her we trust her."

"I trust her. It's all those penises I don't trust," Tank said, glaring at the crowd of boys nearby.

"Agreed," Montana said.

"What do you think we should do?" Tank asked her.

Damn. Now it was on her. Montana looked at Cassie, then shot a glance at Kaia. She hesitated, but it was her time to step up. Tank was asking for her input and giving her influence over this decision. It was a big deal. "I think we should let her go."

Cassie smiled. Tank looked like he was preparing himself for absolutely no sleep for a month. The three of them approached Kaia.

"You can go," Tank said.

Kaia hugged Cassie. "Thanks, Cass."

"It was a group decision," Cassie said.

"Yeah, right," Kaia said, picking up her duffel bag from the ground. "I have to get on the bus before they leave without me."

Kaia hugged Tank, but he was preoccupied putting the fear of God into several boys a few feet away.

Montana noticed the boys quickly avert their eyes. Kaia noticed too. "Dad," she hissed, "stop."

"Stop what?"

"Making everyone afraid to talk to me."

"Not everyone. Just the boys," Tank said, but his expression softened as he pulled her in for another big hug.

"I'm not interested in boys, Dad," Kaia said.

"It's not you I'm worried about, sweetheart," he said. "I was a teenage boy. I know what runs through their minds."

Kaia rolled her eyes. "I play hockey with them. Trust me, they don't see me that way."

But the hint Montana caught in her tone suggested she was disappointed by that. Luckily Tank didn't catch it, or he'd be making the executive decision to put Kaia back in his truck and deal with her preteen angst all summer.

Kaia hugged Montana next. "So, you guys are all coming on the twenty-fifth for pickup, right?" She stared at her.

Her little girl still didn't trust that she wasn't a flight risk. "We will all be here," Montana said.

Kaia waved as she boarded the bus. Tank stood near the door and stopped each of the boys from the hockey team as they boarded. "Don't touch her… Don't touch her… Don't touch her…" he warned.

"I seriously doubt Kaia will have any trouble from those boys at camp and not just because Tank's making them fear for their safety," Cassie said to her.

Montana forced a laugh. "Yeah, Kaia's a tough one. And it's only a month. She will be fine." She waved as Kaia took a seat on the bus.

Her daughter was strong and brave and could handle anything. Kaia *would* be fine. But would Montana be fine without her?

They waited until all of the buses had pulled out of the parking lot before heading toward their vehicles.

"So, you have a big day as well," Tank said, obviously trying to get his mind off chasing after the bus.

"Yeah, I suppose I do." She'd been so preoccupied with thoughts of Kaia leaving that morning she hadn't had much time to stress about the course starting that day.

"It's going to be great," Cassie said. "Everyone returned their waivers, and fees have all been paid." She smiled reassuringly at Montana. "Have fun. Be yourself," she said, then laughed. "Sorry, hard to shake the co-mom advice."

"Thanks, Cass. I'll let you know how it goes," Montana said, climbing onto her motorcycle and reaching for the helmet. She put it on and started the engine, driving away as slow as possible with Tank and Cassie watching.

A half hour later, she stared down into the canyon at the top of the mountain. The fresh air normally filled her with a sense of adventure and serenity. That day she couldn't find either. Coming to Wild River, launching this new venture had seemed like a new beginning, a way to restart her journey in life. But while the pieces of her future were falling into place, not all of them had landed where she'd hoped.

She was happy for Tank and Cassie, but she couldn't say her part-time schedule with her daughter was ideal. She was definitely going to be more than a little lost and lonely not having Kaia around for the next month. Her daughter brought her joy and energy that Montana couldn't quite summon when she was alone. Her partnership with Cassie at SnowTrek was a dream come true. She'd always wanted to teach BASE jumping, but she'd envisioned it a lot further into her future, and she hadn't expected that she'd be teaching because she couldn't indulge.

She could jump now, and no one would know...

I don't think you're up for this.

Tank's words of caution that day ten years ago had only annoyed her. Kaia was four months old, and in that last four months, Montana had barely had a day out of the house, ten minutes by herself, let alone entertained the idea of a jump.

Wild River was feeling claustrophobic. Tank was feeling claustrophobic.

They were trying to make things work for Kaia's sake, but Montana wasn't happy. Not the way she wanted to be. Not the way a new mother was supposed to be. During her pregnancy, she'd followed all the rules, did everything right, avoiding anything even remotely dangerous. Hell, she'd even stopped working out in the third trimester.

She needed to jump that day or she was going to lose her mind. After a lengthy argument, Tank had given up trying to talk her out of it, and she'd climbed the trail to the jump site.

Running. Jumping. Soaring. Everything was once again balanced within her core. Adrenaline, exhilaration, freedom...

Then she'd hit the side of the mountain. Hard. She'd miscalculated her timing, her distance. She didn't even have time to panic or be afraid before her world went black.

I don't think you're up for this.

Noise from the first ATV sounded behind her on the trail, and she released the past on a deep exhale. She had to pull it together. No more self-pity. She had eight trainees that day, expecting her best. Montana Banks, expert BASE jumper. She needed to instill confidence in these new jumpers to trust her and believe in her, despite her own mistake.

She turned away from the view as the ATVs pulled up into the parking area and eight excited, extreme athletes approached. She plastered a smile on her face, determined not to let anyone know how much this was killing her.

EDDIE SHOT OFF another round, then lowered his gun back to the holster at his waist and removed the noise-canceling headphones. The shooting target came closer. Holes in the head, neck, chest and stomach revealed he'd hit his marks. In the stall next to him, his coworker, Adams, swore under his breath. Eddie watched the man's shooting target come closer and joined him in his stall as the guy slammed his headphones to the table.

"Hey, you're getting better," Eddie said.

"How the hell did I graduate from the academy when I couldn't hit the wide side of a bull?" Adams shook his head, taking the target down and balling it. He tossed it into the trash as they left the range.

It wasn't a mystery, really. Adams was one of the smartest guys to opt out of a college degree and go into the academy. While Eddie had struggled with the written components of his exams and courses, Adams had breezed through. Eddie had the physical skills, the instincts and the sharp eye for targets, but Adams could decode threats and identify suspects based on correspondence and patterns of behavior like no one else.

However, he'd never be allowed to leave the office if he couldn't learn to hit an unmoving target.

"Keep practicing, man," Eddie said as they walked across the parking lot. He didn't think Adams's problem was aim; it was ignorance and an unwillingness to shoot to kill. Adams's mother was a teacher and his father a church minister. He was raised in a home that had a more Buddhist approach to life. Eddie doubted Adams had ever killed a mosquito, let alone been able to harm another human, even in self-defense. He'd also lived a rather sheltered life, and unlike Eddie, dinner conversations weren't always about murder or suicide or theft. Eddie hadn't known a time when they didn't have multiple guns in their house. His mother had taken him to the firing range right after his father died and the man was no longer around to stop her.

"I appreciate your help. Hope I didn't take you away from something important."

"Nah. I was just planning on heading into the office, anyway."

"I'm on shift in an hour. Need help with anything?"

Eddie hesitated. He hadn't told his coworkers about his transfer request to the narcotics division, so he went in when he wasn't scheduled to review the drug-related crime files. He could use Adams's help, though, deciphering some of the files. "Sure. Thanks. I'll see you in an hour," Eddie said, climbing into his truck.

Fifty minutes later, he sat across from Adams, hot coffee and a box of donuts on the desk between them. "You requested a transfer, didn't you?" Adams said, scanning the files on Eddie's desk. Known, convicted drug offenders and dealers from all over Alaska.

No sense denying the obvious. He hadn't made his ambitions a big secret, anyway. They all knew he wanted more action. "Yeah, but keep it between us, okay? I haven't heard anything yet, so I'm starting to think the answer is no." He'd only been a trooper for six months. It was ambitious to even think he'd be eligible to transfer and get the promotion yet, but fear of failure had never prevented him from going after what he wanted before.

"You never know. These things take time," Adams said, picking up the latest file on the desk. "What exactly are you looking for with these?"

"A common denominator," Eddie said. "Each of these convicted dealers seem to be operating independently, but the drug they are selling is exactly the same, so it has to be coming from one central dealer."

"Is there something unique about it?"

"It's certainly not your average meth or cocaine. It's a performance-enhancement drug laced with both. Every pill the department has brought in for testing is the same dosage, same quantities." He opened several files and showed Adams the images of the drugs.

"Shit. Those things look like M&M's."

"Exactly why they appeal to kids. It's called Mystic Rush, and eight high-school athletes tested positive for the drug last year before the semester let out for summer. Two junior-high students ended up in the hospital from an overdose, and one died." The drug was designed to dissolve quickly and hit the bloodstream within minutes but took a while to show up in regular drug-screening tests. The high was essentially a shot of adrenaline that improved speed, response time and accuracy. It hit hard and fast and wore off quickly, resulting in the addiction. These athletes were quickly relying on it for the extra boost they needed. Those who competed on college-level teams were using almost daily, and the damage to their heart and lungs as a result was irreparable. Health concerns the drug posed was the major concern, but the reliance on the illegal substance was costing talented athletes their careers when they tested positive or stopped using and their performance was viewed as dropping.

"So, the dealers are targeting schools?"

"Schools, sports organizations and community centers. Unfortunately, no one is giving up their source for the product. Guards down at the docks say nothing is coming in on shipping containers that they've detected."

Adams raised a brow. "It's local made? In Alaska?"

"Seems that way." It was working its way across the state, and so far there hadn't been any reported cases of it in Wild River, but it was only a matter of time. Wild River didn't have a big drug problem, and Eddie hoped to keep it that way, but the local station didn't really have a team dedicated to keeping this shit off the streets. In Anchorage, he could dig deeper, be more involved, try to stop this from spreading to clean communities like his hometown.

"Okay, well, put me to work. What can I do to help?" Adams asked.

"Find the missing link to these dealers, 'cause so far, I haven't found it." Which made his confidence drop. He'd thought maybe if he could prove himself from afar, the narcotics division in Anchorage would see the value in having him on the team, but so far, he hadn't discovered anything that could tie these offenders together. So, maybe he wouldn't be such an asset after all.

Maybe that's why his phone wasn't ringing.

CHAPTER FOUR

WHAT HAD SHE been thinking, inviting Lance over for dinner instead of letting him take her out? She didn't cook. She made her best efforts when Kaia was over, but she doubted the world-champion snowboarder was expecting chicken fingers and mac and cheese in lieu of the steakhouse he'd suggested. He was training for the upcoming competition season, so even his cheat days mostly consisted of clean eating.

Montana pushed her cart through the aisles of the grocery store. So far, she had a can of mushroom soup, chicken breasts and a bag of Doritos. Appetizer, main course and dessert? Not the healthiest...

Reaching the produce section, she picked up a bag of grapes, putting them in the front of the cart next to her purse. She scanned the vegetable options. She could make a veggie platter, cut up some carrots and celery. Side of ranch? Not exactly impressive...

Montana scanned the items along the aisle. She didn't even know what half of this stuff was. Most of the green, leafy stuff all looked alike. Lettuce she could figure out. A Caesar salad couldn't be that hard, but Lance had never ordered one when they went out, always opting for a chop salad or garden side salad along with whatever beast he was eating. Potatoes were safe, but was he eating carbs this week?

She surveyed the spices. Garlic and parsley... Those things made chicken taste good, right? She had no idea. Why the hell was she putting this pressure on herself?

Montana liked to stay healthy by being active, but food was never important to her. She was always on the go. Staying busy was the only way to keep from losing her mind in the small town, and luckily her inability to sit still kept her in shape.

Her lack of culinary skills was not her fault. Neither of her parents liked to cook. They had a meal-delivery service back in Denver.

Montana stopped the cart in the middle of the aisle, reached into her purse for her cell phone and opened a search engine. Wild River was a small town, but someone must have jumped on the meal-box delivery business by now. She didn't want fast food, but something that looked homemade...

She absently reached for a grape and popped it into her mouth as the options loaded.

"You going to pay for that grape?"

She jumped, the grape lodging itself in her throat as she turned toward the sound of Eddie's voice.

His faux-serious expression faded to a teasing grin, then to a look of worry when she started to cough. "Oh, my God. You okay?"

She swallowed hard, and the still fully intact grape slid down her throat. She breathed a sigh of relief. "Yes. Thank you for almost killing me."

"It was a joke. You know, law enforcement and all," he said, gesturing toward his uniform.

It hadn't escaped her notice. The dark navy pants with the stripe down the side and the navy shirt tucked in, nicely hugging his chest and tapered waist, suited him. It was like the uniform was a part of Eddie. It made sense. It was part of who he was. He folded his arms across his chest, and the bulging biceps didn't escape her notice either.

Eddie wasn't a big guy, not like Tank. But he was taller than she was and built solid. Attractive in a nonarrogant kind of way. In fact, his complete lack of ego surprised her, given his chosen profession.

"Yeah, I got that," she said. "I'll make sure to let them know at the register."

"Anyway, you shouldn't eat unwashed produce."

"A few germs never killed anybody."

"That's actually false, but I'm talking about the pesticides. Those grapes aren't organic or grown in a pesticide-free environment." He took them out of her cart and replaced them with new ones—*three dollars more expensive ones.*

She tried one. They did taste better.

Eddie reached for a clove of garlic and some fresh cilantro (or so said the label above it) and put them in his basket. Montana watched as he selected several green peppers and an onion. "What are you making for dinner tonight?" she asked, closing down her Google search. The smells coming from his apartment all the time were better than any delivery service. Maybe he'd let her buy some of whatever he was making.

"Tonight is Grilled Chili-Cilantro Chicken. Why? Want to come over?" He looked just as surprised by the offer as she did.

"I have a date. With Lance. I'm cooking dinner," she said, watching as he selected packets of ground cumin and red-pepper flakes from the spices.

"Chicken fingers and mac and cheese?" he asked, then glancing into her cart. "Grapes and Doritos for dessert?" No judgment, just humor in his voice.

Montana sighed. "So I can't cook. What's your point? There are more important things in life than eating meals that take forever to put together."

"Not for most guys. You are trying to win his heart through his stomach, right?"

No. That hadn't been her motivation at all. Actually, she'd just been wanting to do something, be somewhere there wasn't an audience. Somewhere they might be able to have a conversation without getting interrupted by adoring fans wanting his autograph. Somewhere they might have a connection develop because his eyes weren't wandering to distractions. Somewhere they might be able to take the relationship to another level…if there was one.

"Or was your invite more of a Netflix-and-chill type of thing?" Eddie asked with a raised eyebrow in her silence.

Montana swiped at him, her fingers barely grazing his arm, but the shock of electricity that passed between them had her pulling her hand away quickly. "No. Nothing like that. I thought we'd stay in, that's all."

"Ah. I get it. Well, good luck with dinner. Fire extinguisher is next to the fridge," Eddie said as he started to walk away.

"I won't be needing it," she called after him. She reached for the items he'd selected and added them to her cart. Grilled Chili-Cilantro Chicken didn't sound so hard. There had to be a recipe for it online. She'd follow that. And hers would taste better than Eddie's.

Four hours later, Montana reached for the fire extinguisher as the pan on the stove flamed. She pointed the nozzle and sprayed until the flames gave way to a charcoaled mess. She coughed as she fanned the smoke in her kitchen and went to open the window.

"At least you have the Doritos and grapes," her sister said, appearing at the table behind her.

"I don't have time for you right now." Montana reached for her cell phone and opened the local fast-food delivery app. Enough of this shit. She'd followed the instructions online, and the chicken was still torched and stuck to the bottom of the pan.

"Oh, come on. Don't give up. Cooking can't be that hard," Dani said.

"How would you know? Mom used to have to make you cereal in the morning because you always added the milk to the bowl first and then made a mess everywhere when you added the Frosted Flakes."

Dani laughed. "I did that shit on purpose. If you do things wrong, people don't expect you to do it again. Low expectations—that's the key to happiness."

"Maybe. But right now, I have nothing to serve Lance for dinner, and he will be here in an hour." She scrolled through the delivery options in town.

"Why don't you ask Eddie for help? His apartment smells delicious."

"I'm not asking Eddie."

A knock on her apartment door had her sister disappearing. Shit. Lance better not be early. She needed to talk to her landlord about putting a sign in the lobby about not letting strangers into the building. At least with the buzzer, she had time to prepare for guests. She ran a hand through her hair and checked her reflection in the mirror on the wall before opening the door.

To Eddie.

"Need some help?" The amusement on his face was too much. He'd predicted she'd fail.

Her competitive nature wouldn't admit defeat. Montana closed the door a little so he couldn't see the smoke still filling her apartment. "No. Everything's under control."

"I can smell the burned chicken from my apartment," he said.

Montana glared at him. "And I suppose yours turned out perfectly?"

He nodded. "It did."

"You could just sell me yours." She'd pay any price right

now to avoid having to order something, have it delivered before Lance arrived and get rid of the take-out-container evidence that she was a failure in the kitchen. Impressing Lance with her cooking should be the last thing she concerned herself with, but she wanted him to see her beyond her extreme-athletic abilities. Turns out, she wasn't sure she had any.

Eddie grinned. "But then you'd be lying to Lance."

Damn Eddie and his morals. "I don't have time to go out and rebuy all the ingredients."

"I think I have enough stuff left. Would you like to learn how to cook or not?"

Learning to cook might be overstating; she'd settle for knowing how to make this one meal right now. "Fine. Show me how to make something that smells like yours."

"I'll be right back," he said, returning to his apartment.

Montana waited for him and when he came back carrying a full grocery bag, she stood back as Eddie led the way into her apartment and sprayed an air freshener. "First, we need to get the smell of failure out of here," he said with a wink.

"Man, he's so cute and so sweet coming to your rescue like this."

Shit. Her sister was back.

Behind Eddie's back, Montana made a motion for her to disappear, but Dani was too busy checking out Eddie. She circled around him—super close—and Montana held her breath. Eddie didn't sense anything. Why would he? She was the only one crazy enough to see ghosts. "Dani!" she hissed under her breath as Eddie headed into the kitchen.

Eddie turned toward her with an expectant look. "Did you say something?"

"Um…no."

"Do you have another pan? This one could take a while

to clean," he said, surveying the charred food on the stove and checking his watch.

"Yes, I think so." The deal at Walmart was buy one pan, get the second one half price, and Kaia had convinced her it was a good deal despite Montana's protests that even one pan was being ambitious. Grateful for it now, she bent to retrieve it from the drawer below the sink and caught Eddie's gaze as it dropped to her ass. She stood up quickly and handed it to him. "Here you go."

"Thanks," he said, removing the old one from the stove and replacing it with the new one.

"Mixing bowl?"

"I only have the one. It's in the dishwasher," she said, scanning the kitchen. On the center of the table was a big, porcelain decorative bowl with flowers in it. A housewarming gift from Erika. An eyesore, really, but she hadn't wanted to hurt the other woman's feelings, so she'd displayed it. At least she'd get some use out of it now. She grabbed it, dumped the flowers into the trash and quickly rinsed the bowl. "Will this work?"

Eddie shrugged. "Improvisation. I like it."

"Man, I love a guy who can cook," Dani said, propping her ghost ass onto the counter next to the stove.

Montana's heart raced. Why the hell was she still here? She nodded toward the open window, but her sister continued to ignore her. Damn, she must really be stressed right now. Dani never stuck around when other people were present.

"Get over here," Eddie said, glancing over his shoulder at her.

"Oh, can't I just watch you do it? I'm a great visual learner," Montana said. If she messed this up twice, there'd be no time to figure out a new plan before Lance arrived. Also, she wasn't eager to look like an idiot in front of Eddie.

"Nice try, but I believe in a hands-on approach," he said, his gaze boring into hers.

"He could be hands-on with me anytime," Dani said.

Montana did her best to conceal her annoyance with her sister as she slowly approached the counter. "Okay, well, I mixed all of these ingredients together the first time. I'm not sure what I did wrong."

Eddie surveyed the ingredients on her counter. "Where's the brown sugar?"

"You didn't buy brown sugar at the grocery store!" The recipe had called for it, but Eddie hadn't bought any, so she thought maybe it was one of those optional ingredients.

"I had some already."

"You own brown sugar?"

He shrugged. "I use it in my chocolate zucchini muffins."

Oh, my God. She took a deep breath. "Well, can I borrow some sugar?"

His grin was wide. "Wow, we're like neighbors from the fifties."

"Eddie. Sugar?"

"He could pour some sugar on me anytime," Dani said, breaking into a terrible rendition of the Def Leppard classic.

This was a nightmare.

"I'm actually out," he said. "I used the last of mine, but if you have honey, we can substitute." He went to her pantry. "Ah, bingo!"

The previous tenant must have left it behind, because Montana had absolutely no use for honey, but she kept that to herself. "How do you know these things?" Honey and brown sugar were nothing at all alike.

"Told you—I went to culinary school." Eddie added the honey to the ingredients on the counter.

"This guy is fascinating," Dani said.

"Okay, so let's mix everything together," Eddie said. Montana waited.

"I meant you," he said, taking her hand and drawing her closer.

Montana stared at his hand on hers. Could he feel the pounding of her pulse through her wrist? She swallowed hard, moving her hand away and reaching for the olive oil first.

"Just a teaspoon should do it," Eddie said. "Oh, wait."

She paused. "What's wrong?" She hadn't even started yet.

Eddie reached for the apron that Kaia had bought her as a joke from behind the kitchen door. "This could get messy," he said, looping it over her head. His fingers grazed her neck and goosebumps surfaced on every inch of her body. Her breath caught, and she froze in place as he reached for the apron strings and wrapped them around her waist, stepping closer to tie it in the back. His body was inches from hers, and his dark brown eyes were like pools of chocolate that she found herself drowning in all of a sudden. Had his eyes always been this mesmerizing? So dark they were almost black, but containing kindness and sincerity mixed with an unexplored intensity that swallowed her up.

His gaze dropped to her lips, and she instinctively licked them, causing his expression to change instantly to something she could only identify as lust. He cleared his throat and quickly stepped back. "Okay, that should protect you— your clothes, that is," he said, sounding slightly flustered.

Well, he wasn't the only one. Where the hell had this reaction to him come from? She wasn't attracted to Eddie. He was the exact opposite of her type. Everyone else thought their bickering was actually flirting, but it hadn't felt that way. And she'd certainly never gotten the vibe from him that he was into her. He just liked to tease her and irritate her. Turn her on, apparently.

"Earth to Mon," Dani said, whispering in her ear.

Shit. She was standing there like a moron. "Right. Okay. Mixing the ingredients." Focus on making dinner.

For Lance.

She was partially successful as she repeated the same actions she'd done on her own, except this time adding the honey to the mixture, which made it stick to the chicken, instead of pooling in the bottom of the frying pan and burning quickly. Eddie smiled as she nervously removed the lid after the required cooking time. "Looks just like mine," he said.

Montana blinked as she stared at the delicious-looking, delicious-smelling food. "I did it."

"See? Hands-on approach always works," Eddie said, a hint of something in his voice that had heat rushing to Montana's cheeks. Hands-on. Right. The skin at her neck tingled where his fingers had touched.

Jesus. What was happening to her? He'd barely touched her neck. What if he'd actually touched her? For real? Intentionally? Somewhere a lot more tempting than the back of her neck? And why was she wishing he had?

She looked away quickly. "Thank you for your help," she said, reaching to untie the apron.

"Leave it on. At least until Lance gets here. It's sexy." He cleared his throat. "I mean, it looks more authentic that way," he added with a wink.

The simple gesture he'd done a thousand times before had her knees weakening this time. Dani's dreamy sigh as she watched their interaction was exactly how Montana felt. When had Eddie gotten so hot? Was it just because he'd come to her aid that evening? Or because it was sexy to see his expertise in the kitchen? She didn't care about those things, did she?

Maybe there was an element of damsel-in-distress syndrome in her kick-ass, take-no-prisoner personality after all. She wasn't sure how she felt about that, but right now there was no denying, there were new feelings coursing through her. Feelings spurred by Eddie.

"I should get out of here," Eddie said, leaving the kitchen.

Montana followed, her gaze taking him in. Broad shoulders, strong back, sexy ass in jeans that hugged his body so nicely.

Dani was close on her heels.

"Right. Thanks again. I appreciate the help," she said, as he opened the apartment door and went out into the hall.

"You got it," he said. "Anytime." His voice sounded deeper suddenly, and the word seemed to hold a shit-ton of meaning.

Montana blew out a long breath. It was really hot in here.

"You should be having dinner with him," her sister said as they both watched Eddie go into his apartment next door.

For the first time, it was hard to disagree.

EDDIE CRANKED THE pace of the treadmill and blasted a rock song with a heavy beat from his workout playlist. This would be his second workout of the day, but after spending the last hour with Montana in the close quarters of her kitchen, he needed to let off some pent-up energy. He also had to get the hell out of his apartment. It had been irritating enough that he'd helped her make dinner for another guy; he'd be damned if he sat next door alone while they enjoyed eating it—and did other things that made his stomach turn to think about.

He was pathetic.

His feet hit the conveyor belt with a steady rhythm, and his heart rate increased. Unfortunately, it would take a lot more than loud music and exertion to erase the image of Montana in her painted-on jeans and V-neck sweater from

Eddie's mind. Her shapely hips and thighs, her thin waist that he wanted to wrap his arms around while he helped her at the stove...

That had been the point of the apron—to hide her sexy-as-fuck body so he could concentrate—but he'd been unable to just hand it to her. It was like he'd been on autopilot as he'd draped the apron over her head, reached around her to tie it. He had to have been imagining the look in her eyes when she'd stood there staring at him. It was probably shock over the unexpected gesture.

And he refused to think about the way she'd licked her lips when he'd dared a glance at her mouth.

Shit.

The way she bit her lip as she cut the fresh cilantro and looked nervous as she added the spices to the mixture, second-guessing herself. A woman normally so full of confidence showing a more vulnerable side had done things to him. He'd been wishing for an apron of his own to hide his reaction to her.

Jesus. He had to get his promotion transfer soon. Or find a new place to live. He couldn't run away to the gym every time Lance was visiting. This was the first time Montana had invited the guy over. And she was making an effort to cook for him. Things had to be progressing between them. Maybe even getting serious?

Jealousy curled through him as he thought about the other guy touching Montana, kissing Montana, talking to her, making her laugh. He wanted to be that guy, which was so incredibly stupid. He was not her type.

She wasn't normally *his* type either. But something about her—her confidence, her strength of character to come to Wild River and start her life over, her wild side—Eddie had never been attracted to that in a woman before, but with

Montana, he was drawn to it like a moth to a flame. And he was sure to get burned if he wasn't careful.

The door to the workout room opened a few minutes later, and he had to look twice as he saw Montana enter through the reflection in the mirror.

That was a quick dinner.

Seeing her dressed in her yoga shorts and bra top, he nearly fell off of the treadmill. He grabbed the handles and fought to compose himself as she looked his way. The bright teal matching outfit complemented her sun-kissed skin. Long legs in those tight shorts and the mesh insert at the front of the bra gave him a breath-stealing view of her cleavage. She was shaped like an athlete with the curves of a fitness-magazine model. No wonder she turned heads everywhere she went in Wild River.

She said something, but all he saw were her lips moving. Sexy, still painted a pale pink shade of lipstick lips. She wasn't the type to put on makeup just to go work out, so obviously, Lance hadn't kissed it all off.

The knowledge made him feel a lot better than it should.

He slowed the treadmill and paused his music, removing one earbud. "Sorry, what did you say?"

"I asked if you minded if I work out…with you. Well, like beside you, while you work out," she said, sounding as awkward as he felt. Close quarters in her kitchen, now close quarters in the workout room, while they both got hot and sweaty…

"Nah." He cleared his throat. "Go ahead."

Don't ask about the date. Don't ask about dinner.

"What happened to Lance?" Sure, that was less obvious.

Then a horrific thought struck him. What if Lance was joining her for the workout? Fit couples did that all the time. Workout dates. Maybe they planned to work out first, then shower together, then eat…

Montana sat on a stationary bike next to him. "He got called away. One of his Olympic teammates is in town for tonight only."

The guy had ditched Montana to go hang out with another dude? What the fuck? Eddie wouldn't care who was in town for one night only, he'd never trade the opportunity to be with Montana.

"Did you get a chance to impress him with your cooking skills, at least?" he asked.

"He took a to-go bag," she said, cranking the intensity on her machine.

Was she annoyed by Lance's actions or not? Most women would be pissed. And rightly so. If they'd gone through the trouble of coercing their neighbor into cooking dinner. But Montana wasn't most women. Maybe the thing with Lance was just a casual thing. "Well, his loss." He paused. "The food's not as good reheated," he added quickly.

"I thought you worked out this morning?" she noted.

"Keeping tabs on me?" he asked, starting to run again.

"Hardly. I just saw you go into your apartment earlier. All sweaty," she said, her gaze checking him and his sweat out. He might have been misreading things earlier in her kitchen, but there was no denying the look of attraction on her face now before she quickly diverted her gaze to the mirror. She was definitely checking him out this time. And perhaps even liking what she saw?

Eddie pretended to check his watch. "Yeah, this morning was cardio. Tonight is weights. Just doing a quick warm-up... and done," he said, stopping the treadmill and climbing off.

If she wanted something to ogle, he'd give her something to ogle.

Removing his T-shirt, he headed toward the weight bench.

Seriously, Eddie?

Montana's foot slipped from the stationary bike, sending the pedals into a chaotic spin as she watched Eddie toss his sweaty T-shirt onto the bench press. She was always surprised when she saw him shirtless. He was muscular in an unassuming way, but when he revealed the sculpted chest, biceps and abs, there was no denying he was built like a rock statue of a god.

Even most of the athletes she knew didn't have quite the sculpted body that Eddie did. She'd dated a lot of attractive men in her younger days, all of whom trained hard and focused on creating their best bodies, but no one was quite so chiseled. Tank was a tank, big, solid and all muscle, but she preferred Eddie's leaner look. It made him both sexy as hell and approachable. A dangerous combination.

She kept her gaze down but continued to watch as he straddled the bench, sat and then lowered himself down onto his back. He rubbed his hands together before reaching for the bar. The weights on either side looked impossible to lift, but he lowered and raised the bar with ease.

So, the muscles weren't just for looks.

Then again, what had she expected? Eddie was a cop. He trained and worked out all the time. His safety on the job required him to be strong. Quick. Skilled.

He finished pumping out his reps, then replaced the bar and sat up. He took a gulp of water, wiped his hands on a towel as he stood and approached the chin-up bar.

There was no way to look away as he lifted his body up more reps than she could count, distracted by the bulging biceps and tight core. Sweat poured perfectly down his stomach, and Montana's mouth actually watered.

How was it even possible to have oblique muscles like that? Smooth, tanned, disappearing below the waistband of his sweatpants…

The only other men on earth that seemed to have them were Zac Efron and Channing Tatum, and she'd always assumed they were special effects or computer generated.

"You stopped pedaling," Eddie said as he lowered himself back to ground.

Shit. She forced her attention back to her own workout. She was annoyed at Lance for bailing and had come down to the gym to let off a little steam, not ignite flames of lust by watching Eddie work out.

Besides, that's exactly what he wanted. He wasn't fooling her. He was shirtless and flexing every muscle in his body right now to get her attention.

Well, if that's how he wanted to play it...

Montana climbed off the bike. Approaching the wall, she took down a yoga mat and unrolled it along the mirror. She stood at one end, raised her arms overhead on a long inhale, then lowered them down to the ground on an exhale, walking her hands forward until her body was in plank position, then moving through her yoga flow slowly, until she was in downward dog position.

"Damn." Eddie muttered under his breath.

Then, all she heard as she continued moving gracefully through the motions was the sound of the gym door closing behind Eddie as he left. She assumed it was to go take a cold shower.

Which was exactly what she needed as well.

CHAPTER FIVE

DIVA CURLED AT Montana's fect as she sat on the floor, her back against the sofa in Cassie's living room the following evening. The Siberian husky snored as the credits for the latest hit rom-com rolled on the television. As usual, Cassie was sniffing and wiping a tear from her eye, and Erika was dissecting the plot and expressing her annoyance over the way the heroine had been expected to give it all up to find love.

Rom-coms weren't Montana's thing in general; she preferred action/adventure movies, but these weekly girls' nights were important to her. Spending time with Erika and Cassie helped keep her sane here in Wild River, so she put up with the overly dramatic movies full of over-the-top emotion that made her gag as much as the unrealistic dialogue that no guy would ever speak.

At least not any man she'd ever dated.

Cassie reached for the remote and hit the Pause button. "Well, I thought it was romantic," she said.

"That's because you're so freaking in love right now, it's disgusting," Erika said, readjusting her eye masks that had started to slide down her cheeks.

Cassie raised an eyebrow. "Oh, and you and my brother are an old married couple?" She scoffed. "Hardly."

Erika grinned. "Did I tell you we did it in an empty recovery room two days ago when he stopped by to bring me lunch?"

Montana shook her head. "Never put me in that recovery room," she said, though she suspected Erika and Reed had probably had sex in many unusual and perhaps slightly illegal places all over Wild River. She'd shown up on more than one occasion for her shift at the search and rescue cabin to find the door locked and Erika and Reed supposedly asleep inside. And she knew Erika and Reed's pee schedules couldn't possibly be that in sync, yet every time they hung out, the two of them magically always had to visit a restroom at the same time.

It didn't bother Montana one bit. It was awesome how in love and in lust Erika and Reed were. Cassie's brother definitely pulled out another side to Cassie's best friend. That's why they were perfect together. Erika lit up at the sight of Reed, and he was obviously as crazy about her, but they also complemented one another. They had the whole *opposites attract* thing working for them.

Would she ever find that real connection with someone?

So far she hadn't. But she hadn't really been looking. When she was young she was wild, and free-spirited relationships were all of the casual sort. She'd met Tank years before while in Wild River BASE jumping at the original legal site, and while he'd fallen hard for her, the feelings she'd had for him were admiration, respect, physical attraction and friendship. Even after she discovered she was pregnant and they'd tried to make things work, there hadn't been that real solid, let's-grow-old-together connection. She'd never been able to fully commit to Tank. Something always held her back. Something had been missing.

Then after her BASE-jumping accident, her focus hadn't been on love or finding someone to settle down with. It had been on getting back to the person she'd once been. She'd always thought love and commitment would come to her someday…but she was thirty-four years old, and it was nowhere in sight.

"How are things with Lance?" Erika asked, as though reading her mind.

Montana straightened her legs out in front of her. "Casual. Fun…"

The other women stared at her as though she were completely oblivious to Lance's playboy ways.

"Look, I know the boy will ruin my life if I let him, but don't worry. I'm not in love with him or anything close." Which was disheartening. Lance was exactly her type—adventurous, athletic, gorgeous, spontaneous, slightly unavailable, so she knew not to get too close… If she wasn't getting those butterflies and fanny flutters for Lance, then would she ever?

Eddie had given her both.

A moment of insanity, that's all the night before had been. She refused to read into the twelve-hour attraction to her neighbor. He'd helped her, and he was admittedly stupid hot. That was all there was to it.

"Why not, do you think?" Cassie asked the million-dollar question plaguing her. "I mean, do you think it's just because you have walls up that you know it might not be the best idea to go there with a guy like Lance? Or are you just not feeling him?"

"I'm not sure. Little from column A, little from column B?" How did she explain it to two women so much in love? "I guess I'm being careful not to open myself up just yet, but at the same time, I'm not sure there's any real danger… if that makes any sense?"

"How was your date last night?"

She shifted her position on the floor and avoided their hungry-for-gossip expressions. "It was good." There really wasn't anything juicy to tell. He'd arrived, he'd received a text, and he'd bailed...taking the food with him.

"You know you're talking to two women whose boyfriends work at the bar, right?" Erika called her on her bullshit.

They knew exactly how her evening had gone. "It was a short date," she admitted.

"Did he actually bail on you, after you went through the trouble of cooking for him?" Cassie asked.

Montana waved a hand. "It was nothing, and besides, Eddie did most of the work." She clamped her lips shut. Shit.

"Eddie helped you cook?" Erika's eyes lit up.

"Any new development there?" Cassie asked.

"Where?" Playing dumb would only afford her so long. Cassie threw a couch cushion at her. "With Eddie!"

How did Montana know this question was coming? They really didn't get that a conversation about her love life in any capacity should never logically turn to talking about Eddie. He was her annoying-as-shit neighbor. End of story.

Her palms getting slightly sweaty at the mention of him meant nothing. It was just a physical reaction to having this conversation yet again. "No development. Not even plans for development," she said, reaching for her empty wine glass. "Anyone need a refill?"

They nodded, and she collected the glasses and headed for the kitchen. She knew the minute she was out of earshot, they'd be talking about how crazy she was not to see Eddie as a potential match and how oblivious she must be not to notice Eddie's attraction to her. Neither was true. She saw Eddie's attraction, especially the night before. But she and Eddie together? No way. The guy was the walking definition of *good*. And she was, well, not evil, but definitely mischievous, and she liked herself that way. She wouldn't date a guy who might make her feel like her risk-taking and rule-bending approach to life was wrong.

Montana opened the fridge and took out the wine. As she closed the door, she scanned the pictures of Tank and Cassie and Kaia, plus several with her photobombing in the back, and she sighed. She loved being in her daughter's life and the part-time parenting situation might be all she'd ever be capable of. Their situation worked for all of them, and she adored the coparenting routine they had working. But would there ever be a fourth adult in these pictures, and if so, what would that look like?

Single, she'd only ever had to deal with what was best for her, and dating had been challenging enough. Now, as a *single mom*, things were much different. She didn't think she was looking at relationships with an eye to finding a suitable stepdad for her daughter someday, but maybe subconsciously she was. Maybe that's why her feelings couldn't get any deeper for the playboy snowboarder.

An image of Eddie and the memory of his arms around her in her kitchen as he tied her apron the night before appeared in her mind, and her chest tightened. She poured the wine quickly and headed back into the living room before the temporary insanity from the evening before could once again take over her common sense.

EDDIE WALKED INTO the station on Monday morning only to hear the dreaded words *Captain's looking for you* from his coworker, Angel Sanchez.

A quick mental recap of the last week didn't reveal anything he could be in shit over. "Did he say what it's about?" he asked, dropping his gym bag on the floor next to his desk.

"No. But he didn't look happy," Sanchez said, returning to the mountain of paperwork on his desk. Unlike Eddie,

Sanchez liked to save up his reports and do them all at the beginning of the following month. His desk was always a mess, whereas Eddie's was neat and tidy.

Unfortunately, it meant Sanchez always looked busy and Eddie looked like a slacker from being too efficient. He hoped a transfer to a busier division would help fill the days more. Make him feel useful and confident that he was actually making a difference in the world.

Eddie walked to Captain Clarkson's office and knocked on the partially open door. "You wanted to see me, sir?"

Captain Clarkson looked up from a file on his desk. "Come in and close the door."

Great. Door closed was bad news. But he couldn't remember pissing off the captain in recent weeks. When he'd first joined the department, he'd annoyed the man all the time with his overzealous approach to the job. But Eddie had quickly learned that most of the troopers in Wild River were happy with the slower pace and lack of crime in the resort town. They preferred to leave what they referred to as the *drama* and *excitement* to the local search and rescue crew.

"Have a seat," Captain Clarkson said. He removed his bifocals and sat back in his chair. The buttons on his shirt strained to stay together. They all called him Captain Teddy Bear behind his back. He tried to act tough, but inside he was softhearted and compassionate. And he was quite literally shaped like a teddy bear.

Eddie sat.

"This came for you today." Captain Clarkson slid an unopened envelope toward him.

Eddie's mouth went dry seeing the Alaska Bureau of Alcohol and Drug Enforcement logo in the corner. Here he was waiting for a call or an email…but of course they'd send a letter. More formal and less personal if they were rejecting his application. He stared at it, remembering all the other bad-news and rejection letters he'd received over the years. The anticipation, the waiting, the heart racing at the sight of an answer being so close. Too many times that answer had been no, which made it impossible for him to reach for the envelope. "You open it."

Captain Clarkson stared at him. "You want to catch big, bad drug dealers, but you don't have the balls to open a letter?"

"That's correct, sir."

The captain picked up the envelope and opened it. He scanned it.

Eddie watched and waited. "Well?"

"Well, I think you better find your balls. Fast."

No fucking way. "My application was accepted? The transfer promotion request… I got it?"

His boss handed him the letter. "You're an asshole, Eddie. For three years you drove me crazy with applications and requests for make-up testing every time you failed the written components of your application. You outshine everyone in the academy and surpass all expectations. I finally let you on my team, and now you're leaving us?"

It was so true. Eddie had been persistent with his applications, and he owed Captain Clarkson so much for giving him this opportunity in the first place. The man had gone to bat for him, even when his third written-test scores weren't great, and he'd obviously given him a good reference if his promotion transfer was approved…

Holy shit, his promotion transfer was approved!

He could barely find his voice. "I'm sorry, sir. It's just—"

"It's just that you have huge-ass shoes to fill in your family and you're not going to do that here. I get it. Now, get out of my office before I call Anchorage and tell them to reconsider."

Eddie stood. "Yes, sir. Thank you, sir…for everything."

Eddie stared at the acceptance letter as he sat at his desk moments later. He was being promoted. In two weeks, he was expected to report for duty as a member of the drug enforcement division in Anchorage.

Two weeks.

He had two weeks to get a new place and move an hour away. Two weeks before the career and the future he'd been working hard for began. He could finally embark on a path that might earn him some respect in his family and make his mother proud. He could be formally involved with the investigation into the drug problem in the state. He'd worked his butt off, and it had paid off.

We are happy to accept your application…

He reread the letter, hardly believing it was real. It was really happening. He was leaving Wild River.

Pride and happiness made him sigh with relief, and he ignored the slight uneasiness he felt in the pit of his stomach at the thought of saying goodbye to his favorite neighbor.

Things had changed slightly between them in the last twenty-four hours. He'd felt the shift. Had she felt it, too? Of course it would happen now, when he was leaving. Whatever odd attraction had developed between them was too late.

Life decisions could not be made based on a woman who found him annoying as hell.

CHAPTER SIX

THE MAN WAS definitely in his element.

Montana watched with amusement as Lance signed autographs for a group of female tourists. The professional snowboarder was well loved in Wild River and he didn't seem to tire of the attention. He hadn't revealed much about his past, but she knew from the media that he'd been raised by his father who was also his former snowboarding coach. The man had pushed his son beyond his physical capacity to train and be the best. It had bordered on child abuse, and Lance had eventually fired his father and hired a new coach. The two men hadn't spoken since, but Ralph Baker hadn't made it a secret that he expected his son to fail in that year's winter competitions. A legend in his own right, Lance's father was interviewed almost as much as Lance was, even though he wasn't directly involved in the sport anymore.

But despite Ralph's criticism of his son in the media, the community rallied around their star athlete, and Lance deserved to enjoy the praise and respect he received. Even though he was technically aligned with SnowTrek Tours's direct competition, it wasn't a big deal to Montana. North Mountain Sports Company could have the snow legend as their new spokesperson. SnowTrek Tours wasn't focused on snowboarding adventures anyway.

"Sorry about that," Lance said as the women reluctantly moved on. "I don't even know how they always recognize me."

Montana raised an eyebrow. "You're shitting me, right?"

As if his signature platinum-blond hair wasn't enough, the logoed Olympic clothing he wore everywhere was a dead giveaway. "You look like you're photoshoot-ready at any moment. Of course people recognize you." And even if they didn't know he was a superstar on the slopes, Lance wasn't struggling for female attention. At six foot two and a hundred and seventy pounds, with permanently tanned skin and light green eyes, he was a head-turner.

"Are you saying I need new clothes?"

"I'm saying if you want a night out without adoring fangirls, you might want to consider a change of wardrobe."

Lance looked like he was considering it, then shook his head. "Not going to happen."

"I didn't think so," Montana said with a laugh.

"So, your first training course started last week, right?"

Impressive that he remembered. Maybe he wasn't completely self-absorbed after all. She'd agreed to meet him for drinks that evening, despite her better judgment, as he wanted to make it up to her for bailing on dinner Saturday night. "Yes. A group of eight. They've all completed at least ten skydives but none are experienced BASE jumpers, so I expect to have eight students turn into about five by middle of next week."

Lance leaned on his elbows. "Are the two activities really that different?"

"Absolutely. Jumping from a plane, you have time. You free-fall long enough to get your bearings, get used to the sensation, remember your training. BASE jumping is fast and dirty. The free fall is short, and you need to be alert at all times. The way you position your body, your reaction time—it all matters."

"I don't think I've ever met a woman who is more bad-ass than I am," he said, taking her hand in his.

Montana shifted on the wooden bench. It wasn't the first

time he'd made such a comment, and it left her feeling uneasy. She knew what attracted him to her was just that—her adrenaline-seeking, extreme-sport ways, but she wasn't that woman anymore. Not entirely anyway. "So, what came out of New York?"

Lance shook his head. "I've signed NDAs on top of NDAs. Man, this corporate side of things is shit. I just want to snowboard."

"The price of fame." Montana's cell chimed on the table. She took her hand back and reached for it. "Sorry, it's Kaia."

Lance immediately sat back in the booth as she read quickly.

Camp is going great! First official campfire is tonight. Miss you! Xo

She responded, Great! Love you! Have a fun night.

Knowing her daughter was having fun helped to soothe the sting of not seeing her. Still, she left the phone on the table, in case Kaia texted again. "She just left for camp last week. For a month."

Lance nodded. "Cool…"

"It is. For her. I'm freaking out, but this will be good for her." She'd been reminding herself of that every few minutes since the bus drove away.

Lance scanned the bar. Clearly uninterested.

"My talking about my kid really weirds you out, doesn't it?"

He shrugged. "Nah. I just…kids are just not something I get."

Some days their seven-year age gap was a massive crater between them. Or maybe just their situations in life. Lance was still traveling the world and competing in high-level sports. Montana was learning to adjust to small-town, normal life. "Well, you know I'm a mom…"

"Yeah, I try not to think about it."

Wonderful. This thing with Lance was going nowhere fast. She'd known it all along, but his lack of interest in her beyond her past, exciting career was telling. It had been fun at first, and she'd thought she was okay with just having fun, but facing the inevitable breakup speech, she realized she'd been hoping for more.

Maybe not exactly from Lance…but someone. Which meant, maybe she was ready to put herself out there. Try a real relationship.

Across the bar, a champagne-bottle cork popped, catching her attention. Eddie sat in a booth with several members of the state troopers office. They were all hollering and cheering. Clearly celebrating.

And it must be over something really good. She'd never seen that look of pride and happiness on Eddie's face before.

"Friend of yours?" Lance asked, his obvious dislike of the uniform evident.

"My neighbor."

"Your neighbor's a cop? That's no fun."

"It's not so bad." Eddie had actually been really great when she'd gone missing in the woods months ago. He'd helped Tank and the search and rescue team get into her apartment when no one had heard from her, and his quick thinking bringing one of her pillow cases to the search site for Diva to get her scent was probably what saved her life. She hadn't forgotten that. Eddie had played a huge role in her being found that day.

She watched him laugh and joke with his coworkers now. He had a nice smile. Genuine. Not one ounce of cockiness in his entire body, which was different from someone in his position. Cops needed to be cocky. They dealt with assholes and criminals, putting their lives at risk for the job daily. But Eddie seemed like the most sincere, nonegotistical man she'd ever met.

He was a good guy.

Maybe that was her hesitancy to get close to him. He was good, and the verdict was still out on her.

"Hey…you still with me?" Lance waved a hand in front of her face, and she reluctantly turned her attention back to her date.

Her last one with Lance. She couldn't continue to date him when she didn't see a potential future with him. She was quickly realizing she didn't want to waste any more time.

"Yes, sorry. What were we talking about?" From the corner of her eye, she saw Eddie being dragged toward the dance floor by a woman she didn't recognize. They took turns taking swigs directly from the champagne bottle as they moved in time to the music. His hips swayed, and his feet definitely moved to the beat.

Shit, Eddie could dance, and he looked like a lot of fun when he loosened up…

"I was asking if the launch site would be open on time." Lance said, his gaze drifting past her to a group of women in a nearby booth staring at him.

"Yes, we are on schedule." That's all he would get from her. Her loyalty was with Cassie and making their new venture a success. She didn't trust Lance. He could easily be relaying information back to the executives at North Mountain Sports Company, and Montana wouldn't put Cassie's company at risk from her biggest competitor.

His cell phone rang, and he glanced at it. "Sorry, I've got to get this," he said, picking it up.

"Take your time. I'm going to the ladies' room." Then she was calling it a night. Entertaining herself with Lance was okay, but maybe it was time to start thinking about what she wanted long-term.

Her gaze drifted toward Eddie again as she climbed out of the booth and headed toward the restrooms.

Was Eddie long-term?

Maybe once she ended things with Lance, she could explore that possibility. Take things slow. Get to know him. See how things progressed. She didn't have to rush into something new...but she didn't have to try so hard to prevent something from happening between them, either.

Her step felt lighter as she rounded the corner in the bar and...came up short at the end of a long line of women waiting for the restroom.

There was no way she was standing in a lineup of twenty women when the men's room was free. Tank kept the place spotless, including the men's room, and besides, at one time she'd been part owner of The Drunk Tank, and that gave her special privileges to break the rules, didn't it?

Walking past the waiting women, she opened the door to the men's room and went inside. She ignored the surprised-looking man standing at the urinals and dove into a stall. She peed quickly, and he was gone when she reemerged. She took her time as she washed her hands, then fixed her hair in the mirror.

What should she say to Lance? Saying it was over would imply that they'd had something more serious than they did. Saying she didn't want to see him again seemed a little harsh... Maybe she shouldn't say anything at all and just say no to any future date requests.

If there were any. Remembering the look on his face when she'd mentioned Kaia, maybe they were on the same page. Maybe he wouldn't ask her out again, anyway. Either way, he was leaving soon to train full-time with his snowboarding team and wouldn't be back until Thanksgiving.

Yeah…letting things ride might be the easiest way to play it.

Exiting the bathroom a minute later, she ran into Eddie on his way in. He laughed, shaking his head. "Why am I not surprised to see you come out of there, Montana?"

She blinked. "Since when do you call me by my real name?"

Eddie's slightly drunk smile got wider. "So, you *do* like it?"

She shrugged. "I don't hate it as much as I pretend to." Nope, she was not flirting with Eddie. At least not while she was on another date. She cleared her throat. "What's going on at your table?"

"A celebration."

"Yeah, the drinking champagne straight from the bottle kinda tipped me off to that. What are you celebrating?"

"My promotion. I got accepted to the Alaska Bureau of Alcohol and Drug Enforcement."

"Wow! Congrats! No more trail-security detail for you." Impressive. He'd only been on the force six months, and already he was moving up the ranks.

"And no more listening to my horrible guitar playing for you."

She smiled. "That's definitely a plus. You'll be too busy with the new job to pursue your music career?"

"Oh, no. I'm not giving up my calling just yet. I'll just be in Anchorage," he said, studying her.

Her smile faded. "You're moving?"

Eddie nodded. "In two weeks."

"Shit, that's fast." Eddie drove her batshit crazy as a neighbor, so why was she suddenly feeling sad that she wouldn't have to tell him not to call her Danger anymore?

Too many familiar things changing around her at once, that was all. Kaia gone to camp. A new career. A breakup-sorta-thing with Lance about to happen, and now Eddie moving.

"You okay?" he asked.

"Yeah! Fine!" Too enthusiastic.

"You're not actually going to miss me, are you?" The flicker of interest in his expression made her wonder if she might—and if maybe *he* might miss *her.* Could Erika be right? Was he into her? The attraction had been evident the other night, but was it more than that?

"I don't know." Why had she said that? She should have said no. She should have lied.

He leaned against the wall. His body moving close to hers. The smell of champagne and his soft, inviting cologne lingering in the air between them. "So, you don't exactly hate my guitar playing."

"It will be the thing I miss the least," she said. Her eyes took in his muscular forearm next to her head.

"What will you miss the most?" He leaned even closer. One step toward him, and she would be close enough to kiss him...

"I felt safe having you next door." Where the hell had that confession come from?

Eddie looked just as shocked. His gaze met hers and held. Her entire body tingled, and all of a sudden she was seeing everything everyone else already had. Eddie was not the guy she chose to pin him as. He was sexy and strong and sincere and honest...and just the littlest bit exciting right now. "Are we having a moment?" he asked, his expression searching hers.

They weren't *not* having a moment, but it was too late. He was leaving. In two weeks.

She forced herself to look away from his intense gaze. "Good luck in Anchorage, Eddie," she said and walked away from him before she could do something dumb like admit she might actually like him.

"Hey, wanna ride?" Sanchez asked, sticking his head out of his truck window as he drove past Eddie on Main Street an hour later.

"Nah, it's a beautiful night. I'll walk." Might be one of the last late-night strolls along Main Street he'd have for a while. And the fresh air would help soften the hangover he was no doubt in for the next morning. He wasn't a big drinker, so the mix of champagne and shots that evening would definitely take their toll.

"Okay, man… Congrats again. You deserve this opportunity. Try not to fuck it up."

Eddie laughed. "That's my goal."

Heading toward his apartment building, he took a moment to appreciate his surroundings. Wild River had been home to him for so long. Even after his grandmother and mother and sisters moved to different areas of Alaska outside of the resort town, he'd stayed. The vast, beautiful wilderness combined with the modern, hip vibe of the tourist town had made it a perfect place to live.

But now it was time to move on. Time for a new chapter.

His cell phone chimed, and he read the text from his sister, Katherine.

Congrats, bro! You're almost as cool as me now.

Praise in his family was hard to come by, so he'd take it.

He tucked the phone into his back pocket as he passed SnowTrek Tours. He'd probably miss this part about his current position the most. Patrolling Main Street during the day and catching a glimpse of a certain brunette working inside.

Montana's reaction when he'd told her he was moving

had surprised him. He'd expected her to have popped her own bottle of bubbly at the news, but she'd actually looked disappointed.

She'd felt safe having him live next door. Damn, what an unexpected confession.

He shook his head. She was probably just worried that the new neighbor might be worse. The devil you know, and all that...

He slowed his pace seeing her a few blocks ahead, walking with Lance.

Damn. Don't turn around.

The last thing he needed was for her to think he was stalking her. Again.

Her voice floated back toward him, and it was a sound he would miss. Sharing an apartment wall, he heard it whenever Kaia was around and recognized its absence when the little girl wasn't.

Clearly, Montana was struggling with her new life, but she was determined to make the best of it. He admired that. Admired her.

At first, he'd been concerned for Tank and Kaia and Cassie... Montana's intentions hadn't rung true for him, but she'd proven to be here for all the right reasons, despite how tough it had to be to be unable to do the one thing she loved most.

She was amazing. Putting her daughter first. Her new venture with Cassie first.

He watched her with Lance, and his heart fell. She deserved so much more than that self-absorbed athlete.

Man, he had it worse than he thought he did. Maybe it was for the best that he was headed to Anchorage. At least he wouldn't have to watch her fall for the wrong guy.

A shadow to his left caught his eye, and he turned to see a figure head into the alleyway between the bakery and flower shop. He walked a little faster and saw a man dressed in jeans and a dark hoodie reappear across the street, several paces behind Montana and Lance.

The man was watching them.

Eddie picked up his pace, fighting to get a look at the man's face, but the darkness in the shade of the buildings prevented a clear view.

But the gun the man held was visible enough in the bright beam of the streetlight.

What the hell?

His pulse quickened and adrenaline flowed through him. His training kicked in, and he started to run as the man lifted the gun, pointing it toward Lance and Montana.

"Montana!" he yelled, as he approached.

She and Lance stopped and turned, and a glance toward the man with the gun had Eddie diving...

Next he was free-falling, his body shielding Montana's as they hit the ground.

He felt the bullet pierce his skin before he heard the shot. Searing pain at the base of his spine radiated throughout his entire body as his consciousness wavered.

The ground was unsteady beneath him and dizziness made it hard to focus. Montana's voice sounded far away as she called his name.

He blinked several times, trying not to pass out. His lower body went numb, then the rest of him, and all he could feel was his heart pounding in his chest.

Montana's face above him, her panicked look of terror was the only thing he saw. He reached out to touch her as the world faded in a hazy mist around him.

"Hey...what's up, Danger?" he said before everything went black.

CHAPTER SEVEN

Waking up to bright lights shining in his face was not a good sign. At least he wasn't dead. He didn't think the afterlife was this...noisy.

Voices. Mostly female. Mostly loud. All talking at once.

"Oh, my God, he's awake." His grandmother's voice, then her face peering down at him. "What the hell were you thinking, young man? Jumping in front of a bullet."

"That's kinda my job, Gran," he said, but there was no way she could have heard him. He could barely make out the words. His voice was hoarse, and his ears felt clogged.

"This is why we didn't want you following in our footsteps," Katherine said, stepping closer to the bed. She was still in pissed-off mode. His older sister cycled through emotions when she was scared. First, she pretended it was nothing—he must have been asleep for that reaction—then she was angry, which was the stage they were currently in, based on her tone. Eventually, she'd be upset. He wished he could go back to sleep for the third one. His sister was a hard-ass, and he liked her that way. The few times he'd seen her come apart had nearly destroyed him.

And if she was standing in his hospital room right now, his injuries must be serious. Katherine hated hospitals. She'd refused to visit their father in the hospital years before, until his final days when she'd needed to say goodbye to him.

His mother appeared next to them. "Don't listen to them,

Eddie. You did the right thing. What you were trained to do," she said.

That made him instantly relax. Approval. Good. Finally. He'd only had to get shot to get it, but he'd focus on the positive. He remembered jumping, crashing to the sidewalk and feeling pain in his lower back—and Montana's concerned look. He quickly scanned the room, but she wasn't there now. "Is Montana okay?"

"Yes," his mother said. "She's in the waiting room. She's been here the whole time."

No doubt the hospital—most likely Erika—was bending the rules already, allowing his mother, grandmother and sister in the room all at once, but if he'd had a choice of whose face he wanted to wake up and see, it would have been Montana's. In his deep sleep, he'd dreamt about her...

"The shooter?"

"He got away. Wild River dispatch is still looking for possible suspects, and they're asking for witnesses to come forward. So far no one has. Neither Montana nor the man she was with saw the perpetrator." His mother leaned closer. "Once you're feeling a little better, I'll get them to come in and get your statement."

Not wasting time was important, and the longer the delay before he recounted the events and gave a full description, the less credible his statement would be. The mind forgot or refabricated details the longer they waited.

"What are my injuries?" he asked.

His grandmother looked at his mother. She looked at Katherine. Katherine left the room.

Shit.

"Come on... Someone tell me what's going on."

Erika entered the room before anyone could find the words, and Eddie could see his sister standing outside the door.

Fantastic. She'd brought the doctor in. Not a good sign.

Erika Sheraton was an amazing surgeon and someone Eddie liked to think of as a friend, but while she'd come a long way in her bedside manner since working at Alaska General, she was still able to deliver bad news to patients without batting an eyelash, and right now he felt as though he could use a sugarcoated version of things.

"Hi, Eddie," Erika said, checking his vitals on the machine next to him. "How're you feeling?"

"I don't feel anything." Which was terrifying. At least with pain, he could deal with it. Not knowing why he was numb was daunting.

"We will try to keep it that way for a little while longer to make sure you can get some rest."

"How long have I been here?" Suddenly he realized it felt like days.

"Two days."

It was a worse injury than he thought.

"We did surgery last night. The good news is I was able to remove the bullet. It remained mostly intact, so there aren't any fragments that we are worried about traveling through the bloodstream. The bullet's been handed over to forensics."

So much for hoping it was a flesh wound.

"The bad news is that it hit your spine," Erika said. "The damage was in the lower sacral vertebrae. S4 and S5 to be exact."

He had no idea what that meant.

"As you most likely know, the spinal cord acts like the relay center for the brain, and with these types of injuries, it's common to see a disruption in the signals. Damage to the sacral vertebrae can result in loss of function in both hips and legs. Mobility issues and loss of feeling are common issues," she said.

"Am I paralyzed?" How did his voice sound so calm as

he asked the most terrifying question ever? The pain meds must also be impacting his emotions.

The tear sliding down his grandmother's cheek, or the way his sister kept her eyes downcast, refusing to look at him from the doorway, or the way his mother's face looked anguished should have had his pulse bursting through his veins, but there was no fear at all. Just an unsettling calm that he knew would eventually wear off.

"We don't know yet." Blunt, straightforward. Normally, he liked that about Erika. Not today.

"Why not?"

"We need the swelling to go down before X-rays can assess the extent of the damage. We did everything we could for now. We have you on a high dose of methylprednisolone—a steroid to reduce swelling, with the aim of avoiding any secondary damage to the injury site."

Sounded like quite a lot of damage already.

"You are also on a high dose of morphine, an anti-inflammatory and a strong antibiotic to ward off any chance of infection from surgery. We will continue those for a few days as well."

So many drugs. He barely took pain medication for headaches. No wonder he couldn't feel anything. "So, what now?"

"We just need to wait a few days and hope for the best," Erika said, her voice softening. "I'm sorry I don't have better news. You saved Montana's life. If the bullet had hit her, it would have most definitely hit an internal organ. You truly are a hero."

He'd always expected those words to mean more. As a kid, he dreamed of being a superhero, saving the planet from aliens or monsters. Then, as an adult, he'd wanted to protect people from real dangers. Now he had, and it seemed insanely anticlimactic.

Just him lying in a hospital bed with no way of knowing whether or not he'd walk out of there on his own.

He needed more. Something to hope for, at least. "Your best guess," he asked Erika. "What are the chances I'm… okay?" He couldn't ask if he'd walk again.

Erika shook her head. "You're alive, and honestly, for a little while last night, I wasn't sure even that would be possible. Surgery was touch and go. Your blood pressure and heart rate kept spiking."

Jesus. Sugarcoat *something*, Erika!

Her expression softened as though sensing she'd provided too much detail. "We still have you. That's what matters right now. We will figure out next steps as we gain more clarity regarding the extent of the damage."

Eddie released a deep breath. He should thank her for saving his life and he would…eventually. Right now, he just closed his eyes and hoped that he was still asleep and that the next time he woke up, there would be a better prognosis.

His life may not have ended on the sidewalk two days ago, but there was a significant chance that in that split-moment decision, his future had drastically been sent off course.

MONTANA PACED THE hospital waiting room. She hadn't gone home over the last few days. They were finally allowed to see Eddie, and she was nauseous as she waited her turn. Her stomach churned, and her palms sweat at the recurring memory that refused to leave her. Hearing Eddie call her name, turning to see him lunging toward her, then the gunshot ringing loud in her ears and seeing the blood pooling on the sidewalk. Eddie's blood. Not hers.

It could have been hers.

His family was in the room with him, and she'd just seen

Erika go in, but no one was telling her anything beyond that he was alive and surgery had gone well. The bullet was out.

Bullet. One that could have been lodged in her body.

It could be her in the hospital bed right now. She swallowed the lump in her throat that had kept resurfacing over the last forty-eight hours.

Lance approached with a new coffee. The other three he'd brought her sat cold on the table, but she appreciated the gesture and something to do with her hands. "Thank you," she said, accepting the cup from him.

"Any update?" he asked, taking a sip from his own cup.

"Not yet. His family is still in there, and Erika went in a few minutes ago." She paced back and forth. "Shit, Lance. What if something is really wrong?" Her chest ached thinking that something could have happened to Eddie. So much so that she was starting to think her new attraction to her pesky neighbor might go a little deeper than she'd originally thought.

Though, she knew these feelings were common in survivors after a tragic event. A bonding effect with the person who saved them sometimes mirrored real emotions...

But then, how could she explain away the ones she'd had in the bar before the shooting? Their flirty banter had moved into real-attraction territory. She'd been genuinely upset that Eddie would be moving. Now, she was devastated that his future plans could be derailed or, at the very least, put on hold.

Lance wrapped an arm around her and led her to the sofa. "I'm sure he's going to be fine. Erika is a brilliant surgeon. And Eddie's a cop. His natural instinct was to protect us, so don't for a second feel guilty or responsible about this."

He didn't seem guilty or responsible at all, and that had her slightly on edge. He'd come and gone frequently from the hospital over the last few days, but he claimed to be talking to police, trying to figure out who might have shot at them. He didn't doubt for a second that the shooter had been aiming at him, not Montana, and that in itself unnerved her. Why would someone want to kill Lance? And why was he so confident that someone wanted him dead? Was competitive snowboarding really that cut-throat?

So far, the shooter hadn't been located or identified, and Lance hadn't gotten any real answers about the case from police. They'd spoken to her that night, right after the incident, but she'd been of little help. She hadn't seen the perpetrator before the gunshot cut through the air, and afterwards she was concerned and focused on Eddie. She had no idea who could have shot at them. Or why.

Erika walked toward them, and Montana stood. "How is he?"

"He's awake and stable."

"But is he okay?" *Awake and stable* meant nothing. She'd once been awake and stable, and she'd ended up with a brain injury that consumed so much of her life. Her sister had once been awake and stable, too. Until she'd dry drowned hours later. Those words meant nothing. Reassurance from Erika was what she needed.

"We don't know the extent of the injuries yet." She paused. "There's damage to his lower vertebrae, and until the swelling goes down, we're not sure what his recovery will look like."

Damage to his spine. Montana's heart fell deep into the pit of her stomach. What if he couldn't walk after this? Fresh tears burned her eyes. "Can we see him?"

"He's resting. His family is leaving in a moment, and as soon as he wakes up again, you can go in."

Damn, she was going crazy not seeing him for herself.

She wanted to lay eyes on him, even for just a second, to see for herself that he was…awake and stable.

"Why don't you go home, and I'll call you as soon as he does?" Erika said, nodding toward Montana's still blood-soaked jeans. She'd changed into Lance's sweatshirt and thrown out the destroyed sweater, covered in Eddie's blood, but she'd refused to go home to shower and change.

Lance stood and nodded his agreement. "That's probably for the best."

Erika shot him a look but nodded as well. "Really, Montana, there's nothing you can do for him here. I'll take care of him, I promise," Erika said, sending her a look that said her concern wasn't unjustified and hadn't gone unnoticed.

If Lance read anything more into Montana's concern, he didn't let on. If he sensed her being here for the last two days was anything more than guilt and obligation, he didn't show it.

"Okay," Montana said reluctantly. "But the minute he's ready to see anyone, please call me."

"I will," Erika said as Lance led her toward the front door.

"Hungry?" he said.

"No." And it irritated her that *he* could be, when the man who saved their lives was barely holding on to his own. How could she ever have thought she could have something more with Lance? Now more than ever, it was very clear to her that they weren't suited to one another.

And the torture of the last forty-eight hours revealed that she had more than just throwaway, casual feelings for Eddie.

She stopped in the doorway of the hospital and shook her head. "I can't leave."

Lance looked slightly annoyed as he turned back to look at her. "You heard Erika. There's no point in staying."

There was for her. She didn't want to walk out of here when Eddie couldn't. She didn't want him to wake up and know that she'd left. She cared for him far more than that. He deserved to know that she'd been here every second that he was. She needed that knowledge for herself, too. "I'm going to stay."

Lance checked his watch. "Okay. Well, I'd like to stay with you. You know I would, but I'm leaving in four hours."

Right. His flight to Aspen for training with the Olympic team. He was still leaving, despite everything that happened. Montana wasn't entirely surprised, but it would have gone a long way if he'd considered changing his flight, staying an extra few days. Making sure Eddie was okay. Making sure she was okay.

Especially if he was right in his assumption that the bullet had been meant for him. How could he not want to see Eddie and thank him himself?

Her eyes were wide open now, and she was seeing everything so clearly. She desperately wished it hadn't taken this tragedy for it to happen.

She nodded. "Okay. You go. I'll stay."

He hesitated as he touched her arm.

She folded them across her chest, and he let his hand fall away. "Keep me posted, okay? And tell Eddie thanks and that I hope he recovers quickly."

So insincere, but she nodded. "Of course. Have a safe flight."

"I'll call you when I get settled in Aspen," Lance said.

She wanted to tell him not to bother. She wanted to tell him not to bother calling her ever again, but she was already emotionally exhausted, and her focus was on Eddie right now.

She watched him leave and then headed back to the waiting room, where Erika was still standing. "I knew you couldn't leave," she said. "Come on. His family just left. I'll sneak you in, but only for two minutes, okay?"

So grateful and happy she'd stayed, Montana hugged Erika quickly. "Yes. Two minutes, I promise," she said.

She followed Erika down the hall, and her pulse raced. Her heart beat so loud, even Erika glanced at her. "Are you okay?"

The paramedics had checked her at the site of the accident, and she'd had no injuries, but a heart attack wouldn't surprise her at all with the way her heart had been pounding for the last two days. "I'm okay," she said.

Erika paused outside Eddie's room. "You went through a traumatic experience. Take it easy for a few days, okay? And let me know if you experience any additional stress or depression or anything, all right?"

Montana nodded. Right now all she cared about was seeing Eddie.

"Two minutes," Erika said as Montana entered the room.

Eddie's eyes were closed, but she could tell he was awake by the way his head turned at the sound of the door closing. Hooked to monitors, with an IV in both hands and dressed in a hospital gown, the sight was unsettling and far too familiar. Montana fought the urge to throw up.

His eyes opened slowly, and he looked at her, his expression completely unreadable. A flash of the way he'd looked at her in the bar as they'd flirted appeared in her mind, followed by the slightly desperate way he'd stared up at her as she'd held his body on the sidewalk, and she swallowed hard as emotions threatened to strangle her.

"Hi… How are you?" she asked, moving closer to the bed. He looked pale and tired, his usual energy gone.

She hadn't realized how much she'd liked that about him until it was no longer there. What could she say or do to bring it back? She'd readily be woken up by his terrible guitar playing again anytime. She'd put up with the way he made her feel inadequate for not being able to cook. She craved his overprotective nature—the one that had resulted in him lying there.

"I'm okay," he said, trying to prop himself higher on the bed.

"Can I get you anything? Do you need anything?" Seemed so generic. So bland. He deserved to hear something important, something meaningful from her right now, but she couldn't fabricate the thoughts, let alone vocalize the words.

"Nah, I'm good. Thanks," he said.

The awkward tension lingering on the stale hospital air was nearly suffocating. "I guess the apartment building's been quiet without me, huh?" he said.

"I haven't been there," she said. She pulled the sweatshirt lower, trying to block the blood stains. Maybe she should have gone home and changed. The sight of his own blood on her clothing probably wasn't reassuring.

"You really didn't need to stick around," he mumbled.

"Of course I did. You saved—"

"You know, I'm kinda tired," he interrupted.

Montana swallowed hard. Obviously, he didn't want to talk about the fact that he'd taken a bullet for her, yet it was all she wanted to talk about right now.

"Right. Okay. Well, I wanted to thank you…" The rest of her sentence was choked by the new lump forming in her throat. Nothing she could say would be enough. He was lying here, his future uncertain because he'd saved her.

"Just doing my job," he said, a hardness appearing in his voice.

Was he regretting that? Or regretting the impact it now had on him?

She wouldn't blame him for either. She moved closer and touched his hand. "I'm so sorry, Eddie."

He stiffened. "Yeah. Listen, I'm supposed to be resting, so..."

He wanted her to leave. She desperately wanted to stay.

She stared at him but couldn't find a single trace of the Eddie she knew, the Eddie she recognized...

Come on, Eddie. Come back to life!

It was unfair to expect. After her injury, she was angry, sad, confused. Depression had hit her hard for months as she struggled with her memory loss, the aggravation of not feeling like herself, being unable to function like before. Simple things felt hard. Nothing was as it was before. Helpless and hopeless. Eddie would go through the same myriad of emotions she had. She just hoped his lively spirit would help pull him out of the despair faster.

If that spirit returned.

"Right, yeah, okay. Well, um..." What the hell could she say? Get better? Get some rest? "Can I visit again?" She'd pull up a chair and sleep in it if they'd let her. She wouldn't leave his side. Be there to help in any way she could.

He looked away. "I don't need your pity, Montana, and you don't need to feel any obligation toward me."

That's what he thought? Sure, she was grateful for him— so insanely grateful. But even before this happened, they'd shared a connection, one she still felt.

Obviously, he had other emotions overshadowing any he had for her right now, and that was completely understandable, but she didn't want him to misread her present intentions. "I just want to be here for you...as a friend," she said.

"We're not friends. We were just neighbors," he said.

The blow of dismissive words hit her hard, even though it was his current, justifiable anger speaking. But she wouldn't let him try to push her away. She would be here for him whether he wanted it or not. And not because she felt guilty or responsible—at least, not just because of those things. "I'm here, Eddie. If you need anything. Anything at all. Anytime." She touched his hand gently on the bed, and the same electricity coursed through her at the touch.

He didn't respond. He slowly moved his hand out from beneath hers, and as his eyes closed, Montana could feel his heart closing to her as well.

CHAPTER EIGHT

THE SWELLING WAS down enough to get the MRI.

Eddie forced his heart rate steady. Close, confined spaces were shitty at the best of times. This tight machine about to determine the extent of his injuries had him freaking out.

He'd been an asshole to Montana three days ago, but he hadn't been able to lie there any longer seeing the look of sympathy on her face. She pitied him, felt guilty for what happened.

How could she look at him any other way now? The glimmer of attraction he'd caught on her face the night of the shooting, in the bar, when he'd told her he was leaving, wouldn't be happening again. It felt like a million years ago. Like he'd imagined it.

Whatever attraction she might have started to feel was gone now. An extreme athlete who lived for adventure could never be attracted to a guy who might never walk again.

He'd told Erika not to allow her to visit again. With her around, he couldn't deal with what lay ahead, reminding him about the feelings he had for her. Feelings that he'd had before he'd been shot and feelings that weren't quickly fading. He couldn't deal with the reality that he'd barely had a chance with her before, and now that chance was gone.

He shut his eyes, and tears of anger burned behind his closed lids. He didn't need this machine to tell him his fate. He could feel it. Or rather, he could feel his body shutting down. The morphine wasn't working as well anymore, and pain in his side and core made it difficult to breathe, but his mobility in the lower half of his body was nonexistent on his left side. The right side could move, but barely, and it took more effort than he had in him.

He closed his eyes and steadied his breathing as he lay in the machine, claustrophobia making his heart pound in his ears. Noise-canceling headphones couldn't drown out the terrifying sound of his future being determined.

When Erika entered his room an hour later, he could read it on her face.

"I'm not going to walk again, am I?"

"Do you want to call your family before we discuss the results?" she asked.

"No, I don't." It would be him dealing with the truth. Him having to learn to accept his limitations, his dreams and plans for his future evaporating. His family would only make it worse. "Tell me the truth, Erika."

"The bullet fractured the S4 and S5 vertebrae, as we thought. Mobility on the left side is almost nonexistent, but you still have feeling in that side and you have feeling and slight mobility in the right…"

He nodded. Partial mobility and feeling. He dared to get his hopes up a little.

"Your diagnosis is considered incomplete paralysis and monoplegia, which can be temporary…"

Not the most horrible prognosis so far.

"But full recovery is not expected. Regaining full mobility is possible, and we've seen patients regain their full functioning up to eighteen months after an injury, so we are not ruling that possibility out for you—"

"But…" He heard it coming.

Erika shoved her hands into the pockets of her lab coat.

"But, at this time, the chance of you walking completely on your own again is less than ten percent."

He nodded, his heart hardening. He sat there, hating his body, hating the sight of his unmoving, useless leg, and hating that one split second that had changed his life forever.

"We can start rehab right away and monitor the progress," Erika said. "There are trials and drugs we can start right away as well. We will keep you in for another few weeks. Help you adjust." She paused. "We will do everything we can, but there are no guarantees. I'm sorry, Eddie."

He didn't say anything. She wasn't expecting him to.

Erika and her team would do everything they could for him physically, but it would be up to him to find the strength to heal mentally and emotionally, and right now he wasn't sure he was strong enough.

THE MOOD AT their table at The Drunk Tank was somber as Erika gave them the bad news that evening.

"But the prognosis could be wrong. I mean, there's always the possibility that he will make a full recovery, right?" Even as she said the words, Montana knew the likelihood of it was slim. She'd worked so hard for ten years, and she still hadn't achieved that. Severe injuries rarely worked that way.

Erika shook her head. "I'd love to be wrong in this case, but I don't think so. The bullet did a lot of damage."

Cassie looked devastated. "I just can't believe this is happening to Eddie. He's such a wonderful guy, and he worked so hard to even make it on the police force."

"He'd just gotten his promotion," Montana said. "He was moving to Anchorage." She sipped her martini, staring at the table. Eddie's refusal to allow her to visit him in the hospital hurt, but she understood. He needed time and space to recover, to grieve and to process what he was going through. She wanted to be there for him, but for now she respected his wishes and got her updates from Erika.

Though, she'd been hoping for a much better update from her friend that evening. Meeting for drinks meant they'd either be celebrating or drowning their disappointment. It sucked that it was the latter.

"He still might be able to," Cassie said, but even she didn't sound convinced. "He has some mobility, and there's therapy..."

Erika nodded. "It's not completely hopeless. It will really depend on Eddie. If he can process this quickly and start the healing process sooner rather than later, he has a better shot. His mental attitude will ultimately decide his fate," she said.

Montana sighed. She knew mental fortitude played a huge role in recovery. She'd eventually gathered her strength and determination and used it as fuel to keep getting better, stronger, but she'd had to face the fact that a full recovery was impossible, and Eddie would as well. If he could be strong enough to accept that and want to push for the best possible outcome and not perfection, he would be okay.

"Eddie has a great attitude. He's so sweet and optimistic. I'm sure he will be okay," Cassie said.

Erika and Montana exchanged looks. The guy Montana had seen in the hospital bed three days ago hadn't been the same Eddie they all knew and loved. Based on Erika's expression, she suspected his mood was continuing to spiral downward instead of improving.

"When can he go home?" Montana asked. The apartment building felt so quiet, so lonely without him there. She missed the everyday sounds of him next door. He'd been planning to move, and she'd suspected she would miss him, but she hadn't realized how much until that week when he wasn't there. Though, knowing it was because he was in the hospital made it so much harder.

"Not for a few weeks. We want to start his rehab, and we've recommended a therapist," Erika said. "We want to make sure he's ready."

"I saw his mother and sister in the building talking to a contractor earlier today," she said. She hadn't spoken to them as they'd seemed preoccupied and barely noticed her. They'd met briefly in the hospital and knew she was the woman Eddie had saved, but she didn't think they knew that they'd been neighbors or that lately she'd been developing feelings for him. Talking to them now about all of that would be awkward.

Erika nodded. "Yeah, they want to have the apartment modified for easier mobility before Eddie goes home. They think it will be easier on him if everything is done. He won't have to be there to watch the renovations."

He may not have to watch them, but they would be a part of his life moving forward, and Montana suspected Eddie's homecoming wouldn't be a positive experience for him.

"How are *you* doing?" Erika asked her, concern on her face.

"Me? I'm fine." Erika was worried about her psychological well-being after a tragic incident, but Montana wasn't having recurring nightmares or anxiety about the shooter. She only replayed Eddie's bravery in her mind, and her focus was all on how she could help him.

"You're not freaked out or anything?" Cassie asked, tucking her leg under her on the seat.

"No. Wild River is so much safer than Denver." They had to remember she came from a big city where the likelihood of a random attack was higher and frightened her more than this incident had. "And I don't have any enemies here. I don't think the shooter was aiming for me."

"Lance?" Cassie asked with a frown. "A crazed fan or competitor maybe?"

Montana shrugged. "Who knows? I'm just happy he's away now until Thanksgiving. He's safer at the training camp." She didn't mention that things between them were most definitely over. In light of everything that had happened in recent days, it was hardly significant. As she'd suspected, she hadn't heard from him since he'd left her that day in the hospital, so obviously they were on the same page about where they stood. "I just hope they find the shooter, for Eddie's sake."

Cassie raised her martini glass. "To Eddie and his speedy recovery," she said.

Montana and Erika clinked theirs together with hers. "To Eddie." The man who'd saved her life.

CHAPTER NINE

3 weeks later...

HIS TRUCK HAD sold for six thousand dollars and the wheelchair-accessible van sitting in front of the hospital entrance felt like it cost Eddie his soul. It was white and ugly and the last thing on earth he wanted to drive for the rest of his life.

His rehab and recovery had gone as well as could be expected, with him regaining mobility in his right leg almost completely. So much in fact that it gave him far too much false hope for his left leg. If one could move, why the hell couldn't the other?

Erika and his therapists kept reminding him that his incomplete diagnosis happened a lot more than people realized. He should consider himself lucky, but it was hard to see the silver lining with this eyesore, piece-of-shit van blocking his view of the clouds.

"Ready to go?"

In that thing? Never. He nodded as his driving instructor pushed the accessibility button on the side of the door. The door slid open, and a ramp lowered.

This guy would teach him how to operate the van, and he'd be able to do everything himself. He wouldn't need someone to drive him around town, and his manual wheelchair could be alternated with crutches. He wasn't completely dependent on the chair.

He was lucky. It could be so much worse.

Apparently, if he kept repeating those words to himself, they were eventually supposed to work.

He'd thought the van would be the biggest thing he'd have to adjust to: he'd been wrong. Entering his apartment an hour later, he took in all the necessary upgrades his mother and sister had done to the place.

Guard railings along the walls at waist height. A ramp for easier access to his raised living room. Lowered countertops in the kitchen and railings in the bathroom to assist getting in and out.

Little things. Minor adjustments. That felt so monumental. The simplest actions he'd once taken for granted were now something he had to process. It was difficult to see these upgrades when he still didn't identify as someone who needed them.

But it was time to face the fact that these modifications were a necessary part of what was about to become his modified future.

Tank, Cassie and Montana held up a big Welcome Home sign in the parking lot of the school as they saw the buses pull into the lot. Montana couldn't wait to see Kaia. A month away was far too long, especially since the last three weeks had felt like an eternity. Of course she was also dreading the conversation they'd have to have about the shooting and telling her daughter about Eddie. But first, they'd take her to lunch and listen to all of her fun stories about camp life—and maybe ream her out a little for only sending the one required letter that looked like it had been written before she left for camp, not to mention all the three-word replies to text messages when they had been allowed access to their phones.

"Which bus is she on?" Montana asked Tank.

"Number four. There it is."

"I'm rethinking the sign," Cassie said, though it was her idea. "I thought it was fun, but she might be embarrassed."

"Too late now, and besides, she doesn't embarrass easily," Tank said. "She'll love it."

Kaia *hadn't* embarrassed easily, but now that she was getting older and her interest in boys had clearly started, she might not find the sign as endearing as they'd intended.

They watched the kids get off the bus one by one.

Cassie sniffed. "This was always the saddest part for me. The lifelong friendships made at camp are so important. I always hated the end of summer."

"Yeah. These kids aren't exactly tearful," Montana said as she scanned the faces. In fact, they all looked grumpy. Not sad. Probably tired.

"There she is," Tank said, as Kaia got off the bus and grabbed her oversized duffel bag from the pile on the ground. "Kaia!" he called out.

Kaia glanced their way, and her expression did not scream *Love the sign*, so they all instantly dropped it. She pulled her hoodie up as she trudged toward them, dragging her feet on the gravel.

"Hey, you!" Tank said, taking her bag from her and pulling her in for a hug.

"Hi, Dad," she mumbled.

"Hey, share her!" Montana said with forced enthusiasm, hiding the worry from her voice. Maybe her daughter was really tired or maybe she'd had a fight with a friend, but something was definitely wrong. Her eyes looked heavy, and she looked thinner in the oversize camp sweatshirt. She moved in closer and hugged her next. "Hungry? We were going to go to Snack Shack for lunch." Kaia's favorite.

Kaia shrugged. "I'm really not that hungry. I'd rather just go home."

Cassie shot Montana and Tank a wide-eyed look over

Kaia's head as she crushed her in for a hug. "Milkshakes, at least? I've been craving one since you left," she said.

Kaia nodded. "Okay. Fine," she said, leaving them all behind as she headed toward Tank's truck.

"Do you want to say bye to...?" Cassie's voice trailed as Kaia just kept walking. "Okay. Definitely a different camp experience than I had," she mumbled under her breath.

Two hours later, Kaia's vocabulary had consisted of several *fines*, a dozen *okays* and a lot of uncharacteristic whining. She was tired, she wanted to go home, she wasn't interested in telling them about camp. Tank and Cassie had looked as worried as Montana was about it. Neither of them had ever seen her act this way before. By the time Tank dropped Montana at her apartment building, everyone appeared emotionally exhausted from their attempts to talk to the little girl and keep the mood light, despite her unusually trying attitude.

As Montana unlocked her apartment door, she could hear noises from the one next door. Her heart pounded. Eddie was home. She paused with her key in the door.

Should she knock? Welcome him home?

She'd missed seeing him the past three weeks, had been worried about him, and had been barely satisfied with progress reports about his recovery from Erika, but he hadn't lifted the no-visitation ban.

Well, he couldn't stop her from visiting now. Unless he refused to open the door to her. After the day she'd had with Kaia, that would break her heart. But she desperately craved the sight of him, and Erika had said his therapy had gone well. He was making great progress...

But he'd just got home and maybe needed time to adjust.

Opening her purse, she took out a pen and rummaged around until she found an old receipt. The one from the grocery store four weeks ago—the night he'd helped her cook dinner for Lance. A lifetime ago.

Propping the paper against the wall, she wrote: *Welcome Home.*

What else did she say?

I'm here if you need me? I really want to see you? Please stop avoiding me. You're a jerk for banning me from the hospital?

She crumpled the receipt, tossed it back into her purse and entered her apartment.

"So, how was Kaia's camp experience?"

Montana heard her sister's voice before she'd even turned on the light.

"Not great, apparently." Something had definitely happened to upset her daughter. Maybe Cassie and Tank would have better luck getting her to open up at home once she was rested and wanted to talk. She'd asked them to text or call her if there was any update, but she did feel slightly left out.

It was getting tougher to see Kaia go off with Cassie and Tank when Montana wanted to be there for her as well.

"Why not? Did she get hurt?" Dani asked.

"No, I don't think so… Maybe. She didn't look hurt. She refused to talk about camp or what was bothering her, but she really wasn't herself when we picked her up." Montana put her bag on the kitchen counter and opened the fridge. She'd skipped breakfast, looking forward to lunch with Kaia, so she was starving, yet food didn't appeal to her. She closed the fridge and leaned against the counter. "We're hoping it's just exhaustion and that, once she's had a good night's sleep, she'll be okay."

"Hopefully. That sucks. I always loved camp," Dani said.

"Well, maybe you should have gone with Kaia and kept an eye on her."

"Yeah, that's not how this works."

"How does it work, then? You pick one person to harass for the rest of eternity?" Her irritability was making her lash out at a figment of her overactive brain.

"I don't harass, I—"

"*Visit*, right. I know," she said with a sigh. She rubbed her forehead and neck, tension giving her the start of a migraine.

She reached for her pain medication on the counter, but a loud crash next door had her abandoning the effort to open the childproof lid.

A long silence followed.

"Eddie's back from the hospital?" Dani asked.

"Got home today." She left her apartment and went next door. She knocked on Eddie's door.

Silence.

"Eddie!" she called.

A long pause. Then, "I'm fine."

If she heard one more *fine* that day from people who clearly *weren't* fine, she was going to lose it. She tried the door handle. It was unlocked. She opened it slowly and entered. "I'm coming in!"

"I said I'm fine." His voice was angry, coming from the bathroom.

She swallowed hard as she walked down the short hall. She paused outside the open bathroom door. "Eddie, do you need help?"

"What the hell, Montana? I said I was fine. Please leave."

From the corner of her eye, she saw the wet bathroom floor and the wheelchair overturned. Shit. Help or leave like he asked? "I'm not going to do that. I can help—"

"I don't want your help. I've got this on my own."

She heard him right the wheelchair, so she stayed in the hall, but she refused to leave the apartment without making sure he was okay. Had he hit his head or injured himself in the fall? Her heart was still pounding, and she just wanted to rush in there and make things better for him.

The way her parents were constantly trying to do for her all these years.

Realization of how scared, helpless and desperate they must have felt losing one daughter and almost losing another hit Montana hard. She'd accepted their help because she'd had no choice at times, but she'd often fought hard against it. She hadn't wanted to need them.

Knowing now how it felt on both sides of this equation was eye-opening but only made her feel even more torn in this moment.

What the hell should she do?

"I promise to close my eyes. I won't look at…anything," she said, the attempt at the joke falling flat. Especially when it only served to point out that he was quite possibly naked in there. Heat rose across her chest and neck. Now was definitely not the time to be thinking about sexy Eddie. She didn't need to add lust to the confusing rush of emotions running through her right now. Maybe she should go.

"I'm wearing a towel," he said, and she turned in time to see him prop himself into the chair. Hair wet, a slightly longer beard than he usually wore, bare chest and abs on full display beneath strong, sculpted shoulders and arms that seemed even more defined than before. She continued to stare.

Unfortunately, he took it the wrong way. "Well, now that you've seen for yourself that the handicapped man next door is fine, you can leave."

Her mouth dropped. It had been weeks since the accident, but Eddie's mood and attitude appeared to be worse than when she'd first seen him. Then, he'd seemed defeated, confused and no doubt hiding a great deal of fear, but now he was pure anger. She didn't blame him for being upset, frustrated and irritated, but she wouldn't condone his self-harming talk. "Eddie, don't say shit like that. I came to check on you because we're friends."

"Since when?"

Was he shitting her right now? Before the accident, they'd both been getting friendly. Flirty, in fact. He'd helped her cook—albeit for another guy. Their sexual chemistry had been evident in the workout room, and they'd shared a definite moment in the bar. She'd started feeling more than annoyance for Eddie. So much more. "Since before the accident," she said.

"Accident? That's what you think this was? Some random shooting?" Bitterness echoed in his voice.

"I don't know what it was. I guess *accident*'s not the right word." The attempted shooting was obviously a deliberate action. "Has the department figured anything out yet? Any suspects?" Oddly enough her focus hadn't been on the crime or the shooter these last few weeks. She'd meant what she'd told Erika and Cassie in the bar—she wasn't afraid of a repeat attack. She had no enemies or anyone who'd want to see her hurt.

"No, they don't know who might be responsible," Eddie said, "but I'd bet my life that it was a targeted attack on your boyfriend."

"Lance isn't my boyfriend." Seemed like the dumbest thing to say given the context of the conversation, but she wanted to clarify that much as least.

Eddie scoffed and folded his arms across his chest. "I'd like to finish getting dressed. Can you close the front door on your way out?"

She nodded, dismissed. Still, she lingered a little longer, staring at him, trying to catch even just a glimpse of the fun-loving man she'd gotten to know in recent months, desperately hoping this angry and disappointed man would somehow find a light in all of the darkness he was currently navigating through. She'd been through it herself before, and it wasn't easy. It would be easier with support. If he'd let her be there for him.

"And lock the handle for me, too, please," he said, with no hint of regret to be pushing her away.

Right now, there was nothing she could do but give him space, but her chest and mind were heavy as she locked the door and left the apartment.

Locked out of his apartment and locked out of his life.

HIS ANGER AND resentment filled him so completely that it was impossible not to let it seep out. Hurting Montana was a douchebag thing to do, and he wanted to regret it, but it was necessary. Pushing her away by whatever means was the only kind thing to do. Whatever attraction she'd had to him before the shooting couldn't possibly exist anymore. Now, it was sympathy and gratitude and a feeling of obligation that she felt toward him.

Survivor's attachment was a real thing.

The look in her eyes when she'd seen him had made him shudder. An extreme athlete faced with a very real picture of a damaged person had to be terrifying for her. She may have suffered a severe brain injury, but her body was still physically capable of doing all the things she wanted to do. This real look at what might have been had to have terrified her. Looking at him, remembering how close that bullet had come to hitting her must be making her sick to her stomach.

It made Eddie sick to his stomach. The only time he wasn't feeling sorry for himself was when he allowed himself to remember that if he hadn't acted quickly and dived at the right moment, Montana could be the one going through this. Or worse.

He slammed his fist against the bathroom counter, sending several items scattering. Damn Lance for putting Montana in a dangerous situation. The guy had been questioned by the station twice, and while he agreed that it was possible that the shooter had been aiming at him, he refused to offer anything that might help the investigation. He claimed not to have any idea who might want him hurt...or dead.

Montana had said Lance wasn't her boyfriend. Unfortunately, even in his despairing downward spiral, that had foolishly sent his heart thumping. Which was dangerous. Feelings for Montana before had been stupid. Now they could destroy him completely. She was a train headed straight to wreck his heart if he opened himself up even a little bit.

He sat in front of the mirror and wiped the steam from it. Funny how on the outside he looked completely the same. His bruises had healed. He looked fine. How was that possible when he felt like a completely different person on the inside? Before, he'd been happy, driven, content with his life, and he'd been okay with having to work hard to achieve his goals. Now his ambition and determination seemed to have vanished. Faced with an obstacle that would be nearly impossible to overcome, he'd always relied on his motivation to surge into overdrive, but instead, now that he needed it most, it had shriveled up and slunk away.

He didn't recognize the intensity of negative emotions threatening to swallow him up. Never had he been this angry. Pure, unfiltered anger overshadowed everything else. Luckily even pain.

Eventually he wouldn't be spared that.

CHAPTER TEN

BACK-TO-SCHOOL shopping had always been a day of dread for Montana. Homeschooled for the first half of her life, she'd gotten used to the freedom, but then her parents decided to send them to a real school for junior high, and it had been torture on her. Summer was officially over, and being confined in a classroom seven hours a day was horrible on her adventurous spirit.

The fact that she was five foot eight and took longer to develop than the other girls her age didn't help matters. She was the awkward, new kid—an easy target for mean girls.

But Kaia had asked for her help with back-to-school shopping, and she hadn't seen her daughter since she'd returned from camp that weekend or had the chance to tell her about the shooting, so Montana repressed her own memories and trauma and put on a smiling face.

Unfortunately, Kaia still seemed to be in a funk.

"Why don't you grab the school-supply checklist from the fridge, so you can make sure you don't forget anything?" Cassie said to Kaia as Montana waited near the door.

When the little girl was out of earshot, Cassie pulled her closer. "Oh, my God! She hasn't snapped out of this mood in days. Tank and I are doing everything we can think of, but nothing's working. She's hungry. We make dinner. She refuses to eat. She won't go hang out with friends when they invite her, but then she mopes around the house all day, saying she's bored."

Cassie sounded at the end of her rope. "That's so unlike her."

"I know. That's the hardest part. We've tried talking to her, but she clams up the moment we mention camp." She looked worried. "Tank's about ready to go pay a visit to some of those older boys."

Montana shook her head. "Do not let him do that. She's starting junior high with those kids soon. If Tank embarrasses her like that, there won't be any recovering from it."

Cassie nodded. "Well, hopefully you'll have better luck talking to her today. If you can get her to open up or smile or something, that would be fantastic."

"I'll do my best," Montana said as Kaia reappeared with the school-supply checklist. "Ready to go?"

"Yeah," Kaia said, walking past her, opening the door and going outside.

"Have fun!" Cassie called after them.

Yeah, looked like it was going to be a hoot.

Selfishly, Montana had been looking forward to spending time with Kaia to help drag her out of her own funk. Two days of listening to Eddie next door without being able to go talk to him or see him was driving her crazy. What was worse was that they weren't the usual sounds coming from his apartment—bad guitar playing, old nineties sitcom re-runs, clanging of pots and pans while he cooked. It was mostly silence accented by the sound of his wheelchair against the floor every now and then, and a take-out food delivery exchange at least once a day.

She was desperate to give him the space he needed to recover and get through this, but she wasn't sure how long she could let him wallow in his justifiable but unhealthy self-pity. Had he been to the station yet? Had he figured out what happened next? How this would impact his career? His promotion? Maybe it was still too soon for him, but Montana knew from experience that the longer he allowed himself to stay in this slump, the harder it would be to crawl out of it. Depression was a scary, downward slope, and she didn't want Eddie falling prey to the dark, lonely thoughts she'd once had to face.

Right now, her daughter definitely seemed to be battling some kind of depression of her own.

Montana climbed into the driver seat of Tank's truck and put on her seat belt.

"Why can't we take your motorcycle?" Kaia asked, as she climbed into the passenger side.

"Because your dad—because it's not safe," she self-corrected. At first she'd thought Kaia on the motorcycle was fine, but she could understand where Tank was coming from, and they were a unit in their parenting.

"But it's safe for you?"

"It's safer for me because I've driven one for a long time and I'm in control on the bike—"

"Don't you think it's hypocritical of you and Dad and Cassie to be allowed to do risky stuff but I'm not?"

Jesus. Attitude.

So new and unlike the daughter she knew, it caught Montana off guard, and she simply decided to ignore the question and move on. "So, what's on your list? Can we get everything at the mall, or is there someplace else we should go?"

Kaia folded her arms across her chest and stared out the window. "Whatever."

Whatever. Okay, then.

"Seriously, though, Mom, you and Dad and Cassie are always out doing all these risky things, and I'm expected to be careful, be safe all the time."

Apparently, they were still on this topic.

Montana sighed. What could she say? Because they were all adults and could do whatever they wanted? Seemed hypocritical…even if it was true. She took a deep breath. "Okay, well, what is it that you'd like to do?" Tank was open to allowing Kaia space to be her own person, try new things. Though, Montana hoped this wasn't about motocross again. She'd learned over the last three months that Kaia had once shown an interest in the sport but had changed her mind after the first few lessons. Had Montana's new motorcycle spurred a renewed interest in it?

Kaia turned in her seat. "I don't know! I just think I should be allowed to do things that other kids do without the pressure of being perfect all the time."

Okay, she definitely wasn't equipped for this conversation. Where was this coming from all of a sudden? And what was the motivation behind it? She did understand the pressure of wanting to do the right thing, while being pulled by a desire to do something that might disappoint others, though, so she went with it. "I get it," she said. "It's not always easy choosing between the things you want to do and the things you feel you should. But if you can tell us exactly what it is you're upset about, we can help." So far, no one had been able to help Montana deal with her internal struggles, but Kaia had three very supportive parents who could help her overcome anything she might be going through. If she just let them in.

Kaia looked ready to talk. She shifted on the passenger seat and stared at her hands. She released several deep breaths, and Montana sat quietly, waiting…

Then Kaia shook her head. "It's nothing. Forget it."

Damn. So close.

Kaia retrieved the list of school supplies from her pocket. "We should be able to get all of this at the mall," she said, and silence filled the cab of the truck for the remaining six-minute drive to the busy parking lot across town.

And with each second of silence from her daughter, Montana felt her retreating a little more, and her disappointment in herself grew stronger.

Why couldn't she reach the people who meant so much to her? First Eddie, now Kaia. She was desperate for a way to help both of them.

If only she knew how.

WHEELCHAIR RAMPS. The only time he'd ever noticed them before was when he was writing a ticket because someone had blocked one with their vehicle. Now he needed them himself. Eddie sat at the base of the ramp leading to the front door of Pretty in Pink, the wedding shop on Main Street, and checked his watch. His grandmother was late, as usual. Normally her inability to be on time didn't bother him. Unlike his mother and sisters, he thought it was funny and part of her charm. But, for once, could she be considerate of other people's time?

Sitting in the wheelchair outside the store, he felt thousands of eyes on him. In reality, it might only be a couple, but that was enough to have him seriously on edge. Everyone in Wild River had heard about the shooting by now, and the talk of heroism had died down in recent weeks, replaced by sympathetic gossip about his new disability.

Poor Eddie. He'd worked so hard. Always had bad luck, that one...

Words of the residents echoed in his mind, and he longed to leave town. Go someplace where no one recognized him, no one cared about what he'd done or the tragic aftermath. But where the hell could he disappear to?

The payout from the department for the incident and his long-term disability pay was the only thing keeping him afloat after paying for his new life upgrades, like the van and the modifications to his apartment. Luckily he didn't have major stairs to worry about, his mother had pointed out.

He checked his watch as the store attendant poked her head outside again. For the third time. "If she's not here in five minutes, we'll have to reschedule the fitting," he said. And by reschedule, he meant cancel. It had taken every ounce of his love for the woman to be there that morning.

But it was the first time he'd left the house in days, and being out in the world felt odd. Nothing else had changed in the small town except how he was living in it. Everyone and everything else remained the same. How was that possible when his whole world had been altered so dramatically?

He was about to give up when his grandmother's car sped into the parking stall next to the van. Country music blasting, she smiled and waved at him through the windshield.

He tapped his watch and wheeled up the ramp.

"Sorry, darlin'," she said as she joined him. "Mel had an eye doctor's appointment, you know, where they dilute the pupils to look for signs of cataracts?"

Eddie didn't give a rat's ass. It was really hard to care about anyone else's nonexistent health issues at the moment.

"Anyway, he wasn't allowed to drive after the procedure, so I offered to take him. 'Course they were running late," she said, opening the shop door.

"No problem," Eddie grumbled, wheeling past her. It irritated him that his almost-eighty-year-old grandmother was holding the door open for him. That wasn't the way it was supposed to be.

Would he ever hold a door open for a woman again?

His grandmother sniffed the air and made a face. She bent closer and sniffed again. "Why do you stink?"

Seriously? "Geez, Gran, I don't know. Showering is a bit of a challenge these days."

"Your mother said the construction guys were in right away to make the upgrades to the apartment."

"They were."

"Didn't they put railings in the bathroom?"

"They did," he grumbled.

She eyed him as though there was little excuse for him to be smelly, then.

It wasn't the act of bathing, it was the motivation to give a shit in the first place that had him abandoning personal hygiene. He knew he was wallowing in self-pity— he could smell it on his skin, his hair, his clothing—but he didn't have any idea how to shake himself out of the deep slump he was in.

"Hi. You must be Grace and Eddie," the clerk said, returning to them. She wore a measuring tape around her neck, and he cringed. Why take his pant measurements? Why hem the tuxedo at all? He wasn't concerned about pant length when he wouldn't be standing up, anyway. He had his crutches, but after a week of trying to use them all the time, sores were developing under his arms, so he'd given up and begun to rely on the wheelchair. The crutches were a pain in the ass, anyway, and didn't give him the sense of independence and mobility he'd hoped they would.

"Yes. We are here for the tux fitting. I'm getting married in November," his grandmother said.

"That's wonderful. It's such an inspiration to know that it's never too late for love," the thirtysomething clerk said.

"Exactly," Grace said with an enthusiasm Eddie scoffed at.

"This is her third marriage," he said, unable to let this clerk believe his grandmother was still a pure, innocent little virgin.

His grandmother swiped at the back of his head. "Third time's the charm."

"It better be," he muttered.

"Why don't we get started?" the clerk said, obviously feeling the tension in the air. "What pant and jacket sizes are you?" she asked him.

"Thirty-two waist and forty tall," he mumbled.

"Great," she said. "Why don't you look at sashes and vests over there, and I'll be right back."

Wonderful.

"So, we decided on purple for the wedding party—not a pale, lilac purple but a nice, deep, fall mauve," his grandmother said, moving toward the selection of accents for the tuxedo.

Eddie followed slowly behind. "Didn't you have purple for your first wedding?"

His grandmother shot him a look which he should have heeded. Instead he continued, "I mean, isn't that bad luck? And will you be able to tell the wedding photographs apart?"

Shit, too far. And too late to pull the words back.

The hurt expression on his grandmother's face killed him. This was why he wanted to stay in his apartment. He wasn't in any mood to be around people. He was pissed off at the world, and the fact that everyone else was going ahead, living their lives when his had been permanently derailed was aggravating as fuck. It was selfish and stupid, but he expected the world to stop spinning…at least for a second, while he got used to the shit hand he'd been dealt. He couldn't focus on his future in the force right now, while he was still figuring out the best way to get his laundry done. He couldn't return to work when he wasn't ready to face his coworkers. And he didn't want to think about his grandmother's wedding and what that meant. "I'm sorry," he mumbled.

"You should be," she said, selecting a deep mauve vest. Forcing her enthusiasm again, she displayed it to him. "What do you think? Would you rather a vest or no vest? I'm leaving that up to you before I tell the other groomsmen what to order."

Other groomsmen. Right. Mel's sons and his best friend were also in the wedding party. Men who would walk down the aisle before him and his grandmother. And then stand throughout the ceremony. He swallowed hard. He had to tell her the truth. Confess what had been bothering him the last couple of weeks whenever the topic of the wedding came up. "Listen, Gran, I think maybe you should ask someone else to walk you down the aisle." There was still time to ask someone better able.

She stared at him. Not disappointed. Not hurt. Just uncomprehending. "Why?"

Was she serious? "Isn't it obvious?"

"No. Do you not want me to get married again?" she asked, actually concerned. "Do you think it's silly at my age to be doing this a third time?"

As much as he teased her about it, she knew he didn't. He was happy for her and proud of her for not caring what anyone else thought. For being true to herself and living her life the way she wanted, so why was she making this about her? This was about him. "Of course not."

"Then why, Eddie?"

Damn it! "Because I wanted to walk you down the aisle, not wheel alongside you. I wanted the focus to be on you and your special day, not on my tragedy. I wanted everyone staring at the beautiful bride, not her poor grandson who may never walk again."

"You think you're going to steal the day?" She scoffed

on a laugh. "Obviously, you have not seen me in my dress," she said.

Jesus! Why couldn't she take this seriously? "Grandma!"

Stunned by his uncharacteristic outburst and raised voice, she dropped the vest.

"I can't do this. And I don't understand why you're so calm about this. Acting like everything is natural, normal and fine when it isn't. Do you see me?"

She nodded. "Of course I see you."

"Then, why are you not devastated by this?" He gestured to the chair, and anger made his chest tighten. *He* was devastated. Devastated that the career path he'd wanted for so long was being derailed. Devastated that the simplest tasks, the things he'd taken for granted, like showering, were now a chore that required more thought and effort than he was capable of. Devastated that he couldn't be the same person anymore. Devastated that something as simple as walking his grandmother down the aisle at her wedding now was a complicated mess of making sure the venue aisles were wide enough to accommodate him and the chair.

So why was his grandmother acting so calm about all of this? Why wasn't she as upset as he was?

His grandmother approached and touched his shoulder. "I'm not devastated by this at all," she said softly, deep emotion evident in her voice.

Emotion so strong, Eddie struggled to keep his own in check.

"Because I can't be devastated when I'm so incredibly happy that you didn't die. That I still have you. We could have lost you a month ago, but you are still here. And I'm so damn grateful for that that I can't find it in myself to feel anything but," she said, kissing the top of his head.

The lump in Eddie's throat prevented him from responding. He'd been an asshole. His own despair was making it impossible for him to see the positive in his situation. He was still alive. He was still able to be there with his grandmother on her special day, and it might take a while, but he had to start seeing the gift he'd been given instead of focusing on what had been taken away.

It was the only way he'd survive having survived.

CHAPTER ELEVEN

SNOWTREK TOURS WAS busier than usual when Montana entered the office the next day. Cassie was going over a winter-camping expedition with a group of ten people all crowded around her desk, while Mike, one of their full-time tour guides, answered phone calls, the landline switchboard continuously lighting up. He shot her a *Nice of you to join us* look as she hurried to her desk, where a couple sat waiting for her.

"Hi. Sorry to keep you waiting," she said, removing her jacket and hanging it on the back of her chair. She sat and logged into her computer quickly. "What can I help you with?"

The woman smiled cautiously and the man next to her squeezed her hand. "It's okay, honey."

The woman took a deep breath and nodded. "We were looking to book a bungee-jumping excursion. Sometime in the next few weeks."

Okay, that explained the nerves. "First-timers?" she asked with a smile. This was one of the aspects of her job at SnowTrek Tours that didn't stress her out. Helping others—especially first-timers—book exciting adventures was exhilarating to her. Her passion when booking others was genuine and, she hoped, contagious.

"Yes. Neither of us have gone before. We aren't really the extreme-sports type," the man said.

"Not yet," Montana said with a wink, checking their

online-booking system. They partnered with the best bungee-jumping company in Alaska for their tours, and they booked quickly. She frowned. "Sorry. I'm not seeing any availabilities until November—late November."

The woman looked sad. Genuinely sad.

Wow, she'd really been looking forward to this. Montana understood, and it was probably one of those spur-of-the-moment, impulsive things where if they didn't do it right away, they'd chicken out. "Winter may not sound like a great time to go, but it's actually fantastic. The plunge is off a bridge that overlooks an amazing waterfall, and once the water starts to freeze, it's even more breathtaking."

"No. November doesn't work for us," the man said.

"Are you sure there's nothing sooner?" the woman asked. "Maybe they could squeeze us in?"

"I'll keep checking, but we book our tours on a tight schedule so that we can accommodate as many people as possible." She hesitated. She didn't like sending customers to North Mountain Sports Company, but they did work with several different companies that offered the activity. "Um, have you checked with North Mountain Sports Company? They might have availability," she whispered.

The woman shook her head. "No. Definitely not. SnowTrek Tours played a huge part in us meeting last year, so we want to book with you and Cassie."

Loyal customers had helped SnowTrek survive the big chain store's opening, and that was a testament to Cassie and the amazing company reputation she'd built. "Oh, wow. That's awesome. How did you meet?"

The man took a deep breath, and the woman stared at her hands.

"If it's a personal story, no worries," Montana said quickly. "You don't have to share."

"No. It's just, um…" The man couldn't seem to find the words.

Montana's heart raced. Clearly this booking meant a lot more to these two than just wanting to be adventurous.

"We met on a hike with a spiritual leader," the woman said. "SnowTrek Tours organized the event. It was a peaceful-passage ceremony at the top of Suncrest Mountain."

A peaceful-passage ceremony? "I'm sorry, I'm not familiar—"

"It's a ceremony that helps you make peace with a terminal illness."

Montana's chest tightened so hard, she could barely breathe. "Oh. I'm…" What? What could she say?

The man smiled slowly. "It was the best day of my life," he said. "I met Amber, and we've been together every day since."

Amber beamed at him. "Living every second we have left." She turned to Montana. "We both have stage five colon cancer. Surgeries haven't worked, and the cancer has spread to my lymphatic system, and Frank's to his pancreas." She pulled out a folded piece of paper—a list. "We are working through our bucket list in record time," she said with a small laugh.

Montana scanned the items. Some they'd already crossed off; too many were yet to be fulfilled. "This is a great list," she said over the lump in her throat.

"We're trying to be brave and do the things we still can, before it's too late."

"We're not dead yet," Frank said.

Obviously finding acceptance in their situation had been part of their process, but it broke Montana's heart to see two young people in love, facing the end of their time together.

"Anyway, neither of us is likely to make it until late

November," Amber said, suddenly finding strength in her voice. "So, if there are any cancellations…"

Montana nodded quickly. "You know what? I think there just was," she said, making a note on her calendar to call the Harrisons and rebook them on a free excursion of their choice anytime. "How about Thursday at four o'clock?" she said to the couple.

"Perfect," Amber said.

The man just smiled and squeezed his love's hand.

Montana completed the booking, saw them out and then went in the back to cry.

Living every moment they had left….

Definitely put so much into perspective for her. Could she start to appreciate living every moment she'd been given and help Eddie do the same?

EDDIE'S PHONE LIT UP more now than ever. Before the shooting, he'd heard from his mom or sisters once a month. They were all busy with their own lives and while they were a close family, they hadn't needed to check in with one another so much before.

They were driving him crazy now.

Especially Leslie. She'd recently been assigned a high-profile client that required twenty-four-hour protection, therefore she hadn't been able to come to Wild River after the shooting, but she was certainly making up for it with the frequent phone calls.

He hit the Ignore button and sent her to voice mail, but a second later, she texted.

Don't ignore me.

Then the phone rang again.

"Leslie, I'm just about to head out," he answered.

"Bullshit. You've only left your apartment once in six days."

He blinked, pulling his cell phone away to look at it. "Are you tracking my phone?"

"Maybe."

"That's a violation of privacy."

"It's called being a concerned sister. No one would convict me for it, especially since I'm obviously right to be concerned about you," she said.

"I'm fine. Getting around these days is a little more time-consuming. And damn, you know, I let my gym membership expire, so there's that. And I'm on leave from work, so there's really not a whole hell of lot to do." What did they expect from him? That he'd be running his usual errands, going out to hang out with his coworkers and friends, living his life as though everything was the same as it was before?

The hardest part about this whole thing was that everyone was acting completely normal. He'd just like someone to acknowledge the fact that this sucked. He didn't regret his actions, he didn't want a medal for bravery, he just wanted someone to say that it was okay to be mad, it was understandable to feel lost and afraid right now. And to give him the time and space he needed to figure it all out.

"You're depressed, and you're wallowing," Leslie said.

"Bye, Leslie."

"Hang up on me, and I'll log in to the video camera I had the contractors install in the apartment while they were doing the modifications."

"You didn't..." Eddie scanned the room, before hearing her laugh.

Unexpectedly, it made his own face crack. Just a little.

"No, you idiot, I didn't. And I haven't put a tracker on your phone, either, but you just confirmed my suspicions."

He released a deep breath. "Look, I'm fine. I'm adjusting."

"Apparently, your idea of adjusting is turning into a complete asshole."

Wow, so much for a concerned sister calling to check in.

"I heard you weren't exactly nice to Gran at the tuxedo fitting," she said.

That was true, and he did feel bad about it. He'd sent flowers to apologize, but he couldn't take back his sour mood that day—or his shitty attitude with Montana a few days before. His sister was right. He was turning into an asshole, but he couldn't stop it. He wanted to be that optimistic guy who looked at his new situation with positivity, but all he could muster was the strength to move from the bedroom to the living room and back again. "I apologized. We're cool." His grandmother deserved his love and respect, and she'd get nothing but going forward. And he wouldn't leave the house if he wasn't capable of that. No more hurting people he cared about.

"Eddie, if you need to talk to someone, there are some really great therapists in the department." Ones she'd refused to talk to years before, after her fiancé, a fellow state trooper, had died on the job. Drunk driver in a high-speed chase had T-boned Dawson's vehicle on their wedding day. He'd died at the scene, and Leslie had never been the same. She'd moved on with her life and slowly started to get over the tragedy, but if anyone understood a fraction of what he was going through, the dangers of the job and the risks they took and the consequences attached, it was her.

But like her, a therapist wasn't something he was quite ready for yet. The ones at the hospital hadn't helped. He needed to find a way out of this darkness on his own. "Yeah, I'll think about it," he mumbled. Then the smell of smoke made him sit straighter.

What was burning? He glanced into the kitchen, but he hadn't used the stove or oven in weeks. The empty take-out bags all around his apartment had their own disgusting scent, but that wasn't it.

The sound of the smoke detector next door echoed loudly through his apartment wall. Montana was cooking? Or trying to?

Damn, if Lance was coming to dinner again that evening, his sister would see how fast Eddie could leave his apartment when sufficiently motivated.

"Hey, I'll call you back," he said.

"No, you won't, but that's fine. Just get help," Leslie said.

He disconnected the call and left the apartment, then knocked loudly on Montana's door. The wailing continued inside her apartment, so he knocked again. Louder.

When she opened it, he could barely see her in the thick cloud of smoke. "What are you doing?"

"Cooking?"

He moved past her into the apartment and headed for the kitchen. Grabbing a dish towel from the stove, he waved it beneath the smoke detector in the hall as Montana continued to open all the windows.

The noise ceased, but he kept waving it as the smoke disappeared outside.

He shivered as the space quickly cooled with the fall mountain breeze blowing through, but then he was instantly grateful for the chill in the air as Montana came into better view.

Dressed in yoga pants and a bra top, his mouth watered, and his tongue went dry at the same time. Fuck, she was hot, even if she couldn't boil water. Long, sexy, shapely calf muscles and thighs leading up to curvy hips, hugged tight by the blue fabric, had his eyes moving slowly upward, taking it all in. Her tight stomach and full chest, long arms and neck. Like a dancer. Shit, just the sight of her had him going hard. Something that hadn't happened in weeks.

Happy to know he was still capable of it, but he put the dish towel on his lap to cover up the evidence.

"Thank you," she said. "Sorry if the noise interrupted your evening."

Funny, she didn't look sorry at all. She actually looked pleased with herself—for what exactly? She folded her arms across her body in the cool air, and the action had her breasts squeezing together, giving him an even more tempting view of her cleavage.

She caught his stare and grinned.

Was she doing this on purpose? "What were you making?" He went into the kitchen and opened the lid on the pot. Water. Or at least there used to be water in the pot. Now it was empty and charred. "There's nothing in here."

She looked slightly sheepish. "Okay...so maybe I wasn't cooking."

He frowned. Had he been set up? "Did you just try to burn down the building to get me over here?"

"What if I did?" Her voice held a daring, challenging tone that instantly sparked something to life inside him.

"I'm reporting you to the apartment board," he said, but his mood had been lifted for the first time in weeks. She'd wanted to see him, even though he'd been an asshole before.

"You'd get me evicted?" she asked, her gaze definitely flirty. More flirty than was safe. He felt himself twitch beneath the dish towel. Time to go.

He cleared his throat as he moved past her toward the door. "Just be careful," he said. "Some of us can't get out of the building as fast as we used to," he said, surprised that there wasn't even a hint of bitterness in the joke.

She nodded, looking slightly disappointed but not completely derailed. "At least I know how to get you out of your apartment."

His pulse raced. "There might be easier, less dangerous ways."

Why the hell had he said that? He didn't want to give Montana false hope or the wrong impression. Leaving the door open for her to reach out to him again wasn't smart. He couldn't hang out with her anymore. Obviously, he still wanted to.

"Yeah, but they're not as much fun," she said as he went back into the hall. She leaned against the doorframe, and her soft expression was void of pity or guilt. Just beautiful, sexy Montana looking at him with an unconcealed interest that he'd only gotten a glimpse of before.

He had to be careful not to let himself believe it.

But he did take the opportunity to allow his eyes to scan her body once more, so he could survive on the memory of it for quite some time...

"Can I have my dish towel back?" she asked, the knowing look on her face as she held out her hand made it difficult not to smile as a slight embarrassment washed over him.

"No," he said, turning away from her and heading back to his apartment.

She laughed. "Just neighbors, huh? Good night, Eddie."

CHAPTER TWELVE

HE COULDN'T AVOID the station or his coworkers forever. Still, Eddie sat in his van, staring at the building. How could he go inside like this? How could he face everyone? The shooting had changed his career and future on the force. He wasn't even sure if there would still be a position for him, active duty he was still capable of, or if he'd ever get his confidence back to even try.

He wasn't afraid. He wasn't suffering from nightmares or PTSD symptoms from the incident. He'd done what he was trained to do, and he'd done the right thing in the moment. But he didn't want to return to a job that he couldn't be great at. His motivation for pushing so hard to join the force in the first place had been his confidence that he could be a really great officer. But, without that certainty anymore, could he realistically stay in the job?

Several of his coworkers had visited him a few times in the hospital, but he'd sent them away. It had been a jerk move, but surely, they hadn't wanted to see him lying there—helpless, uncertain, useless... It only reminded them of the danger of the job they did every day.

The last thing he'd wanted to be was a cautionary tale.

Lying in the hospital, he replayed every second of that moment over and over in his mind. Had he acted the right way? Could he have done something differently?

But from all angles, the only thing that could have been different was that it would have been Montana bleeding on the sidewalk, unable to walk—or worse—if he hadn't done what he did, as quickly as he did.

If he needed a silver lining, that was it. And it was actually a pretty damn good one. All night, he'd kept the memory of her in his mind—the sexy body, the teasing flirtation, how clear it was that she wasn't going to make it easy for him to push her away.

Shit. He ran a hand through his hair. What the hell was he going to do about his neighbor? He couldn't have her, but his body definitely wanted her. She was dangerous in the way she'd been able to spark life back into him the night before. A man could start to crave that feeling...and a stupid man might seek it out.

He sighed as he removed his seat belt. Better go in before anyone saw him sitting out there like a moron.

He did want to find out if the station had found any leads on suspects in the shooting yet. Adams had texted him several times, but there hadn't been any progress. His captain had signed off on his leave and was giving him the time and space he'd requested, but he owed his boss a check-in and a discussion about next steps.

He went inside and immediately wanted to turn the chair around and leave. Inside the station was a big banner that read *Welcome Back, Eddie* and on his desk were balloons, flowers, and boxes of cookies and cupcakes. Some from his coworkers. Others from locals in town who'd heard about the incident.

Damn, Adams must have told everyone he was planning to come in that day. He'd only texted Adams about it to see if he could pull the files on the incident for him to take a look at.

Overwhelmed by the kindness and generosity but also slightly embarrassed, Eddie continued past his desk and moved quickly to his captain's office. He hesitated before knocking twice on the slightly open door.

"It's open," came the captain's voice from inside.

Eddie pushed the door open and entered. "Hey, Captain Clarkson—"

"Eddie! Great to see you. Come on in," the man said, standing and closing the door behind him. Then he took Eddie's hand and shook it. "The department is honored to have you serve our community," he said, serious and somber.

Shit. He was treating him like a hero. Eddie wasn't sure what he'd expected exactly, but this just made him even more uncomfortable. He wanted everyone to be normal around him. Ride his ass. Bust his balls. Not this. "Um, thank you. I thought it might be time to stop by."

"Absolutely. Your desk is ready whenever you are."

Desk. Right. He'd be limited to that from now on. No more patrols. No stakeouts. No arrests. He hadn't realized his job in Wild River could get even less desirable. Now, he longed to be monitoring the trail to the jump site. "I'm not sure what my future here looks like, yet," he said.

Captain Clarkson nodded. "Of course. We will figure it out, though. We definitely don't want to lose you as a member of the team."

A member of the team. But in what capacity? He could kiss his transfer to the narcotics division in Anchorage goodbye. They wouldn't want him now. But he wasn't ready to hear that yet, so he asked, "Any leads on the shooter?"

"Not yet. We haven't been able to find a match for the bullet in our existing database. Unfortunately, no one saw the person—except you. The description is vague, and not a single camera along Main Street caught a clear image. Not of the shooter, anyway..." He turned his monitor to face Eddie and called up security-camera footage of that night. "Are you ready to see this?"

Probably not. Eddie nodded.

Captain Clarkson hit Play, and Eddie leaned closer. He saw Montana and Lance walk past the bakery, laughing and talking. His chest tightened, and the reaction was almost comical. This wasn't going to be the tough part to watch, yet it was still difficult to see Montana with the other guy.

Was she still seeing Lance? She'd said he wasn't her boyfriend. And would she have been flirting with him the night before if they were still seeing one another? He hadn't seen the other guy come or go, hadn't heard his voice through the walls...

He saw himself appear on the screen, and he held his breath as he leaned closer. He was running, then jumping, followed by the crash to the ground, his body shielding Montana's before falling limp.

His heart pounded in his chest as he stared at the screen. Not at himself lying on the ground but at Montana and the way she cradled his body, the way she touched his face, the terrified expression on her face as she yelled to Lance to call 9-1-1 but then stayed focused on Eddie.

Shit. He was in trouble.

Anyone in Montana's situation, in that moment, would react exactly the same.

He had to keep reminding himself that.

Captain Clarkson stopped the footage as the first emergency flashing lights appeared on the screen. "That save should have been impossible," he said, shaking his head. "I've watched this footage a dozen times. So have the other guys. Eddie, you must have flown through the air to pull that off," the man said.

"Adrenaline, I guess," he said. Adrenaline that would have given him extra strength and speed for anyone? Or just Montana?

"It was definitely something. We spoke with both Montana and Lance, but they weren't able to offer a lot of help. Lance did agree that the shooter was most likely targeting him, but he had no idea who might want him hurt or dead."

"Have we talked to his teammates on the Olympic team? Former competitors? North Mountain Sports Company executives?" Maybe his sponsorship deals were going south? Maybe someone didn't want to see him compete that year? Lance's skills on the slopes made him a definite target, and his arrogant nature didn't make him the most likable.

What did Montana see in this guy, anyway? Obviously she was attracted to sporty, confident bad boys. Eddie didn't check any of those boxes, yet she hadn't exactly been subtle in her attraction to him the night before.

"Eddie, you still with me?" Captain Clarkson waved a hand in front of his distracted, far-off gaze.

"Sorry, yes... What did you say?"

"I said we were hoping maybe you'd be interested in being part of the investigation. Questioning everyone you mentioned, gathering new leads..."

Was he ready for that? Investigating his own shooting might be jumping in a little headfirst, too fast. "I'm sorry, Captain. I don't think that's a great idea." He hadn't even decided if he was coming back to the job.

If Captain Clarkson was disappointed, he hid it well. "Totally understandable. We move at your pace, Eddie. Okay?"

What was his pace? First, he needed to make a decision about whether he had a future on the force. Then they could move forward with a reintegration plan.

"We're still in need of volunteers for the Haunted Trail," Captain Clarkson said. "If you're interested?"

Eddie hesitated. The Haunted Trail was the station's annual event that they'd been hosting since Eddie was a kid. They used an old barnlike structure on an acreage just outside of town with woodsy trails for a spooky Halloween event with proceeds donated to local charities. Eddie had participated the last two years. It wasn't exactly active duty, but it was a way to reconnect with the guys, get back to living and being involved in the community without any pressure or expectations. It was something he could do right now when he was feeling like there was little else he could fill his days with... Maybe if he got involved, it might provide some needed clarity. "Okay. Yes, sir. I'm happy to help."

Happy might be an overstatement, but he hoped to eventually get there.

ONCE THE CRAZY idea came to her, there was no talking herself out of it.

Since meeting Amber and Frank the day before, Montana had renewed determination to bring Eddie back to the land of the living. Like her, he'd been given a second chance, and neither of them were going to squander a second of it by focusing on the things they couldn't do.

She'd made a few calls, pulled some strings and told Cassie she needed to take the day off. Now, she just had to get Eddie out of his apartment and into the van.

Was she strong enough to lift him if she was reduced to knocking him out and dragging him the whole way?

She knocked on his apartment door, unwilling to be deterred by a shitty attitude or excuses. She missed her annoying yet charmingly seductive neighbor, and this was the only hope she had of getting him back.

He opened it, leaning on a crutch, a piece of toast in his mouth. "Hi."

Good. No chair today. That was definitely a good sign. Also, no shirt. Her gaze wandered the length of his torso... *Focus, Montana. You're on a mission.*

She whipped her gaze back to his face, forbidding herself to look elsewhere, otherwise there might be a new crazy plan. "I need you to come someplace with me," she said.

He looked confused. "Where?"

"I'm not telling you."

"You want me to go somewhere with you, but you won't tell me where?"

"Exactly."

"Yeah, that doesn't sound like something I'm going to do," he said, but there was just enough of a hint of intrigue in his voice that she pushed on, as he continued to eat his toast.

"Why not? Afraid?"

"Absolutely," he said.

A grin tugged at the corner of her mouth. "Good. You should be. But, you know, fear is really just the same emotional reaction as excitement. It's how you process the feeling of adrenaline that matters."

He sighed. "What is this about? Are you trying to drag me to therapy or some support group?"

She grabbed the piece of what looked like homemade bread from his hand and took a bite at his surprised look. God, it was delicious. "Not that either is a bad idea, but no," she said after swallowing the carbs. "I have my own approach to healing, and I want you to be brave enough to give it a try." She handed him back his breakfast.

He hesitated.

"Come on, Eddie. What else do you have planned for the day? Self-pity at ten? Wallowing at eleven thirty? Nap at two? I know that's not how you want to live the rest of your life. I know that's not who you are. So, put on a shirt—" *for the love of all that is good and holy* "—and come with me," she said.

She waited and watched the sexy chest muscles rise and

fall in a deep sigh. "Fine. Give me a minute," he said, stepping back to let her in.

She'd expected a mess inside the apartment. Take-out containers all over the place. A pungent smell. A blanket and pillow fort on the couch that he'd prefer to stay buried under, so she was shocked as she looked around.

The place was spotless, and damn if the smell of homemade bread wasn't still lingering in the air.

Eddie was starting to feel better. She smiled. Maybe today wouldn't be as challenging after all. It had only taken a minute and a half to talk him into coming on this blind adventure with her. She'd factored fifteen minutes into her planning, so she was already ahead of schedule.

He reappeared wearing a tight black T-shirt, a hoodie thrown over one arm. His hair was combed and gelled, and she could smell his cologne from across the room. He was gorgeous, and her pulse raced at the thought of what they were about to do.

Five minutes later, they were in his van, and she was behind the wheel. The bigger vehicle was actually quite intimidating, but she'd never admit that to him. She adjusted the mirrors and the seat.

"Hey, don't mess with my settings," Eddie said in mock annoyance.

"You're taller than I am, and this thing is a little more complicated than I'm used to."

"Well, why don't you let me drive?"

"Because you don't know where we're going," she said, pulling out of the parking stall.

"Where *are* we going?"

"Told you—it's a surprise." She turned to glance at him. "Sit back and relax. It's a bit of a drive."

"A bit of a drive to where?"

"I'm not telling you. Stop asking," she said, heading

down Main Street toward the exit for the highway. As she passed the spot of the shooting, her hands tightened on the steering wheel. She'd purposely jogged an extra couple of blocks to work every day to avoid having to run past the place where Eddie almost died. Where *she* could have died...

She dared a quick glance at him now. Would he be upset seeing it? Remembering?

He wasn't even looking out the window. He was staring at her. "What?" she asked nervously, unable to decipher his expression.

"How did you start to heal after your injury? Did someone kidnap you like this, or did you try therapy and support groups?"

Normally her response to the question would be to say that she wasn't quite sure if she was healed, but since meeting Amber and Frank and learning about their tragic love story and quest to fulfill their bucket lists, Montana knew she had come a long way. Denying the success and progress she'd made in her own healing was unfair. It was time to give herself the credit she deserved to be at this point in life after her setback, and it was time to appreciate what she had around her, instead of constantly striving for that elusive happiness she thought would come with having her old life back.

"Actually, all of the above," she said. "I had a lot of friends who disappeared when it became clear that I wouldn't be out on cliffs with them anymore. But a few good ones stuck with me and helped me get moving again. That said, I did go to therapy for years. In fact, I attend a support group here in Wild River." It was the first time she'd told anyone, and it felt good to tell Eddie.

"Really? Does it help?"

She laughed. "It does, actually. While my issues are

different than most people's in the room, we are all still struggling with something, and that common denominator brings us all together on a basic level of just trying to survive each day."

He nodded. "You still struggle?"

"Yep." Though the struggles seemed to change over the years. At first, it was regaining her memory and being able to live independently. Then, it was trying to figure out what was next for her and finding a way back to Kaia. Since being in Wild River, she'd been putting the pieces in place for a new future, and now the struggle was finding true happiness. Reevaluating what she wanted most, what she *truly* wanted most. For years she'd thought she'd known the answer, but lately it didn't seem so clear.

Since the shooting, she hadn't felt the suffocating disappointment over not being able to jump anymore. The issues with Kaia and the tragedy with Eddie had taken priority in her mind, and while they were challenges, they gave her focus and made her realize she was entirely capable of putting her former passion on the back burner when there were more important things for her to take care of—more important things that mattered to her.

For the first time, she was seeing that BASE jumping had once defined who she was. The circle of people she associated with. Her identity had been tied to it. But the sport was just a sport. It wasn't who she was.

"I feel like you just went on a journey and left me behind," Eddie said gently.

She'd been quiet, lost in her own thoughts. "That's exactly what just happened," she said. "Sorry. I've just had a lot of things put into perspective lately." She smiled at him and the intensity in his dark eyes had her returning her attention to the road quickly. She was doing this for him, yet all of a sudden, this adventure trip was meaning so much to her. "Thank you for coming along," she said. "And for trusting me."

He nodded. "I didn't think you'd really give me a choice. I could see you plotting how you were going to knock me out and drag me to the van."

She laughed hard at the entirely too accurate truth.

Half an hour later, she took the exit for Palmer, and Eddie scanned their surroundings. "I thought we were heading into Anchorage. What's out here?"

"You'll see." Her palms sweat against the steering wheel. *Maybe this wasn't such a great idea.*

The closer she came to actually executing her plan, a slight panic crept into her chest. Would Eddie go along with this? Was he well enough? She'd cleared it with Erika the day before, so she knew he was fine physically, but mentally—was he ready for something this extreme? She wasn't sure anything less would work to snap him out of his slump.

She drove onto the Palmer Municipal Airport lot, and Eddie frowned. "Are we flying somewhere?"

"Sort of," she said.

"Were we planning to buy clothes when we get to wherever we're going?" he joked, but she heard the nervousness in his voice.

She didn't answer as she pulled up in front of the building for Alaska Skydive Adventures. "No clothes needed," she said with forced enthusiasm. She wouldn't back out now, and she wouldn't let Eddie back out, either.

"What are we doing here?"

"What do you think we're doing here?" she said, unbuckling her seat belt. "Come on."

Eddie shook his head, and his hand instinctively covered his seat belt buckle. "Montana, I was shot six weeks ago. I don't think this is a good idea."

"I happen to know your doctor, and she said you are all clear," she said.

"Okay, let me rephrase. Even if I hadn't just gotten shot six weeks ago, I still wouldn't think this is a good idea."

"You said you'd come on this adventure with me."

"When I thought we were going for frozen yogurt or something. Shit, even a surprise vacation would meet with no arguments right now, but this? Are you for real? You want me to skydive when I can barely even walk?"

She leaned closer and met his gaze square on. "Why walk when you can fly?"

FLY. RIGHT. OR FALL to his death. He'd already come close enough to that once this year. Tempting fate a second time seemed a little stupid.

Eddie made no motion to get out as he watched Montana walk around the front of the vehicle. The woman was insane. He struggled to get out of bed on his own in the morning, and he could barely function without pain medication, and she wanted him to throw his body out of a plane?

She opened the back door and retrieved his crutches. "Come on," she said, opening the passenger door.

"Nope," he said, not budging.

"Do I have to take your seat belt off myself?" she asked.

And despite the tense situation, Eddie felt himself get slightly hard at the idea of Montana leaning over him to unlatch the buckle. Shit. He had to keep his attraction to her in check. She was trying to trick him into a crazy stunt. "Montana, I appreciate the gesture, I really do. But have you even thought this through? How am I supposed to jump out of a plane?"

"We're signed up for a tandem jump. You'll be fine," she said.

"And what happens when I hit the ground?" He'd never

gone skydiving before, but he'd seen it, and the landing didn't look all that soft. Running seemed to be a requirement.

"I've arranged for a crash-mat landing. You'll fall into a nice inflatable pillow," she said with a look that said *Bring on your excuses 'cause I've got an answer for everything.*

He searched for another plausible reason why this was a horrible idea, but all he could come up with made him look like a wimp.

Which he was actually fine with.

"Our plane's waiting," she said, tapping an invisible watch.

Eddie sighed as he removed the seat belt and lifted himself out of the van, accepting the crutches from her. "I'll watch you jump, but there's no way I'm doing this."

"We'll see," she said as she closed the van door and locked the vehicle.

As they walked toward the building, Eddie could see the small airplane on the runway with the Alaska Skydive Adventure logo on the side. He'd only ever been in a plane that small once. A seaplane, when he'd traveled to northern Alaska with some friends after graduating high school. He'd been sick then, even without the terror of jumping to contend with. Montana could drag him all the way out here—he might even get inside the plane since the idea of watching her in action was kinda intriguing—but there was no way in hell he'd be free-falling that day.

"I didn't know you still did this," he said as they made their way inside.

"I haven't since I've been here, but my support group suggested it. Skydiving, zip-lining, bungee jumping. All things I can still do that might give the same thrill as BASE jumping."

"Will it?" He didn't think so. Montana had progressed

from all of those activities to BASE jumping. She'd never get the same high from these activities. Adrenaline junkies suffered the same affliction as other addicts. The high of each new dangerous activity eventually weakened or wore off, leaving them searching for the next thing to take them even higher.

Montana didn't answer. Instead she smiled as they reached two men in matching Alaska Skydive jackets. "Hi. I'm Montana Banks. I called yesterday."

Yesterday? So this was as spur of the moment as it appeared. How had she gotten it all arranged so quickly?

The first guy stepped forward and shook her hand. "Hey, I'm Tom, and this is Alex." He indicated the other guy. "So great to meet you. I'm a big fan," he said. His appreciative gaze swept over Montana, and an unsettling feeling washed over Eddie.

Fantastic. Another adrenaline junkie with full capacity of all his limbs.

"Uh, thank you. This is my..." Montana hesitated "...friend, Eddie Sanders."

Friend. Why did that irritate him? A few days ago he'd claimed they were no more than neighbors. He still needed to apologize for his mood and harsh words that day.

Tom turned to him and said, "Ready to do this?"

Eddie shook his head. "Nope. I'm not jumping today. I'm just here to watch this crazy one." He wasn't a fan of heights or falling—or willingly tempting fate.

The guy nodded. "It's daunting to be sure. But compared to your chosen career, this is a lot less dangerous."

So, Montana had filled them in.

"Let's get you both geared up," Alex said, stepping forward. "There are separate change rooms to the right. Montana, you know the drill by now. I'll help Eddie."

Was no one listening to him? He wasn't doing this. He

hadn't even signed a waiver or anything. Getting geared up seemed a little premature. "Yeah, I'm not in," he said.

Montana looked at the guys. "Can we have a sec?"

"Sure thing," Tom said. "I'll print out the waivers and tell the pilot to prepare."

They really thought he was doing this.

When the guys were out of earshot, Montana turned to him. "Eddie, I need this," she said, the vulnerability in her blue eyes rocking him to the core. *Vulnerable* was not a word he'd ever use to describe Montana. Even through her challenges of relocating to Wild River, rekindling her relationship with her daughter and ex-boyfriend, and starting her own venture in a partnership with a woman who was essentially parenting her daughter most of the time, Montana had navigated the rapids with ease and grace and confidence. She was afraid of nothing. Hell, she'd been shot at, something that would have had a lot of people needing therapy to feel safe again, and she was hardly fazed by it.

So this new dimension to her had him floundering. But one look outside at the tiny plane on the tarmac had his common sense restored. "You can go. I'm not stopping you." He paused. "I'll even go up in the plane."

Disappointment clouded her expression. "I'm not doing it if you don't."

Damn it! "I saved your life. Isn't that enough?"

"That was last month," she said with a grin that meant she knew she was going to get her way.

"This is insane. Even for you," he mumbled, knowing protests were useless. He may be down and out lately, uncertain about his future on the police force and struggling to get this new version of life working for him in some way, but he could never say no to her for long.

"Insane can be good sometimes," she said, waving the guys back over. "We're ready to gear up," she said.

"Great! Eddie, let's get you into a harness and get you both up in the air," Alex said enthusiastically.

Eddie tried to keep from throwing up as Montana disappeared into the women's changeroom and he followed the guy into the men's. Most people contemplated shit like this for months, years, before they actually took the literal leap. He'd had all of five minutes. Could he really do it? He'd hate to get up there and chicken out.

Though, he doubted that was a possibility with Montana next to him.

Fifteen minutes later, Eddie signed away his rights to sue if this went horribly wrong, and they boarded the plane. Harnessed into his safety gear, Eddie took a seat as far from the door as possible as Montana climbed in behind him. If only excitement was truly contagious. She was actually glowing with anticipation, which would have completely stolen his breath, if he could find it in the first place.

Sweat pooled on his lower back, and his veins should've been exploding with the blood rushing through them. He was seconds away from an anxiety attack as the plane door closed and the four of them buckled into the cramped space and the plane took off the runway.

"We're going up to thirteen thousand feet," Tom said.

"Awesome," Montana said. "About sixty seconds of freefall," she told him.

"Awesome," he mumbled, trying to steady his breath. A minute could feel like an excruciatingly long time.

This would be fine. And if it wasn't fine, at least in an hour from now, it would all be over. He could file a restraining order against his crazy, hot-as-shit neighbor and continue to be grateful he was alive in the safety of his apartment.

"Look at the gorgeous view," Montana said, leaning closer.

The smell of her honey-scented hair and soft vanilla-scented skin filled his senses in their proximity, and it helped to distract him from the task at hand—a little. More so than the breathtaking view below. He'd get plenty of time to appreciate that once they were falling in midair.

For now, his gaze took in Montana, possibly for the last time. Her beautiful, high cheekbones seemed even more prominent, colored in a deep rose blush that was all natural. Man, she was gorgeous. So far out of his league. He wasn't sure what had spurred that day's outing, but he was happy to be around her, despite the terrifying circumstances. Which was terrifying in itself. Pushing her away would be impossible when she refused to let him, so now the focus would be on protecting his heart.

Not falling hard and fast for her would be the hardest challenge of his life.

She turned her attention away from the window and caught him staring. Her smile was warm and genuine, and he already felt like the battle of preserving his heart was lost.

"We're at altitude," Alex said and Eddie's heart was instantly in his throat. All this stress couldn't be good for his recovery plan. How had Erika signed off on this? He needed a new doctor.

Tom opened the plane door, and the noise of the wind speeding past made him gulp.

Montana laughed. "Did you just gulp?"

"I did." Zero ego or pride left in that moment. He was scared shitless, and he was man enough to admit it. He peered over the side, taking in the scenery. The boreal forest below him, mountain peaks at eye level, and water cascading from a waterfall on one side coursing into a running river would at least be a beautiful way to die.

But even if he really wanted to do this, how exactly was

this supposed to work? He eyed the parachute pack. His spine was recovered, but the effect of the opening parachute would surely have a jarring impact. And it was a long way down. Especially if he was in pain.

Alex must have read his concerns. "Don't worry about the chute opening. You'll just feel like you're floating back up a little, before continuing the slower decent."

Luckily he'd have someone else operating the chute. Right now he could barely remember to breathe.

"Okay, let's get ready," Tom said.

Shit. No. What the hell was he thinking, agreeing to this? Moment of insanity brought on by an irresistible woman, but his common sense had returned in the nick of time. "You know what...?" Eddie stopped as Montana stood and removed the oversize hoodie she'd been wearing.

Wait. What was she doing?

Under her harness, she was wearing a bikini top. One that tied at the top and the back.

Eddie's mouth went completely dry. "What are you doing?" he asked as she lowered the sweatpants she wore down over her hips. Beautiful, shapely, curvy hips. He glared at the other guys who were openly staring.

"It's free if we jump naked," she said. "Clothes off." She folded her arms across her seminaked body and raised an eyebrow in challenge.

Suddenly the free fall wasn't the most terrifying aspect of the day. He was already feeling himself grow hard... How the hell was he supposed to tandem-jump from an airplane with Montana's sexy naked body soaring through the air without embarrassing himself? In his anxious state, he hadn't even stopped to question it when Alex had instructed him to put the gear on under his clothing. He shook his head. "Nope. I'm not strapping myself to some naked dude," he said.

Montana moved closer. "You won't be strapped to one of the guys. You'll be strapped to me."

Holy shit.

"So, clothes off," she said with a sexy grin as she reached for the base of his T-shirt. Her fingers tickled his abs as she lifted it slowly, allowing him time to protest.

He didn't. He couldn't. Not when she was standing there almost completely naked. Instead, he lifted his arms and allowed her to remove the shirt. He undid his jeans and lifted his body with his arms as she removed his pants. Her eyes widened slowly as she saw his semi pressing against the underwear. "It still works," he said, feeling all embarrassment disappear as her face flushed. "Sure *you* want to do this?" he asked.

"Absolutely," she said, removing his underwear as well and trying and failing to divert her eyes from his penis. "Don't worry, that won't last long."

The complete and utter insanity of the situation had him almost forgetting about the part where he was about to free-fall out of a plane.

"Okay, we're reaching the jump zone," Tom said.

Montana reached behind and untied the bikini top, letting it fall away, then removed her panties slowly, suggestively.

Eddie was both completely turned on and scared to death at the same time.

The two guys harnessed them together for the tandem jump and he could feel Montana's breasts pressed against his back. Her naked skin touching every inch of his. The fall over the forest and waterfall below was the last thing on his mind in that moment. She was so beautiful, exciting, adventurous… His chest tightened. She was not-so-slowly bringing him back to life.

By trying to kill him, he thought, daring a glance over the side of the plane. His grip on his harness tightened.

"On three?" she asked.

"On three," he said, shutting his eyes tight.

"Open your eyes. You don't want to miss this," she said.

He slowly opened them.

"Whenever you're ready," Alex told Montana.

She gave him the thumbs-up. "One," she said in his ear.

"Two," Eddie said.

"Three," they said together as they fell forward out of the plane, sending their bodies into freefall. Montana screamed in joy, but all sound died on Eddie's lips as they fell fast and free, the wind zooming past them.

"Isn't this amazing?" she yelled.

It really was, but he couldn't find the words. He was flying over the most beautiful scenery in Alaska, with a woman he was insanely attracted to. Naked. Even in his wildest dreams, he'd never thought this would be happening.

But now that the initial shock was over, he could appreciate the experience. Except for the way his entire body jiggled and his skin flapped in the wind. When she'd removed her clothing on the plane, he'd assumed this would be a sensuous experience. Nothing could be further from reality. He started to laugh as he glanced back and saw he wasn't the only one with body parts doing some hilarious shit.

"Told you the hard-on wouldn't last," Montana said as she started to laugh as well.

Then their laughter was uncontrollable. His stomach ached, and tears were running down his cheeks as he experienced the wildest sixty seconds of his life. He hadn't laughed in weeks, and the pure joy radiating through him was as unexpected as that day's events.

He had Montana to thank.

"I'll be pulling the chute in ten seconds," she said, composing herself long enough to prepare him.

Eddie braced himself, but as the guy had said, once she pulled the chute, he felt as though he were once again floating upward. Another exhilarating feeling.

The chute slowed their trek toward the ground, and he was relieved to see the crash mat in sight. He relaxed and took in his surroundings, embracing the experience he may never have again and tried to steady his heartbeat, thundering over being so close and connected to Montana.

Several minutes later, they landed on the mat and Montana unhooked their harnesses. Her face was flushed and excitement shone in her eyes. It took all his strength not to grab her and kiss her.

"Holy shit," he said. "That was quite a ride."

"Cool, right?"

"Yeah...pretty fucking cool," he said. *She* was pretty fucking cool, and he needed more of her in his life. More of these experiences and opportunities that she brought. And he'd take her anyway he could have her, even if it meant dealing with the heartache of unreciprocated love. He needed her in his life, even if it was just as a friend.

But her gaze was full of attraction and desire as her eyes flitted from his lips to his eyes and back again. "Yes."

"Yes, what?" he asked.

"The answer to your question from before. This was as exhilarating as BASE jumping."

"WELL, IT'S OFFICIAL. You are a member of SANS." Montana placed the framed certificate announcing Eddie as the newest member of the Society for Advancement of Naked Skydiving on the shelf above his television. She couldn't believe he'd actually gone through with the crazy scheme of hers. They'd both been on a high the entire drive back to Wild River.

Adrenaline-induced endorphins weren't the only thing coursing through her body, though. The intimacy of the naked jump—despite its humor—had her body on fire for him. The closeness and connection of doing an extreme sport together had her craving him. All of him. But, up until a few hours ago, he'd been hell-bent on pushing her away. They'd made progress that day, but was he really ready for more? She wouldn't go too far too fast and risk setting them back.

But as she went to join him on the sofa, Eddie reached for her.

Montana moved toward him and only hesitated a fraction of a second when he pulled her down on his lap. His hands wrapped around her legs, pulling her into him as his expression searched hers. His dark, gorgeous eyes full of desire had her swallowing hard.

After the exhilarating jump together, her pulse had yet to steady, and she knew this excitement had nothing to do with the free fall. She couldn't remember the last time her adrenaline had soared so high. She wanted Eddie. So damn much, it terrified her.

His hand cupped her face as he moved closer. "I'm going to kiss you," he said.

She nodded quickly, unable to find her voice.

He slowly closed the gap between their faces, his gaze locked with hers. His eyes closed as his mouth connected with hers. She held her breath as she savored the taste of Eddie's full, soft lips. So warm, inviting, yet demanding and taking the lead.

She wrapped her arms around his neck as she pressed her body closer. This had to be the best kiss of her life. She pressed her mouth to his and slid her tongue along his bottom lip. His mouth parted and she explored it with her tongue.

Eddie's hand caressed her face, then moved down her neck, over her exposed collarbone to her shoulder. He squeezed tight as though trying to hold himself back from allowing the hand to travel further over her body.

He was policing himself, but there was no need. He could touch her anywhere and everywhere.

Montana reached for the hand and lowered it over her breast.

Eddie moaned against her mouth as his hand squeezed and massaged her breast beneath her T-shirt. His breathing quickened, and Montana's body was on fire. His kiss, his touch, was driving her mad. She wanted him. Her body awakened, and she tingled everywhere. She clutched her thighs tighter together as she deepened the kiss even more.

If they kept this up, she'd come from first base alone.

Did Eddie want to go further?

She'd noticed his semi hard-on on the plane as she'd removed her clothing. Now she could feel it under her ass, but was he ready to do this?

Was *she* really ready?

She moved away slowly, licking the taste of him from her lips.

Eddie's eyes opened, and the intensity in his expression almost scared her. Before he'd been fun, annoying, cute Eddie. Now he was sexy as all fuck, serious and tempting. "What's wrong?" he asked as she stared at him, caught up in the unexpected emotions raging through her.

"Nothing. I just... I want you." Blurting out the obvious was the only thing she could do.

"I want you, Montana." He paused, glancing down at his lap. "I'm not sure how..."

Well, if that was all that was stopping him... "Leave

that to me." She gently climbed off his lap and bent to unbuckle his jeans. Her hands shook slightly as he watched. "Lift up," she said.

He did, allowing her to remove the jeans and underwear, as she had on the plane. He was already hard, and she took the opportunity to gently stroke him. Eddie's eyes closed, and his head fell back. Feeling herself grow wet just by the simple act of turning him on even more, she clenched her thighs together.

"Damn, Montana…"

She removed his shirt next and kissed his body. Starting at his shoulder, she moved her way inward, kissing his neck, down his chest, over to the other shoulder…then downward over his abs and lower.

She saw his hands tighten their grip on the fabric of the couch on either side of him and saw his cock straining. He was as close as she was.

Standing, she reached for the base of her T-shirt, slowly— *torturously on purpose* slowly—lifting it up and over her head. She let it fall to the floor with Eddie's discarded clothing, liking the way it looked tangled up with his. A small thing that suggested so much intimacy.

"You are gorgeous, Montana. Like, breathtakingly gorgeous," Eddie said.

She unbuttoned her jeans and wiggled her hips free of the denim, pulling them down slowly, then stepping out of them. She kicked them to the side, standing in front of Eddie in just her bra and underwear.

She desperately wanted to remove the rest of her clothes, climb onto his lap and seek relief from the intense desire radiating through her body, but she also wanted this first time with him to be special. They were moving so fast, but she didn't want to put on the brakes. That day had been incredible, and this felt right.

She turned around and slowly backed toward him until her legs were inches from his. Then slowly she started rotating her hips, seductively, tempting. She dared a peek over her shoulder at him and laughed seeing his mouth agape.

He slammed his lips together quickly and composed himself, sitting straighter on the couch. "Sorry. This is unexpected."

"Would you like me to stop?" Maybe he wasn't a striptease kind of guy.

"Hell no," he answered, reaching out gently to touch her hip, before letting her resume her teasing display.

She continued the figure-eight motion with her hips, standing on tiptoes to reach higher as her arms moved in the air. She'd only ever taken a stiletto-striptease class once in support of her friend's pole-dancing studio opening in Denver years before, but she could bluff her way through this, and Eddie didn't seem to mind that she wasn't a professional.

She reached behind her back and unclasped the bra. She slowly removed the straps over her shoulders and slid the fabric down her arms, letting it fall to the floor at her feet.

She turned around, and Eddie took her in. All of her.

The look of appreciation and respect and admiration coming from him, despite the primal reaction happening to his body, made Eddie so deserving of this time and attention she was giving all for him, and it was empowering as fuck.

She ran her hands down her sides, over her hips, then back upward over her stomach, her rib cage and over her breasts, stopping to massage them, before continuing up and around her neck.

"Jesus," she heard him mutter under his breath.

She turned around again and backed up until she was sitting on his lap. She rotated her hips against him, grinding slightly, creating enough friction that she could feel him spasm against her ass.

She swallowed hard, desperate to have him inside of her. She was wet and ready for him. Still, she resisted the urge.

She lay back against him, resting her head in the crook of his neck and ran her hands over her body again, dipping one hand into her underwear, touching herself. She moaned slightly, and Eddie's lips were instantly at her neck, kissing, licking, tasting. "Can I touch you?" he whispered into her ear.

"Yes, please…" She could come quickly by her own hand, but she craved his fingers to explore her.

He cupped her breasts, massaging gently at first, then harder. His fingers pinched her nipples, and she swallowed hard, her breathing labored as she continued to rotate her hips against him. She was driving them both insane, and she was enjoying every excruciating minute of it.

Eddie's hands caressed her stomach and hips, then one hand dipped into her underwear. Her legs parted, and his fingers dipped lower, entering her body.

"Oh, my God, Eddie. I'm so close already."

"Can I have you, Montana?"

Something in his tone made her shiver. He wasn't just asking for her body right now—he was asking for *her*. All of her. Normally that would have her retreating, but this time it didn't scare her at all. She wanted him too. All of *him*. "Yes," she whispered, happy that it sounded strong and confident.

"Condoms are in the bedroom. Bedside table," he said. "Should we go in there?"

"No. I'll be right back." Slowly, she stood and when she came back with the condom, she handed it to him. "My hands are shaking too much."

He opened it and slid it on, then reached for her hands. "We don't have to do this," he said.

"When have you ever known me to turn down an adventure?" she asked, climbing onto his lap and straddling him. Her thighs hugged his, and she pressed her body against him, feeling his hard cock press against her pelvis. "Damn, Eddie…"

He lifted her body with ease, setting her slowly back down on top of him. He moaned as she tightened her body, clenching around his erect cock. "This is going to last about as long as that free fall did," he said.

She was already coming. She moved painfully slow. Back and forth, up and down, just a few times and felt her orgasm ripple through her core. Intense, sharp, pleasurable waves radiated through her. She kissed Eddie hard and bit down on his lower lip as her orgasm peaked.

"I thought we'd get at least sixty seconds," Eddie said with a teasing grin, and she immediately felt her heart open to him. She'd seen him at his lowest these last few weeks, but bringing back that grin and seeing more sides to him had been one of the best journeys she'd ever been on. She'd never known a high quite like Eddie.

"You're fucking sexy," she muttered, grinding faster and harder against him. The faster she could make him come, the sooner they could do this again.

Eddie seemed to read her mind. "This first time will be quick, but the next one will last all night."

Montana's body throbbed in anticipation, eager for Eddie to deliver on that promise.

As EARLY-MORNING DUSK appeared outside his bedroom window, they hadn't yet slept a wink and Eddie was wide awake as he snuggled next to Montana in his bed. He traced his finger from one freckle to another, creating different patterns on her shoulder.

"I love your freckles," he said.

She scoffed. "No one likes freckles."

"I do. In fact, it was the first thing I noticed about you."

"Bullshit," she said, swiping at him.

Eddie laughed. "Okay, so maybe it wasn't the first thing." He lowered his lips to her shoulder and kissed it. "This one here is my favorite," he said, pointing to a tiny brown dot near her collarbone.

"You have a favorite?"

He sounded like a moron. He didn't care. He did have a favorite freckle, and Montana seemed over-the-moon happy about it, and making her happy was the only mission he was on currently. He never claimed to have game or be the most confident guy in the room, but he was sincere... and now he was lying in bed with the most intoxicatingly beautiful woman in the world.

"This one is shaped like a butterfly," he said.

"Great... Aren't oddly shaped brown spots potentially skin cancer?"

"Not this one," he said.

"You're probably right. I've been back and forth to medical facilities, seeing different doctors for so long, they've examined every inch of me. I'm sure they would have discovered something serious by now. So far, it's just my brain that's broken. Other than that, I'm in top shape."

Eddie touched her cheek. "No part of you is broken. You're exactly as you are because you're perfect this way." He knew she'd been through a lot in the last ten years, and now her journey to recovery was just another thing drawing him to her. If she'd made her way back, made amazing medical progress when it wasn't guaranteed or expected, maybe he could make bigger strides toward recovery as well.

Either way, she was a source of inspiration and hope—along with so much more.

He'd always been attracted to her and the last few weeks had challenged him and forced him to acknowledge that his life might never be the same. She'd been here, despite his attempt to push her away.

He could easily fall for a woman like Montana, but feeling her attraction for him had him quickly in trouble. There was no turning back, but she could so easily break him. And right now, he wasn't sure he'd recover from that.

"I'm not sure I actually thanked you for the skydiving experience," he said. "It was incredible."

"So, you'd do it again?"

"Naked? No. But fully clothed? Maybe."

She laughed. "I made you go naked so that you'd stress about that and the jumping itself wouldn't seem so scary."

"Oh, was that the reason? I thought you wanted to check out the goods before you decided whether or not to sleep with me."

"Oh, believe me, I checked out the goods. But as you quickly learned, there is nothing sexy about naked skydiving," she said.

"Obviously this wasn't your first naked adventure." He wasn't jealous, just completely in awe of her. Nothing scared her, and she backed down from nothing.

"Nope. My first time was when I participated in a world-record attempt with twelve other skydivers. I'd always said I wouldn't do it. It was kinda my own worst fear, I guess, but when they asked me to join for the record-breaking attempt, the challenge of it won out over my insecurities."

"Did you break the record?"

"We didn't that year. Missed it by six seconds, but the group did eventually beat it. I'd moved on to BASE jumping by then."

He heard the dull longing in her voice—the same as whenever she mentioned her passion. "You really miss it, huh?"

She nodded. "Yep."

"Is it just the high or the challenge? Or something else?" He wanted to understand her better. He totally understood wanting to do something with every fiber of his being and struggling to get there, but he wondered what drove Montana. What motivated her.

"I used to think that's all it was, but I'm starting to realize it was so much more than that. Growing up, I was a bit awkward. Shy and kept to myself. I was into science and sports, but mostly individual activities. I wasn't exactly popular." She paused. "Finding a community of like-minded people, first with skydiving and then BASE jumping, I finally felt connected to others, and my identity was wrapped up in the sport for a long time. I trained with other jumpers. I hung out with other jumpers. And while everyone was so different, we had that shared passion in common, and it really felt like a family…"

"I get that." It was similar on the force. The men and women he worked with on a daily basis shared his commitment to serving and protecting the community. They'd trained for the worst together, and they were a family.

"After my injury took me out of the game, I lost that. I mean, I still spoke to some of them, but I wasn't really one of them anymore. It felt different, and not only did I lose the community I'd come to depend on, I lost my identity. If I wasn't *Montana Banks, expert BASE-jumping daredevil* anymore, who was I? Who *am* I?"

Eddie swallowed hard. He had so many answers to that, but the words stuck in his throat. Telling her exactly who he saw when he looked at her would send her packing. "Who do you want to be?" he asked instead.

"A good mom to Kaia, a successful business owner..." Her voice trailed, and he knew those answers were the ones she knew she was supposed to say, but deep down she was still struggling to find herself and find that sense of family and community that she'd relied on for her self-worth and identity before.

"Well, you're doing both," he said. "And maybe someday you'll get back to BASE jumping."

"I've given up on that hope."

Had she really, though? "How are the new trial drugs working?" he asked.

"Good," she said but there was hesitancy in her voice.

"But?"

"But not well enough."

"How do you know? I thought you weren't due for a new scan for another month. Erika wanted to let the drugs do their thing for at least eight weeks, right?"

She stared at him in disbelief.

"What? I listen," he said with a laugh. Since the night she'd gone missing in the woods, she'd been open with him about her diagnosis. It was her way of reassuring him that she was fine and didn't need a babysitter, but he'd liked the updates. Since his injury, he'd been too focused on himself. "Are you feeling okay? Any recent memory lapses?"

"Yeah. No, I'm feeling fine. It's just...my sister hasn't disappeared."

He frowned. "Your sister?" She'd never really discussed her family before. He knew she was originally from Denver and her parents didn't approve of her being here in Wild River. She barely spoke about them, but he knew from something Tank had said that Montana's sister had died.

"She died in a swimming accident at sixteen, but she's... lingered ever since my accident."

"You see her ghost?"

"I see her, I talk to her, I fight with her, I laugh with her..." Her voice trailed again. "Am I crazy, Eddie? I am, right?"

He laughed, pulling her tighter. "While that might explain what you're doing here in bed with me, you're not crazy for seeing your sister's spirit."

She propped herself up on an elbow to look at him. "You believe in ghosts?"

He hesitated, choosing his next words carefully. "I don't think we know everything that's out there or what's possible. What our senses can pick up on. You're obviously experiencing something. Whether that's a real spirit visiting from the afterlife or your own subconscious talking to you, who knows? But I'm not one to judge or rule out the possibility that maybe you are still connected to your sister in some subconscious way." After his father died, he used to sit in his old truck for hours, listening to the old CDs they'd listened to together, chewing the tobacco his father had hidden in the glove compartment so his mother wouldn't find it. While his sisters had shared their own bonds with their dad, he'd felt closer to him in that truck than anywhere else.

Montana cuddled closer. "You have two sisters, right?"

"Yes. PITA 1 and PITA 2."

"Oh, come on. I met one of them when she and your mom were here doing the renovations to the apartment. She seemed...nice."

He laughed. "Love how you hesitated. That's exactly how I'd describe her." He brushed her hair away from her face. "She's actually blunt and intense, but she means well. She's never been great with emotion or feelings, but she's always been there for me. When/if I needed or wanted her help or not." He wouldn't describe his relationship with either sister as super close. Their father had been the one that really tied them all together, and once he was gone, they all kinda lived independently in the same house. But they were there for one another when it mattered.

"What about your other sister?"

"She works personal-security detail in LA."

"A bodyguard? Impressive."

"She's a beast in a five-foot-six, hundred-pound body. She had to work hard to prove that her size didn't mean she couldn't protect someone effectively. But she's not only a genius and security-hack wizard, which makes her valuable to any company, she's also a black belt in karate and jujitsu and military-trained with a weapon. She's kick-ass, but never tell her I said that."

"I hear it runs in the family. Your mom was a state trooper as well, right?"

"Wow. You've been listening, too." He'd only mentioned these things to her in passing. The fact that she'd paid attention meant something to him and gave him hope that the spark and connection between them went beyond the physical for her as well. "Yes. She was Alaska's second female state trooper."

"So you grew up with all women but no traditional feminine role model?"

"My grandmother is very much the domestic, stay-at-home, typical-of-her-era kind of woman, so it took her a long time to come to terms with the fact that she had three daughters—and two granddaughters—all of whom chose masculine careers, as she calls them."

"Obviously she raised very strong women. That's nothing to be ashamed of."

"Oh, she's proud—now. Actually, I think she likes being

the only real girly-girl in the family. She gets all the attention that way. We dote on her and put up with her demands." He smiled. "Like attending an elaborate wedding."

"She's getting married? At her age?"

"It's actually marriage number three, if she goes through with it, and wedding number five."

"How…?"

"She left two at the altar."

"Like, literally?"

"She broke one engagement off on the plane to Hawaii, but because everyone was flying to a destination wedding, they still threw the party on the beach for all the guests and just skipped the ceremony and vows. And the other, instead of saying her vows, she called the guy out for cheating right there in church." His grandmother was nothing if not ballsy.

Montana laughed. "I think I love her."

"I think she'd really like you." He paused, clearing his throat. She'd cued him up for the perfect opportunity. Still, he hesitated. They hadn't really defined this thing between them. It could be a casual one-night stand for her. He wanted it to be more, but meeting his family—his entire family at a big event—might be too much, too soon. He didn't want to scare her off.

She was quiet, as though sensing he was holding something back. He wanted to invite her, but he was nervous. He didn't want to get rejected or put her on the spot, where she might feel obligated, but the woman *was* in his bed, naked. She might say yes to be his date for a wedding. "Hey, I was wondering, if you're not busy…"

"I'm not," she said quickly.

He grinned, relief flowing through him. She'd been waiting for him to ask. She wasn't scared off by the idea of being seen with him at a family function, and her actual eagerness warmed him to the core. She was a special woman. "I haven't even told you what day it is yet," he said.

"Doesn't matter," she said, snuggling closer. "Whenever it is, I'm free."

Eddie smiled as his eyes got heavy. He wrapped his arms tight around Montana as they drifted off to sleep.

He had a date for his grandmother's wedding. And not just any date but the woman of his most fantastic dreams.

CHAPTER THIRTEEN

MAIN STREET WAS in full Halloween mode the next day as Montana jogged her usual route to work. It seemed overnight the storefronts had transformed their back to school promotions into haunting, spooky displays. Orange and white lights, black tarps as backdrops for gruesome and scary decorations, and Halloween favorites playing on the outdoor speakers definitely reminded patrons that the event was fast approaching. Wild River really got into the spirit of things. The small town seemed to go big for all kinds of activities and events in an effort to appeal to tourists.

Montana passed the small local theatre house and saw costumes for sale in the window. Sexy Witch, Sexy Bunny, Sexy Superhero... Pass.

Halloween had never been something she'd celebrated as a kid. Her parents weren't into it, and therefore she and Dani had never dressed up or done the trick or treating thing...

Kaia would probably want to participate in the local events, though, so Montana would make an effort for her.

She stopped outside SnowTrek Tours and stretched. When she turned around, Cassie was standing in a partially decorated window with a werewolf mask on her face. Montana jumped, then laughed. Obviously Cass was into this whole spooktacular thing. Not a huge surprise, really.

She opened the door and went inside. "Hey. I guess we're decorating for Halloween?"

"Of course. The business association hands out awards

for the best window displays each year. There's different categories," Cassie said, standing on a ladder to hang a strand of pumpkin lights along the top of the window. "And on Halloween, the stores usually stay open late to hand out treats to the kids."

"Sounds fun," she said as Tank appeared outside, carrying a box of what looked like severed body parts. Montana shook her head. Nope. She didn't get the appeal of this holiday at all, but she opened the door for him.

"Thanks," he said, setting the box down near the window.

"Ohh! Severed limbs—awesome!"

Montana laughed at Cassie's excitement over the grotesque decorations. "I assume we're entering the Terrifying category?"

"Yep, but not too gory. Don't want to scare the kids away."

"So, I guess Kaia's into all of this too, huh?" she asked Tank. She'd seen photos of Kaia in Halloween costumes over the years, but she wasn't sure at what age kids grew out of it.

"She lives for Halloween," Tank said. "She's been practicing her zombie makeup application for weeks." Tank's cell phone rang, and he moved away to answer. "It's the school. Just a sec."

"A zombie. Great." Montana just hoped it wasn't Sexy Zombie. "What can I help with?" she asked Cassie.

"You can start spraying the fake blood on the window," she said.

"No. I meant *actual* SnowTrek Tours work. I'll leave the decorating to you two," Montana said as Tank rejoined them. He looked pissed as he tucked the phone away. "What's wrong?"

"Kaia was caught skipping school."

Cassie nearly fell off the ladder as she swung to face Tank. "She *what*?"

"Yeah, apparently Principal Lee caught her at the mall when she popped over there before lunch to pick up some Halloween supplies for the school dance."

"At the mall? That's twenty blocks from the school. How did she get there?" Cassie asked.

"Public bus, apparently," Tank sighed.

Montana looked back and forth between their annoyed expressions. "So, this is a big deal?" She'd cut class all the time in junior high and high school. Cassie and Tank surely must have as well. All kids did it.

"You bet it is," Tank said.

"Oh. Okay."

He stared at her. "Seriously? You don't think so?"

The right answer was *Yes, of course I think so*. Unfortunately, that would be a lie. "Well, not really. This is the first time, right? And we've all done it. It's part of growing up," Montana said with a shrug.

"She had a math test this morning," Cassie said. "It was ten percent of her grade."

Okay, so that made it a little worse. "Can she retake it?"

"That's not the point," Tank said. "This isn't like her. Her behavior lately is not at all like her." His expression suggested Kaia's new behavior was somehow Montana's fault.

"Why are you looking at me like that?"

"I'm waiting for you to see that this is a problem."

"I do see that her behavior is strange lately…" Though, admittedly she hadn't spent a lot time with Kaia before the past six months, and she honestly believed maybe it was natural preteen hormones and drama. Tank was making too big a deal over it, and blaming her wasn't cool. "I'm just saying that cutting class isn't a major offense. She wasn't shoplifting at the mall or anything."

Cassie even looked slightly disappointed in her take on it as she climbed down from the ladder. "You're right. It's not the worst thing she could do...*but* we need to address this as though it was. Otherwise, what's next?"

Oh, come on. Skipping class wasn't a gateway to criminal activity. Tank and Cassie needed to settle down a little. "Kaia's a good kid. She made an arguably bad choice today."

"Arguably?" Tank said, eyebrow raised.

"Put the accusing eyebrow away. I didn't tell her cutting class was okay. And I won't, if that's how we're playing it. I'm just saying that I don't agree that it's as big a deal as you two are making it out to be."

Tank sighed. "Well, I guess we disagree on that. Either way, she's grounded."

Cassie nodded.

"For how long?" Montana asked, annoyed that this was the first parenting thing they weren't really agreeing on and yet Cassie and Tank had majority vote on how to deal with it. They needed a fourth to balance things out.

An image of Eddie appeared in her mind, but she sighed. He'd side with Tank and Cassie on this. So maybe she *was* the one who was wrong about it.

"A month and no Halloween," he said.

A month? Was her ex serious right now?

Even Cassie looked like she wanted to argue that point, but she reluctantly nodded. "That will definitely make her stop and consider her actions next time."

"Look, I agree to the grounding." Not that they'd asked her opinion. "But banning Halloween seems harsh." Tank had just said two minutes ago how important Halloween was to her.

"Punishments aren't supposed to be easy. On kids...or parents. I don't like this either, but she made her choice today." His tone softened. "Look, you know life wasn't easy on me as a kid, and I made choices in the past that weren't always the best. Kaia has the good fortune of having three people in her life who can guide her, help her make the right decisions. We need to stay strong with her, now more than ever. This shit's not going to get easier as she gets older," Tank said, touching her shoulder. "And I'm sorry if I seemed to suggest that you might be having an influence on her."

Montana nodded, accepting the apology, but the unsettling feeling in the pit of her gut told her that maybe Tank was right.

She wanted only the best for her daughter; therefore, maybe there did need to be some changes in their relationship.

From now on, mother first, friend second.

"Hey, Danger, if you chop any harder, you're going to pierce the cutting board," Eddie said, as he wheeled his chair into his kitchen and gently took the knife from Montana. He turned her to face him. "What's going on?" She'd seemed on edge since she'd arrived an hour before with a bag of groceries to make the Grilled Chile-Cilantro Chicken he'd taught her to make. She hadn't wanted to talk about it, but clearly she was upset.

She sighed. "It's Kaia."

"She okay?" Eddie knew that the little girl had been different since returning from camp, but Montana hadn't said much about it in days.

"She skipped class yesterday," she said.

"That's not like her. Where did she go?"

"The mall."

"With other kids?"

"By herself."

"Okay, that's a little concerning."

Montana looked pensive. "Which part?"

"All of it, but the by herself thing is probably the thing I'd be most concerned about," he said.

"Right, 'cause all kids cut class sometimes." Montana shrugged, but he could see an internal battle going on in her brain, as though she was questioning her own take on the subject.

"I didn't," he said.

"Shocking," she said, swiping a dish towel at him. "I guess I'm worried that maybe I'm not a great influence on her."

"Bullshit. Did Tank say that?" Didn't sound like something the man would say, but if Kaia was acting out, Tank might be looking for a reason or excuse to try to make sense of it or deal with it.

"Not in those exact words…and he did apologize after for implying it, but it's been nagging me ever since that maybe he's right. I'm not exactly the most disciplinary when it comes to Kaia. I let her get away with everything, really, and at first, I didn't see anything wrong with her cutting class."

She looked genuinely disappointed in herself, and Eddie took her hand and pulled her down onto his lap. "Hey, don't beat yourself up over that. There are a ton of different parenting styles. Not one is better than the other, and Kaia is benefiting from having you in her life." So was he, but that was a conversation for another time. "And it's natural to question yourself. That's a sign of a good parent," he said, touching her cheek.

"I just don't want to mess things up, you know? Cass and Tank were raising her just fine before I showed up, and I can't deny the coincidental change in attitude."

He kissed her forehead. "Things are different for her

now. She's adjusting and probably trying to pit the three of you against one another to get what she wants sometimes. See how far she can push you. But just keep setting boundaries, and she'll be fine."

"How do you know so much about parenting?"

"I don't. But I know she has a mother who is sacrificing a lot to be here for her. A mother who would do anything for her and who loves her—and goes to bat for her even when she makes a mistake. Believe me, that will mean a lot to her even if, in the end, you still decide that Tank's right in his punishment."

Montana released a deep breath and cuddled into his chest. "How do you always know the right thing to say to make me feel better?" she asked, her gaze burning into his.

Because he cared about her more and more each day and he'd do anything to bring a smile back to her face. Because he respected the sacrifices she was making to be there for her daughter and he admired all the strength and determination in her. Because the fiery passion she ignited in him gave him clarity into who she truly was and he was falling in love with every part of her. But he'd promised himself he'd take it slow for both their sakes, so his expression gave way to a teasing grin as he held back the things he wanted to say to her and instead simply said, "I was just trying to save my very expensive cutting board."

CHAPTER FOURTEEN

KAIA STRUGGLED UNDER the weight of the massive pumpkin as they waited for the elevator the following week. Montana balanced two smaller ones in her arms. "I hope you know how to do this," she told Kaia.

Kaia looked at her in shock. "You've never carved a pumpkin before?"

"Never." And she wouldn't be now, except that it was the first thing in a long time that had gotten an excited reaction out of Kaia. Montana would even don a costume if it meant finally drawing the little girl out of the shell she'd retreated into since returning from camp. Unfortunately, any chance of using Halloween as a way to connect with Kaia had been lessened since she was grounded and would have to miss the festivities. But, they could still carve the pumpkins, Montana had reasoned at the grocery store.

"My parents didn't really get into any traditions and holidays," she explained. Even before her sister died, their family didn't put a lot of emphasis on celebrating things the way other families did. Even Thanksgiving and Christmas weren't a big deal. Her mother was an only child, raised by an unconventional mother—Montana's skydiving, thrill-seeking grandmother—and her father was estranged from his family because they were Mormon, and with his younger, adventurous streak, he'd decided to leave the community at age eighteen. Growing up, it had been only the four of them together most of the time. Then the three of them after Dani died.

"But you went trick or treating, right?" Kaia asked. "Your parents didn't stop you from doing that."

Damn, this topic had taken a turn a lot quicker than she'd expected. She'd had a feeling the little girl would try to get her to change Tank's mind about allowing her to go trick or treating, but Montana was adamant that she would stick to Tank's rules, no matter how strict she thought them to be.

That was why Kaia had agreed to this whole pumpkin-carving idea. She was trying to bait her. Eddie was right—Kaia really was testing the waters.

For now, Montana would avoid getting pulled into the tougher conversation. Maybe if Kaia had fun that evening, she'd start to open up. All of their prodding and questioning and disciplining her recent crappy attitude and decision-making certainly wasn't working. She'd try a new approach. "Nope. No trick or treating, either," she said simply, pretending not to catch the little girl's drift.

The elevator doors opened, and they got in.

"Dad's being a jerk," Kaia blurted out as the doors closed.

Montana of six months ago would have tried to make Kaia feel better by letting the insult of her father slide, but the Montana she was today was quickly learning not to be manipulated by her eleven-year-old. "Well, so are you. Maybe change *your* attitude and your dad's will change, too," she said as lightheartedly as possible.

Kaia's jaw dropped. But then she gave what some might consider a small grin. "Fair enough."

Montana did an internal happy dance at the tiny victory. She'd let Kaia know that she and Tank were a team and she couldn't run to her complaining about her dad. Problems they could discuss—absolutely. But she wasn't here to validate any negativity Kaia had about Tank or Cassie.

The only way they would survive the teen years was by setting boundaries now.

Wow, those dull parenting books Tank had supplied her with might actually be paying off.

Her cell phone chimed in her pocket, and she struggled to retrieve it, balancing a pumpkin between her hip and the elevator wall.

A text from Lance?

First one since he'd left to train with his team over a month ago. She read quickly:

Missing you a bit lately.

"Wow, that's romantic," Kaia said, reading the text behind her.

"Hey! Privacy," she said, though Kaia's words had perfectly summed up her thoughts. She tucked the phone away without replying. She hadn't officially ended things with Lance, though the last time they were together in the hospital should have tipped him off that she was losing interest. And they hadn't spoken by phone or text or Skype since he'd left, so she'd assumed the conversation to break things off was unnecessary.

"Are you still dating him?" Kaia asked.

"No. Not really. He's away with his Olympic team, training for winter competitions, so we've just let things kinda die off."

"Does *he* know that?" she asked pointedly.

"Okay, okay. I'll be sure to inform him," Montana said as the doors opened on her floor.

They climbed off the elevator and the smell of cinnamon and pumpkin reached them. Kaia turned to look at her. "Did you bake?"

Montana laughed.

And laughed some more as she unlocked her apartment door. "That would be Eddie," she said, and just saying his name had her cheeks flushing slightly. The two of them had been practically inseparable that past week when Montana wasn't at work or with Kaia, but she hadn't told anyone about them yet. She wasn't sure how to define what was happening between them, and part of her liked keeping things a secret for now. It made it even more fun and exciting.

But Kaia caught the flushed cheeks. "Oh, my God. Have you and Eddie finally...?"

"Finally what?" she asked. Had mind-blowing sex? Absolutely. Discussed when they would do it again? Not quite. Since the first time had been so impulsive and after an intense skydiving experience, they both seemed slightly unsure if they should keep doing it or move back a few paces to a more natural dating progression. Dinner at his place every night usually resulted in lots of making out and talking. And cuddling and more making out. That was as far as they'd gone since the first time, but Montana was definitely ready for more.

"Netflix and *chilled*," Kaia said with a grin.

How the hell did she know what that meant? And no, they hadn't watched anything on Netflix. But this wasn't a conversation she was going to have with her daughter. "No, we did not," she answered. It wasn't a lie. "But we might have started to see one another...sort of."

She opened the door and went inside, but Kaia wasn't behind her. "Kaia?" She went back out into the hall just as Eddie opened his apartment door.

"Hi," he said to Kaia, then a secret little smile was sent her way.

Damn, the flush turned into full-blown flames coursing through her. He looked hot in a pair of jeans and tight fitting T-shirt. His hair was messy, the way it was after each heavy make-out session after she'd run her hands through it.

"Hey, Eddie. Mom and I were wondering if you'd like to come over and carve pumpkins with us."

They were? Montana's heart raced. She and Eddie had just moved into new territory they hadn't yet defined. Friends with benefits? They hadn't really had a second date outside the apartment, if the first could even be labeled as a date. It was more like a kidnapping. She wasn't sure how she felt about him hanging out with her and her daughter together, though the smell of pumpkin pie coming from his apartment suggested he might be better at this pumpkin-carving thing than she was, and it would definitely be fun...

"Right, Mom?" Kaia asked when she hadn't said anything.

"Yeah. I mean, if you're not busy, you're welcome to join us." Why was she feeling like a shy, tongue-tied schoolgirl all of a sudden? They'd jumped out of a plane together—naked.

Eddie, too, looked slightly hesitant.

Of course. He'd just had sex with her. That didn't mean he was ready to jump into stepdad role. She wanted to reassure him that was the last thing this was but wasn't sure how to say it, especially in front of Kaia, in a way that sounded casual and noncommittal but also not opposed. Because she wasn't. Which was absolutely terrifying to her, so it would most definitely have him running for the hills. Her thoughts ricocheted, and she reined them back in. "You don't have to," she said.

"Well, I am skilled with a pumpkin-carving tool," he said, moving away from the door to let them see the row of pumpkins he'd already carved in his own apartment. "Had a lot of time on my hands," he said with a wink. "Just give me a sec to get the pies out, and I'll be right over."

"Great!" Kaia said, walking past Montana into her apartment. She set her pumpkin down on the living-room coffee table.

Montana closed the door. "What was that?" she asked.

"What? You didn't want him to come over?" The teasing glint in her daughter's eyes made her instantly feel better. *There* was the little girl she recognized—the little shit disturber. "Besides, didn't you smell that pie? I'm hoping he'll share."

Montana laughed, setting down her pumpkins next to Kaia's and unpacking the stencils and carving tools from the shopping bags.

She was hoping for more than just pie that evening.

TRYING TO FOCUS on carving a spider into the humongous pumpkin was a challenge when his gaze and attention kept drifting across the table toward Montana. She was butchering a traditional pumpkin face, but he doubted it was from being distracted by him. Probably more lack of skill with the carving tool. He couldn't believe this was the first time she'd done this.

It also hadn't escaped him that this was the first time she was celebrating seasonal activities with her daughter. And they'd invited him.

Correction: *Kaia* had invited him.

But Montana seemed to enjoy having him and his pie there. She was doing more eating than carving.

And despite the initial awkwardness over the invite, he was loving being there as well.

She'd mentioned that Kaia had been withdrawn and distant lately, but the little girl seemed to be having fun that evening. Grossed out by the gooey insides of the pumpkin, she shrieked and reached for a napkin. "So gross!"

"Hey, don't throw it away. I'll take it," he said.

Montana looked at him. "For what? Do you use it in the pie?"

"No. I, uh…" He hesitated, unsure whether to tell her. He didn't want the pressure of expectation if he still wasn't ready to go back to work, but this was different—it was just community volunteering. "The station hosts a Haunted Trail event every year, and I said I'd help out. Hence the pumpkins in my apartment. We use them to mark each station along the trail."

"That's great," Montana said casually, but he knew she was trying hard to hide her pleasure that he was taking steps to get back out there and return to the career he loved.

"So, why do you need the pumpkin guts?" Kaia asked, trying to get the mushy, slimy goo off her hands and into a bowl.

"For brains," he said.

Her eyes widened. "That's what it was all those years?"

Eddie laughed. "Yep." He paused. "Hey, now that you know the inside scoop, maybe you'd like to volunteer this year? We need a ton of people to pull it off." The troopers dragged family members and friends to participate every year, but Eddie knew his mother and sister wouldn't do it. Neither of them were huge fans of Halloween, not appreciating the excuse for people to act crazier than usual. Police calls doubled on Halloween. But that's why the station held the event—to give people something fun and in the spirit of the season but safe to do instead.

"Really?" Kaia said. "That would be so cool!" She stopped, then her expression turned to disappointment. "But unfortunately, I'm not sure I can." She stared into her hollowed-out pumpkin. "I'm kinda grounded."

Shit. He'd forgotten.

Montana cleared her throat. "Well, seeing as how you'd be doing a nice thing, volunteering with the police station…"

And clearly in a place where she couldn't get into trouble.

"…I'll talk to your dad about it and see if he will lift the punishment just for that," Montana said.

Kaia beamed and wrapped her pumpkin-goo-covered hands around Montana's neck. "Thank you!"

"No guarantees," Montana warned. "I just said I'll talk to him, but if he says no, the answer's no."

"Okay," Kaia said, still squeezing her.

Over Kaia's head, Montana's gaze met Eddie's, and the look of gratitude mixed with pure desire had his mouth going dry.

Thank you, she mouthed.

Eddie's heart raced as he winked at her. As much as he liked her kid, he hoped Kaia wasn't spending the night that evening.

HE GOT HIS WISH.

Tank arrived a little after nine to pick Kaia up, and when his gaze landed on Eddie, there was nothing but a knowing smirk on the other guy's face. "Hey, man. How are you?" he asked. Eddie would definitely be hearing about this—from Tank and just about every dude in Wild River.

He didn't care.

"I'm great," he said. More than great, actually. That evening had been the first time since they'd had sex that he and Montana had hung out and had to keep things casual and PG because they had an audience. Oddly enough, the secret looks and casual touches they'd exchanged all evening had been more sexually charged than the full-on make-out sessions they'd been enjoying.

He couldn't wait to be alone with her. They'd agreed to take a step back and take things slower, but he was over that, and he suspected so was she.

Kaia nudged her mother forward. "Ask him," she whispered.

Tank looked slightly wary but mostly pleased to see his daughter in a better mood. "What's going on?"

Kaia looked pleadingly at Montana, and Montana sighed. "Well, I was going to talk to you about this tomorrow, but someone is clearly impatient, so…" She hesitated. "Eddie invited her to volunteer at the station's Haunted Trail event this year. He said they need a ton of helpers to run different stations."

"He said I could be the victim in the spider-web exhibit," Kaia said, nearly bouncing with excitement.

To his credit, Tank looked like he might say no, but they all knew he wouldn't.

Still, he asked all the right questions before deciding. "What time is the commitment? Halloween is Wednesday night, and I don't want you out too late on a school night."

Kaia looked at Eddie for the answer.

"It would be from five thirty until about ten thirty, eleven at the latest. We run a family/kid-friendly version earlier in the evening, and then it gets spookier later in the night for adults," he said.

"She'd be safe in that area of the trail?"

"Absolutely. There are three volunteers per station." One state trooper manned the entrance of each station, while the volunteers ran the show inside and several others walked the trail all evening to make sure everything went smoothly.

"You'd be there with her the whole time?" Tank asked.

The fact that he trusted his daughter's safety to him had

Eddie's shoulders straightening. "Absolutely." He'd make sure the spider-web station was easily accessible with his chair, and he'd keep an eye on her—not infringe on her fun but make sure she was okay.

Tank still hesitated.

"Please, Dad. I'm sorry for my attitude lately and for skipping class… It won't happen again, I promise," she said, folding her hands in front of her face and sending him a pleading look.

Montana looked just as pleadingly at Tank. She'd made progress with Kaia that evening, and Eddie knew she wanted to keep the good momentum going.

"Okay," Tank said, then held up a hand when Kaia got ready to pounce in excitement. "On one condition."

"Anything," she said.

"Someone gets me a piece of pumpkin pie to go," he said with a grin. "Damn, Eddie, I could smell it from the lobby."

"Hey! Why do you assume Eddie baked the pie?" Montana asked with fake hurt, hands on her hips. "Maybe I made it."

Tank laughed and laughed.

Five minutes later, Montana hugged them both goodbye, and Eddie's heart was nearly exploding out of his chest. With Kaia around and the focus on pumpkin carving, it had been easier to keep his thoughts PG. Not easy. But *easier*.

Now they were alone. And his gaze swept over her tight jeans and soft-looking V-neck sweater that accentuated her full breasts and tiny waist. Her makeup-free face had never looked more radiant, and the way she'd butchered her poor pumpkin with its crooked, uneven expression made her that much more endearing and irresistible to him.

Montana seemed to take a really long time closing the door, but when she finally turned the lock and turned around to face him, he headed straight toward her.

Grabbing her around her waist, he pulled her down onto his lap. "Hi," he said. "I'm going to kiss you now."

"You don't always have to give me a heads-up," she said as his mouth met hers. She wrapped her arms around his neck, moving even closer. She tasted like pumpkin spice, and the scent of the fall air still lingered on her clothes and her hair. She was addictive, and he wasn't sure he'd ever stop kissing her.

"I've been craving this since I left you the other morning," she murmured against his lips before going back in.

"Well, why didn't you come get it?" he asked.

"Just because you live next door doesn't mean I can be presumptuous."

"You can presume anything. Anytime," he said, kissing her again.

He was hard already, and the way her body was pressed against his, her fingers tangling in the back of his hair, her breath shallow, he knew she was just as turned on as he was. "I've been craving something else as well," he said.

She grinned. "Oh, yeah?"

His hand covered her breast. "I know we said we'd move slower, but I'm not sure I can do that anymore."

"Thank God. I thought I was going to have to do something drastic like bungee jumping naked or something to get your clothes off again."

"No drastic measures required. All you have to do is ask."

She kissed his mouth, then his earlobe, then his neck. "Okay, Eddie, can I take your clothes off, please?" she whispered in his ear, and goosebumps surfaced on every inch of his body.

"Yes," he said. "And do it fast."

She wiggled free of his grip and climbed off his lap. She knelt in front of him and wedged her body between his legs, reaching for the button on his jeans. His breath was already labored in anticipation of being naked with her again. Their long, heavy make-out sessions weren't enough. Her sultry gaze locked with his, she undid the jeans and pulled them off, tossing them on the floor.

His dick was already rock hard. He was always turned on when he was around her, and he didn't think his desire for her would ever start to fade.

She slid her hands up the inside of his thighs and ran her fingertips along his groin, teasingly slow, before sliding both hands beneath the waistband of his underwear. One hand cupped him, while the other wrapped around him.

He swallowed hard, and his body tensed at her touch. She gently stroked him beneath the fabric and he was desperate for more. He moaned. Damn, it felt so good. He'd been fantasizing about her hands on him since the first time they'd had sex.

He removed his underwear and threw them aside. "Those have to go," he said.

"Agreed," she said, lowering her head to him. She licked the top of his cock, slowly, running her tongue along the length of his shaft before circling the tip. Precum escaped, and he gripped the chair. She was so crazy sexy. All the time. But right now, he couldn't take his eyes off her.

She took him into her mouth and glanced up at him, and her expression nearly put him over the edge. Her mouth was soft, warm and wet, and the way she eagerly wanted to pleasure him was driving him insane.

"Montana."

She sucked and licked and pumped him with her hand as he fought the orgasm and pleasure erupting inside of him. He didn't want to come just yet. He wanted this to last. But damn, it felt so fucking good.

"Can we slow down a little?"

She removed her mouth from him slowly, and he instantly regretted the decision. The deep burning coursing through him demanded release. He was so close to the edge already. She kissed along his inner thighs, coming so close to his cock, then backing away again. Her hand stroked him up and down. Slow and teasingly. Not enough pressure to make him come but just enough to keep him erect and throbbing.

She moved closer between his legs. Gripping his upper thighs with her hands, she kissed his chest, his abs and lower. Her tongue traced the shape of his muscles and the lower she went, the more excruciating the desire pulsing through him. "Montana, put me in your mouth again," he said, his voice hoarse.

"I thought you wanted to go slow?"

"I'm not sure I can take slow."

She grinned up at him as she teased the top of his cock with her tongue, flicking gently. "Unfortunately, you're not in control…"

Fuck that.

Gently, but firmly, he gripped her ribcage and moved closer to the edge of the chair. He pushed her slowly backward onto the floor and allowed himself to topple on top of her, protecting the back of her head as they hit the living room floor together.

She gasped in surprise at the reversal, as his hands massaged her breasts through the fabric of her sweater and he wedged himself between her thighs, pressing his cock against her.

"What was that about control?" he asked, grasping both her wrists together with one hand and placing them over her head. With his other hand, he dipped inside the tight jeans that had him drooling all evening with the way they hugged her hips and ass so perfectly.

She wasn't wearing any fucking underwear. She was going to be the end of him. "You've been commando all evening?"

She grinned. "It's laundry day."

"I'll be sure to keep the machines busy all week." He slipped a finger inside her wet, warm body, and the effect on him was almost as intoxicating as it was on her. She moaned and grabbed a hold of his shoulders, her back arching to get closer to him.

Knowing that he could turn her on made him feel powerful again. Capable, strong, sexy...

He moved lower down her body and gripped the waistband on the jeans. She raised her hips to allow him to lower the fabric down over her hips and thighs, then she let her knees drop to the sides, giving him full access to her body. He took a moment to just look at her...all of her. Exposed and vulnerable but still so confident. He'd never met anyone who balanced the dichotomy so perfectly. She was always so in control, so giving it up to him in that moment told him that this connection went further than just the physical. She trusted him, and damn, that was empowering.

His gaze met hers as he buried his face between her legs. She gasped, and her moan of pleasure made him throb as his lips met her opening. He kissed gently at first, giving her the same torturous pleasure she'd given him. Then he licked along the folds as he dipped a finger deep inside of her body. She tasted so good. He couldn't remember ever feeling as insatiable as he licked and sucked and explored every inch of her with his tongue.

"Jesus, Eddie..."

Her back arched closer to him, demanding more instant relief, but he pressed a palm to her pelvis, holding her where he wanted her. He was in control now.

He put another finger inside as his tongue flicked against

her clit…over and over, bringing her closer and closer to the edge.

Her hands flailed out around her body, looking for something to grab hold of, and finally her fingers buried into his hair, pressing his head into her body. "I'm so close." Her legs shook at her sides, but he wasn't about to let her come that fast. He moved his head away and removed his fingers from her body.

She moaned. "Fuck, Eddie…"

"You were planning on teasing me before, weren't you?" he asked, licking the inside of her right thigh, then the left one.

Her breathing was labored as she fought to control the tremble of her body. "No. I'd never do that to you."

He laughed as his lips moved higher, kissing along her inner thighs, along her pelvis, up her stomach and over the valley between her breasts. His cock pressed against her as his mouth found her right nipple. He circled it with his tongue, before taking it into his mouth. He bit gently, and her hands tangled in his hair. She pulled gently, and he bit a little harder.

She rocked her hips against him, desperate for friction. Any kind of release.

He moved to the left breast and continued to torture her with a combination of gentle sucking and little bites until he couldn't take it anymore, either. He needed release, and he wanted to give her a mind-blowing orgasm.

Leaving another trail all over her body as he went, he returned his mouth to her opening. His hands pushed her thighs apart, his fingers digging deep into her flesh as he licked desperately at her clit, making her wetter and wetter.

"Eddie, please don't stop this time. I'm too close."

He had no intention of stopping this time. He quickened his actions, dipping two fingers back inside her body. He felt her clench around them as her entire body trembled beneath him. She moaned in pleasurable release, and her body slowly relaxed.

He raised his head to look at her, and the look of satiation on her beautiful, flushed face filled him with even more confidence. "Was that okay?" he asked, though he knew the answer. She couldn't fake the way her body had convulsed around him.

"More than okay," she said, sitting up and reversing their position. She straddled him and slid her hands beneath his T-shirt as she lowered her mouth to his. She kissed him hard and long, before moving away and shimmying lower.

When her mouth took his cock this time, he thought he might instantly explode, but she gently sucked and licked, keeping him so close to the edge to enjoy the sensations without it ending too fast. His dick throbbed at her touch, her eagerness to please, the way she lovingly pleasured him…

He felt himself spasm, and there was no holding it back any longer. "Montana, I'm coming," he said.

She didn't stop.

Eddie felt the waves of his orgasm crush him, almost drown him as he fought for a breath. Damn, it was incredible. She was incredible. His body trembled as the orgasm peaked, then gradually receded.

She lifted her head and smiled at him as she moved higher to cuddle into him on the living-room floor. "Was that okay?" she asked.

"It was perfect," he said, holding her tight and kissing the top of her head.

She was perfect. And he was so screwed.

CHAPTER FIFTEEN

"Can I Skype with Grandma and Grandpa to show them my Halloween costume?" Kaia asked as Montana returned from handing out candy at her apartment door a few weeks later.

Or rather, giving the kids in apartment 4C her stash of oversize chocolate bars because she hadn't expected trick or treaters in an apartment building and was caught completely off guard when kids started knocking on the door that evening. She had two bars left and three cans of Diet Coke, then she was out. She'd head down to SnowTrek Tours and help Cassie give out candy there while Kaia was helping out at the Haunted Trail event.

"Um, sure," she said. Should she give Kaia another heads-up that her parents weren't exactly into the Halloween thing and they probably wouldn't get the scary, realistic-looking zombie makeup job Cassie had helped her perfect? Maybe they'd pretend for Kaia's sake.

A minute later, her mother's blood-curdling scream could have come straight from a horror movie. Montana hurried over as Kaia tried to get her to calm down. "It's okay, Grandma. It's just makeup," she said.

"Good heavens, why would you do that?"

Montana shot her daughter a *Told you so* look.

"It's part of my Halloween costume," Kaia said, standing to show them the ripped, blood-stained clothes.

"Halloween is tonight?" Montana heard her father ask.

"Yes, Grandpa. It's October thirty-first every year," Kaia said with a laugh. "Don't you have trick or treaters?"

"We don't answer the door to strangers—big or small," he said.

Montana remembered hiding out in the basement of their house with her parents and sister on Halloween nights, watching movies, ignoring the ringing doorbell. Maybe it should have bothered her not to participate in the festivities like the other kids did, but she and Dani had popcorn and full-size candy bars and pop, and the family had their own fun evening together, so she really hadn't felt like she was missing out on anything. They'd always been on the move, seeking out one new adventure after another, so the slower pace of that family movie night had been special.

"Who did that to your face? Your mother?" Montana's mother asked, disapproval evident.

As if. Kaia genuinely looked like she'd just climbed out of a grave. Gray and purple makeup paled her complexion with a creepy undertone effect. Facial prosthetics covered in blood gave the look of gashes along her forehead and cheeks, and black eyeliner applied thick around her eyes completed the terrifying look. No number of YouTube tutorials would have helped Montana pull off something like this.

"No, my stepmom—I guess you could call her—Cassie, did it," Kaia said. "Dad's girlfriend."

"Ahh," came the reply on the screen.

Ah, the undecipherable *ahh*. Montana had never known exactly what that simple word meant when her mother said it, but it was never good. It was usually the response to something she was disappointed about or didn't understand. When she didn't want to start an argument or give a real opinion on an issue but she wanted Montana to know that she wasn't completely on board with an idea.

Kaia's excitement dampened, and Montana jumped in. "I think it looks so great. Super scary. And she did most of it herself, which is quite impressive, don't you think?"

Come on, Mom and Dad. Take a hint.

She'd warned Kaia that this grandparenting thing was going to be new for them, and they would need some time to figure it out, but Montana hoped that her daughter could feel their love for her, despite not showing it in the most traditional of ways.

"Oh, yes, well, makeup artistry is a growing industry," her father said.

There you go. Was that so hard?

Kaia beamed, and Montana continued with something she knew would appeal to her mother. "She offered to volunteer with a Haunted Trail event tonight. Proceeds go to the youth shelter in town." Eleanor Banks had to approve of volunteer work, at least.

Her head bobbed up and down on the screen. "Yes, okay. Now, that makes more sense."

"I still don't love the idea of Halloween, though," her father said. "It's bad enough out there every other night of the year, but Halloween just gives teenagers an excuse to get into trouble."

"Well, not Kaia," Montana said. She hadn't told her parents about Kaia's attitude lately or that she'd skipped school. Kaia was a wonderful kid, and she might be going through some stuff right now, but Montana only sang her daughter's praises. Public shaming of her wrongdoings wasn't something Montana ever planned on.

"Yeah, it's with the police station. And Mom's boyfriend will be there," Kaia said.

Montana's eyes widened, and she slid off camera. Unfortunately, she could still see her parents' faces. Surprise and confusion and the normal disapproval flashed in succession. If Kaia noticed, she didn't act like she had.

"Boyfriend?" Eleanor said.

"Yeah, you know. Eddie. The cop who saved her life."

"Saved her life?"

Montana was desperately waving her hands and shaking her head on the other side of the monitor. She hadn't told her parents about any of that yet. She hadn't told them a whole hell of a lot since she'd been there. They didn't know her exact role and job description with SnowTrek Tours. They didn't know she was a support member of the search and rescue crew, and they didn't know about her getting lost in the woods months before or the shooting incident.

Or about her dating life.

They knew absolutely nothing, and Montana had been planning on keeping it that way for as long as possible.

Kaia looked confused as she glanced back and forth between the computer monitor and Montana.

"What do you mean *saved her life*, darling?" she heard her father ask.

Kaia looked panicked. "Oh, it was nothing. Just a shooting on Main Street."

"Shooting?" Her mother's voice had gone up an entire octave. Montana was in so much shit.

She shut her eyes tight as her front door opened and Eddie entered.

"Kaia, can we chat with your mom for a minute? Alone?" her mother asked.

"Hello, hel…" Eddie stopped and shot her a quizzical look, when she put her finger to her lips.

My parents, she mouthed.

He nodded and quickly hid out by the door. Lucky bastard.

Lucky *gorgeous* bastard, dressed in his state trooper

uniform, clean-shaven for the first time in weeks with his dark hair gelled back. He looked like Sexy Cop, and she wished he could blow off the Halloween event and they could spend the evening role playing. She could definitely think of a few uses for those handcuffs.

"Sure. Eddie's here so I have to get going anyway," Kaia said. "Bye!" She blew them both a kiss as she moved away from the laptop.

Right. Shit. Her parents.

Kaia looked sheepish as she approached Montana. "Am I grounded again?" she whispered as she hugged her good-bye.

"No, but *I* might be," Montana said, hugging her daughter a little longer, not wanting to let go and to have to face the music.

"So, YOUR GRANDPARENTS had no idea about the shooting, huh?" Eddie asked Kaia as they drove to the Haunted Trail site.

"Nope. I think Mom's going to kill me."

"Aw, she didn't seem upset with you." Freaked out to face her parents, but not upset with Kaia. They hadn't had a chance to talk, with her parents waiting on Skype, but the look she sent him as he left, one that said she wished they were alone so she could tear his uniform off, made him less annoyed that she hadn't told her parents about *him* yet, either.

Besides, how could he be annoyed? He hadn't exactly told his family he was seeing anyone, either. He still hadn't told his grandmother that he'd be bringing a date to the wedding after all. They each had their reasons for not revealing the relationship. His was because he couldn't deal with his sisters' teasing that he'd eventually have to endure. He suspected hers was that her parents seemed to be having a hard time with her being in Wild River. They weren't completely on board with her recent life choices and they worried about her living on her own and being so far away from them, so she obviously didn't want to give them more cause for concern. He understood. He just hoped it wasn't because she wasn't sure about the two of them together yet, because *he* was definitely feeling sure.

The last few weeks with Montana had been amazing. His attraction to her kept growing stronger. He looked forward to seeing her every day and missed her when they weren't together. Playing it cool had never been his forte, but he was desperately trying not to scare her away with the intensity of his feelings for her.

"I don't know why she'd be afraid to tell them things," Kaia said, gazing out the window. "They are her parents."

"Well, do you tell your parents everything?" he asked. He knew the answer was no, and he hoped that maybe Kaia could see how her mother could understand what she was going through.

"I guess not," Kaia said. She looked about to say something else on the subject, but Eddie turned into the lot of the Haunted Trail, and she didn't. "Are we here?" she asked instead, looking around at the empty lot and field around them.

Eddie laughed. "Yes. The trail starts in that creepy-looking barn over there," he said, pointing to it.

"Oh, cool," she said, already climbing out of the van.

He grabbed his crutches from the back and got out, then led the way to the dimly lit trail entrance that guided visitors toward the creepy barn. Donation bins lined the trail and skull-shaped lights illuminated the path. Only the event volunteers had arrived so far. "Go on in," he said, opening the door for Kaia.

"Wow, it looks super cool in here," Kaia said as she entered. The makeshift thirty-by-thirty space was painted all black—walls, ceilings and floor—with the exception of stripes of iridescent, fluorescent paint that gave the room its ominous glow and provided lighting for participants. The station put up the same structure each year, but the interior stations of spooky surprises changed from year to year to keep the trail fresh and exciting for regulars who attended as part of their Halloween traditions.

"You think so?" he asked, looking around.

"Absolutely. Can I check it all out?" she asked.

"Of course."

She pushed through one curtain of ripped garbage bags hanging from the ceiling to check out the first scary exhibit along the tour. He heard her chat with Al, the trooper running that station, and then heard her *Oh, gross!* when she saw the floating eyeballs in the punch and the severed fingers dipped in a blood-red-colored rich chocolate.

"They may be gross, but they are delicious," Eddie said, joining her as she picked one up. "Hey, Al."

The other man nodded his greeting. "Good to see you, Eddie."

"You made these?" Kaia asked him.

"Yep." He'd made most of the edibles and gross-out stuff that year, with the help of YouTube, having more time to do it than anyone else. It had felt good giving back to the department in some way while he was on leave. "Take your time looking around, and when you're ready, I'll show you to your station out on the trail," he said.

"Awesome." Kaia made her way through the interior setup, and he heard her laugh and shriek as she moved from one to the next. The volunteers were happy to have a test run before the crowds started to show up.

"Hey, Eddie. Good to see you," Adams said from behind his own station in the corner. He was dressed as a mad scientist in a white lab coat covered in fake blood and guts. His naturally dark hair was sprayed white and stuck out in all directions as though he'd been electrocuted. Thick black glasses, broken and held together with medical tape in the middle, completed the look. It actually suited the guy.

"Hey, what are you carving up over here?" he asked, moving closer to peer into the specimen jars containing brains and organs floating in a yellow gellike goo.

"Captain Clarkson," Adams said, pulling the sheet back to reveal the captain's head poking up through a hole on the table, while a fake disemboweled body lay on the examination table.

Eddie laughed. "Never looked better, sir."

"I don't know how you assholes rope me into these gruesome displays every year," Captain Clarkson grumbled, but Eddie knew for a fact that he was always the first one to sign up for a volunteer station—the gorier, the better. He practically funded the event himself. His kids were older now, but he'd been doing this every year since they were young enough to be terrified by it. "How are you feeling?" he asked.

"Better," Eddie said and meant it.

"Better as in ready to return to work?" the captain asked.

Eddie was afraid to ask in what capacity or to promise anything he wasn't entirely ready for, and the event wasn't really the place to discuss his future on the force, so he said, "Better as in I've been thinking about it."

His captain nodded. "Good."

"Eddie, I'm ready," Kaia said, joining them. "Oh, sick!" she said, seeing the guts and gore of the exhibit.

"What do you think? Too scary?" Adams asked her.

"Just perfect scary," she said.

"You look great. That's amazing zombie makeup. Did you do it yourself?" Adams asked.

Kaia beamed at the praise. "Cassie helped."

"I hear you're trapped in the spider web this year," Captain Clarkson said. "That's a fun one."

"Yes. Want to hear my scream? I've been practicing," she said.

"Absolutely," he said.

Eddie grinned as she let out the blood-curdling sound that chilled his veins.

Damn, he'd believe that.

After suitable praise on her performance, Eddie led her out and through the outside exhibits along the dimly lit trail. She shivered and moved a little closer to him. "You're going to be sticking nearby, right?" she asked, looking all around her as they walked.

"I promised your dad I would, but don't worry, I won't crowd you," he said with a wink.

"It's totally cool if you want to stay close," she said casually, but he heard the note of fear in her voice at the idea of being out there by herself.

"I'll be right outside the exhibit, directing people toward your brilliant performance," he said.

"Great." She paused and coughed. "Hey, I just wanted to say thank you for saving my mom. I think it's really great that you two are, well, you know..." she said with a shrug.

Did he? He knew what he wanted to be happening with Montana, and he suspected they were on the same page. He could feel her attraction to him growing stronger each time they were intimate, but he hoped it was more than just amazing chemistry. He was starting to catch major feelings for the woman, and he hoped he was having the same effect on her heart. "Thank you, and it was no problem."

Kaia eyed his crutches. "I'd say it was a huge problem. You risked so much—your life—for her. You must really like her."

And it was kinda his job, but the truth was he wasn't sure he would have reacted as quickly if the bullet had been flying toward anyone else.

"Here we are. Your web," he said, stopping by her exhibit setup.

Kaia's eyes lit up at the bungee cord spider web, spray-painted a shade of silver, and the oversize, mechanical jumping spider on the floor next to it. "That is so cool!" She moved closer and stepped on a spot on the floor that read *Beware of Spider: Don't Step Here!* The spider jumped toward the web, and Kaia shrieked in happy surprise. "This is going to be so fun!" She ran toward him and hugged him. "Thanks for asking me to help, Eddie."

"Hey, you were made for this," he said. "Whenever you're ready, climb onto the web…and I'll just be over here watching people pee themselves."

Two hours later, he'd heard countless screams and tons of nervous laughter echoing all around him on the trail. Between groups, he snapped a photo of Kaia in the web and sent it to Montana.

You might have a movie star on your hands, he texted along with the image.

Good thing we know a bodyguard in LA ;) So thrilled that she's having fun, came her reply.

Are you having fun with the trick or treaters?

I could think of things that would be more fun…

Such as?

Ripping that uniform off you.

He grinned. So she had been eyeballing him.

Later?

Count on it.

Seeing another group approach on the trail, Eddie reluctantly put his text flirting on hold and tucked the phone into his pocket. "New group," he told Kaia.

On cue, her pleas for help started, growing more frantic as the group got closer. A group of junior-high and high-school students. No parental figures with them. They were laughing and joking as they stopped in front of Kaia's exhibit.

Eddie watched closely as Kaia suddenly didn't look to be having as much fun. Maybe they were kids she knew... but why would she be embarrassed? She was killing it with her performance. She continued to play the part, but Eddie could sense she was uneasy.

Two of the junior-high-age boys spoke to her, and she ignored them.

One reached for the bungee cords on the web and shook them, tossing her off balance. She told him to stop.

Eddie couldn't hear what they were saying, but their tone and demeanor suggested teasing and taunting. He didn't like it. He moved closer, but before he could tell them to scram, they saw him approach and moved on down the trail.

"Hey, everything okay?" he asked Kaia. She looked visibly shaken, and he glared after the boys. "You didn't get hurt when they were shaking the web, did you?"

"Yeah, no, I'm fine. Just some jerks from school," she said, fixing one of the cords that had come loose before climbing back into position.

"Well, I'm not far away if they come back," he said.

She smiled gratefully at him, and he sensed whatever was going on with her might have something to do with those jerks from school. Might explain the withdrawn behavior and the cutting class. "Thanks, Eddie," she said.

He moved away again as a new group approached on the trail. "Okay, you're on. Let's hear that scream," he said with a wink, and she visibly relaxed as she got ready to act scared shitless.

Confident she was okay, he moved back out of the way and radioed up the trail to his coworker, Sanchez, who was hiding behind a tree with a hockey mask and really loud and very real-looking chain saw. "Hey, man, there's a group of teenagers approaching. Do me a favor, will you?"

WHEN HE RETURNED to his job on the force, Eddie would be needing a new uniform. New shirt buttons at least. True to her word, she'd ripped the sexy uniform from his body the minute they found themselves alone at his place the night before.

Now, the uniform lay discarded in a heap along with her clothes on his bedroom floor, and Montana smiled as she rolled over in the bed next to him. "Good morning," she said, prying one of his eyelids open.

Eddie laughed sleepily. "Why are you awake? We barely slept last night."

Bad Cop, Good Cop, Sexy Cop, Naked Cop—it had taken a while to fulfill all the cop fantasies she hadn't known she had. "I have to go to work," she said. She'd rather stay in bed with him all day. It was cold and rainy outside. The perfect day to stay wrapped up together in these bedsheets, order take-out and stay naked all day. But she needed to help Cassie with the holiday-adventure tour package brochures.

Now that Halloween was over, they were full steam ahead on bringing in the holiday tourists bookings. Winter was one of SnowTrek Tours's busier seasons, and this would be Montana's first winter in Wild River. She'd actually been kinda dreading the shortened days with twenty hours of darkness and the frigid temperatures, but now that she had Eddie to snuggle the long winter nights away with, she was actually looking forward to it.

In fact, she was looking forward to her new future a lot more now. Feelings of fear and uncertainty about whether she was doing the right thing and in the right place were slowly fading…fading a little more each day as her feelings grew for Eddie.

She had everything she needed here in Wild River.

Of course, convincing her parents of that was something she was giving up on. The Skype chat the night before had gone exactly like every other. They thought she was making a mistake by continuing to pursue her dangerous career, as they put it. They weren't convinced that the doctors here in Wild River were as good as the ones in Denver. They thought a new romantic relationship would be added stress on her and now thought Wild River was a dangerous ghetto because of the shooting.

She'd tried to tell them that she was happier and safer here surrounded by an amazing support system, which included Eddie, but it had fallen on deaf ears. Luckily, she'd learned over the years to take her parents' advice and ignore most of it. She was grateful for all they'd done for her after her accident, but she really was okay now, and she wished they could see it for themselves.

She was feeling better than she had in a really long time.

Dani hadn't been around in a while, either, so if she was a result of an overstressed mind, then that was a good sign.

Who knew the magic cure she'd been searching for to start feeling like her life was back on track was her annoying cop next-door neighbor?

Eddie pulled her closer and nuzzled her neck. "I don't want you to go."

That made two of them.

She ran a hand over his bare chest, then down over his washboard abs, then lower. He may have just woken up, but a certain part of him was wide awake already. "Sorry, it has a mind of its own," he said.

Her hand wrapped around him. "Don't apologize. I'm glad I can have this effect on you," she whispered, stroking slowly, up and down...

Eddie growled as he rolled on top of her and pinned her hands above her head on the pillow. "You, Montana Banks, drive me absolutely insane, and I never want that to stop," he said, kissing her.

An hour later, she finally got out of his bed. Not because she wanted to but because she had exactly sixteen minutes to get to work.

Eddie lay on his side, watching her get dressed. "Can you do that slower, please?"

She laughed, picking up a pillow and throwing it at him. "Because of you and your morning wood, I'm going to be late." She pulled on her jeans and reached for her sweater on the floor. "Damn. I wore this last night..." She turned to Eddie's closet. "I'm stealing your shirt," she said, reaching for the smallest white button-down she could find and putting it on.

"You can keep it. It looks hotter on you," Eddie said as she tucked it into her jeans.

It could come in handy for a striptease outfit sure to drive him wild later... Damn, the temptation to call in sick and dive back into bed with him was strong, but she had to go. She crawled onto the bed and kissed him, savoring the taste of him, committing it to memory for the long, busy day ahead. "I'll see you tonight?"

"Not even a question," he said, squeezing her ass in her jeans.

She got up and slid her feet into her shoes.

"Oh, I did mean to tell you something, but you didn't really give me a chance last night before tearing my uniform to shreds," he said, sounding slightly more serious, despite the joke.

"What's up?"

"I don't think it's anything to worry about...but there were some boys on the trail last night, and they seemed to be giving Kaia a hard time."

Her chest tightened, and her mama-bear instincts were on full alert. Funny, for years, she hadn't really possessed a maternal instinct, but it hadn't taken long to develop. "Which boys?"

"I don't know their names. Just some junior-high and high-school kids. Kaia recognized them. She said it was nothing, but maybe it's a conversation you want to have? Just to be sure," he added.

Montana nodded as she returned to the bed and kissed him again. "Thank you for letting me know." She checked her watch and groaned. "Please don't make me go to work."

Grabbing the front of the shirt, he pulled her in for another kiss. "I'll be right here when you get back."

She sighed and broke away from him, hurrying toward the door before she changed her mind and stayed. "Stay naked," she said with a wink.

Four minutes late, she entered SnowTrek Tours, out of breath. "Sorry I'm late."

Cassie waved a hand. "I thought for sure you'd be at least an hour more." She eyed the outfit as Montana hung her jacket on a hook. "Cute shirt. Eddie's?"

So much for fooling Cassie. "Maybe."

"Thank him again for including Kaia last night. She was

so happy when she got home. Almost like precamp Kaia," Cassie said, opening the proofs of the new winter brochure as Montana took a seat next to her.

"Yeah, she had a great time." She hesitated. "But there was one thing that happened that I want to talk to you and Tank about."

Cassie immediately looked worried. "What is it?"

"Well, apparently there were some boys that were teasing her…harassing her a little."

"Those little assholes!"

"Exactly."

"It's the same ones from camp and on her hockey team, I bet," Cassie said, full-on annoyed. "They were being jerks to her at hockey practice last week, too."

So, it *was* a problem. Montana had been hoping it was just a one-off, with Halloween and being hyped up on too much sugar. "Anyway, Eddie dealt with them." She grinned. "Apparently, one of them had to run home to change his jeans after the other volunteers on the hike were through scaring them."

Cassie's smile was wide, and Montana appreciated the restraint not to say they all told her so. They'd all seen the connection between her and Eddie so much faster than she had. "Eddie's incredible. Have I mentioned how happy I am that you two are dating?"

"About six hundred times already." She paused, then brought the conversation back to Kaia. "Except, we thought maybe it's a bigger deal. Maybe Kaia's being bullied by these kids."

"Bullied? Kaia? But she's so awesome. Smart, confident, unique…" Cassie's face fell. "Shit. Exactly the target for bullies."

Unfortunately, Montana knew all about it. She'd been a target for bullies once she started attending a real school.

She'd always been taller than all the kids, so nicknames like Amazon and Giant had been the start of it, then her body hadn't developed as fast as the other girls in junior high, and she'd always worn her hair short, so they'd teased her about her sexuality.

The only thing that had prevented the bullying from turning into something Montana couldn't handle was her sister. Unlike Montana, Dani was the popular girl in her grade and among her friends. She was petite and cute, and her body developed at the same rate as the other girls'. She was like the others—she liked makeup and hair-care products and boys and gossip. Dani fit in. And because no one wanted to be on Dani's shit list, they weren't too nasty to Montana. Always holding back the really insulting comments on the tip of their tongues or pretending to be joking when Dani caught the behavior.

After her sister died, things got a lot worse. Dani had always stuck up for her, but once Dani was gone, Montana was the odd one with the dead sister.

"Should we talk to Kaia about it together?" Cassie asked.

"Actually, I was wondering if you guys would mind if maybe I spoke to her first. I've been there, and I can definitely identify with what's she's going through, if it is in fact bullying." Cassie had grown up cool and sporty and popular, and Tank—well, no one had ever dared to mess with him, so the two of them might be able to sympathize, but they couldn't relate.

Cassie's eyes were wide in disbelief but she nodded. "Of course, yeah. You should talk to her," she said, but she continued to look at Montana with an odd expression.

"What?"

"Nothing. It's just hard to envision anyone bullying you," Cassie said.

Montana laughed wryly. "I wasn't always this badass," she said with a wink.

The day flew by, and as tempting as it was to head straight back to Eddie's and fall back into bed, Montana had motherly responsibilities that took priority that evening.

"Any requests for dinner?" she asked Kaia when she picked her up from Tank and Cassie's. "We're eating out, obviously," Montana said, hoping to get a smile out of her daughter.

It worked, and once again Montana was grateful for Eddie. Kaia seemed to really be coming around after the Haunted Trail, despite the incident with the boys.

"I'm cool with anything—uh, except the Snack Shack," she added quickly.

The place where most of the teenagers hung out. Montana took it as the perfect segue into the conversation she wanted to have. "No problem, we can go to the diner instead." The place where all the older crowd sat and drank too much coffee and talked about local news all day. No worry of running into the kids Kaia wanted to avoid over there.

"Perfect," she said.

"So, I wanted to talk to you about something Eddie mentioned…"

"He told you about those dumbasses the other night, huh?" She didn't seem upset, just slightly annoyed at the mention of said dumbasses.

Montana let the swear word slide as she nodded. "Yeah, he did. And I just wanted to ask you if that's a recurring thing with those guys. Are they always…dumbasses?" Keep it casual. Light. She wanted Kaia to open up to her. Tell her what was going on. "Do they bully you at school?"

Kaia shrugged and gazed out the window.

Shit. She was losing her.

"I mean, I knew guys like that in school." She paused. "In fact, I was bullied quite a bit by both guys and girls all throughout junior high and high school."

Kaia frowned as she looked at her in disbelief. "No way were you ever bullied."

Montana laughed. "I love that I give that impression of being bully-proof, but it's true. I was tall and awkward as a kid and into a lot of different things."

Kaia turned in the passenger seat to face her, intrigued. "Like what?"

Wow, she was really going to come across as a dork, but if her daughter wanted to know the truth, she'd confess her deep, dark secret. "Well, for one, I had an obsession with aliens as a kid."

Kaia's mouth dropped. "You? Aliens? Like from outer space? Little green men with antennae and UFOs and stuff?"

"Yes! Stop judging," Montana said turning onto Main Street. "I was totally into them as a kid." She'd never told anyone about her fascination with extraterrestrials before now, and she'd have taken the memory of her geeky years to the grave if she wasn't trying to help Kaia. "Anyway, the point is I was different. And kids don't always like other kids who are different. Who speak their minds and are confident in their individuality."

She waited for Kaia to confess that this was a problem for her, too. With those boys. But she just continued to stare at her. "So, you really thought aliens existed?"

"There's more proof that they do than that they don't…" She shook her head. "You're missing my point. I'm trying to say that I get it. I understand what it's like to be picked on."

Realization dawned on Kaia's face. "Oh…right. Yeah."

"And I'm here if you want to talk about it. Anytime. You can tell me anything," she said, reaching across and touching her daughter's cheek. She hadn't known it was possible to love someone as much as she loved her daughter. Being away from her for so long would always be her greatest regret. She'd thought she was doing the right thing at the time, for both their sakes, but now she saw the error in that. It was too late to change the past, but she had control over her future, and from now on, nothing would take her away from Kaia.

"Thanks, Mom, but I'd rather not talk about it right now, if that's okay."

Not right now, but not never. Montana would take it. "Okay... And you know, I'm happy to kick some dumbass ass if needed," she said.

Kaia laughed and the sound warmed Montana's heart. "I'll be sure to let you know."

Finally, it seemed they were getting the old Kaia back.

CHAPTER SIXTEEN

EDDIE'S ARMS WRAPPED tight around her, Montana had never felt so completely relaxed. As the latest action movie's credits rolled on his television screen, he reached for the remote and turned it off. If asked, she'd never be able to recount the plot to anyone. There may have been more kissing than watching. And she wasn't complaining.

"So…" he said slowly. "Your parents aren't big on Halloween. What about other holidays? Christmas? Thanksgiving?"

Montana knew why Eddie was asking. Now that Kaia had spilled the beans about everything she'd been up to since arriving in town, how long would her parents hold off on making a trip to Wild River?

Her parents in Wild River—the thought made her stomach twist. There was so much they still didn't know, and now they wouldn't just be visiting with Tank and Kaia and Cassie and seeing her new life here firsthand, they'd be meeting her…boyfriend?

They hadn't really labeled their relationship, but things were moving rather quickly between her and Eddie. Her feelings were growing all the time. Thanksgiving was only a few weeks away, so a visit at that time made sense—not that she'd be the one to suggest it. It wasn't that she didn't want them there. Life was just less complicated this way, but her ability to hold them off was coming to an end. "Um, let's just say, this year, they will most likely make an effort to celebrate the holidays."

He looked nervous. "You think they will visit?"

"Maybe. We haven't discussed it yet, but if not Thanksgiving, definitely Christmas." She snuggled closer to him. "Would you be ready to meet them? No pressure." It was probably too soon, and she wouldn't be offended if he said no.

But he nodded. "Yeah, of course. If you want me to. I know they will already have a lot of surprises to deal with."

"That's my fault, I know. I just can't be honest with them. They're far too judgmental, and they will never think I've made the right choice. Even if they see how well I'm doing here."

"They don't think you made the right decision being here? That's crazy. Of course you did. Kaia's here."

"Kaia is the easy sell. Once they meet her in person, they'll consider moving here themselves." That she was sure of. So much so, it almost unnerved her. "It's the BASE-jumping site that they will disapprove of. They will be pissed, actually."

"Why? Everyone in town is obsessed with it, and it quite possibly saved SnowTrek Tours. I mean, it's insane, and I'll never do it, so please don't ask," he said, hugging her tighter, "but you've really accomplished a lot here."

"They won't see it that way. They want me to leave BASE jumping in the past. They'll be annoyed that I'm even teaching others." They'd think she hadn't learned her lesson about extreme sports. They'd say she was enabling others to potentially get hurt.

"That protective, huh?"

"They weren't always. We never really focused on holidays and traditions, but we were always traveling to exotic, cool places. Their philosophy was that every day was special, a new opportunity to try something amazing. My sister and I were fairly adventurous from a young age. I remember my first zip-lining experience through the rainforest when I was three years old. Later, we skied and hiked and surfed... But my sister's death changed everything."

"I get that."

"I do, too, but that doesn't make it any less irritating," she said. "After Dani died, we stopped traveling and doing anything even slightly risky or dangerous. Life was suddenly such a contrast to what it had been before, and I felt lost without Dani and smothered by my parents."

"So, you rebelled?"

"Something like that. I just wanted to start living again. I wanted to do all the things that I knew Dani would have wanted to. She was never afraid of anything, and I wanted to be just like her. My parents saw that in me, and it terrified them." She paused. "Dani's issues with drugs and alcohol aren't something I've ever battled, but my parents are unable to accept that I can be an adrenaline junkie without looking for highs elsewhere." She rested her head against Eddie's chest and breathed in the smell of him. She loved being right there in his arms. She was strong and independent, but she liked the feeling of safety and security she found in his embrace.

"Well, for what it's worth, I think you are incredible, and I think if they come here and see all the progress you've made with your healing and with Kaia—and they meet the handsome man you're dating—they might start to realize they're the ones who are wrong, and maybe they might start living their lives to the fullest again, too."

Her eyes felt heavy as she listened to Eddie's optimistic hope. "It's a nice thought," she said. Unfortunately, she knew her parents, and it would take erasing the tragedies of the past for them to see a different future.

But they didn't need to approve of her new lifestyle. They just had to accept it.

IF HE COULD offer optimistic life advice to Montana, he needed to start applying that same philosophy to his own. Two months ago his life had changed, and he wasn't sure where he was going anymore. Plans he'd set for himself had been derailed, and he'd lost all motivation to keep moving forward. His self-worth and happiness had always come from proving people wrong about him and succeeding when he was told repeatedly he wouldn't.

But what was there left to prove?

He'd achieved his goal of becoming a state trooper, his application to the drug division in Anchorage had been accepted, and he'd literally saved someone's life. On the bucket list of police-career achievements, he'd unlocked them all.

It was time to acknowledge that he'd made it and, despite this setback, he'd continue making it.

After all, he was arguably the happiest he'd been in his life right now. Holding Montana in his arms, he felt complete. He didn't need to prove anything to her. She wasn't pushing him to return to work, but he knew she'd support his decision—whatever it was.

Being around her made him feel invincible.

He stroked her upper arm as they lay on his couch together, his emotions so strong and so on the surface, it was hard not to tell her how he was feeling. He was falling in love with her. In fact, he was already in love with her.

But it was too soon to say it. She'd think he was crazy. Maybe he was, but this thing with her was different than any other relationship he'd ever had in the past. They connected on levels he'd never expected. They were so different from one another, and neither of them fit the description of what they each thought they were looking for in a partner. On paper, anyway. But love wasn't supposed to make sense.

She wanted him to meet her parents. That was encouraging. But what would they think about him? Would they see his disability as a weakness, an inability to give their daughter everything she longed for and deserved, or would they hope that being with him would give Montana a reason to slow down a little and take fewer risks?

Neither was ideal. He wanted them to like him, respect him, for who he was, and see how crazy about their daughter he was.

He breathed in the soft scent of her hair and savored the feel of her body pressed against his on the couch. She was breathing deep and easy, her chest rising and falling gently. She felt safe with him. She *was* safe with him.

But was safe something she craved without knowing it? Or would the security of a relationship with him bore her eventually?

She wasn't someone who needed or wanted protection. She was an independent free spirit. Her parents may not have recognized how capable she was, but Eddie saw it. If she was here with him, it was because she wanted to be— not because she needed to be.

Which was both amazing and terrifying, because what happened if she decided she no longer wanted to be?

For now, he'd take every day, every minute he had with her and hope that the worst thing that could happen to him had already happened that year and there were only good things, unexpectedly amazing things, waiting for him if he continued to be brave enough to go after what he wanted.

MONTANA WOKE TO the sound of running water. She yawned and stretched out on Eddie's sofa and cuddled into the cushion under her head, breathing in the scent of him on the fabric. When was the last midafternoon nap she'd had? Probably when she was a toddler. Her body didn't know how to completely shut down and relax. Eddie definitely brought out a different side of her, one that could slow down a little and relax. One that didn't need constant stimulation. One that didn't need to always be on.

One she was starting to like.

She was starting to really like *him*. There had always been a fiery tension between them, and obviously their physical connection was strong. But it was so much deeper than that. He made her feel comfortable being uncomfortable. She'd been driving herself crazy with her difficulty adjusting to life in Wild River since she arrived. She expected to feel good about being here all the time, just because it was the right thing to do. But Eddie taught her that it was okay to not always feel like she was making the right decision, to question her choices, but to acknowledge that the difficult ones were often the most important. Change had never scared her, uncertainty had been intriguing. She liked knowing her life or her day could be altered at any moment. And the normalcy and routine in Wild River had been unsettling at first. But it was okay to feel uncomfortable and to embrace the fact that discomfort often meant growth.

Eddie was good for her. He balanced her. He kept her grounded, and for the first time in her life, she was okay with her feet being firmly planted on the ground. Which was also unsettling and uncomfortable, but in the best way.

The water shut off, and Montana stood, stretched, pulled Eddie's discarded T-shirt on and went into the bathroom.

Eddie was in the bathtub, bubbles all around him, up to

his neck, his head the only thing visible. She laughed. "You look comfy," she said.

"There's room in here for two," he said.

So tempting… Hot water, slippery bubbles, wet skin against skin. She checked her watch and forced her body to settle down. "I would, but I have to get to the station. I'm on shift tonight." She'd applied to be a support member of the search and rescue team two days after arriving in Wild River. At the time, she'd been desperate for anything and everything to fill up her days, knowing she'd need the distraction and to keep busy if she was going to be happy in the small town. But now, she'd rather laze around here all day with Eddie. She walked toward him and squatted next to the tub. She dipped an arm into the bubbles and under the water, touching his wet chest and abs and moving lower to gently massage his penis. Already semihard, it sprung to life immediately. "Trust me, I'd rather be in there," she said. She felt her own body reacting to her teasing touch as well. She'd never known pleasure like she had, being intimate with Eddie.

Eddie leaned forward and kissed her, gently, then with more intensity—a deep, burning passion sizzling between their mouths.

He quickly reached for her, grabbing her with one arm around her waist, and the next thing she knew, she was falling into the bathtub. She gasped in surprise at the luke-warm water. "The water's freezing," she said, sputtering and wiping the bubbles from her face.

Eddie wrapped an arm around her, pulling her back into him. He kissed her neck as his other hand cupped her breast through the wet, thin fabric of the shirt. "Let's warm it up," he said, pinching the nipple.

Montana leaned back against him, splashing water and bubbles over the side of the bathtub. She pressed her bare ass against his lower stomach and spread her legs over his. Her hand found his cock, standing erect between her spread legs, and she started to stroke it again. The lubrication from the water and bubbles made the motion flow, and within seconds, she could feel the skin tighten and the veins straining.

Eddie continued massaging both of her breasts, his mouth leaving kisses on her neck and ear and collarbone. Her nipples were rock hard beneath his touch, and she was so wet and ready and craving to be pleasured. "Eddie, touch me, please," she said, opening her legs even wider.

Keeping one hand on her breast, Eddie dipped the other hand between her legs. The simplest, gentlest touch had her body spasming already. He ran a finger over her clit, downward slowly toward her folds. He massaged them softly, and her mouth went dry as the sensation grew stronger. The ache for him was almost too much. She thought she might come just from his soft, grazing touch. "Inside, Eddie." She needed something to clench, to relieve some of the ache overwhelming her.

He dipped a finger inside, but it wasn't enough. She reached down with her other hand and guided two more inside her body. "How bad do you want me inside of you right now?" he murmured against her ear.

"So fucking badly." She pumped him harder, up and down, circling the tip of his cock with her thumb. "I don't think I'll ever get enough of you," she said.

"Good. 'Cause I'm not planning on letting you go," he said.

Her body trembled and a deep warmness radiated through her core at his words. She knew his feelings for her were getting stronger. She could feel their connection deepening. And the idea that they could both be so equally into one another had her excited.

She tightened her grip around him and pumped even faster, desperate for him to quicken his pace as well. "Faster, Eddie," she said.

His hand squeezed her breast, and he held her tight and firm against his body as he moved his fingers in and out while his thumb rubbed against her clit. They were both breathing hard. Fast and shallow breaths in sync as they came together in a frenzy of passion.

Montana's orgasm erupted through her, making her body shake. She could feel Eddie coming, and it made her own pleasure that much more intense. His head fell into the hollow of her neck as he shuddered his own release beneath her. "Damn. That was the best bubble bath I've ever had," he said.

She sighed in relief as she lay back into him and took his hands in hers. "Next time the water needs to be warmer," she said, kissing his hands.

Arriving late at the station, she snuck in sheepishly, avoiding Erika's perceptive gaze. "Sorry I'm late," she said, not feeling the least bit remorseful for lingering a little longer with Eddie.

"No problem. I just have to perform surgery on a seventy-eight-year-old woman in an hour, but I'll just explain to her that you were having sex with your boyfriend, and I'm sure she'll totally understand," Erika said, but her tone was teasing.

"Eddie's not..."

Erika raised an eyebrow. "He's not what?"

Montana joined her behind the desk. She sat and propped one foot up on the desk, lacing up her hiking boots. In her rush, she'd just run out of her apartment with them untied. "We haven't defined things, yet." But maybe they should. Normally the idea of vocalizing a commitment would terrify her, but this time, it didn't.

"But things are going well?" Erika asked, standing and reaching for her coat behind the door.

Montana couldn't keep the smile off of her face. "Really well," she said. Fantastic even. It almost made her worry. Whenever things were going well, there was always that dreaded fear that her happiness could be shattered or taken away.

"I won't say I told you so, but…" Erika said.

"Don't you have an old lady waiting for you?"

"All I'm saying is, it's nice to see you so in love. Welcome to the club," she said as she dipped out of the cabin.

Montana stared at the door as Erika closed it. In love. Was she? She'd never had feelings like this before. Not even for Tank… She swallowed hard as the realization hit her.

Damn. She was completely head over heels in love with Eddie Sanders.

CHAPTER SEVENTEEN

THE DRUNK TANK was quieter than usual when Eddie entered the next day, but then it was only four o'clock in the afternoon. A few guys played pool at the tables in the back, and a dart league had just finished up, so several team members lingered, having a beer in a booth along the wall. Classic rock played from the speakers as usual, and the faint scent of floor cleaner lingered in the air.

It was the perfect opportunity to speak to Tank, but Eddie almost lost his nerve, seeing the guy behind the bar. He'd known Tank for years. They were friends. Sort of. Definitely closer since he'd assisted with Montana's rescue months before, and he knew Tank knew about him and Montana hooking up and dating, but would he be okay with them being in a real relationship?

Normally, Eddie wouldn't care what an ex-boyfriend had to say on the matter, but this was different. Montana and Tank had a kid together, and they were still really close. Being with Montana would mean spending a lot of time with Kaia and Tank and Cassie, so Eddie hoped the other man was cool with it.

"Hey, man, how are you?" Tank asked, leaning against the bar as he approached in his chair. The crutches were great, but he was developing more sores under his arms from using them too often, so he needed to balance out his usage with the chair. He had to reluctantly admit that the chair was more convenient. He didn't tire as easily, and everyone in town had gotten used to seeing him in it, so he didn't feel as weird about it anymore.

Montana had definitely played a part in him learning to accept his new normal.

"Great. Definitely feeling a lot better," he said.

"I bet." Tank's knowing grin had Eddie clearing his throat. "What can I get you?"

"Um, just a soda, please."

Tank poured the fountain drink and slid it toward him. "We're not allowed to give out straws anymore, except these paper ones that dissolve in your drink. Would you care for some recycled paper in your soda?"

Eddie shook his head. "I'll pass," he said.

"Good call. Have you heard any updates about the case, yet? Any new leads or suspects?" Tank asked.

It wasn't what he'd come to talk about, but he appreciated the delay. Unfortunately, he didn't have any news. The lead investigator on the case had questioned some of Lance's training partners and a few other snowboarders in the community, but no one was able to provide any clues into the case. They'd even spoken to the North Mountain Sports Company executives working with Lance on his new brand of snowboards, but that business relationship seemed to be thriving. With Lance out of town, there hadn't been any other incidents involving his safety, so they weren't getting much traction on finding the perpetrator. "Not yet. It's like the guy just vanished after firing the shot. Storefront cameras didn't catch a good view of him, and there's been no other shootings or related incidents." Wild River had gone back to being the safe, quiet community they all loved.

"You think it was a man, though?" Tank asked.

Eddie shrugged. "We think so, but it's not confirmed or anything. Why?"

Tank stacked beer glasses on the shelf behind the bar.

"Just don't think the department should rule out any dis-gruntled ex-girlfriends of that Lance guy. He's certainly got that player vibe to him."

Obviously Tank wasn't impressed with Lance either, which made Eddie feel better. "Yeah, good point." He paused. Since they were loosely on the topic of his ex's dating life… "Hey, I was actually hoping to talk to you about something."

"Yeah?"

"Yeah. Well, you know that Montana and I are…to-gether." He wasn't going to go into more detail that that.

Tank folded enormous biceps across his chest and nod-ded. "Sure."

"And spending time with her means spending time with Kaia."

"Right."

"So, I just wanted to…"

"Get my blessing?" Tank looked slightly surprised, but there was definitely a look of respect in the other guy's ex-pression as well.

"I guess that's the best way to put it." Not that he'd be ending things with Montana if Tank had an issue with it, but it would be a challenge they'd need to deal with.

"Things are getting serious between you two, huh?" he asked.

"I think so. For me, anyway." It was odd to admit his feelings to Montana's ex, but he wouldn't lie to the guy, and he did want Tank to know he was serious about Mon-tana. He was in love with her, and while he'd keep that lit-tle confession to himself for now, he didn't want anyone to assume they were just having a casual fling when it was so much more.

"Hey, man, as long as you two are happy, and you prom-ise not to hurt her, I'm totally cool."

Eddie's shoulders relaxed. That was an easy promise to make.

"She seems a lot more relaxed lately, and Kaia likes you, so we're all good," Tank said.

"Great. Thanks, Tank. Means a lot."

Tank nodded. "Sure thing." He glanced toward the front door as it opened and his expression changed. "But, uh, heads-up, it's not me you're going to need approval from. It's them."

Eddie turned to see an older man, dressed in a suit and tie, and a woman that looked like an older version of Montana enter. Polished and prim, they looked out of place and severely uncomfortable as they took in the bar.

No questioning who they were, though. Shit.

Talking to Tank had been tough enough. Eddie wasn't exactly ready to meet the Bankses, especially without Montana to do proper instructions. He looked around for a quick escape. This was definitely not the impression he'd been hoping to give. Sitting in his wheelchair in a mostly empty bar, in the middle of the afternoon. Thank God he hadn't ordered alcohol.

He took a deep breath. Montana was amazing. How bad could her parents be?

Tank straightened his *We have the right to refuse service to assholes* sign on the bar as they approached.

"That bad, huh?" Eddie muttered under his breath.

Tank nodded. "Let's just say they never liked *me* much. I wish you better luck, man."

Eddie had a feeling he would need it.

"HI, IS MONTANA BANKS HERE?"

Stocking the back shelves with new winter camping gear, Montana froze at the sound of her father's voice at the front of SnowTrek Tours. What the hell was he doing here? She'd noticed a few missed FaceTime calls from her parents that day, but it wasn't unusual for her to avoid their calls. Unfortunately, they weren't texters, and they also disliked talking to her voice mail. Impersonal, they said. What they really meant was it was harder to keep tabs when they couldn't see her or hear her voice.

But, shit! They'd been calling that day to let her know they were in Wild River?

Her heart raced as she turned in a circle, looking for an escape.

Damn stockroom didn't have a back door into the alley—not even a window she could crawl out through. She took a breath, ran a hand through her hair and straightened her clothes.

"Yeah, she's in the back," she heard Mike say.

If only Cassie had been working, she'd know not to sell her out that quickly to her parents without checking with her first.

"I'll get her for you," Mike said.

He poked his head around the side of the door. "Hey, there's a couple out here, asking for you. The lady looks a lot like you."

"Those are my parents," she hissed.

"Oh, wow! Yeah, I totally see the resemblance."

Montana sighed. "Tell them I'll be right out." She needed a minute.

When Mike went back out front, she sat on a box of winter sleeping bags, and her mind reeled. Coming unannounced was a bad sign. They'd wanted to catch her off guard. But why were they here? To talk her into moving back to Denver? There was no doubt in her mind that was their motive. Obviously their Skype chat hadn't put their mind at ease, and they were done trying to talk sense into her long distance.

But, they were here. There would be no more avoiding them. And why should she? She was a grown woman who could make her own decisions. Time to be honest and straightforward with them. She'd made a life here in Wild River, and she wasn't going back to Denver. She plastered her best fake smile as she went out front. "Mom? Dad?" Faked surprise as she walked toward them. "What a surprise."

Her mother rushed forward to hug her, then pulled back, scanning her as though checking to make sure she still had all her limbs intact. Montana was surprised she didn't count all of her fingers and toes. "Darling, you look…"

What? She waited.

Her mother Eleanor's face went from concerned to relieved to confused.

No doubt she'd expected to see Montana looking tired and stressed, like she usually did. But right now, Montana was neither of those things. She was happy and relaxed and feeling better than she had in a long time.

"You look good," her mother said.

"You do, too." Montana turned to her father. "Hi, Dad."

He stepped forward and hugged her quickly, then he scanned the store. "So, this is where you work?"

Uh-oh. No more hiding the BASE-jumping site. There were promo photos of her at Suncrest Peak hanging on the wall behind them. "Yes. Actually, I've partnered with the owner to launch a new BASE-jumping site here in Wild River." Like pulling off a Band-Aid. Only this Band-Aid was covering a deep, gaping gash that hadn't yet healed at all, and now she was immediately open and vulnerable.

Her parents' expressions said it all.

Mike must have felt the tension loom over the room like a storm cloud because he chose that moment to duck out.

"Going for coffee. Anyone want…? I'll just bring some ex-tras," he said, letting the door close behind him.

"You're BASE jumping again?" her father asked.

"No. I'm teaching others," Montana said, moving to grab a brochure from the desk. She held it out to them, but nei-ther reached for it. They blamed the sport entirely for her accident. They couldn't understand that she took the risk, and that despite all her training and knowledge and safety precautions, shit happened sometimes.

They used to get it, but then her sister's death had made them afraid of every new adventure. It made Montana sad to think about all the opportunities that they were letting fear hold them back from experiencing.

She tucked the brochure back and pointed to the enlarged poster of her on the wall. "This is the new jump site—it's at Snowcrest Peak. Remember, Dad? We found that place together years ago on a trip here." He had to remember that day. They'd hiked all day and had discovered the gorgeous peak almost by accident. He'd claimed it was the most beau-tiful scenery on earth.

He did remember. She could see it on his face, yet he shook his head. "No. I don't. So, you've started a partner-ship?"

"That's right."

"What about the bar?" her mother asked.

"I sold my half to Tank," she said. She'd basically given him the bar for a dollar. She'd invested in it years before, and Tank had more than repaid her the initial investment. She'd signed the legal-sale papers months ago to sever that particular tie between them so Tank could move on with his life with Cassie. But her parents wouldn't get that.

Her father looked annoyed. "You signed the papers, even though our lawyers advised against it?"

"That was years ago when I wasn't of sound enough

mind to sign them." *According to them*, she thought. "I'm fine now."

Her father scoffed.

Eleanor placed a hand gently on his arm. "William…"

He turned to look at his wife. "What? She's obviously not fine if she's up here in the middle of nowhere making a ton of life decisions without even discussing them with us."

Wow. Nothing had changed. They still talked about her like she wasn't even in the room. "It's my life, Dad." She may have needed their help before, but she was okay now. They had to see that.

"A life you almost lost several times. Lost in the woods? A shooting? You can't be serious about feeling safe here," her mother chimed in. Her tone was gentle but authoritative.

"I *do* feel safe here. And happy," she said. That would be the hardest part for them to get. But it shouldn't be. Her daughter was here. She had a great career opportunity here.

Eddie was here.

Eleanor sighed. "Okay, well, what about your treatments? You haven't really been keeping us updated."

Meaning they didn't have full access to her medical reports anymore. "I'm seeing a specialist here and a support group—"

"We think you should come home," William said with finality, obviously not wanting to hear anything she had to say.

No beating around the bush or sugarcoating their reason for being there.

"I don't see how going home is going to help," Montana said calmly. "The doctors there have done all they can."

"Exactly. And you're obviously still not well enough to be living out here on your own," her father said.

"I got lost in the woods, Dad, not in my own kitchen,"

Montana argued. "And it was a simple mistake that could have happened to anyone in that part of the outback."

"But it didn't happen to anyone," he said.

Her mother stepped in. "Honey, we are only trying to do what's best for you."

"No. You're trying to stop me from living my life, and it's time you both admitted this isn't about me. It's about Dani," Montana said.

Her mother's face paled, and her father stared at the floor. "Your sister's death could have been avoided," Eleanor said quietly. "She should never have been in the pool that day…"

"Alcohol and drugs only made the problem worse, but she was always so reckless…" Her father's voice was angry, but also full of remorse.

Montana's chest tightened. She hated talking about her sister. It always made all three of them feel horrible, and she couldn't imagine how hard it must be on her parents to have lost a child. As a parent now herself, she got it. But she refused to continue living in the shadow of her sister's mistakes. "Well, I'm not Dani, and I survived my accident. *Accidents* happen for a reason. I still have a purpose, Dad," Montana said, touching her father's shoulder gently.

"Opening a BASE-jumping location? That's what you think your purpose is?" he asked.

"No. Being here for Kaia. I can be in her life now."

"That's what you thought before," her mother said gently. "And look what happened. You put her in danger."

"But that was—"

"No. You made the right choice for that baby's sake years ago, and I trust, if you care enough about her now, that you'll make the same choice and not put her at risk by being here," her mother said.

Montana's mouth dropped. They were using Kaia and

Montana's guilt to force her to leave? That was a new low, even for them. "Do you really think I would put her at risk?" she said, her own annoyance and determination not to be manipulated rising.

"Yes, darling. We do," Eleanor said, gentler now.

"Coming back home doesn't mean you can't still stay in contact, but think of Kaia and what's best for her," William said.

Montana squared her shoulders. Her strength returning. "Me being here is what's best for her. And it's what's best for *me*. I'm not going back to Denver." She hoped she sounded as resolute as she felt. She wasn't a child anymore, and she wasn't unable to make her own decisions based on her injury anymore. Her parents needed to realize they couldn't continue to run her life. "I'm glad you're here. Stay and see for yourself," she said.

Her father looked ready to argue, but the front door opened, and the three of them turned toward it as Lance entered.

"Fuck my life," Montana muttered under her breath. This had to be the worst timing ever. And what the hell was with everyone and their surprise visits? Lance wasn't supposed to be back in Wild River until Thanksgiving.

"Hey," he said, glancing between her and her parents. Obviously he sensed the awkward tension between them.

"Hi, Lance. What—what are you doing here?" she asked, tightly.

"I had a break in training for a few days, so I thought I'd come back…"

Her parents were staring at him in awe.

Shit. Of course they recognized the Olympic snowboarder. They may not hit the slopes much themselves anymore, but they were huge Olympics fans.

Lance turned to them. "Hi. I assume you're Montana's

parents?" He stepped forward and reached for her father's hand. "I'm Lance—"

"Baker," her father said, nodding enthusiastically. "I know who you are." His demeanor had completely changed as he pumped Lance's hand. "I'm William Banks, and this is my wife, Eleanor."

"Pleasure to meet you both," Lance said.

Montana felt uneasy watching the exchange. Of course her dad would be impressed by Lance. And unfortunately, Montana had yet to end things with him, which made this all very awkward.

"How do you know our daughter?" her mother asked, sending her a sidelong glance.

Lance smiled. "We're dating," he said.

Both of her parents turned to look at her. For the first time since they'd walked in, their expressions weren't ones of disapproval or annoyance.

They looked impressed.

Shit. Her argument that she and Lance were just friends died on her lips.

"Montana, why didn't you tell us?" her mother whispered, moving closer to her as her father and Lance immediately started talking about snowboarding.

Montana hesitated, looking at them, then turned her attention back to her mother. "Because we aren't really dating. Not anymore. And we were never serious, anyway." But for some reason it seemed that if they were, her parents might be a little less reluctant to get on board with her being there. Her father looked starstruck as he questioned Lance about his training and the upcoming winter games, and her mother looked like if only she was a few years younger... It was a complete one-eighty from the people who'd been trying to convince her to leave Wild River two minutes ago.

"He's even better looking in person," Eleanor said. "Taller. Definitely more muscular."

Oh, God. "Look, Mom, I told you on Skype the other day that I'm kinda seeing someone else… Eddie, remember?" Montana whispered. She didn't want Lance finding out this way, and she really hated to burst her dad's bubble, but things with Lance were over.

As soon as she told him.

What a mess. She should have broken that dating rule of not ending things over the phone or by text. But he'd only sent her that one lame-ass message in two months, and she'd assumed he'd already moved on as well.

She took a deep breath. Well, she'd just have to explain all of this to her parents and introduce them to Eddie right away. Then they could see for themselves.

Her stomach knotted at the thought.

Would they be as warm and friendly to the man who'd saved her life?

He was meeting the parents.

Officially.

And he was freaking the fuck out. Eddie stared into his closet knowing no matter what he wore, all the Bankses would notice was his wheelchair. Better than being invisible to them like he had been in the bar. They'd spoken to Tank and had barely acknowledged him. He'd been tempted to introduce himself, but they were tense and awkward enough being around Tank for the first time in years. Besides, he hadn't known exactly what to say.

Montana's text asking him to join them all for dinner that evening had him panicking. The Bankses had once been hell-bent on convincing Montana to return to Colorado— were they still on that mission? Was dinner an attempt at a reverse intervention?

He'd be joining her, Tank, Cassie and Kaia at the steak house on Main Street in an hour, and he was desperate to make a good first impression. He couldn't exactly launch into a confession about how much he cared about their daughter at the dinner table, but somehow he had to prove to them that he was worthy of her affection. It was important to him.

Montana inviting him was a good sign. She'd told him she wanted him to meet her parents, so obviously having them show up unexpectedly hadn't changed how she felt about him.

He reached for a dress shirt and black pants and gave himself a pep talk before heading out. Still, he was nauseous as he scanned the steak house twenty minutes later. Spotting them near the window, he hesitated. Three small steps led up to the platform of tables along the window overlooking the view of the mountains. The best seats in the house.

Ones he couldn't get to quite so easily. He didn't see a ramp anywhere. Damn, he knew he should have taken the crutches instead.

Montana saw him and waved and everyone turned his way. She looked slightly flustered and desperate but happy to see him. Cassie and Tank looked relieved to see him, too. No doubt they expected him to be in the hot seat that evening, taking the pressure off them.

The Bankses just stared at him. He didn't know them well enough to decipher their expressions. Unfortunately, judgment was easy to recognize.

Kaia got up from the table and hurried toward him as he headed their way. "Hi. Want some help?"

"Uh…" He surveyed the steps. "I was thinking I'd just go get the crutches," he told her.

"I can get them. Are they in the van?" Kaia asked.

"They're at home," Eddie said.

"Why don't we just move to a different table?" Cassie asked, standing.

Oh, Jesus. "No, no. I've got this," Eddie said, shooting Tank a look when the guy stood up to help.

Tank sat his ass back down.

Reaching for the railings on either side of the stairs, Eddie propped himself up and hopped up the three small stairs with ease. He sat on the edge of the seat next to Montana and reached down to grab the chair, hoisting it effortlessly up onto the platform, placing it against the wall and as out of the way of waitstaff as possible.

"Impressive," Tank said with a grin.

Montana's expression echoed the sentiment, and Eddie squeezed her knee gently under the table. She'd never have to worry about him embarrassing her. Being with her, his confidence was quickly returning, and he was determined to show the Bankses he was man enough for their daughter.

"Mom, Dad, this is Eddie Sanders, the guy I was telling you about. The man who saved my life," Montana said. "Eddie, my parents—Eleanor and William."

Eddie shifted uncomfortably. He knew what she said was meant to be flattering, a compliment, but he would have preferred if she'd introduced him as her boyfriend— or friend at least. She made it sound like she was dating him because he'd saved her life, and while he knew that wasn't true, her parents would no doubt think it was her motivation.

He refused to let it bother him as he extended a hand. "Nice to meet you both," he said.

"Yes, it's a pleasure," her father said, reaching for the drink menu. "Anyone care for a whiskey?"

"I'll join you," Tank said.

Eddie hesitated. He wanted to connect with the man, but he was driving. "I'll have to pass. I'm driving."

Montana's mother stared at him. "You can drive?"

"Mom..."

Eddie laughed. "It's okay," he told Montana. "I actually still have feeling in my right leg and eighty percent mobility." Discussing his injury wasn't what he wanted to do, but it was obviously an issue for them, and he wouldn't shy away from it. He had a disability. They'd have to accept that.

"He has a cool van," Kaia said, sending a wide smile his way.

Cool and *van* seemed like an oxymoron, but he was grateful for Kaia's attempt.

"Speaking of cool vans," Eleanor said, "Cassie, I've noticed several tour vans throughout town this afternoon with the name of your company on the side. Business must be doing well."

Cassie nodded, and Eddie was grateful that the attention was on someone else for the moment. He picked up his menu and scanned it.

"Yes, and I actually have Montana to thank for that," Cassie said. "It took me a while to get on board with the BASE-jumping idea, but she was right. We are now able to offer adventure packages that our competitors can't."

"Competitors like North Mountain Sports Company?" Mr. Banks said, flagging the waitress.

"Exactly," Cassie said. "When they first opened this year, I'll admit I was worried they'd put me out of business."

"Still, they have a pretty impressive spokesperson," William said.

Eddie glanced at Montana at the mention of Lance. She shifted in her seat and avoided his gaze. Had she told her parents that she'd dated Lance? She hadn't told them about him, and he knew they were a lot more serious than she and Lance had been.

"That depends on your viewpoint," Tank chimed in.

"I think a gold medalist is impressive no matter your viewpoint," Mr. Banks said.

Obviously the man couldn't read a room. No one at the table appreciated Lance's involvement with the big chain company that had almost run SnowTrek Tours out of business.

"Agree to disagree," Tank said, wrapping an arm around Cassie, and settling deeper in his chair, obviously choosing to evacuate the awkward conversation.

Eddie hoped someone would change the subject, but unfortunately the Bankses thought Lance Baker was the most fascinating thing in Wild River. They talked about the guy's achievements and how excited they were to see him in that year's winter games.

Montana remained quiet, looking more and more uneasy, while Eddie bit his tongue. This was the guy who'd gotten their daughter shot at. Had they forgotten that? Or maybe Montana hadn't given them all the details. She was definitely acting weird that evening. He couldn't read her at all.

"We actually had the pleasure of meeting him this afternoon," William said.

Eddie's head swung toward Montana. "Lance is back in town?" Could anyone else hear the jealousy in his voice?

Montana nodded, sucking in her lower lip. "Apparently, he had a break in training, so he came home for a few days," she said. Her gaze met his and silently pleaded with him to understand, to not get upset and to see the odd predicament she was in.

Eddie looked away. She hadn't ended things with the guy. If she had, he wouldn't have gone to SnowTrek Tours to see her. And why hadn't she mentioned it to him? His gut twisted, and he couldn't wait for dinner to be over.

He sat back and tried his best to act normal for the rest of the evening, but inside he was slowly closing off. The longer the dinner went on, the more obvious it was they weren't connecting. They talked to Tank about the bar, they talked to Kaia about school, they even discussed the possibility of a Christmas snowmobiling tour with Cassie, but their lack of interest in him was clear to everyone at the table.

And unfortunately, there was nothing he could do to gain the Bankses' approval if they thought Lance Baker was a better fit for their daughter.

And their approval normally wouldn't matter—except now, worry was slowly seeping in that Montana might agree with their opinion.

"TOLD YOU MY parents were a little over the top," Montana said, glancing nervously at Eddie. The dinner hadn't exactly gone the way she'd hoped. Maybe introducing Eddie to them in a group setting hadn't been the best idea, but she'd been nervous about it, and having Tank and Cassie's support had made her feel less stressed.

Man, had that backfired.

"They were nice," he said, his gaze lost out the passenger-side window of his van.

"They really are when you get to know them," she said, reaching across to hold his hand. He made no motion to link his fingers with hers or bring her hand to his lips. She cleared her throat. "I'm sorry about the whole Lance thing. I had no idea they would spend the entire evening fangirling about him."

"You knew he was back in town?"

Shit. "I told you. He got back earlier today. He stopped by SnowTrek Tours right when my parents were there. It was a complete surprise." She'd been ambushed by two un-expected arrivals within a matter of minutes. She'd pan-icked and hadn't exactly dealt with either situation the way she should have.

"You obviously didn't tell him about you and me..."

"There was no time, Eddie. He left for training while you were still in the hospital, and I didn't want to break things off by phone or text, and I honestly didn't think there was anything to break off. We weren't exclusive or any-thing." They hadn't had the same relationship as she had with Eddie. "I should have said something to Lance when he showed up earlier today, but my parents stole the con-versation, falling all over..." Shit, this wasn't helping. "No excuses, I should have made it clear I was no longer inter-ested." Before getting involved with Eddie. Before starting to fall in love with Eddie.

She pulled the van into the apartment-complex parking lot. Shutting off the vehicle, she turned to face him. "Lis-ten, I'm sorry. I should have handled everything better, but I'm going to talk to my parents about us. Tell them how you saved my life—twice."

"Because that's the only way they will accept me, right? Only if I'm the hero of the day will they be okay with me." The hurt in his voice made her wince. Her parents had barely acknowledged Eddie at dinner. They weren't rude, but they certainly hadn't been welcoming and warm. It was not the first meeting she'd envisioned. Nothing like the way they'd embraced Lance with open arms.

"No. That's not true," she said, but she wasn't even con-vincing herself.

"Really? I saw the way they were suddenly nice to Tank once the incident in the woods came out, and how he and Diva saved you then. Damn, they just want a hero for their damsel-in-distress daughter."

She moved back as though slapped, letting her hand fall away from his. "What the hell, Eddie? Is that what you think I am?"

He sighed. "No."

Not exactly convincing, either. "Look, the woods thing—that was my fault, but being shot at wasn't. And no one asked you to jump in the way." She was starting to see that her appreciation for his actions was only making things worse. He wanted her love, not her appreciation for what he'd done.

He had it, but all of a sudden he was pulling back. Because she hadn't been clear about how she felt. She'd gone about things the wrong way.

"Well, the good news is I'm not able to anymore," he said, reaching for the door handle.

She blocked him. "Hey, stop this. What does it matter what my parents think?" She'd moved to Wild River without them on board, she'd started a business venture without consulting them. What did their opinion on her love life matter?

"A lot," Eddie said. "Family is kinda a big deal to me. You know that. I want to be with someone whose parents approve of the relationship."

Old-fashioned Eddie. So freaking amazing and considerate, but… "That's not always so important. Not to me, anyway. And I told you, they will love you once they get to know you."

"They love Lance already," he said.

"But I don't!"

"Have you told Lance that?"

"Lance and I were never serious." Still making excuses, but it was true. "We were casual…not like you and I," she said softly, squeezing his hand, desperate for some kind of reassurance from him. Anything.

Eddie sat silent.

"Come on, Eddie. You know we have something special. I love being with you."

His gaze pushed straight through the windshield as he asked. "For how long?"

Her heart raced. "What do you mean?"

"How long can you do this without starting to feel trapped? I can't be everything you need, Montana. In the last few weeks, I've tried to convince myself that this change in my life was okay, that things might not be what I'd planned, but they could still be good. *I* could still be good. You helped convince me of that. You brought me back to life… But, I was fooling myself and you into thinking I could be the guy for you."

"No, Eddie—"

"Let me finish, please."

She clamped her lips together, fighting the protests forming, but feeling him slip away in the seconds.

"I'm not going to walk again. That means not being able to do a lot of things. And for most women, that might be okay, but you're going to resent my limitations and how they limit you."

She couldn't stay silent and listen to this bullshit. "What limitation? I can't BASE jump anymore because of my own issues. But I can do everything else—and I don't need you doing it all with me."

"I want to do it with you!" he said, exasperated. "I want to give you everything. But you can't honestly tell me that I can be everything you need. You live for adventure and excitement. Are you going to trade in your motorcycle for this van?"

She wasn't sure how to answer. She hadn't thought Eddie wanted her to change, but maybe he'd need her to in order for him to feel better about himself. Maybe her actions would only make him feel worse about his own limitations, as he put them. She'd thought she could pull him through, help him see that nothing was impossible, but she was assuming he wanted that.

"I didn't think so," he said. He reached across the seat and gently touched her cheek. "It's okay, Montana. You deserve it all, and your parents believe that, I believe that. You need someone like Lance. I was never going to be the right person for you."

Tears burned the back of her eyes. "What are you saying, Eddie?" He couldn't possibly be breaking up with her because of the shitty evening they'd just had. Unfortunately, she knew it went so much deeper than that, and she wasn't equipped to argue with him, prove him wrong. She knew she was falling in love with him, but could she convince him of that?

Until he was ready to accept himself as he was, he'd never believe that anyone else—that *she*—was more than just accepting but one hundred percent in for whatever life and its challenges lay ahead of them.

"I think we should be thankful for the fun we've had together but recognize it for what it was before one of us gets hurt." One of them *was* getting hurt. Right now. Her stomach turned, and her chest tightened. What could she say? She couldn't believe this was actually happening. The day before, things had been perfect between them. She was almost ready to tell him that she loved him.

Now he was walking away? "I don't want that," she said.

Eddie's head dropped, and he sighed. "Me neither. But I think I need that. I'm sorry, Montana." He caressed her cheek, the look in his eyes pained as he let his hand fall away.

He reached for the door handle, and this time she didn't stop him. She had no idea what to say to make him feel better, to make him understand that she'd messed up but wanted to fix things. He wouldn't believe it. Her actions, not ending things with Lance, not telling her parents the truth about how much he meant to her, spoke louder than any of her hollow words and excuses right now.

She wanted to tell him she loved him, but how could she say *I love you* when he'd just said goodbye?

THE WALL BETWEEN them had never felt so thick.

Eddie lay in bed, staring at the ceiling. The hollowness in his chest was a big gaping hole that he wasn't sure how to heal. Walking away before one of them got hurt had happened a little too late.

What the hell had he been thinking, falling for her? Allowing her to start having feelings for him? And accepting that the free-spirited, wild beauty next door could ever be happy with a straitlaced, boring guy like him?

Her parents hadn't needed to say anything. He could see it in their faces that they didn't get it. Their daughter and him together hadn't made sense to them at all. And they knew Montana better than anyone.

Her pained expression in the van had nearly broken him. Hurting her was the last thing he wanted to do. Damn, he wanted to protect her, keep her safe, prevent anything bad from ever happening to her...and that's why he had to walk away now. Before things got even more complicated and she felt compelled to see them through.

He didn't want a relationship based on sympathy or guilt. He knew in his heart that it was more than that. But how much more, and for how long?

Lance was back now. And the fact that Montana hadn't ended things with the other man was telling. She hadn't been sure about them. She hadn't been ready to commit to him.

Unfortunately, Eddie had been sure. He'd been ready to commit, and now all he was left with were emotions he had no idea what to do with and a heart he wasn't sure would ever heal. Even before he knew how great the two of them could be together, Montana had left her mark on him.

Now, there'd be no getting over her.

CHAPTER EIGHTEEN

GETTING HIT BY a snowplow couldn't possibly feel worse than the aching throughout her body the next morning as Montana entered the Wild River Resort Hotel. Meeting her parents for brunch was the last thing she wanted to do, but she was desperate to prove to them that living here was the right thing, the best choice for her. Let them see that she was doing great. If she bailed, they'd assume something was wrong.

They'd be right, but she didn't need them knowing that.

All evening after leaving Eddie, she'd wrestled with her conflicting emotions. She was in love with Eddie. More than she'd ever realized, until she was in her apartment missing him, replaying their argument and the painful evening that hadn't gone at all to plan. But she couldn't convince him that she was into him, into them…at least, not until she ended things officially with Lance and confessed the strength of her feelings to her parents.

And as tough as it was to climb out of bed after a sleepless night, she'd needed to get out of the building. Being that close to Eddie and not being able to go to him, to see him, to make things better, was killing her. She hadn't heard him at all the night before—not the usual sounds of the television replaying old episodes of sitcoms or the sound of his shower running or his terrible guitar playing. And she hadn't heard anything from the apartment that morning, either. She was worried about him, but she knew going to check on him would only make things a million times worse.

She entered the dining room of the resort and looked around. The place didn't fit in Wild River. The not-so-subtle elegance and high-end feel was a stark contrast to the wild Alaskan town and surroundings. This place was for wealthy tourists only, and the price tag on an evening for one of the rooms made sure no undesirables stayed there, tainting the decor and ambience with their long hair and untrimmed mountain beards. Wild River was smart to cater to all kinds of tourists, but Montana had stayed there for several nights when she'd first moved to town, and while it was a spectacular resort, it hadn't been her style.

Her parents' style? Very much so.

"Can I help you, ma'am?" the hostess at the front asked.

"Yes...hi. I'm meeting my parents for brunch. Last name Banks," she said, looking around.

"Yes, right. The rest of the Banks party is here." Was it Montana's imagination, or did the woman's eyes light up, followed by a flash of jealousy? "Right this way, please."

Montana followed her into the restaurant, past dozens of elegantly decorated tables of lovely dressed people. The ceiling-to-floor window walls and circular style of the room assured that every diner had a breathtaking view of the mountains. She glanced down at her dress pants and sweater. Maybe she should have dressed fancier, but she was exhausted and heartbroken and in no mood to put on a show for her parents. She wanted to convince them that she was doing great here, but she wasn't going to pretend to be something or someone she wasn't.

"Just to the right," the hostess said, standing back to allow Montana to turn a corner around the center bar.

She did and stopped.

Lance and her father were laughing over what she could

only assume was a glass of brandy. At ten thirty in the morning. Wonderful. Her father reserved his early-morning alcohol splurges on people he liked or people he wanted to impress.

Her mother was snapping a photo of them with her cell phone.

Montana hung back, watching the interaction. Lance was exactly the kind of guy she would have dated years ago. Exactly the guy she would have been excited to introduce to her parents. She'd never really fallen for any of those guys, though, just like she felt nothing for Lance. She'd always liked the idea of those guys more than the men themselves. The way the idea of Lance had appealed to her. A snowboarder with a zest for adventure, free-spirited and up for the next challenge. She'd thought that was what she'd been looking for.

Which explained why she'd never found what she was looking for, back then.

When she looked at Lance, she saw a gorgeous, fun guy, but she didn't see a future. Not the way she did when she saw Eddie. Lance made her feel excited, but Eddie made her feel alive, even in those moments of quiet, getting lost in the moments together. Eddie gave her a glimpse of the happily ever after that Tank and Cassie had, that Erika and Reed had. A relationship full of passion that only two people truly connected on all levels can achieve.

Eddie was her person. Not Lance.

She approached the table, knowing she couldn't put off the inevitable. "Hi, everyone," Montana said as pleasantly as possible as she joined them.

"Oh, hey, darling. Look who we saw in the lobby this morning promoting his new line of snowboards," her father said.

Good. At least they hadn't sought Lance out purposely

for this family brunch. Although, she didn't doubt for a second that her father had exchanged personal contact information with the professional snowboarder. Well, there was nothing preventing the two of them from being friends.

"You do know this guy is a competitor for my company, right?" she said, trying to keep her tone and focus light. Like her thing with Lance had been all along.

"Ugh, business is boring," her father said.

Since when?

He was always about business. All the time. Since her sister died, her parents had given up all the things that had once made them happiest—traveling, exploring the world— and both had settled into corporate jobs in the city, letting their days slip away under piles of spreadsheets and board meetings.

It was actually nice to see them outside the city for a change. Wild River was once a place they'd enjoyed together as a family. And her father's face lit up as he discussed the upcoming winter games with Lance. As awkward as this might be for her, her parents seemed to be having an unexpectedly good time. They'd maybe even forgotten the plight of the daughter they wanted to drag back to Denver.

"Sit. Have a mimosa," her mother said, gesturing to the empty seat next to Lance, as the men took theirs again.

What choice did she have? She couldn't exactly break up with the guy in front of her parents, and this had just been a coincidence. Lance couldn't possibly have really wanted to spend more time with her parents—could he?

He looked completely at ease sitting there now, chatting up her father, like he belonged. Like he was one of them. He definitely suited the environment of this resort and her parents' expectations.

How would Eddie look sitting there that morning? He wouldn't be comfortable or relaxed. He wouldn't have a million snowboarding stories to trade with her father, and she knew without ever having to ask the question that he wasn't a huge fan of brandy first thing in the morning—or ever.

Lance squeezed her arm gently and leaned in to kiss her cheek as she sat next to him. Montana tensed and ignored her mother's beaming smile across from her. She forced her own polite smile, then scanned the restaurant for their waiter.

A mimosa—or three—sounded great right about now.

As the men continued to chat, her mother leaned toward her and whispered. "You know, sweetheart, your father and I may have been wrong to think that you couldn't handle life here on your own." She glanced toward Lance. "Maybe Wild River isn't such a bad place for you to be after all," she said with a wink.

Montana sighed as she nodded. Her parents had done a one-eighty in their thinking rather quickly. And she'd be happy about it, if she knew it had everything to do with her and what she'd been able to accomplish and nothing to do with the fact they thought she could be in a relationship with someone they worshipped and approved of.

A PIZZA BOX with cold, leftover food inside sat open on the floor next to the couch, and as Eddie opened his eyes, he blindly reached inside for a slice. The television was on but muted, and not even reruns of "Gilligan's Island" were cheering him up that morning. The evening before had brought him to an all-new low. The ups and downs of the last three months were making him dizzy like a roller-coaster ride he'd been on far too long.

Things with Montana had been going great, but what had he expected? That she'd actually fall in love with him? When she had guys like Lance falling over themselves for her attention? Guys who could give her everything she wanted out of life.

Well, maybe not the love and attention he wanted to give her.

Her parents had made their opinion quite clear about who they wanted to see their daughter with. And Montana might rebel against her parents on a lot of things, but even she had to see it, or she would eventually.

Better to break things off now before he really got hurt.

As though it could get worse than this.

Hell, weeks ago he'd thought he'd been at his absolute lowest. Now, he knew the tragedy of being shot and losing the job he'd fought hard for was nothing compared to losing the one thing in his life that made him happy right now, that gave him purpose, inspired him to be better, try harder.

A knock on the door made him hold his breath. He hadn't buzzed anyone in, so he assumed it must be Montana. He didn't want to talk to her. He was desperate to talk to her, actually, but he couldn't. Not that day. Maybe once the sting of the situation subsided, once the intense longing dulled to a tolerable ache, they could be...friends.

Who was he kidding? How could he ever be around her and not want to touch her, hold her hand, kiss her, tell her everything he felt for her?

There was a second knock, followed by, "Eddie, you in there?"

He shot straight up. "Kaia?"

"Can I come in?" she called through the door.

"Um, sure. Just a second," he said. Was she alone? Or was this a setup by Montana? Why would Kaia be here alone? Yet, he knew Montana had left an hour ago. "You alone?" he called out, then cringed. If that wasn't a creepy-sounding question, he didn't know what was. "I mean is Tank with you?" he asked, reaching for his T-shirt and pulling it on. He picked up the pizza box, closed the lid and put it on the table.

"It's just me," she said.

"How'd you get into the building?"

"I have a key."

Made sense. He climbed into the chair and opened the door a second later. "Come on in."

She entered, and he closed the door behind her. "I think your mom went to meet your grandparents at the resort," he said. He'd heard them planning it the night before at dinner, and it hadn't escaped his notice that no one had invited him.

"I know. I said I was feeling sick this morning so I wouldn't have to go."

So, he wasn't the only one who got nauseous at the thought of the Banks. Which was exactly another reason why he and Montana could never work. He didn't like the way the couple treated Montana, or their unwillingness to acknowledge Kaia until recently, or the way they looked at him as though, even if he could walk, he still would never be good enough for their daughter.

He hated that they were right.

"*Are* you sick?" he asked. She didn't look it. Maybe a little flustered and nervous, but not sick.

"I lied," she said.

"Okay. So, what's up?" he asked when she wasn't immediately forthcoming with the reason for her visit.

"I need to talk to you about something, but you have to promise me you won't tell anyone I told you." It came out on a long rush of breath.

Parenting was admittedly something he had zero knowledge about, but even he knew he might not be able to deliver on a promise like that, depending on what she was about to say. "Well, um, I can promise that whatever it is, I'll help you do the right thing."

She studied him, seemingly thinking about it. "But I'm afraid that I'm going to get someone in trouble."

"If someone did something wrong, you're not getting them in trouble by talking about it. That's on them. Do the crime…" His voice trailed. His police-officer voice ran deep, and he hadn't realized how brutal of a hit it had been to have his career on hold until that moment. "Anyway, I want to help if I can, but just like you coming to me, I may have to choose the right thing for me to do."

She nodded slowly. "Okay, I guess that's fair." Still, she bit her lip and didn't seem in a rush to continue.

"Are you hungry? Thirsty?"

"I'll get us drinks," she said, going into the kitchen. He heard his fridge open then close as she returned with two sodas.

He sat back on the sofa and opened the pizza box. "Day-old pizza?"

"I'll pass," she said.

"Good call." He waited. Still, she was quiet. Contemplating. He didn't want her changing her mind, but he also didn't want to push. "Do your parents know where you are?"

She shook her head, looking guilty. "I told Dad I was going to see Mom and my grandparents, and I will, so I wasn't lying, but I needed to see you first. Alone. And you and Mom are pretty much always together when I see you…"

That wouldn't be the case anymore. His gut twisted. "Okay, well, once we chat, I'll drive you to the resort if your mom's not back."

"Okay." Kaia took a deep breath. "I know where the drugs are coming from," she said quickly. "The new ones that everyone is using to be better at sports and stuff."

Eddie leaned forward but tried not to act too eager for

more. He didn't want to spook her. "Okay... You've seen the drugs?"

She nodded. "Yeah. At the summer camp. And now the boys at school are distributing them. I didn't say anything before, but some of my friends on the hockey team are thinking about using them, and I'm worried about them."

Maybe even a boy she liked... "Do you have some?"

"I only accepted some at camp so that they wouldn't make fun of me, but I didn't use any. I threw them down the toilet."

"Good. That's good." He reserved the *Say no to drugs* speech. She obviously was smart enough. Tank was raising her right. So was Montana in the time she'd been involved. Yet, he couldn't understand why she wouldn't go to them with this info. They were both coolheaded parents—they'd know how to deal with this.

He'd leave the parenting to them. He would just collect the necessary info to bring to the station. "And the drugs at camp are the same kind authorities confiscated at the high school in Anchorage?" The sport enhancer laced with other narcotics was becoming an epidemic among young athletes. It was dangerous and illegal, and too many promising high-school athletes had blown their scholarship opportunities by using the year before. Eddie hoped they could get these drugs off the street and out of the schools in time to prevent more kids from ruining their lives over a desire to fit in or desperation to be the best.

"Yes, I think so. They look the same as the ones I saw on the news. Mystic Rush? Bright-colored pills that look like candy?" she said, toying with the rim of her soda can.

"Do you have any left?"

She shook her head. "Mom and Dad would kill me if they found drugs."

"I think they'd believe you were smart enough not to take

any. And you're brave being here, now," he said reassuringly. "How much are the boys at school selling them for?"

"Five dollars a pill for first-time buyers, then the price goes up to twenty dollars a pill once people are hooked."

That's how it worked. "Have you heard the boys talking about where they got the drug? Who's supplying them with it?" The boys were in trouble for trafficking, but the department was more interested in the person supplying the kids, bringing the new drug to Alaska and Wild River.

Kaia shook her head, but she refused to meet his gaze.

"Kaia, this is important. Your friends are in over their heads, and they may not think this drug is a big deal, but it's dangerous. It already killed several kids in Anchorage last year, and a lot of lives are being destroyed. If you know anything that could help, it's important for you to tell me."

She sighed. "I didn't hear the boys talk about it. They are pretty secretive about the whole thing. They don't want to lose their territory to other sellers."

Their *territory*. Shit. These kids were treating it like a business already. Eddie hated to see smart, talented kids corrupted like this.

"But," she continued, "I think I saw the man at camp." She hesitated. "We took the kayaks out after curfew one night. I know we shouldn't have done it, and I would never do it again."

He believed her. She looked kinda shaken by what might have happened that night. "You okay, Kaia? Did anything happen? Other than the drugs?" His chest tightened, and he was ready to kick some junior-high-boy ass.

Her cheeks flushed slightly, and he was instantly ready to drive to the home of any boy who might have touched one hair on the girl's head...

"It was nothing, really. Tommy, this boy I sorta like, the

one who gave me the pills, he tried to kiss me when we were alone in a kayak, but I stopped him."

Eddie nodded. "Did he hurt you? Or pressure you?"

Tears appeared in her eyes, before she stubbornly wiped them away. "He laughed and said I was just a child."

Obviously that hurt. "He's wrong, Kaia. You are more mature than any of them. Mature and strong. I'm proud of you."

Even she looked slightly weirded out by that, and he cleared his throat. "Sorry, that was weird."

But she smiled. "It was actually kinda cool. For a second, you almost sounded like stepdad material."

His stomach dropped. He and Montana had never gotten that far into discussions of their relationship. They hadn't put a label on it. But Eddie had hoped things were headed in that direction. In those hopes, he'd given thought to what it meant to date a single mom: being with Montana meant being a big part of Kaia's life. It hadn't scared him, and the more he'd thought about it, the more he'd liked the idea. How would Kaia feel when she found out he and Montana had cooled things—frosted things, actually?

Right now, they had to focus on the drugs. "So, out in the kayaks, that's where Tommy met up with the dealer?"

"Yes, on the other side of the lake. We weren't supposed to go that far, but he wouldn't listen to me. He docked the kayak and got out. I waited in the boat, but I could see the older man he was talking to."

"You could see clearly in the dark?"

"Yes. They had flashlights."

"Did you know him? Recognize him?"

"Not really, but he did look familiar. He was tall, about six four—not quite as tall as my dad."

"No one's as tall as your dad," Eddie said in an attempt to break the tension, but his body remained tight, his spine tingling with the realization that he might be close to helping catch this lowlife the department had been looking for.

"That's true, but this man was close. He wasn't big like Dad, though. He was skinny, like really unhealthy skinny."

"Drug use, most likely."

"He had longish white hair and no facial hair."

Eddie nodded. So far nothing extremely telling. "Do you remember what he was wearing?"

"Looked like a tracksuit..."

"Did you see any logos or anything on it?" A company brand would at least give him a starting point.

But she shook her head. "No, sorry. It was too dark."

"Okay, well, thank you, Kaia. I really appreciate you trusting me with this."

She looked worried again. "If Tommy gets in trouble, he'll know it was me who ratted him out. I was the only one there that night."

"Don't worry. I'm not after Tommy. My hope is that if we can catch the dealer, the inflow of drugs will stop. Tommy might not get off without some sort of punishment, but I'll make sure before we approach him there's no reason for him to think it was you. Deal?"

"Deal," she said, looking relieved. "Thanks, Eddie."

"Anytime, Kaia. Now, let's get you to your mom." He climbed into his chair, and two minutes later they were in the van.

As soon as Kaia was delivered safely to Montana, Eddie needed to get to the station.

"Hey, honey, I thought you weren't feeling up to brunch?" Montana asked as Kaia joined them in the restaurant. It didn't escape her notice the way her mother assessed Kaia's choice of clothing. Jeans and hoodie, baseball cap covering her long, dark hair; she looked perfect to Montana. Her mother's opinion didn't matter, and she hoped Kaia didn't notice the disapproving frown.

Or Lance's obvious annoyance at the sight of her daughter. How on earth had she dated a guy who liked to pretend Kaia didn't exist? She was more and more annoyed with herself over the casual fling with Lance the more she compared him to Eddie.

"I was feeling better," she said, but Montana could tell something was up.

"Did your dad drop you off?" She looked around but didn't see him.

Kaia shook her head. "Eddie did," she said, nodding toward the restaurant entrance where Eddie was leaving.

Montana's heart thundered in her chest. Eddie was there? Shit. He'd obviously seen Lance having brunch with them. She sighed. This kept getting worse. She frowned as she turned back to Kaia. "What were you doing with Eddie? Is everything okay?"

"Can we talk about it later?" Kaia asked, glancing nervously at her grandparents.

"Sure…okay." Probably best not to have a serious conversation in front of an audience, anyway.

"Are you hungry?" her father asked.

"Not really," Kaia said, but she did reach for a piece of toast from the basket.

Montana studied her daughter. There was definitely something wrong. Had Eddie told her about their argument? About things being…over? No, she refused to believe that they were really over, and he'd never tell Kaia. He'd leave that discussion for her.

"Lance and I were just talking about a ski day during the holidays," her father said to Kaia. "I hear you're a natural on a snowboard."

The fact that her father was interested in developing a

better relationship with Kaia filled Montana with hope that their family was starting to reconnect and come together after all the years of little contact. Her parents making an effort was great—if only their plans didn't include Lance.

Montana's future plans sure didn't and she'd need to talk to her parents soon.

Kaia looked slightly confused by the idea as well. "We are all spending the holidays together?" she asked Montana.

"We'll talk about that later, too," Montana told her.

Lance shot her an odd look, but then his attention was caught elsewhere. "Oh, excuse me. I have to get going," he said, standing rather abruptly. "Mr. and Mrs. Banks, it was a pleasure. I hope to see more of you both. Montana, I'll call you later."

Shit, so much for talking to him.

He bent to kiss her cheek, and she pretended to cough and pulled away, aware of Kaia's *What the hell is happening?* look.

Montana had a lot of awkward conversations ahead of her.

"Okay, yeah. We should meet for a drink or something later." No matter what happened with Eddie, Lance was definitely not the one for her. If her father liked him so much, her father could date him.

Lance left the table, and Montana turned her attention back to Kaia. "Sorry, I know that was awkward. I'll definitely explain later," she whispered.

Kaia nodded, but her attention was still on Lance, who was now...talking to his father? She recognized him from the media. Odd. Montana didn't think the two men spoke.

In fairness, it looked more like an argument. The older man was up close in Lance's face. Toe to toe. Their similar height putting them nose to nose. His father's long white hair was pulled back into a low ponytail, giving them a view of the angry scowl on his face. He said something, but Montana couldn't hear what it was from that distance, just the raised voices.

Lance grabbed the man's arm roughly and said something before walking away. Wow, she'd never seen this side of him before. He was usually so relaxed and under control, even under stressful situations like his competitions or North Mountain Sports Company events. Whatever his father had said had clearly gotten to him.

"Who was Lance arguing with?" Kaia whispered, a note of fear in her voice.

"Oh, don't worry, that's just his dad. Their relationship is complicated, I think," Montana reassured her, but even she felt uneasy, an unsettled feeling in the pit of her stomach as the older man turned to look in their direction. His intense stare seemed to narrow in on Kaia, and the little girl moved closer, as Montana instinctively put a protective arm around her.

What the hell?

He turned and left before Montana could go over to him and demand an explanation for the way he was staring at her daughter.

"You okay?" she asked Kaia.

Kaia nodded quickly. "He was just odd—the way he was staring at us. That's all."

Odd indeed. So odd that Montana wasn't waiting to find out what it was about. She stood. "I'll be right back."

Kaia grabbed her hand. "Where are you going?"

"I just need to talk to Lance for a minute. I'm going to see if I can catch him outside. Stay here with Grandma and Grandpa, okay?" she said, with her best reassuring smile.

"Okay. Be careful."

Montana frowned. Be careful? Something had definitely unnerved Kaia about the older man.

She left the restaurant and headed toward the lobby, scanning for Lance or his father. To find one and avoid the other. She caught sight of Lance outside and picked up her pace to catch him before he got onto a shuttle bus headed back toward town. "Hey, Lance," she called, pushing through the revolving doors.

A blast of cold air hit her as she'd left her jacket inside. She wrapped her arms around her body as she jogged toward him.

"Hey, what are you doing out here?" His tone definitely sounded like he was trying to sound okay, unfazed by the argument he must suspect she'd noticed.

"I, uh, wanted to make sure you were okay." It wasn't exactly the reason, but she needed to broach the conversation carefully. She sensed the animosity between the two men was something Lance tried to make light of, but that's not what she'd just witnessed. If it hadn't seemed to affect Kaia, she wouldn't care.

"Oh, yeah, I'm fine. Just have to get back to North Mountain Sports for some meetings."

"On a Sunday?"

"Executives are in town," he said, checking his watch. "But we'll grab a drink later, right?"

"Actually, no." No time like the present to have this conversation. "I don't think you and I should see each other anymore."

He frowned. "Really? Since when?"

Wow, he really thought a relationship could survive one half-hearted text in over a month and casual dates that had been going nowhere fast? "Well, since you were gone, I guess. Actually, Eddie and I were dating."

He nodded. "Okay, that's a little unexpected. Don't you think you should have mentioned that?"

Seriously? With the way they'd left things at the hospital and the lack of communication between them? No, he was right. Just like Eddie was right. She should have made a clean break of things. "Yes, I should have. I just thought we were keeping things fun…"

"But not anymore?"

"No."

He stepped forward, and his expression was actually one of disappointment.

Oh, shit. What was happening? He was supposed to not care. He was the playboy snowboarding god of the mountains. He wasn't ready to be serious with anyone. Especially not her—a single mom, former extreme athlete.

"I can't say I'm not upset. Like I said in my text, I started to really miss you when I was away. Maybe my feelings were stronger than I'd realized."

Either way, hers weren't. And this was coming a little too late…or maybe she'd never have reciprocated the feelings he was now claiming to have.

"Sorry, Lance," she said, rubbing her arms for heat.

He nodded slowly. "And this change…it's because you have feelings for Eddie?"

She swallowed hard. "Yes." Ones she knew were not just going to go away. Ones she desperately wanted to confess to him, to see if maybe they could start over…

"Okay, then…" He turned to walk away, but she stopped him. Breaking things off hadn't been the reason she'd chased after him. Though, she was relieved to have one tough conversation out of the way. "Wait, um, about your dad just now…"

Annoyance, then a flash of anger appeared on his face. "My father's and my business is none of yours," he said, storming away to board the shuttle bus, leaving her standing there, uneasiness growing stronger. What was he hiding? Was this feud with his father more than the older man's anger over Lance firing him?

Montana shivered and headed back inside the resort.

At least whatever had been happening between them was officially over, and there was no reason Ralph Baker would ever be near Kaia.

CHAPTER NINETEEN

IT WAS THE last training day of the season before the weather was too inconsistent to bring new jumping groups to the peak for the Fundamentals of BASE course, and Montana wished she had the same enthusiasm for this group as she had for the others. They all deserved her at her best, but the last forty-eight hours had been emotionally exhausting. She missed Eddie, she'd pissed off Lance and subsequently her father in the process, and something was definitely up with Kaia again, despite her daughter's insistence otherwise.

She was meeting Cassie and Tank at the bar that evening for a parents' meeting to discuss how to approach the situation with the little girl. Three heads were better than one, and she was so grateful for the two of them to navigate this journey with.

The group had only consisted of six participants, but she anticipated at least four of them would return in the spring for the next level that would have them soaring over the mountainside. As they all dispersed, Montana climbed onto an ATV and rounded out the pack as they headed back down the muddy trails toward town.

But even the noise of the all-terrain vehicle didn't help to drown out her own troublesome thoughts. Returning home the day before, she'd wanted to talk to Eddie. The breakfast mimosas and the clarity she'd found that day gave her confidence and courage to go to him and tell him how she felt, and she was hoping to coerce him into telling her why

Kaia had gone to see him, but Eddie's van hadn't been in his usual stall, so she'd tried to keep herself busy cleaning the apartment, doing laundry, even cooking the one meal he'd taught her, all while checking for his vehicle or listening for sounds of him next door. But by midnight, he still wasn't home. She hadn't been able to break up with Lance by text message, so she sure as hell couldn't tell Eddie she loved him through one.

She suspected he was at the station, which she was happy about. He was ready to go back to work. He was feeling better, ready to continue his life.

She hoped it wasn't too late to be a part of it.

Her cell phone vibrated in her pocket, and she pulled the ATV to the side of the trail, flagging the rest of the group to continue on. She cut the engine and reached for the phone. Tank's cell number lit up the screen. "Hey."

"Did you pick up Kaia from school today?"

Her eyes widened. Shit, had she mixed up their days? She'd been so preoccupied that it was possible, but a quick mental tally revealed that no, it was definitely not her day to pick her daughter up. "No. It's not my day. I just finished up a training course. Everything okay?"

"I don't know. She didn't get off the school bus ten minutes ago, and I thought maybe I'd messed up our schedule."

"No. She's not with me." Her pulse started to race, and she forced a calming breath. "Maybe she was going to a friend's house today?"

"Maybe," he said, but he didn't sound convinced. "She may have told me but I forgot. Whenever I try her cell, it goes straight to voice mail, so I'll call around to some parents."

"Let me know what you find out. Please."

"Of course," he said before the line went dead.

An hour later, he opened the front door of his house right

as she reached for the doorknob. The worried expression on his face was a mirror image of her own. "Still nothing?"

"No. And she's not answering her phone or messages." Tank said, instantly redialing Kaia's cell phone.

Even Diva paced the hallway back and forth, sensing something was wrong. The husky brushed against Montana's leg and gave a small whimper as she lay on the floor, ears still perked and tail swiping nervously.

"I even tried blocking my number to see if she was just ignoring us for some reason, but still nothing," Cassie said, joining them in the entryway.

"Was she in school today, or did she skip class again?" Maybe if she thought the school had called them to rat her out, she'd be nervous to come home or answer them. Preteen minds didn't always make the best, logical choices.

"She was there. We called her teacher already. She said she saw her head out to the bus with the other kids after the last bell," Cassie said, biting her lip and peering out the front door, scanning up and down the street. "We checked the mall and the Snack Shack already, and Reed's heading over to the station now to see if she had a wilderness-training thing she forgot to tell us about. Where else could she be?"

Montana had stopped by her place before coming to Tank and Cassie's, but Kaia wasn't there either. "Have you tried tracing the GPS on the phone?"

Tank and Cassie exchanged guilty looks.

Her heart fell into the pit of her stomach. "What?"

"She said it was an invasion of her privacy and gave a very compelling argument about why it should be disabled," Cassie said.

"How about *our* very compelling argument that we are the parents and we can track her ass all day long, every day, to make sure she's safe?" Montana sighed. Since when was she the hard-ass parent? And the fact that Tank and Cassie hadn't discussed this with her prior to doing it annoyed her. She needed to step up more and be more vocal. Sure, in the past she was the lenient one, but if the last few months had taught her anything, it was that Kaia's strong will and determined, stubborn nature needed to be matched not caved to.

"I know. It was dumb. Lesson learned not to get schooled by our kid anymore," Tank said, looking devastated and severely on edge, so Montana let the lecture about coparenting communication slide for now.

"Well, do you think she did that on purpose? Do you think she was planning this—whatever this is—and that's why she didn't want us to know where she was?" Montana's mind immediately went to that kid that she had a crush on, and she started to pace.

Tank either read her mind or he'd had a similar feeling. "Don't worry—I called that Tommy kid's parents. They are on a dart league at the bar. They're away in Florida for a funeral. Tommy's with them."

"What about those other boys that Eddie mentioned were bothering her at the Haunted Trail event?"

"She said they weren't bugging her anymore since Eddie put the fear of crazed, chain-saw-wielding madmen in hockey masks into them."

The mention of Eddie had Montana feeling even worse. He'd helped Kaia that night. He'd be such a great role model for their daughter. Her gaze landed on the photo she'd bombed of Tank and Cassie and Kaia on the fridge, and her chest tightened. She could see Eddie as the fourth adult in their family photos. "So, where could she be?"

"I don't know, but this is out of character," Tank said.

"A lot has been out of character lately," Montana said. She told them about the brunch the day before, and Kaia's reaction to Lance's father and the way the old guy had stared at her. "She seemed nervous. Scared, even."

Tank's fists clenched at his sides as he paced the living room, dialing one new parent after another.

"Has she ever met Lance's dad before?" Cassie asked.

"*I* haven't even met his dad. Since Lance fired him as a coach, the two men haven't spoken—at least that's what Lance said. They were definitely arguing, though…" The way he'd gone on the extreme defensive when she'd asked him about it the day before had the hair on the back of her neck standing up now. There was definitely something going on… Could Kaia somehow know something about it? "I'm going to the police station," she said, heading for the front door.

"She's only been gone an hour. Will they do something this quickly?" Cassie asked, right on her heels.

Tank followed, the cell phone to his ear, the sound of Kaia's phone ringing and her not answering terrifying all three of them.

Montana swallowed hard. "The station might not, but Eddie will."

EDDIE HADN'T LEFT his desk at the station for over twenty-four hours. Six half-empty coffee cups littered the space between folders of convicted drug dealers in the state and beyond. Words started to blur on the page, made even more difficult to read due to his dyslexia, but despite the exhaustion creeping in from hours of research, he was feeling better than he had in days. Working again was giving him back some of what the breakup with Montana had taken away.

Some.

Staying busy and away from the apartment building kept him from being consumed by thoughts of her—or the sight of Lance having brunch with her family the day before. So much for ending things with the other guy. Eddie backing away seemed to have given Montana the green light to continue pursuing a relationship with Lance instead.

Which was for the best, really, and all he had to do was keep repeating that to himself whenever the urge to reach out to Montana was overwhelmingly tempting.

Like every five minutes, when he wasn't engrossed in a police file.

Unfortunately, he'd yet to make a physical-description match to the man Kaia had described. Research into Olympic coaches hadn't provided much clarity, either. The only recent scandals were stories about sabotaged efforts or, like in Lance's case, big public disputes after a high-profile firing. Drug-testing policies in these elite-level sports were intense and taken very seriously.

The day before, he'd taken a break from the files and had stopped by both the community hall where most of the teens hung out on the weekend and the Snack Shack to ask around about the drugs showing up at camp and at the school, but he'd been informed that Tommy was away with his family, and of course all the other kids claimed to know nothing about it.

Apparently, Kaia was the only one brave enough to come forward.

Eddie ran a hand over his face and blinked the tiredness from his eyes. More coffee. He needed more coffee.

He went down the hall to the vending machine and waited for the dark roast to brew. He still wasn't sure what to do about telling Montana and Tank and Cassie about Kaia coming to him with the lead. He hoped to talk to the little girl again and convince her that telling her parents herself was the right thing to do.

"Eddie!" Montana's voice made him drop the coffee cup as he reached for it.

"Shit," he mumbled as hot coffee hit his legs. He reached for the cup and several napkins, happy to have a distraction while he composed himself over the unexpected sight of her. He hadn't showered in three days, and he was now smelling like dark-roast coffee. Probably an improvement, though.

"Sorry for startling you," she said, quickly helping him clean the dark liquid.

"No problem," he said, staring at her. Damn, he'd missed seeing her, being near her, touching her these last few days. He couldn't avoid his apartment forever, and he had no idea how he'd survive run-ins with her without feeling the sting of disappointment and regret each time. It was so strong now, it was a sucker punch to the gut.

Then, the sight of Tank and Cassie coming down the hall told him she wasn't there because she missed him. "What's wrong?" he asked, his gut twisting, now for a different reason.

"Kaia's missing," she said.

"What do you mean *missing*? How long? When was the last time any of you saw her?" he asked, his head swiveling between the three of them.

"This morning when she left for school," Tank said. The man looked wrecked as he texted on his cell phone.

"The teacher saw her a few hours ago, though, getting on the bus, or at least heading to the buses," Cassie said, her voice thick with emotion.

"Okay, so only a few hours." He felt a little better. Not much. "Obviously, you've tried friends and hangouts?" It wasn't really a question. He knew they'd have exhausted all other possibilities before coming to the station.

"Yes. We're worried, Eddie." The deep concern in Montana's dark eyes made him instantly want to fix things.

He was no longer tired as he headed back to his cubicle.

"Follow me." At his desk, Eddie grabbed a pen and paper. "What was she wearing this morning?"

"Her usual—jeans, ball cap, sweatshirt..." Tank said. "Colors?"

"Blue—light blue hat and black hoodie," Cassie said. "I remember because she was looking for her green one in the laundry. I said she couldn't wear the same hoodie to school four days in a row, so she wore the black one."

"Great. This is helpful, Cass," Eddie said. "Was she upset this morning? Other than about the hoodie?" He doubted Kaia would run away but he needed to eliminate all possibilities.

Tank and Cassie shook their heads. "No. She seemed fine," Tank said, as a call came in to his cell. "It's Reed," he told them before taking the call. "Hey, man. Any sign of her at the station?"

They all listened. Waited. Hopeful.

"Okay. Thanks, anyway." Tank sighed as he disconnected the call. "Nope. He's going to head to the hospital. He said he texted Erika already, and she said she hadn't seen her."

Relief and fear washed over Eddie, and he could tell the rest of them were battling with the same conflicting emotions. "Okay, any idea where else she might have gone?"

They all shook their heads.

"There was an incident yesterday at brunch with Lance's dad," Montana blurted out. She looked sheepish, but right now, the fact that she appeared to still be seeing the guy and he was integrating into her family took a back seat.

"What happened?" Eddie asked.

"I don't think it's anything, really, but Kaia saw them fighting at the resort. It was the way she looked at his dad that stood out." Montana shivered. "And the way he stared at her." She shook her head. "Probably nothing, but it was as though he knew her or something."

Eddie's heart raced. "She looked at him as though she'd seen him before as well?" he asked, typing *Ralph Baker* into a Google search as he asked. The man was notorious for being a loudmouth and disgruntled ex-coach. He was constantly on the media discrediting his son's talent. Real nice guy.

"Yeah…" Montana said.

The image loaded on the screen, but the man really wasn't a fit for Kaia's description. That's why Eddie had already dismissed the idea. Still, he turned the monitor to Montana. "This guy?"

She leaned closer and frowned. "That must be a really old picture. He's skinny now, with long—"

"White hair," Eddie finished. Shit. Of course the man would be older now. He hadn't been coaching his son for a few years, and this picture was from the last winter Olympics.

"What's going on, Eddie? What do you know about it?" Tank asked, stopping his pacing.

"Kaia saw this man at camp. She said he's the one supplying the kids with the new performance-enhancement drug that's been circulating," Eddie said. That's all he'd say for now. The late-night kayak trip was irrelevant, and he didn't want them focused on other issues, just finding Kaia immediately.

"Was she…?" Cassie looked devastated.

Eddie shook his head. "No. She's an amazing kid. She didn't use. But she was afraid and was very brave to come to me and tell me." He'd keep reminding them that ultimately she'd done the best thing by going to authorities.

But Montana still looked confused and pained. "When did she talk to you? Why didn't you tell me?"

Eddie cleared his throat and shifted. Discussing their fallout in front of Tank and Cassie was uncomfortable. They must already feel the tension in the air—or maybe their own worry was overshadowing it. "She told me yesterday," he said. "Before I dropped her off at the resort to meet you."

Their gazes met and held for a long beat before Montana nodded. "Well, can you help? Do you think Lance's father could have…done something? Does he know police are looking for him? Would he know Kaia might have seen him?"

"He shouldn't suspect Kaia of anything, so I'm not sure he's the guy, but he's definitely our first suspect," Eddie said. He turned to Montana and kept his voice as steady and unemotional as possible. "We're going to need to talk to Lance."

THE FEAR COURSING through her outweighed the awkwardness of the situation as Lance joined them in the police station office two hours later. Montana's fear and annoyance level with him that it had taken three phone calls and a text to even get him to respond and then it had taken him so long to get there had skyrocketed to an unhealthy level. "What took you so long?" she asked as he entered.

"I was in a meeting."

Her eyes widened, and her arm instinctively flung out to her side in time to hold Tank back from advancing on the guy and tearing him apart. They'd all been going crazy with worry. "I told you this was an emergency."

Lance's look suggested this was an emergency for *her*. Not him. And she wasn't sure if he was being selfish or vindictive over the fact that she'd ended things. He couldn't possibly be that petty, which meant he was thoughtless.

"I am sorry," he said. "Any update on Kaia?" he asked

as he sat next to her at Eddie's desk. He reached for her hand, and Montana moved it away.

If Eddie noticed either gesture, he didn't show it.

He'd looked tired and stressed when she'd first entered the station, and it had taken all her strength not to hug him, kiss him, ask him if they could rewind back to before her parents showed up and things got complicated, but her focus right now was on Kaia and only Kaia. There would be plenty of time to talk once Kaia was home. Safe.

Captain Clarkson had joined them, but the older man let Eddie take the lead. He sat back in a chair, studying Lance with the intensity of a human lie detector, and Montana was so grateful that the station was taking this seriously.

"No—not yet." Eddie said, leaning forward. "I need to ask you some questions."

Lance sat straighter. "Of course. I'm not sure what I can do, but if it can help Kaia…" he said, but Montana detected an edge in his voice.

"Kaia said she saw your dad dealing drugs at the summer camp."

Straight-shooting Eddie hit his mark when Lance looked completely caught off guard. "What?" He uncrossed and recrossed his leg over the other knee, trying to look relaxed, but she could tell he was anything but. "Was she sure it was my father?"

"Yes," Montana said. "She described him perfectly to Eddie yesterday, right before seeing him with you at the resort." Talk about timing. If Kaia hadn't seen him, would they have been able to put two and two together? The idea that they might not have leads about where she could be right now made her shiver.

"Is your father selling this new performance-enhancing drug, Mystic Rush, here in Wild River?" Eddie asked.

"I don't know anything about what my father is doing. I

don't have a relationship with him." Lance's tone was cold. Unfeeling. Shut down.

He knew something. Montana could tell. He hadn't said he hadn't heard about the drug or that his father couldn't possibly be involved. She wanted to shake the truth out of him, and from the corner of her eye, she saw Tank and Cassie struggling not to strangle him as well. Their kid was missing, and he was clearly lying.

"Except to argue with him at a high-end resort?" Eddie asked.

Man, he was so incredible right now. Authoritative. In command. He was such an amazing cop, but right now the stakes were also personal. In so many ways.

"Look, I wasn't expecting to see him there. He caught me off guard, and we argued." Lance ran a hand over his bleached-blond hair and sighed. "I didn't know I was being called in for questioning."

"What did your father want?" Eddie wasn't letting up. If Montana didn't already love him, she'd be falling hard and fast for him now.

"What he always wants. To be my manager again," Lance said.

"So, you know nothing about his involvement with the drugs?"

Lance hesitated.

Eddie sat forward, and Captain Clarkson stood and leaned against the desk.

"Lance, Kaia could be in trouble. If you know any-thing…please," Montana begged.

Tank moved closer, taking a more aggressive approach as he laid a hand on Lance's shoulder, and Montana wasn't sure which appealed to Lance's sensitivity, but he sighed, before saying, "Yes, fine, okay. I know of his involvement with selling these drugs. It was one of the reasons I fired him years ago. I wanted no part in it."

"You never took the drugs yourself?" Eddie asked.

"Once. But only in training. They worked. Too well. And I'm not an idiot. I've worked my ass off to get where I am in the sport. I'm not about to throw it all away because my father thinks I'm slipping, that my talent and skill are waning." The bitterness in his voice was something Montana had never heard before, so off-brand for his laid-back snowboarder persona.

"Do you know where he is?" Eddie asked.

Lance's jaw tightened. "I know where they make the drugs. It's on the other side of the lake near the summer camp. But I don't know the exact location."

Eddie was already on the move as though he knew exactly what Lance was talking about. Montana wondered how much more Kaia had confessed to and confided in Eddie. The thought both made her chest tighten and her heart hurt. Eddie had connected with Kaia, enough that her little girl had gone to Eddie with this, instead of her parents. She understood. Eddie was the definition of good and right, and hell, Montana had even gotten ahead of herself, envisioning him in their lives someday. "I'll put in the official word, and Tank, can you get the search and rescue for assistance? If their operation is in the woods, we could use the backup."

Tank was already dialing the station.

"Look, my father is a lot of things, but he's not a kidnapper. I don't think he'd do something to Kaia."

Montana swung toward him. "You don't *think*? That's not good enough. My daughter could be in danger right now."

Tank looked close to knocking Lance out, and no one would blame him if he did.

"I hope you're right," Eddie told him. "But either way, we're headed out there."

Montana's gaze met Cassie's, and the double mama-bear stare would make anyone who messed with their daughter afraid.

EDDIE DIDN'T NEED any Mystic Rush to have his blood pumping and adrenaline coursing through his veins as they approached the area of the woods where the drug operation was taking place. He leaned on his crutches as he directed the members of his team to surround the small cabin where Ralph Baker and his crew allegedly were. Snow was falling in small flakes all around them, and smoke from a woodstove belched into the air on the chilled evening. The windows were boarded up, and there was only one door leading in and out.

A drug lab disguised as a hunting cabin—across the lake from a kids' summer camp.

Tank approached, his body literally vibrating. "What do you want us to do?"

The fact that the man hadn't already charged the door and murdered Ralph Baker was a surprise, but Tank was deferring to Eddie's lead. They all were. Even Captain Clarkson seemed okay with letting him lead this rescue-and-bust mission. Unfortunately, this was as far as he could go. The rest was up to the team.

"Um, you'll have to ask your guys to pull back. This could get dangerous, and they are unarmed. They've done their job getting us in here." The Wild River Search and Rescue team had provided the transportation and designed the safest, fastest route to the cabin. Eddie tapped Tank's arm. "If Kaia is in there, we will get her out safely," he said.

Tank looked reluctant to retreat, but common sense got

the better of the guy's emotion as he backed down and signaled Reed and the rest of the S&R team to retreat.

Within seconds, Eddie's team of officers had the cabin surrounded, and Eddie took a deep breath. Now or never.

He hoped they weren't too late. If Kaia was in there, if that man had hurt her...

He raised his hand to signal the team, and they moved in. Within seconds, the cabin door was kicked in, and Ralph Baker and two of his associates were surrounded by armed officers, forced to surrender.

Eddie entered the cabin and looked around. Drugs were boiling on an old woodstove, and an assembly line for cooling, shaping and packaging was set up on the counters. A gun sat on the table, the same brand and make as the one that had been used in the shooting.

Shit. This guy wasn't just pushing drugs in the athletic community—he was a hell of lot more dangerous. And the attack on Lance's life was obviously connected to this drug case. If the man was capable of shooting at his own son...

"Kaia!" Eddie couldn't see her anywhere inside the cabin. He searched the bathroom and the small bedroom, but she wasn't inside. Maybe she wasn't there... Maybe Lance had been right.

But then he saw her unicorn key chain with her name on it lying on the cabin floor. The one that used to hang from her backpack.

His heart rate spiked as he picked it up and hurried back outside, grabbing Ralph Baker by the collar of his jacket. "Where's Kaia?"

"Who?" the old man asked as he was being handcuffed. His long hair fell into his face, and his eyes were red and bloodshot, pupils dilated. He reeked of smoke and bad breath.

Eddie held up the key chain. "The little girl. Kaia. We know she was here."

Seeing it, Tank stepped forward, his long stride full of intimidation. "Where is my daughter? I'm only going to ask once."

Ralph looked at Eddie for protection, but Eddie just looked away. For once maybe he wouldn't play so close to the rule book. "Look, that kid is an animal. She was on her way to the police station when we picked her up. Threatened to turn us in, claimed she knew all about the drugs. I recognized her from the camp and then with my son…"

"Where is she?" Eddie demanded.

"I don't know… The minute we got here, she bit me and took off," he said, showing his bandaged right hand. "I sent one of my guys out after her, but he couldn't find her."

Damn, Kaia was a beast. She'd been coming to the station to report Ralph Baker and had told him so. She'd even gotten away from the man herself. Such a brave kid. Something that felt a whole hell of a lot like pride mixed with relief in Eddie's chest. "Which guy?" he asked.

Ralph nodded to a shorter, younger guy being held. They'd question him further about which direction Kaia had headed in and where he'd lost track of her.

Tank hesitated a second longer, hovering above the guy. Ralph tucked his head into his shoulders, preparing for a punch, but Tank moved away, radioing his team. "She's out here in the woods."

Eddie allowed Sanchez to lead Ralph away and turned to Tank. "The main thing is that she got away," he told him. "Don't worry, we'll find her."

Unfortunately, after hours searching the woods, they still hadn't.

WHEN SHE'D APPLIED to the search and rescue team, Montana had never imagined that her first real search would be for her own daughter. Moving slowly through the trees along the lake as the wind and snow picked up that night, she knew this would be her first and last. She loved the thought of helping other people, but if the pounding in her chest and the pulsing through her veins was any indication, this volunteer position was not for her.

Tank had to be going out of his mind as well, but he was acting clearheaded and calm as he led Diva through the trails. The dog could barely contain herself to move slow as she followed Kaia's scent.

They'd find her. Montana had no doubt that they would. But it was dark and scary in these woods, and sure, Kaia was strong and capable, but she was also still a little girl. Montana's own time alone in the woods months before had definitely been one of the more terrifying episodes in her life.

But Kaia had only been out there for five hours. She'd been dressed for the frigid temperatures and forecasted snow that day, and a search of the cabin hadn't come up with any of her belongings, so she had her backpack and everything with her. Unfortunately, the cell reception was nonexistent, so all attempts to call her were futile.

Thank God Eddie had put all of this together so quickly. Montana was already losing her mind. She'd be a complete mess if this search took much longer.

She glanced across the trails toward him now. He'd commandeered one of Baker's ATVs and was combing through the wider trails. Montana felt a whole hell of a lot safer and more confident with him there. Would her debt of gratitude to Eddie ever stop growing? Her feelings certainly hadn't. Being away from him the last few days had only solidified how she felt about him.

Diva barked, and Montana's shoulders sagged with relief. She'd found something.

Two more barks, and then she was leading Tank closer

to the water's edge. There was a small drop-off at this point in the trail, and the light dusting of snow they'd had all evening might make the slope slippery...

They followed Diva through the trees into the small clearing on the other side, and Montana saw her daughter's bright blue scarf tied around a tree branch, obviously as high as she could climb. Underneath was a shelter made of brush and overgrowth, and the smell of a fire drifted toward her.

Diva was the first one to reach the shelter, but Tank and Montana were close behind. Inside, Kaia was sitting, fully dressed, except for the scarf, with her science textbook on her lap, the dog licking her cheek. Relief on her face, she jumped up and ran to them. "Oh, thank God."

Tank and Montana both dropped to the ground to hug her.

"It's okay. You're safe now," Montana said.

Tank's emotions were written all over his face and prevented him from speaking. He just continued to hug Kaia as Diva joined them, dancing excitedly from paw to paw.

"Sorry I worried you," Kaia said. "I was going to the police. I recognized Lance's dad from..." Her voice trailed as she grew nervous having to tell them what she'd been hiding.

Tank nodded. "We know what happened. And we're not upset."

"Not at all," Montana reassured. "You were doing the right thing going to Eddie, but know that you can always come to us as well. With anything."

"Anything," Tank repeated.

Kaia hugged them both tight again and petted Diva affectionately before going back into the shelter.

"What were you doing in here, anyway?" Montana asked through tears of relief.

"Studying. I have a test tomorrow. I wasn't sure if you guys would find me this fast, but I wanted to at least be prepared, just in case," she said, closing the book and putting it in her backpack.

The rest of the team joined them and looks of relief and amusement were on everyone's faces. "We should have known not to be worried," Reed said, but the obvious relief in his voice revealed he'd been as terrified as everyone else. "Look at you. Cassie should hire you to take groups out for winter camping."

Montana shook her head. "Not yet, but you definitely have a future at SnowTrek Tours whenever you want it."

Tank radioed the station where Erika and Cassie were waiting. "We found her," he said. "Totally fine. In fact, she might want to stay out here for a few days. You should see her setup." Pride in Tank's voice echoed exactly how she felt.

"You are truly incredible," Montana said, hugging Kaia again tight. She was safe. She was okay. But Montana still hadn't completely relaxed. The idea that someone had tried to abduct her daughter made her blood boil—and it all had to do with Lance and those horrible drugs. "You weren't scared at all?"

Kaia nodded. "I was at first, but once I got away, I knew they wouldn't find me here. They'd been planning on packing up their shop and moving it, so I figured they'd be more concerned with getting away. And they don't know these woods like I do."

Eddie appeared at the entrance of the shelter, leaning on his crutches, and Kaia nearly knocked him over as she ran to hug him.

Jealousy and a sense of longing radiated through Montana's core. *She* wanted to hug Eddie and thank him…and never let him go.

"You did it! You caught the bad guy, right?" Kaia asked him.

"Yeah, kiddo. Thanks to you and your bravery, we caught him," Eddie said, wrapping an arm around Kaia. His gaze met Montana's, his expression intense and full of complicated emotions. Ones that matched her own.

If only she knew what to do about them.

CHAPTER TWENTY

"If we'd known you were capable of solving cases this fast, maybe we'd have promoted you sooner," Captain Clarkson said back at the station late that night. Ralph Baker and his associates were in custody, and they'd initiated the process of tracing his gun to the scene of the shooting.

"I'm just glad this was the case I was able to solve as fast as we did." Eddie would never admit how terrifying the last twenty-four hours had been. He hadn't slept in almost four days, but he was still wide-eyed and buzzing. The crash was coming soon, but now that it was all over, he'd have a chance to sleep.

"Yeah, I'd say saving your girlfriend's kid ranks up there as a priority," Captain Clarkson said with a grin. "Bet it gets you some bonus points at home as well."

Eddie glanced down at his lap. Captain Clarkson was right. The look he'd shared with Montana out there in the woods told him her feelings for him were still as strong as his were for her. She'd looked grateful for his help in locating Kaia so quickly, but there had been so many more layers of emotion in the brief exchange between them. She wasn't seeing Lance anymore, having officially ended things with him, but Eddie couldn't reopen that door. Three days away from her, and the hurt and disappointment hadn't dimmed even a little. If they tried again and things didn't work out, he'd never recover. "Yeah, things with Montana were just casual. I'm not sure there's anything there anymore." The lie was one he would have to get used to repeating.

Captain Clarkson studied him. "And you're good? That's okay with you? You both thought it was just a casual thing?"

His captain thought he'd been dumped. Eddie almost smiled—it *was* the most logical assumption. What guy in their right mind would ever end things with a woman like Montana? One who was smart enough to know she was out of his league. "Absolutely," he said.

"In that case, what I'm about to say will be much easier."

Eddie frowned, his heart picking up pace.

"They still want you in Anchorage. Your position may be…modified, but they were impressed by your abilities on this one and would still love to have you."

Eddie's jaw dropped. His dream job hadn't been lost because of his accident? He cleared his throat. "So…they still want to promote me?"

"Yes. And I want to lose you even less than I did before, so I'd been hoping your relationship with Montana might make you consider staying." Captain Clarkson shrugged as he collapsed into his chair behind his desk. "But if there isn't one, I guess I can go ahead and finish the transfer paperwork?"

Yes. Absolutely yes. This was what he wanted. This was something he'd thought he'd lost. Yes, finish the paperwork and let him get to Anchorage and away from Montana, so that the burning need to be with her could start to fade. "Can I think about it?" Damn.

Captain Clarkson nodded. "Maybe not so casual, huh?"

HER PARENTS WERE waiting in her apartment when Montana entered just before midnight. She'd called them as soon as she'd gotten back to cell service range, but they were still anxious and slightly on edge. "How is she?" her mother asked, hugging her tight.

"She's good," Montana said. Now that her adrenaline had subsided and the fear had dissipated, she was exhausted, but she hadn't wanted to leave Tank and Cassie's until Kaia was safely asleep in her bed. "She was studying by campfire," she said with a tired laugh, as she removed her coat and flung it over the back of a chair.

Her father chuckled softly. "She reminds me of you so much," he said.

Montana sat on the arm of the chair her dad was sitting in. "Really? I'm not sure I was ever as competent as Kaia is already." Her daughter had done all the right things out there in the woods to keep herself safe, calm and visible until help arrived. She was brave and smart and capable.

Her father took Montana's hand in his. "Oh, you were— still are. But I mean her spirit," he said. "She's so full of life, and she's up for any adventure, just like you."

Across the room, her mother smiled. "And we're sorry that we tried to curtail that…after your sister died. We were just so devastated and worried about losing you, too," she said.

"I know, Mom." She did know, and she hadn't let her parents' fear stop her from living her life the way she wanted. And she couldn't let it now, either. "I'm not moving back to Denver. Not now or ever," she said gently.

Her father squeezed her hand. "We don't want you to. You are exactly where you should be."

"We're proud of you, darling," her mother said, moving closer as they wrapped Montana in a group hug.

The sound of the elevator doors opening in the hallway had her pulse racing, then the sound of Eddie unlocking his apartment door made her chest tighten. She'd only had a moment to thank him out in the woods, but it had been brief and not exactly private. She wanted to thank him properly, but her parents were there.

"Is that Eddie?" William asked.

"Um, yeah. I think so," she said.

Eleanor stood. "Let's go see him. I want to thank him," she said, heading for the door.

"No, Mom. It's late…"

Her father stood as well. "He's obviously still awake."

Montana sighed. There would be no deterring them. "Okay," she said, following them out into the hall.

Her father stood back from Eddie's apartment door and gestured for her to knock. She knocked gently and waited. "We really shouldn't be bothering him."

"I thought you were seeing him," her mother said. "This shouldn't be a bother."

Montana stared openmouthed at her mom. Was she serious right now? Their arrival in town had upset everything, and now they were cool with Eddie?

Eddie opened the door, and a look of surprise flashed on his face. "Hi…"

"Hi. Sorry, I know it's late, but my parents—and I—just wanted to thank you again," she said. Damn, all she wanted to do was rush forward into his arms, cuddle into him and show him how grateful she was for him—and how in love she was with him.

"Yes, that's right," her father said from behind her. He stepped forward and extended a hand to Eddie. "We can't thank you enough for…everything. You're an amazing officer, and we're proud to know you," he said. "Montana's lucky to have you living next door…and in her life."

Eddie nodded, surprised at the unexpected gesture. "Thank you, sir."

Eleanor smiled as she reached out to gently touch Eddie's arm, her own emotions making it too difficult to echo the sentiment.

"We leave tomorrow to head back to Denver, but we hope to see you at Thanksgiving," William said.

Eddie nodded politely. "Have a safe trip home."

It didn't escape her notice that he didn't comment on Thanksgiving, and Montana stared at the man she loved, waiting, hoping, for what she wasn't sure. He looked exhausted but happy, and she couldn't help but wonder if maybe he wasn't struggling like she was. It took all her strength not to beg him to reconsider their relationship, the two of them together, but he didn't seem to be having the same issue.

"Well, uh…" he said.

Montana blinked and shook her head quickly. "Right. We'll let you get some rest. That was all we came over for," she said. "To thank you. Again."

"Okay… Good night," Eddie said, closing the door.

Montana hesitated, staring at the door, then she slowly followed her parents back to her apartment and went inside.

THE DRUNK TANK was busy and loud the following weekend. A dart tournament had an influx of visitors to the town, and they all seemed to be in the bar that evening. Normally, Montana liked when the town was bustling with activity and excitement, but she'd been hoping for a laid-back, quiet girls' night with Erika and Cassie. Her parents had already gone home, and SnowTrek Tours had been fairly quiet with her BASE-jumping course having wrapped up the week before, so she was feeling slightly lost again. She really wasn't in a partying mood, but being home alone was worse.

She still hadn't decided which was harder—being next door to Eddie when he wasn't there and feeling the empty loneliness of missing the sight and sounds of him as they passed casually in the hallways, or when he was home and the wall between their apartments felt impenetrable.

"Why don't you go over there?"

"What?"

"Go talk to him," Erika said, nodding toward the opposite side of The Drunk Tank where Eddie sat now with a few coworkers.

Obviously her friends had seen right through her attempt at pretending not to notice him. "I don't want to interrupt his night out. And besides, things are still kinda tense."

Cassie rolled her eyes. "And I thought Tank and I were stubborn. You two are even worse."

"Hey! This is not my fault. Eddie's the one who broke things off. He's not interested in being with me." Which she'd need to keep reminding herself if she continued drinking Tank's famous Crantinis. She pushed the half-filled glass away.

Erika scoffed. "Are you blind? He keeps staring over here at you as much as you're staring at him."

"No, he's not," she said. She'd been desperately hoping to catch his eye, to see if there was anything there—see if he was regretting his words that day in the truck as much as she was regretting letting him push her away. When he'd helped them find Kaia, she'd thought maybe...

"Do you want me to call out to him?" Erika said, pushing herself up in the booth and getting ready to flag him down.

Montana reached across, grabbed her T-shirt and yanked her back down in her seat. "No. Seriously, I'm not sure where we stand, and I'm not eager to be shut down again." Eddie's life had changed a lot over the last few months. He was adjusting. And maybe she'd simply helped him get to a better place, and now he didn't need her anymore. Maybe his excuses in the truck were a way to soften the truth: that he didn't see himself being happy with someone like her.

"Hey, so I heard that the gun they found in the cabin was a match for the gun the night of the shooting," Cassie said.

Erika nodded. "The bullet I removed from Eddie's body is a match."

Montana winced at the mention of the injury and the bullet—and Eddie's body. Damn, she missed that body.

"I can't believe Lance's father was actually trying to shoot him," Cassie said.

Neither could Montana have if she hadn't met the man, but she couldn't say she was surprised. Ralph Baker was rumored to be a control freak who didn't handle failure or rejection well. He'd pushed Lance to his breaking point as a kid, wanting him to be the best, and Lance's refusal to be involved with the illegal performance-enhancement drug had been a betrayal in Ralph Baker's mind. Montana was just happy that the guy was behind bars and his drugs were no longer a threat to her family or their community.

"Have you talked to Lance?" Erika asked her.

"No. He texted to say sorry about his father, but we'd ended things before, so…" She didn't want to talk about Lance. Her friends had been right about him—he wasn't the right man for her, and she hadn't really given him a second thought. Eddie, on the other hand, she couldn't stop thinking about.

Montana checked her watch. "I have to pee, then I think I'll call it a night." She'd been wanting to escape since Eddie and the others had walked in, but she didn't want it to look like she had trouble being around him.

She'd already started to look for a new apartment. She couldn't continue sharing a wall with him when she wanted to share so much more—her heart, her bed, her life… Damn, she'd fallen hard for him. So hard. And what he did—saving her, saving her daughter—it only made the hole in her heart created by his absence that much bigger.

She climbed out of the booth and made sure to hold her head high and add an extra sway to her hips as she passed Eddie's table. The girls might be right. She could certainly feel his eyes burning into the back of her as she passed, so she took a slight detour and paused near the old jukebox. She pretended to survey the song choices, keeping an ear to their table.

"How does it feel to single-handedly take down a major drug dealer?" she heard the state trooper they called Sanchez ask.

"I had help," Eddie said.

"Yeah, an eleven-year-old kid. Crazy," Sanchez said.

Montana's heart swelled with pride at the thought of her daughter's incredible bravery. Since the investigation was over and Ralph Baker was facing jail time, they seemed to have the old Kaia back. Precamp Kaia. And the boys involved in the dealing were being dealt with as juveniles, so they'd most likely get community service, but the surprising thing was how relieved those kids seemed that this was over. They'd known what they were doing was wrong, but they'd been afraid and caught up in the criminal activity and weren't sure how to get themselves out.

"Kaia's pretty amazing," she heard Eddie say.

"Well, Captain's pissed at the thought of losing you," Adams said, and Montana's ears perked. Losing him?

"Yeah, we're going to miss you, man, but you more than earned the position in Anchorage," Sanchez said.

Eddie was going to Anchorage? He was still up for the promotion to the drug division. Montana was simultaneously thrilled for him and devastated for herself. She'd thought maybe, eventually, he might have a change of heart about them, but he wouldn't if he was away.

Having heard enough—more than she wanted to—she ducked into the ladies' room and took a deep breath as she leaned against the bathroom door. Disappointment escaped her on a long exhale.

Eddie was leaving and moving on with his life. It was over between them. He'd sacrificed so much for her already, and he deserved this opportunity, this chance to have what he thought he'd lost.

And she somehow needed to find a way to let the man she loved go, even if it broke her heart.

BREAKUPS IN A small town had to be so much worse than breakups in a big city where waves of strangers and the fast-paced lifestyle could help sweep away lingering feelings. Eddie hadn't really faced the challenge of living in prox-imity to an ex-girlfriend before, but even if they weren't building mates, Wild River was small enough that he'd see Montana all the time, anyway.

That was one reason Anchorage was appealing. An hour drive between them would at least make awkward encoun-ters like running into her at the bar less frequent.

It wouldn't erase her from his thoughts, though.

Despite working again and hanging out with his cowork-ers and hitting the gym daily—the one across town, not the one in his building—he couldn't shake her from his mind.

Seeing her now, across the bar, was the ultimate torture.

There should be a law against looking that beautiful after a breakup. Dressed in a pair of black leather leggings and a loose-fitting red sweater that hung off one shoulder, ex-posing his favorite freckle to the world, Montana shined brighter than the neon lights in the room. How was he sup-posed to get over her?

He watched as she reached for her coat in the booth.

She was leaving.

A feeling like panic set into his chest, and he instinc-tively shuffled his way out of his own booth and grabbed his crutches from against the wall. "I'll be back," he told his coworkers. He just wanted to make sure she wasn't walking home alone.

The heels of her boots echoed against the wooden bar floor as she waved goodbye to Erika and Cassie and headed toward the front door.

Eddie followed, his eyes drawn to her curvy ass still visible under the puffy, bomber-style jacket she wore. Then he noticed the helmet.

She was still driving the bike?

Sure, they'd only had a light dusting of powdery snow several times that winter so far, and the ground was dry that evening, but how long was she planning on keeping the motorcycle out of storage?

She pushed through the door, and he saw it parked outside.

"Hey, am I going to have to commandeer that bike to get you to stop driving it?" he called after her.

She turned to face him, and his heart pounded in his chest as she said, "Somehow I don't think this bike's getting all your things to Anchorage."

Damn, she'd heard. He had no idea what to say, and her conflicted expression mirrored exactly how he felt.

When his silence lasted a fraction too long, she climbed on and started the engine. "Bye, Eddie."

And his tortured heart could do nothing but watch her drive away.

CHAPTER TWENTY-ONE

EDDIE'S GRANDMOTHER WAS getting married in four hours, and in her imagination Montana had already crashed the wedding thirteen times. He hadn't exactly uninvited her to the wedding as his date, but she assumed she wasn't still expected to go. Or that he wanted her to go.

But she *desperately* wanted to go.

Weddings weren't her thing, but she wanted to be with Eddie. They'd barely spoken since the rescue and Lance's father's arrest, and she had no idea if he was still planning to take the job in Anchorage or not. He didn't owe her an explanation or clarification. He'd certainly done enough for her, but she longed for something from him. Anything.

She rinsed her coffee cup in the sink, and it nearly slipped out of her hands when she saw Eddie leave the building and head toward his van. His garment bag was draped over his lap as he got into the van, and Montana's heart ached as she watched him drive away.

"Why are you being so stubborn?"

Ah, so her sister was finally back. "Why don't you ask Eddie why he's being so stubborn?" Why was this on her? Eddie was the one who'd put the brakes on the relationship—not her. "And where the hell have you been, anyway?"

Her sister grinned, propping herself up on the kitchen counter. "Missed me?"

"No, of course not. I just thought maybe you were gone

for good this time." Truth was that idea had terrified Montana. It had felt odd not seeing Dani while things were going well with Eddie, and she'd been craving support since they'd ended things.

"According to your doctor, I'm your subconscious, so I come back when you need me to talk sense into you," Dani said.

"Look, I'm not the one in control here. Eddie doesn't want to be with me." He'd had plenty of opportunity to tell her otherwise.

"Come on, Montana. You know Eddie is crazy about you. He only pushed you away because he feels like he's not good enough for you. Mom and Dad didn't help."

"Funny that you stayed away during *their* visit," Montana said with a raised eyebrow.

"We're talking about your issues, not mine. All I'm saying is that you're not one to not chase after what you want."

"What do you want me to do? Run after his van? Confess my undying love for him?"

"Yes!"

Montana set the mug in the cupboard and turned away from the sink. "Call me crazy, but I'm not in the habit of putting myself out there like that."

"Why not?"

"Because I'm afraid of getting hurt, that's why!"

"You? Since when do you let fear stop you from doing anything? You're the most fearless person I know."

Maybe at one time, but since arriving in Wild River, she'd learned that there were very different kinds of risks in life. Some cost more than others. "My body and my heart are two very different things."

Her sister shot her a look of sympathy. "You haven't put yourself out there or opened up to anyone since I died."

"That's not true…" She'd put herself out there and

opened up to Eddie, hadn't she? Maybe not when it truly mattered.

"I know this is tough on you, but you have to learn to trust and be willing to get hurt. Otherwise, you won't ever be truly happy. I died from my accident. You didn't, and I know that you think your limitations define you, but they don't. You are more than just an extreme athlete."

She'd started to see that when she was with Eddie. Being in Wild River, close to Kaia, and taking on the new challenges of parenting had helped her realize that, but now she was struggling to remember it. "Like what?"

"Are you serious? You're running your own training camp and working with the best adventure tourism company in Wild River."

"But that's because it's still something I know. Something I'm still technically good at. Relationships are not my forte."

"I disagree. Since you've been here you've made some really fantastic friends in Cassie and Erika—female friends! That's something that you weren't great at before. You've developed an amazing coparenting relationship with Tank, and Kaia is benefiting from that. And Kaia! Oh, my God, Montana, you've become the best version of yourself in the way you are with her."

"You think?" She felt it, too. Being a parent had changed her in so many ways, and she knew Dani was right. She was a good mom. At first she wasn't sure if she could be or would be what Kaia needed, but she believed she now was. Their connection had grown so much and continued to grow.

"You know I do," Dani said gently. She reached out as though to touch Montana but settled for a warm, encouraging smile instead. "And if you can make these changes in yourself to grow in these other important ways, you can figure things out with Eddie."

Montana was quiet for a long moment. What her sister said was true, but how could she go after Eddie when he'd made it quite obvious that a relationship with her wasn't what he wanted? No matter what his reason, whether he wasn't ready to open up or if he was simply trying to protect her, it didn't matter. "What if he doesn't want me?"

"Mon, that guy has been head over heels for you since you moved in next door to him."

Montana swallowed hard. Memories of the last six months came flooding back—the flirty banter, the accidental touches that resulted in unexpected sparks, the connection between them the first time they'd kissed, the way Eddie made her feel when he made love to her, held her, listened to her, looked at her... She wanted that feeling again. She straightened her shoulders, feeling her determination and confidence coming back. "What do I do?"

Dani laughed. "You're asking a sixteen-year-old ghost for advice on men and relationships?"

Her sister had a point. "Okay, well at least help me decide what to wear to crash this wedding," she said.

"*That* I can do," Dani said.

EDDIE ENTERED THE bridal dressing room at the back of the venue twenty minutes before the ceremony was scheduled to start. He leaned against the wall and watched as his sister Leslie snapped several photos of their grandmother in her wedding dress and ballet flats. Gran was right to assume that Leslie would eventually agree to the job. Of course Leslie had flown into Anchorage earlier that day and was leaving tomorrow. They all knew being in Wild River was tough on her, even though she refused to open up and talk about her fiancé's death, so no one gave her shit about her infrequent, whirlwind trips.

Eddie was just happy she'd made it home for the event.

"One looking into the mirror..." his sister said, refocusing her camera lens "...and then glance over your shoulder."

As she did, his grandmother spotted him in the room. "Is it time?" she asked.

"Almost," he said, moving toward them.

Leslie checked her watch, a thick, black-strapped military-looking thing that didn't go with her purple dress and fancy hairstyle at all but that she wore all the time. "I'll go take a few shots of Melvin at the altar," she said, hugging her grandmother tight. "See you out there," she told him as she passed on her way out of the room.

"Wow. You are stunning," he told his grandmother as the door closed behind Leslie.

His grandmother smiled, but she looked nervous as hell. Fifth wedding—successful or not—and she was still nervous. "You like Mel, don't you?"

"Yes, I do. He's a great guy." A little crazy to be marrying into their family, but he'd fit right in.

"But is he *the one*?"

Eddie couldn't suppress the laugh and his grandmother scowled at him, then her face gave way to laughter as well. "I guess if he's not, maybe the next one will be," she said.

Eddie reached for her hand. "All I know is that I haven't seen you this happy with someone in a very long time. Definitely more than the others. I think you found him this time, Gran." His words had meant to reassure her, but they'd also reinforced the big, gaping hole in his heart and the empty space reserved next to him at the table that evening. He'd toured the reception area earlier that day, and seeing Montana's place card next to his had resulted in a lot more emotion than he'd expected to feel being there without her.

His grandmother squeezed his hand. "You know, speaking of finding the right one…"

He shook his head, but kept his tone light as he said, "Nope. No trying to matchmake today. This is your day. We'll worry about me later."

"Okay, but—"

"Gran…"

She sighed but nodded. "Fine. But the conversation's not over." She stared at him for a long moment. "I'm happy you decided to wear your uniform," she said, tears of joy forming in her eyes.

"Do not cry. Those fake eyelashes you sent me out to buy last minute aren't the best quality," he said, desperate to lighten the mood and his heart. He heard the music start to play in the great hall. "Ready to do this?"

"I am," she said. She held his hand tight as they took their positions at the back of the room and the traditional wedding march started to play.

Everyone stood as they made their way down the aisle, and as usual, his grandmother was right. All eyes were on her as she made her way toward Mel. Nothing and no one could steal the show from her.

MONTANA SAT ON her motorcycle outside the wedding venue. Could she really do this? Go after what she wanted, risk putting her heart on the line? Seeing Eddie leave earlier that day for the wedding without her had made the crack in her heart that much deeper.

She took a deep breath and squared her shoulders. He'd invited her to be his date that evening, and she was going through with it. She'd prove to him how she felt about him, and if he was moving to Anchorage, they'd figure something out, but she wanted to be with him.

She removed her helmet, ran a hand through her hair

and climbed off the bike. She removed her riding boots and shimmied out of the leather pants she wore under her red, knee-length dress, then slipped into a pair of heels. She removed her leather jacket and shivered as she hurried inside.

The venue was beautiful, elegantly decorated with varying shades of purple and white accents throughout. An archway covered in flowers and twinkle lights led the way into the reception area. She'd missed the ceremony on purpose. She didn't want her unexpected arrival to steal any of the focus from the bride and groom or Eddie's responsibility to the event. But now, she could hear the music playing and the sounds of laughter floating out of the room, so maybe her entrance could go unnoticed.

She took several calming breaths as she stood under the archway, scanning the room. A private two-seater table for the bride and groom was set up in the center, and tables of eight draped in white satin with flowers and tea lights floating in glass bowls surrounded it. Some guests were enjoying dessert and champagne, chatting amongst themselves, while others were already on the dance floor.

A gift table along the far wall made her panic slightly.

Damn it! In her apprehension and second guessing, she'd forgotten a gift, and if she thought about it long enough, she'd allow it to be her excuse to leave.

But then spotting Eddie at a table, near the dance floor, nursing a drink, she swallowed hard. He looked so amazing in his state-trooper uniform, his medal of bravery catching the dim, romantic lighting in the room. His dark hair was gelled back, and his five-o'clock shadow was the perfect length. She missed that stubble between her hands, the way it tickled her cheek and left a razor burn after a night of passion. She missed those strong arms wrapped around her, and she missed the way he made her laugh, made her feel complete. She missed him so damn much.

Too much to walk out now.

If he rejected her, at least she would know that she'd given it her best shot.

Head held high, she walked on slightly unsteady knees toward the table. Her palms sweat, and her hands trembled slightly at her sides. Eyes turned to look at her in curiosity, but her gaze met Eddie's grandmother's on the dance floor, and the already-radiant bride beamed even more. She nodded, giving Montana the courage to continue her trek toward the man she was in love with.

She stopped behind his chair and cleared her throat. "Excuse me, but I'm looking for my date. He forgot to pick me up," she said in the most pissed-off tone she could muster.

Eddie's head swiveled around so fast he nearly spilled his drink, and his eyes widened at the sight of her. "Danger," he muttered.

She held her breath. Waiting. Would he be happy to see her standing there? Or would he be upset that she was crashing his family event?

His expression revealed nothing at first, as his gaze slid the length of her, taking in the knee-length, formfitting dress and four-inch heels that were supposed to make her feel confident and powerful...

"He must have been an idiot," he said, his voice sounding hoarse.

Relief flowed through her, but she wasn't completely relaxed yet. "He can be stubborn sometimes, but the thing is, I'd take fighting with him any day over laughing with anyone else. And I'd take a chance on getting my heart broken by him any day of the week."

He turned around to face her completely, and his chest rose and fell. "Montana, I'm happy to see you..." He ran a hand over his face. "I've been going crazy not seeing you."

That made two of them.

"But I meant what I said about us not working—"

"And I mean what I say when I call bullshit," she said. She'd made it this far. There was no turning back now. The way he was looking at her, the way he'd confessed to missing her gave her the needed confidence to continue. "You love me, Eddie Sanders. I know you do because I'm in love with you, too. And I don't think it's possible to be so completely head over heels in love, to feel this deep, intense connection with someone, if they don't feel it, too."

He was staring at her. His gaze searching hers. His own emotions so clear on his handsome face that they confirmed everything she'd been hoping for. "You love me?" he said finally.

"Yes. And you love me." She said it with even more confidence in case he still wasn't getting it.

The music had changed to a slow song, but the couples on the dance floor had stopped their swaying to turn to look at them.

Eddie's face gave way to a slow smile as he reached for her. He gripped her waist and pulled her down onto his lap. "And you thought I didn't know that?" he asked, cupping her face between his hands.

"I thought maybe you might need a push into admitting it," she whispered, as his face inched closer to hers.

His gaze flitted between her eyes and her lips. "I'm going to kiss you now," he said and her heart felt like it might explode.

Audience or not, she wrapped her arms around his neck and pressed her lips to his, a satisfying sigh escaping her at the feel of his warm, welcoming mouth. She'd been missing this so much, and now that she was back in Eddie's arms, he wouldn't be pushing her away again.

He reluctantly broke away. "You're sure this is what you want?"

"You are what I want."

He touched her cheek, still slightly hesitant to go all in. "I'm not a bad boy…"

She laughed. "Bad boys got me shot and my daughter abducted. I'm seeing the error in my ways."

"Well, just as long as you stay wild and never change."

"Think you can handle that?" she asked, moving closer to him. Suddenly, she couldn't get close enough.

"It's a challenge I'm very much looking forward to," he said, kissing her again. "Now, dance with me so that all these people can stop staring at us?" he asked, rolling them out onto the dance floor.

Montana laughed as Eddie spun them around the floor, high on the adrenaline that can only come from being in love.

EPILOGUE

MONTANA PARKED HER motorcycle in front of the hospital and checked her watch as she hurried inside. Thirty-six seconds until her appointment with Erika. One she'd almost canceled a dozen times for a dozen made-up reasons.

Faced with another clinical drug option that could reduce or eliminate her hallucinations, would she go for it?

She hadn't known the answer weeks ago when Eddie had asked her, and she still didn't now.

"You are the queen of arriving right at the last minute," Erika said, meeting her in the lobby.

"I like to keep you guessing," Montana said. She'd also had trouble getting out of Eddie's bed. Since the wedding two days ago, they'd barely been able to tear their bodies away from one another long enough to go to the bathroom. If possible, their connection was even stronger now. They definitely appreciated what they had together and knew it was real. Together, they made sense.

Erika eyed the motorcycle helmet and leather clothing. "I'm not even going to say anything…" She sucked in her bottom lip, then pursed her lips together.

Montana waited.

"But there is snow on the ground."

"Thought you weren't going to say anything," Montana said with a grin. "Don't worry, I'm just driving it to a storage facility. Eddie's picking me up there in an hour." He was at the station, and Montana was almost more nervous about his meeting with Captain Clarkson than she was about her doctor's appointment.

She swallowed hard. They'd make it work if he moved to Anchorage. It was only an hour away by train. She'd spend the weekends there with him on the alternate weekends when Kaia was with Tank and Cass. He'd come back here to visit. His family was still here.

She wasn't losing him. They were both getting everything they wanted.

Still, the knot in her stomach grew, knowing he was across town accepting the new promotion and that, within a few weeks, he wouldn't be just a wall away anymore.

She followed Erika into her office and took the seat across from her.

"So, all your tests look good. No real change."

Montana nodded. She'd gotten used to hearing that. It used to bother her that her progress had essentially reached its potential, but now, as long as she wasn't digressing, she was happy. She was able to live a completely independent, fulfilled, happy life. She was lucky. It had taken her far too long to realize just *how* lucky.

"We do have a new drug we can try," Erika said, opening the file on her desk. "The one I mentioned to you a few months ago when it was still in trials. It's been FDA-approved. Early results show significant improvement in the reduction and—in some cases—the elimination of auditory and visual hallucinations in the trial patients."

"So, you think it will work?" Will make her sister disappear. For good.

"I'm confident it will, yes," Erika said.

A few months ago, this would have been an easy yes. Now she was looking for reasons to reconsider. "Side effects?"

"No different from the drugs you're currently on," Erika

said, sensing her hesitation. She reached across the desk and touched Montana's hand. "You don't have to do it."

Montana was silent for a long moment. If this drug could eliminate her hallucinations, maybe it could help her memory grow even stronger. Maybe she could make even more progress with her recovery. For so long, she'd been waiting for an opportunity like this. Could she really turn down a chance to heal even more?

She shook her head slowly. "I don't think I can do it."

Erika smiled as she closed her folder. "Cool. Well, I'll see you in three months."

"I'll see you tonight at The Drunk Tank," Montana said with a laugh as she stood.

"Figure of speech," Erika said, seeing her out. "Enjoy your last ride on that thing," she said, nodding toward the motorcycle parked illegally in the fire lane.

Unfortunately, all Montana could think about was how she was planning to enjoy her last few days having Eddie as her neighbor.

EDDIE STARED AT the transfer and promotion papers on the desk in front of him.

Captain Clarkson sat, watching him.

This should be so easy. Pick up the pen. Sign the papers. Be on his way to Anchorage next week. So, why was he hesitating?

Because two nights ago everything changed for him. In truth, things had been changing for him for a while now. He'd always known what he wanted to do with his life, and he'd always known it wouldn't come easy. What he hadn't expected was a tall, gorgeous bombshell to walk into his life and turn it all upside down. He'd tried pushing her away, claiming it was the best thing for her, that she deserved better, but he knew he'd been afraid. Afraid that he'd disappoint her, but also that he might have to choose.

He stared at the choice in front of him now, memories of the night before, lying in bed with her in his arms while she slept, and then waking up to her that morning, the only thing on his mind. She loved him. He loved her. They'd talked all night about this decision. They'd make the long-distance thing work. It was barely even a long distance. A little over an hour was nothing.

"We're not forcing you to go," Captain Clarkson said, only adding to Eddie's confused heart. He knew the department wanted him to stay, but what did *he* want? If he could have it all, what would make him happiest in the end?

He picked up the pen, and the tip hovered above the line.

Then he put it down. "I want to stay," he said.

The sigh of relief from the other man erased any doubt still lingering. This was the right thing to do.

"You're turning down the promotion?"

He nodded slowly. The money had never been his driving motivation for the new position; it had just been a perk. He'd wanted to do more, give more, by being involved in things that made a real difference in the community. "I want to stay in Wild River, but I want to start a juvenile drug-education program."

Captain Clarkson sat back in his chair and nodded. "Okay. Yeah, let's talk about that. There's obviously going to be a lot of paperwork involved, and a lot of ground-floor work to launch something like that, but it's been done in other communities, so I don't see why we couldn't do it here."

Eddie felt his hope rise and any anxiety he'd been battling evaporate. Indecision was always the worst. But he'd made a decision, and it was the right one. He wanted to be here with Montana. Full-time. A part-time relationship with her would never be enough.

"Can I ask if this change of heart has anything to do with a certain neighbor of yours?"

"Nah, but it has everything to do with the woman I'm in love with," he said with a grin as he left the office.

MONTANA TOOK HER time locking the storage unit. She could heard Eddie's van running in the lot behind her, but she wasn't sure she was ready to hear him say that it was official, that he was leaving Wild River.

Having him next door had driven her batshit crazy, but even during the times he was playing his horrible guitar or singing the wrong lyrics to songs, or making her jealous and/or hungry with the delicious smells coming through the vents of her apartment, she'd always had a thing for him. Not having him so close all the time would be hard.

But this wasn't about her. It was about Eddie and what he deserved, and this promotion and opportunity meant everything to him. He'd almost been forced to give it up once before for her. She'd never expect him to again.

She took a deep breath and forced a smile, one that turned a hundred percent genuine when her gaze landed on him through the windshield of the van. Damn, he was so sexy. Dressed in his uniform, his hair messy, the stubble along his jawline just the right length. Her heart quickened at the sight of him. She wouldn't waste a second of their remaining time together being sad or anxious or depressed about it. Anchorage was only an hour away, and in the summer months on her motorcycle, she'd cut that time in half.

She opened the passenger door and climbed in, and he immediately reached for her. "I missed you."

Think of how much they'd miss one another when he

moved. She shook the thought away as she laughed. "You saw me two hours ago."

"Too long," he said, cupping the back of her head with his hand and drawing her face toward his.

The smell of his cologne and the warmth of his breath against her cold cheek made her shiver as she wrapped her arms around his neck and moved closer. His lips met hers, and she savored the feel of them, the taste, trying to commit it all to memory, trying to slow down time. The week would fly by, their time together already slipping away too fast, and she was desperate to live in each and every moment. She wanted to be with him as much as possible in the next week and deepen their growing connection, so the distance had no chance of severing the ties between them.

He kissed her harder, more urgently. She could sense his apprehension and need to get in as much of this physical touch as possible before they had to rely on phones and Skype chats. It was with major reluctance that she pulled back and took a deep breath. "How did it go?"

He smiled and he looked so freaking happy, she couldn't be upset. This was what he'd wanted for so long. "Good, but I want to hear about your appointment first." He studied her, looking deep into her eyes.

"It was good. No significant changes on my tests. Erika said the new drug is available now, and that it's showed significant success in the trial candidates."

"No more hallucinations?" he asked gently, running his thumb along her jawline.

"She said there was a very good chance that they would go away." She paused. "But I said no."

Eddie's smile was full of understanding.

"I've decided to let my sister stick around," she said, knowing it was really the only choice. She'd lost her sister once before, beyond her control, and whether what she was seeing now was real or just a product of her head injury and a manifestation of her stress or deepest emotions, she couldn't willingly give her up.

"I think you made the right choice," Eddie said, and his words meant everything. "Um, so, what about me? Do you think you'd be okay with me sticking around?"

Her eyes widened, then narrowed as she frowned. "What? Didn't you sign the transfer papers?"

"No."

Her pulse raced. "Why not? Eddie, this was what you wanted. What you worked so hard for…"

He touched her cheek and kissed her nose. "I decided I want it all. A job I love where I can make a difference to the community I love and get to be with the woman I love."

She gulped the lump in her throat, her mind narrowing in on the last part of his sentence. He loved her. She knew it, and she didn't need him to give up his promotion to prove it.

"That's you, in case there was any doubt," he added in her conflicted silence.

She laughed, and a strangled sounding sob escaped as well. Embarrassed by the intense emotions she hadn't been expecting, she looked away and wiped her eye.

"Hey, this is what I want. I want you. I love you."

This time, she knew he meant it. This really was what he wanted. "I love you," she whispered.

Eddie's familiar grin made her heart soar. "That didn't sound very convincing."

She flung her arms around him once more and hugged him tight, then moved back to kiss him again. "Take me home, and I'll show you instead," she murmured against his mouth.

Eddie reluctantly pulled away, but as he threw the van in

gear, his hand tightened on hers, and Montana knew they'd be home in record time.

Home.

Home was where her heart was, and Wild River would always be her home.

* * * * *

ACKNOWLEDGMENTS

THIS BOOK WAS so fun to write and I continue to be grateful for the amazing opportunity to do what I love as a career. Thank you to my agent, Jill Marsal, and my wonderful editors, Susan Swinwood and Kate Studer, for all the notes and feedback that made this book stronger. As always, thank you to my husband and son for giving me the time and space to be creative and for always being a source of support and encouragement when the words refuse to cooperate. And a huge thank-you to my readers—without you, none of this would be possible.

A WILD RIVER RETREAT

CHAPTER ONE

KENDRA PHILLIPS MUST have dozed off in the hour-long staff meeting that could have been an office memo, because there was no way her boss had just said they were going on a team-building weekend in the Alaskan wilderness. The only "survival training" with her coworkers that appealed to her was battling it out for a new sales lead.

She sat straighter and cleared her throat, ignoring the eye rolls from her colleagues as she asked, "Um...excuse me, Roger, is this team-building trip in Wild River mandatory?"

Her boss's expression was one she'd seen a thousand times. Her father used to wear the same raised eyebrow and wrinkled top lip when he was presenting her with a "choice" but the only appropriate decision was the one he wanted her to make. "Well, I can't force anyone to participate, because everyone needs to sign an individual waiver from SnowTrek Tours, but it is *highly* recommended that all staff participate."

In other words, it was mandatory. "Of course, I'm happy to attend. I was just asking for the room," she said.

That weekend, she'd been planning on working on several new accounts she was targeting. As one of Webber Pharmaceuticals' top sales representatives three quarters in a row, she'd hoped to continue her winning streak and prompt her boss to finally promote her to senior sales executive. The promotion meant that Kendra would manage the sales reps. It also meant she'd get a significant pay raise. Roger had dangled the position like a gold necklace in front of a cat burglar for months now, and with several of their senior team members, including himself, about to move into VP positions in the coming weeks, he'd have to make a decision soon.

But until then, she couldn't ease up or take her foot off the gas.

She'd just have to find time to work around the survival training. Surely they'd have some downtime she could use to do her follow-ups? Was there cell service in the Alaskan wild? How long could her laptop battery last?

"Here is the information packet with all the details of the training—what to bring, what to expect…" Roger handed the packets around the table and no one looked particularly excited, but Kendra's eyes widened as she scanned the printout.

A pocketknife, a water bottle and a piece of rope. That was all they were allowed to bring.

She raised her hand.

Roger was already looking at her as though expecting she'd need clarification. "Question, Kendra?"

"Yeah…um, this list isn't set in stone, right? I mean, they can't really expect us all to go off the grid completely for two days, can they?" She laughed nervously, absentmindedly clutching her cell phone tighter. In this one-hour meeting alone, she'd missed three calls from potential clients. Three sales that could have gone to a competitor. The pharmaceutical business didn't take a day off… And to be out of reach for a whole weekend? *Okay, just breathe. Save the anxiety attack for the privacy of your own office.*

"Of course not," Roger said.

Huge sigh of relief.

"The guides will be prepared with emergency supplies

and a cell phone in case there are legitimate calls that you need to make," he continued.

"Well, everyone's definition of emergency is different..." To her, lost sales resulting in a lost promotion was a big enough reason to borrow a cell phone for an hour or two.

"The idea is to unplug."

Unplug.

May as well tell her not to breathe.

"Look, we can all be successful when we have all the tools available," Roger said. "This weekend I want to test resourcefulness among the team. How you adapt in new surroundings and situations will show me—and more important, yourselves—what you're truly capable of, beyond self-limiting beliefs."

Kendra nodded slowly. Okay, so it was essentially another opportunity to prove herself. If she framed the weekend that way, she wouldn't lose her mind. "Okay, yes, you're absolutely right, Roger."

"I know," he said with a smile. "And before you all rush off, I have another announcement to make."

Kendra held her breath. Here it was—the promotion announcement. She had to have this. No one else sitting around that table put in the hours she did, or made the sacrifice of putting their career above all else, the way she did. She deserved to be promoted, and it would soften the blow of having to head out to Wild River that weekend to rough it in the woods. Without any contact with civilization.

"As you all know, there are two openings for new senior sales executive positions, and I'm happy to announce that I have filled one of those already," Roger said.

Kendra sat taller, her acceptance speech turning over in her mind.

What a wonderful surprise! Thank you, Roger. I'm so happy that I can continue to be a valuable member of the team... I completely agree that the team really could benefit from survival training...

But instead of calling her name, Roger turned toward the opening boardroom door. "Ah, here he is now."

He?

Kendra's head swung toward the door so fast her neck cramped.

"Ow," she muttered, rubbing it as the man entered.

Crisp brown leather shoes; perfectly tailored, slim-fit navy dress pants with a brown belt; light blue dress shirt opened at the collar; and a sports coat that fit like he was born in it. The new hire joined her boss at the head of the boardroom table.

Her mouth gaped as her eyes scrolled up to meet his and her arm flopped back onto her lap.

Nolan Lawless was standing in the office boardroom.

The man she'd spent an amazing week with at a sales conference, only for him to ghost her for three months, had just stolen her promotion.

Because of course he had.

NOLAN HAD KNOWN walking into the boardroom at Webber Pharmaceuticals and seeing Kendra again would be challenging, but he'd told himself that he couldn't turn down a job opportunity he'd been busting his ass for just because it would mean working with a woman who'd led him on and disappointed him three months ago.

Unfortunately, he hadn't expected the intensity of the tug in his chest at seeing her surprised, annoyed and embarrassed expression as their eyes met across the boardroom table.

Met and held as though locked in an unspoken battle of who'd blink first.

He did.

So much for showing up confident and unfazed, but damn, she was even more beautiful than he remembered. Dressed in a dark charcoal suit and white blouse, her straight, silky blond hair swept into a high ponytail, she was intimidatingly professional—which was what had attracted him to her in the first place at the conference in Seattle. But he also knew the fun and relaxed side hidden beneath her polished exterior, and that knowledge had him wiping his sweaty palms on his lap.

Nolan could hardly resist this intoxicating woman, but he had no choice. He hoped anyone hearing his pounding heart would assume he was simply nervous to be starting a more senior level position at a new company.

"Everyone, welcome Nolan Lawless," his new boss, Roger, said.

Everyone around the table applauded, but Kendra kept her hands clutched tight in her lap. She avoided Nolan's gaze and continued to shift in her seat like she had ants in her underwear.

Great, now he was thinking about her underwear...the pale pink silky ones that had somehow ended up on the ceiling fan of the conference hotel room. Had she ever gotten them back? He liked to think they were still there—the only remaining evidence of their wild, whirlwind affair.

He felt his neck grow hot and he shook the memories of their time together away. He wasn't the one who should be sweating and uncomfortable. That honor was hers. She was the one who'd made him believe that what they had that week in Seattle was real. More than just a physical connection or a fling to bring excitement to an otherwise boring work trip. She had wanted more, as well...or so she'd claimed.

Then she'd given him a bogus phone number.

So no, he shouldn't be the one feeling awkward in this situation at all. She should. He was mature enough to move on.

"Nolan comes to us from Pharmatech in Juneau, where he was the top sales rep last quarter," Roger told the group.

Did Kendra just scoff? Well, Miss Top Sales Rep was in for some competition now.

"We agree that his joining the team here at Webber Pharmaceuticals will be mutually beneficial," Roger continued. "Nolan can grow in this position while bringing a more intimate approach to the sales process."

Intimate. Funny word choice. He'd already been intimate with one element of Webber Pharmaceuticals. As well as vulnerable and open…

Roger was staring at him. Waiting.

Shit, right, he should say something. He cleared his throat as quietly as possible. "Yes, that's right. I'm excited to work with this amazing award-winning team and hope I can bring a fresh approach to the table."

Another scoff from Kendra?

He'd totally call her out on it if it wasn't his first five minutes with the company. No one else seemed to notice. Maybe they were all used to her not being a team player.

"Nolan will start officially next week, but he will be joining us for the team-building event this weekend," Roger said.

He what? His head swung toward Roger. "Well, I'm not really officially part of the team just yet…" He'd only accepted the company's offer the week before and moved from Juneau to Anchorage in record time. He'd planned on using the next few days to talk himself up to the challenge of pretending not to be infatuated with one of his sales staff. How the hell was he supposed to be impartial to her, treat her fairly, when she wasn't just another coworker?

It terrified him that this one detail of the job could completely throw him off his game when he knew he could excel here. He'd needed a few more days to figure out how he was going to handle seeing Kendra every day, knowing he couldn't be with her.

But Roger was adamant. "What better way to get acquainted with the team than jumping right out of your comfort zone and into a challenge?"

That was the problem. He'd jumped right out of his comfort zone three months ago when he'd met Kendra, and unfortunately, she'd allowed him to crash. He didn't need a repeat of that disappointment so soon.

KENDRA'S FINGERS FLEW over her cell phone as she hurried out of the boardroom and down the hall to her office. Everyone else was greeting their new team member, but she'd had that pleasure already, so she'd faked needing to be on a conference call to skip out without question from Roger.

You'll never guess what happened.

Her best friend Nisha's reply was immediate:

YOU GOT THE PROMOTION?!

Kendra felt another sharp kick to her stomach at the mention of surprisingly the least devastating thing to happen in the last hour. She'd thought for sure she was going to get it. She'd been confident enough to tell Nisha about the possibility, and now she had to tell her friend that she'd been overlooked...for a man. And not just any man. One who'd been on her mind relentlessly for three months. One she'd talked to her best friend about for three months. One she'd really missed for three months.

Three long months of silence.

And he hadn't even looked the slightest bit embarrassed or apologetic standing up there in the boardroom. She'd felt his eyes on her the whole time. What kind of uncaring, sadistic freak was he?

An amazingly sexy one who'd made her body and heart react in ways it never had before. Damn it! Before meeting Nolan, her main priority—scratch that—her *only* priority had been her career. She loved her job, she was good at it, and at twenty-six, she'd been at the point in her life where it was unapologetically her sole focus. Then she'd opened herself up to the possibility that a career wasn't the only thing she wanted. It had shocked the hell out of her to realize that she was interested in a relationship. Seems it only took meeting a man she couldn't resist to open her eyes to the fact that not only *could* she have it all, but that she wanted it all.

And then she was left with a void that hadn't existed before.

No promotion. A new boss.

The sad-face emoji Nisha sent in reply partially mirrored how she felt: unhappy and disappointed, but also annoyed and conflicted. Three offices down the hall, Nolan would soon be settling in and casting a shadow over her in the process. Working with the first man she'd ever really had feelings for was going to be torture. Her office had once been a second home, a place where she felt confident and secure. Now she felt as though it were being invaded...just like her heart had been.

She hesitated briefly, then hit Send on the next message.

It gets worse. It's the guy from Seattle.

Her cell phone rang immediately and Kendra closed her office door before answering. "Hey, Nish..."

"The love-at-first-sight guy is your new boss?" Her friend's disbelief came out in a shrill tone.

Kendra winced. Maybe she had to stop being so open with her friend. It was embarrassing that her gut feelings about situations and people were so off. From now on, she'd tell Nisha things *after* they happened. No more counting unhatched chickens for dinner.

"What the hell am I going to do? Working with him is going to be very difficult." Understatement. Especially since seeing him hadn't triggered feelings of rage or resentment. It had only brought back memories of how freaking great they'd been together.

Sure, it had only been a week. But it had been the best week of her life.

They'd met the first day of the pharmaceutical conference at the registration desk. She'd been dripping Seattle raindrops from her hair when he turned to her and joked, "Rainy enough for you?"

"I'm from Alaska, so the rain doesn't bother me. It's a nice break from all the snow," Kendra said, receiving her badge and attendee schedule.

"You're from Alaska?" Nolan's voice had warmed her right away, and when she'd turned and met his friendly smile, she'd been hooked. Never one to believe in love at first sight, she'd definitely started to question her stance on the subject.

"Yes, Anchorage. Where are you from?"

"Juneau."

Had the planets actually aligned in her favor? A guy who was hot as hell *and* lived in her state? In her field of work? They weren't exactly neighbors—Anchorage and Juneau were separated by a twelve-hour drive and a ferry ride—but she was already mapping the route in her mind and juggling her vacation days.

"Which company are you here with?" And was he traveling with coworkers or was he up for a conference buddy? She wasn't prepared to share her leads…but someone to sit next to at the sessions and have meals with would be nice. Maybe explore the city with in the evenings after the networking sessions wrapped up.

"Pharmatech." He glanced at her badge. "Wow—Webber Pharmaceuticals. Impressive. I think we might currently be up for the same client, actually."

Interesting. Her competitive spirit was piqued, only enhancing her interest in the guy. "Well, then, my condolences in advance."

His grin was downright drool-worthy as he nodded. "Stiff competition for sure. Actually, I've been interested in working for Webber for years. Applied a few times."

"Really? And relocating to Anchorage wouldn't be a problem for you…and your family?" Okay, she was fishing. Could he tell? He wasn't wearing a wedding ring, but that didn't mean he wasn't blissfully betrothed with six adorable children.

If he sensed the intention behind her question, he didn't seem to mind as he answered, "No family to consider. I mean, I have a family, like parents and stuff…just not wife, kids…that kind of thing." He cleared his throat awkwardly.

If she was still asleep on the plane and this was all a dream, Kendra was going to be severely pissed off when she woke up.

But it hadn't been a dream. It had been the start of an amazing week together. They'd attended most of the same presentations and met up for lunch. They'd had dinner together every night and stayed up all hours talking and walking along the pier. And then their final night: they'd spent it together…in each other's arms. She'd never been some-one who opened herself up easily, but it had felt natural and right with Nolan. It had seemed like she'd known him her entire life. Thinking that her life had changed that week had both terrified and excited her. They connected on so many levels—emotional *and* physical. He was the first man she'd met and been genuinely interested in who wasn't at all intimidated or put off by her drive and ambition. In fact, Nolan had been attracted to it.

He'd hinted about seeing each other again when they got back to Alaska, and she'd eagerly agreed that she'd like to continue what they'd started that week. Figure out the dis-tance thing somehow. She'd been more optimistic and ex-cited about it than she'd been about anything in so long… Could she have found Mr. Right?

And then her fantasy had evaporated when she never heard from him again.

Until now.

Had she read the situation completely wrong? Or had winning the client they'd been competing for cost her the guy? She didn't want to believe that Nolan would be a sore loser, but admittedly she really didn't know him after a week, despite their connection.

"When does he start?" Nisha asked, breaking into her thoughts.

"Next week, but get this—Roger's sending us on a sur-vival training team-building thing this weekend. How am I going to survive this?" she groaned, rolling her eyes to-ward the ceiling, hoping to find the answer written there.

"This is actually perfect," Nisha said.

Had her best friend lost her mind? "Did you not hear me? Wilderness survival training—two full days…" She gulped. "And nights stuck with *him*."

"Exactly. Think of it as bypassing the frying pan and leaping right on into the flames."

Her friend's analogy was spot-on. Kendra *was* terrified of getting burned again.

"You're going to go on that wilderness survival training and you're going to show Mr. Heartless that you are completely fine, that you are strong and competent, and you haven't given him a second thought since Seattle."

Kendra nodded, swallowing hard. But she had given him a second thought. A lot of second thoughts. As much as she was annoyed by his ghosting, she couldn't help but feel that what they'd shared was real. She hadn't imagined it, had she? Her instincts really couldn't be that off, could they?

She hoped not, as she was going to need them to survive the Alaskan wilderness that weekend.

"So, did little Miss Wrong Number faint when she saw you walk into her office?"

No, but Nolan almost had. His cell phone cradled between his shoulder and chin, Nolan collapsed into the chair of his soon-to-be new office before confessing the truth to his best friend. "Man, I did not think it was going to be so hard seeing her again, but damn..." Being fourteen hours away hadn't helped erase her from his thoughts and now she was just a short hallway walk away.

"But you held it together, right?"

"Barely," he mumbled. His buddy didn't get it. Married to his high school sweetheart with a baby on the way, Matt had never experienced the heartache of wanting someone and being rejected.

And she looked even more beautiful than in his memories—that certainly hadn't helped mend his broken heart. She'd blushed when he walked in the room, which reminded him of another encounter that had her flushed and sweaty...

A night of passion like none he'd ever experienced before. It had completely caught him off guard in the best way; for the first time in years, he'd allowed himself to fall.

And then Kendra had let him fall further, down a dark hole of second-guessing and doubt.

"Well, don't lose sight of your goals," Matt was saying. "You busted ass for years for this opportunity. You can't throw it away on some woman."

If only she'd been just some woman. "Yeah, yeah, I know. It'll be fine. We're both adults." Now coworkers who'd seen each other naked, who'd spent all hours of the night tangled up in one another. Who'd had a hard time saying goodbye as she'd left his hotel room, knowing they were headed to different sides of Alaska. Damn, he'd replayed those final moments together so many times, and not once could he detect hesitation from her when she said she wanted to keep in touch, see him again. He prided himself on being good at reading people, so what had he missed?

He swallowed hard. "We just need to survive this team-building event this weekend in Wild River." Tents. Close quarters. Stressful situations. All the ingredients for a recipe for disaster.

"Hey, you got this, man." But even Matt's confidence sounded like it was wavering. Everyone knew feelings were less difficult to ignore in the light of day. Come sunset, all bets were off. "You're wiser now," he said. "Don't let her play you this time."

Nolan suspected it was easier said than done. He'd fallen hook, line and sinker for her the first time and that was before he knew how incredible she was.

"I don't plan on it," he said, but he was unsure if that call was his to make. The heart wanted what it wanted. Though Kendra's quick exit from the boardroom told him she might not be interested in playing any kind of games with him anymore. And while that should give him a sense of relief, it didn't.

"The good news is that at least now you can put this whole thing to rest," Matt said.

Nolan frowned. Seemed to him this whole thing was just beginning. "What do you mean?"

"Well, you can't exactly date her now anyway if you're her boss, right?"

His stomach dropped as though he'd plunged on a roller coaster. He hadn't really thought about it. He'd been too focused on getting through their first face-to-face encounter since the last time he saw her—when he'd kissed her so long in the hotel hallway that her taxi to the airport had almost left without her. But Matt was right. "That's true," Nolan said.

And that should make things at least a little easier... So why did he suddenly feel less excited about this opportunity he'd just moved across Alaska for?

CHAPTER TWO

SNOWTREK TOURS WAS one of the best adventure tourism companies in Alaska. It might have been located in the heart of the ski resort town of Wild River, but its reputation for providing one-of-a-kind, adrenaline-filled experiences for all athletic abilities was second to none.

Still, that knowledge did not put her mind at ease as Kendra stood on the uneven, slightly muddy ground of "base camp" late Friday afternoon with only her water bottle, a new pocketknife and the required piece of rope as the company's tour guides unloaded the emergency-only supplies from the van. Not that there was much to unload. Just a few extra water bottles, a first aid kit, a flare gun and walkie-talkies.

Her boss had *actually* signed the eight of them up for real wilderness survival training. Albeit a shortened two-day version, it was still going to be a challenge, not some comfy glamping trip with inflatable beds and shower facilities.

Kendra was about to spend a lot of time with Nolan and she was going to look…well, like someone who hadn't had proper hygiene maintenance for two days. Not that he seemed to care what she looked like. He'd barely glanced her way at all on the uncomfortable drive from Anchorage to Wild River, where they'd carpooled in several SUVs. He'd sat in the front seat and made comfortable, idle chitchat with their boss while she'd sat cramped between two other male sales reps in the back seat.

She dared a quick peek at him now and immediately wished she hadn't. Dressed in a pair of gray sweatpants and a tight black Under Armour T-shirt, running shoes on his feet and a Seattle Mariners baseball hat—*the* baseball hat he'd bought in Seattle that week—he looked too gorgeous to her broken heart. Sunglasses on, she couldn't tell if he was looking at her or at the guides as they called everyone in for a briefing. Secretly she hoped the guides made him hand the sunglasses over, like they had with all their other personal items back at the shop. Without her own sunglasses, she was at a disadvantage, not being able to hide her emotions behind dark lenses.

"Okay, is everyone excited to get started?" Cassie Reynolds, the owner of SnowTrek Tours, asked the group. So much energy in her five-foot-nothing frame. She looked actually pumped to be spending two nights out there, roughing it.

A low rumble of forced enthusiasm came from the group, but Cassie wasn't dissuaded as she launched into the safety briefing.

Kendra tried to focus on information that could actually save her life, but her attention was elsewhere. For the next forty-eight hours there would be no getting away from Nolan. No avoiding him. How was he feeling about this? Could he really just be okay forgetting about their time together and not even addressing it? Did Cassie have any really useful tips, like how to survive close quarters with an ex-lover?

"And before anyone panics, you won't be taking on the next two days alone. We are going to pair everyone up for the weekend's challenges," Cassie's colleague, Mike something-or-other—she'd been distracted during the introductions—said. "The key is to work together. Push one another. Help each other. Use your strengths and lean on your partner in areas where you might not be as strong. Your success out here this weekend depends on your ability to work as a team. And to make things more fun, along the way, you'll be competing against the other teams for points."

Cassie nodded as she stepped forward again. "That's right, and keep in mind that while this course is the beginner, shortened version of our certification course, it will be demanding. Some of you may not be able to keep up, and that's okay, but we hope you'll have fun and learn some new skills. Most of all, you'll learn about yourselves as you become more aware of your perseverance and strength."

Roger nodded as he glanced at the group.

Kendra stood straighter and forced herself to forget about Nolan and focus on her own goals. This was another test of her abilities and she was determined to shine. She would show her boss that she could adapt, be resourceful, think outside the box—whatever it took to prove that she deserved the other, still available, senior sales position.

"The list of challenges for each team are the same: building a reliable shelter from your surroundings, surviving a simulated emergency, navigating an orienteering course and outlasting an isolation training exercise," Mike said, reading from a clipboard.

He started announcing the teams, and Kendra's pulse grew faster with each pairing. She didn't hear her name or Nolan's…until they were the only two left.

"The fourth and final team are Kendra and Nolan," Mike said.

No! Her hand shot up at the same time that Nolan said, "I'm not sure that pairing is such a good idea."

Cassie grinned as she glanced between the two of them. A sparkle in her blue eyes suggested she knew what they were trying to hide. "Is there conflict or tension between you two at the office?"

Roger was studying them intently, so Kendra forced a smile as she shook her head. It wasn't a lie—the tension had happened *outside* the office and it was more of a sexual nature... No one in the office knew about their previous encounter. At least Kendra had kept it to herself.

"No..." Nolan said slowly, clearly choosing his words carefully so he wouldn't sound alarm bells the first week on the job. "More like differences in how we communicate."

Like by *not* communicating? Was he serious? That was *his* problem. She communicated quite well. "Actually, I think it's more of a difference of opinion on communication frequency."

Nolan shot her an odd look, which she pretended to ignore.

"Do you two know one another?" Roger asked.

"Sort of."

"Not really," Kendra lied. "We just know *of* one another."

Cassie nodded. "Perfect. Then I think that this pairing is great. Use this weekend to overcome any preconceived notions you might have about one another and this...communication issue. You'll see your working relationship in the office will be that much stronger."

Damn. Looked like they were stuck together. Nolan reluctantly shuffled across the group to stand next to Kendra. She took a large step away from him to keep a safe distance between them.

"Does anyone have any questions before we start the first challenge?" Mike asked the group.

Against her better judgement, Kendra raised her hand. "What if your partner just disappears on you?"

Nolan let out an annoyed sigh next to her.

Good, be irritated. She was. She was irritated that he hadn't even had the decency to text her to say he wasn't interested. Irritated that after three months of zero contact, he had the balls to apply for a position he knew she'd been working her ass off to get. And irritated that he seemed perfectly content to just sweep their history under the boardroom rug.

"Well, the key is to stay together," Mike said.

"Right…but what if, for example, your partner doesn't give you the right coordinates to follow and you're just left to wander the great unknown alone?" Nolan asked.

What the hell was that about?

Mike frowned, looking back and forth between the two of them. "Well, again, the key is to stick together and not leave one another stranded…" He spoke slowly and carefully and then looked at the rest of the group. "Anyone have any other questions *not* related to the first and most important rule of staying together?"

Everyone shook their heads.

"Nope," Kendra mumbled.

"All good," Nolan said.

"Great. Then, let's get started. First challenge is building your shelter. You can use anything from nature to construct a lean-to or debris hut that will serve as a place to sleep and rest during breaks, so make sure it's sturdy and will last through various elements for at least the next two days," Mike said. "This challenge will be timed and then each team's shelter will be awarded points based on sturdiness, practicality and overall usefulness. Time starts…" he clicked a stopwatch "…now!"

Kendra looked at Nolan, but he was already scanning the area around them.

Okay, guess they weren't going to talk strategy. Or talk at all.

She looked at the other teams, already moving quickly to complete the challenge, and her competitive spirit flared.

She squared her shoulders. Game face on. She could do

this. Cavemen had done it before YouTube tutorials. She could figure this out. How hard could it be?

Kendra headed toward an area of the forest where scattered tree branches lay on the ground, broken off from windstorms. Ignoring the dirt and sharp edges, she collected as many as she could hold and carried them back to the campsite.

Now what? Making a lean-to sounded like it required something like a thick tree to position her branches against...but there were none in their sanctioned area. What was the other option? A debris hut. What the hell was that?

Across from her, Nolan squatted next to a pile of leaves, bark and pine needles. He started to work, positioning a long branch against an old tree stump, then making an A-frame from two more branches and tying the three together with his piece of rope.

Ah, that was what the rope was for. Got it.

Kendra found another tree stump and repeated Nolan's actions. Luckily, other groups were doing it, too, so it wouldn't look like she'd had to copy him. This actually wasn't so hard. She looked around to see if Roger was taking notice, but he was busy working on his own shelter with Alan, an older rep from their company.

She started to place her other sticks along the side when Nolan turned to face her. "What are you doing?" he asked.

The first words were spoken and she felt slightly victorious that he'd broken the silence first. "Making my shelter."

"*This* is our shelter," he said, tightly.

She pointed at his debris hut. "That's *your* shelter." Then pointed at her own. "*This* will be mine."

He placed his hands on his hips and her eyes dipped to where his shirt had risen to expose the side of his stomach. An image of running her tongue along that exact oblique muscle appeared in her mind and she quickly averted her eyes. "We're supposed to build one together as a team," he said.

"I don't remember that being part of the rules."

"Then you weren't listening."

That was probably true... Still, the company couldn't force them to stay in the same shelter if she wasn't comfortable with it.

Kendra narrowed her eyes. "I'm not sleeping with you." Again.

Lying next to him in a cramped debris hut with just branches and moss and a fire to keep them warm seemed like a disastrous idea. Too many nights she'd dreamt of being in his arms when she was nowhere near him. She was terrified she'd confess her feelings in her sleep or worse... curl into him during the night. His rejection was embarrassing enough. She didn't need him waking her up by rolling her body off him in the middle of the night.

He sighed. "Look, if it makes you feel better, we'll put up a divider so you can have your space—which you obviously want..." His eyes burned into hers.

"What's that supposed to mean?"

He shook his head. "Nothing. Look, I'm not a good loser, and I think I remember that you like to succeed, as well, but we won't if we don't meet the challenges."

She clenched her teeth and sucked in a deep breath. "Fine, but we need a thick divider."

"Fine," he said, going back to work.

Kendra stared at his ass as he bent to pick up more branches to prop against the main support beam to create walls. God, that ass should be illegal. And what was it about gray, loose-fitting sweatpants on a man that turned her primal? It had to be the wilderness and the fresh air. Though it was really attractive that he seemed to know his way around the forest...

"You going to help or stare at my ass all day?" he asked without even turning back to look at her.

Was he giving her a choice?

HER "HMPH" ALMOST made him smile. So she had been checking him out. Good. She could get a good look at what she'd casually thrown away.

Unfortunately, he was getting a good look, as well…at what he couldn't have.

He watched from the corner of his eye as Kendra disappeared into the bush to gather more debris for insulation. The combination of her looking so goddamn sexy in tight blue leggings and a fitted sweatshirt and being so unapproachable with her standoffish attitude had him conflicted with what to say or do. The ride out to Wild River had been intense as he'd tried to maintain a casual conversation with his new boss, but he'd felt her glaring into the back of his head from the back seat.

And she hadn't exactly been thrilled about them partnering up.

Even if she hadn't raised a fuss, he'd been planning on having a divider in their shelter. There was no way in hell he could lie in close quarters with her out there in the magnificently beautiful outback, under the promised starry sky, and not be tempted to touch her, kiss her, ask her what the hell had happened after she'd left his hotel room the morning after the best night of his life.

She returned and dropped an armful of leaves and moss onto the ground, then set to work insulating the shelter. She was literally inches from him but seemed a million miles away. Despite the heat of the midday summer sun beating down on him, the coldness radiating from her made him shiver.

Where was the woman he'd met in Seattle? The one who

was so warm and outgoing that he'd stayed up long into the night talking with her. The one he felt he knew better after just one week than people he'd known his entire life. They hadn't just gotten to know each other on a surface level, they'd shared their goals and passions, and they'd had so many things in common.

Now they felt like strangers.

He had to say something. The silence was killing him, but she obviously wasn't interested in getting personal again...

"So I heard you landed the account." It had almost given him a reason to reach out—to congratulate her on the win— but he'd resisted. The hurt part of him wondered if that had been her strategy: get close to him so he'd back off the account. But it had only fueled him to push harder, and deep down he knew that wasn't Kendra's way. She'd hate to have gotten the account by default. She'd gotten it because she was a kick-ass sales rep and Webber Pharmaceuticals was the best option for the client. That was why Nolan had been so eager to work there himself. "Congratulations," he added.

"Told you I would," she said, weaving the moss through the branches to hold it in place.

"So modest," he mumbled under his breath.

She turned toward him and opened her mouth to say something, but Cassie and Mike moved into the center of the clearing.

"Time's up!" Mike called, hitting the stopwatch.

"Step away from your shelters," Cassie said.

The awkward silence fell between them again as they waited for their debris hut to be inspected. Nolan wasn't worried—he knew they'd crushed the challenge. He and Kendra worked well together, and they would continue to succeed if they could put aside their differences and personal history.

Unfortunately, that was hard for him to do when he knew they were good together, period.

"Great job on the shelter," Mike told them after his assessment. "You two are leading in points."

"Yay!" he said turning to Kendra for a high five.

Impulsively, her hand connected with his and she smiled widely. But her smile quickly faded and he was back to wondering if he'd imagined that entire week in Seattle.

"Next up is your simulated emergency," Mike told them. "Who'd like to be the injured one?"

By the glares Kendra had been shooting him—between lustful gazes at his body—he figured she'd like to give him a real injury. "I think I should be the medic," he said.

She crossed her arms in annoyance. Of course she had a problem with it. No doubt, no matter what he chose, she would have argued. "Why do I have to be the damsel in distress?"

"Because I have three different first aid training qualifications, so I think we could nail this one." Of course, they'd all been Boy Scout badges, but he'd keep that to himself.

She hesitated, obviously torn between wanting to win the challenge and not wanting to let him win this argument. "Well, I think that would be cheating." She turned to Mike. "I'll be the medic. What's his injury?"

Besides a broken heart?

Mike scanned the clipboard. "Each team has been randomly assigned something different. Your team has a sprained ankle that leaves one of you immobilized a mile from camp."

"So we pretend he hobbled here and I wrap his ankle?" She shrugged. "Sounds easy enough."

Mike laughed. "No. The four of us hike out a mile and

then he fakes his injury. Cassie and I will assess the challenge by how the two of you deal with it from that point."

Her eyes widened with panic.

"Care to change positions now?" Nolan caught his choice of words a second too late. No doubt they were both thinking of a lot of different positions they'd tried during their night of passion. His cheeks flamed as he remembered one in particular. "I mean, can I be the medic?"

She shook her head. "Nope. I've got this."

He sighed. "Kendra, stop being so stubborn. I'm like two hundred pounds."

"Well, lucky for you, size isn't everything," she whispered with an evil grin.

Wow. The blows just kept coming...

Fine. If she wanted to lose this challenge, it was on her.

CHAPTER THREE

TWENTY MINUTES LATER, Kendra was rethinking her decision, made purely out of spite and pride. They'd completed their one-mile hike away from camp and she was already winded. A mile on a treadmill did not prepare someone for a mile of uneven wilderness trail. She drained the contents of her water bottle and turned to Nolan. "Okay, let's go." The faster they completed this one, the better.

Nolan nodded and then immediately launched into his award-worthy performance. "Ow...oh, the pain!" he said dramatically, falling to the ground, holding his ankle.

Cassie smirked as Mike made a note on his clipboard.

Kendra hid a grin. He was funny. That was one of the things about him that she hadn't been expecting, but she was totally attracted to humor. He had an endearing goofy side that she suspected he didn't reveal to everyone and that had made her feel special. He'd had her laughing all week and it had made the conference so much more fun.

But his rejection wasn't so hilarious, and she needed to remember that anytime she let her guard slip. This man just wasn't into her and she needed to protect herself this time.

"I said, ow, I think I sprained an ankle." He lifted his leg in the air when she continued to stand there, lost in her memories.

"I thought it was the other ankle," she said.

"Oh, right," he said, switching legs.

Game time. Game face. Focus on completing this challenge better than the other teams. "Can you stand?" she asked. If he leaned on her, she could support his weight back to camp. Of course, that would require touching him.

He glanced at Mike, but the guide shook his head.

No? What the hell did he mean *no*? What was she supposed to do—carry him?

Oh snap.

Nolan looked equally as nervous, but also a little smug as he said, "Apparently, I can't stand."

Okay, don't panic. Do not let them see you sweat.

She crouched on the ground in front of him and glanced over her shoulder. "Give me your hands," she said, reaching over her shoulders.

"You're going to piggyback me?"

"Well, I can't exactly toss you over one shoulder, now, can I?"

"Okay…" He reached forward and took both of her hands in his. Immediately, her flesh tingled at the contact. His were warm and slightly sweaty—the only indication that he might be nervous.

She was. And not because of the challenge. In seconds, he'd have his arms around her neck and his legs wrapped around her waist. Not exactly the sexiest or manliest of positions, but they'd be body to body. Full contact. Maybe she should switch with him. Let him take over on this one. The mile hike out there had nearly killed her; this wasn't going to be any easier.

Mike and Cassie were watching. Waiting. Assessing.

She wouldn't wuss out now. She could do this. Mind over matter.

"Kendra, are we doing this today or…?" Nolan asked.

Right, time to get moving.

She linked her arms beneath his thighs and stood, lifting him off the ground and shifting her weight forward so as not to tumble backward. She swayed to the right and took a few quick steps to regain her balance. Damn, only two hundred pounds? She couldn't remember him feeling this heavy when he was lying on top of her.

Nope, not going to think about that now.

"You sure you got this?" he asked.

"Yes," she grunted. Unfortunately, his arms around her neck, his hands falling in front of her chest were throwing her off a lot more than she'd expected. Those hands had explored every inch of her body...over and over and over. Strong and confident. Pleasuring her and leaving her wanting more...

"We can switch."

"I said, I got this." As long as she didn't think about how sexy his hamstring muscles felt beneath her hands or think about how his chest and abs were pressed against her back.

Sweat instantly pooled on her forehead and she wished for a third arm to wipe it away.

Damn, this was a lot harder than she'd expected.

"Want me to sing or something?" he asked.

"I want you to stop talking," she said, hoisting him a little higher. She picked up her pace, allowing his weight to propel her forward down the slightly sloped trail. They were at least smart enough to walk out in a direction that was uphill—it made the trek back easier.

But the hot sun was relentless with little tree cover and she was panting pretty good by the quarter-of-a-mile mark.

Water would be helpful, but her bottle was empty and she'd die of thirst before she'd ask him for some of his.

"You doing okay?" he asked, and the concern in his voice was almost enough to weaken her to the point of admitting defeat. But only almost.

"Totally fine," she said, her inability to breathe making a liar out of her.

Halfway there. She could do this. If only her mouth didn't feel like a desert. If only that sun would fuck off behind a cloud or something.

Her vision started to blur slightly and the trees around her started to move...coming closer, then looming overhead... Then they disappeared completely, along with her consciousness.

IF THERE WAS an award for stubbornness that weekend, Kendra would win it.

Nolan applied the ice pack to her forehead and waved a smelling salt under her nose as she lay out cold on the trail about a quarter mile from camp. To her credit, she'd almost made it, but he wanted to ream her out for passing out instead of quitting.

Never in his life had he met a woman so determined to succeed. Her no-quit attitude was hot as hell even if in this case it was a little misguided.

Her eyes opened slowly and she smiled up at him. "Hey, you."

Shit, had she hit her head when she'd collapsed, sending them both falling to the ground? There was no sign of her annoyance or irritation with him now. Instead, there was the woman he'd started to fall for. Beautiful, warm, open...deceiving.

Must remember that last one.

"Hey...you passed out." He handed her a water bottle and her eyes widened as she sat up quickly and scanned the trail.

Mike and Cassie watched on carefully from a distance. Turned out their simulated emergency had turned into a real one and they were assessing *his* actions now instead.

"No, I didn't," Kendra said.

"Are you narcoleptic, then? Otherwise you passed out

from dehydration because you overdid it," he said, pressing the water bottle to her stubborn, sexy-as-hell lips.

She glared at him over the rim of the bottle, but she drank. Then she shook her head and started to stand. "Okay, I'm good. Jump back on," she said, crouching in front of him again.

She wasn't a quitter, he'd give her that. Too bad that trait obviously didn't apply to her relationships. Instead of accepting her outstretched hands this time, he quickly scooped her up and into his arms.

Her mouth dropped when her face was just inches from his. "Do you want to get punched?"

"Not particularly," he said, readjusting her in his arms. She was light, but she was hard to hold on to when she was squirming to get down like a toddler throwing a fit.

"Well, then, put me back down."

His grip on her only tightened as he started walking toward camp. "Change of challenge—they are assessing us on this new situation." He nodded toward Cassie and Mike, who looked more interested in this turn of events than evaluating. "We need to do what we would actually do in this scenario. We're being judged, remember?" But, shit, could he actually carry her the rest of the way back to camp when the familiar smell of her was filling his senses now? When her neck was this close to his face and making him remember everything he shouldn't be? He'd been able to hold his breath when she'd been carrying him. He couldn't now. Both of them passing out in the one challenge would surely cost them a few points. In fact, they really needed to impress Cassie and Mike to make up for Kendra's blunder.

"Fine," she grumbled. She turned her head and refused to look at him the rest of the way back to camp. It was fine by him, because if he had to look into those gorgeous brown eyes this close up or see her absentmindedly lick her lips, he just might say screw the challenge and kiss her to remind her what she'd been missing these last three months.

In record time, Nolan set her onto the ground at their campsite and struggled for breath. Sweat dripped down his forehead and he could taste it above his upper lip.

"Out of shape?" she asked.

"Says the woman who passed out carrying me," he said.

"I made it most of the way and you're definitely sweating more than I was."

Ignoring the temptation to be lured into her verbal sparring, he bent next to her and removed his shirt.

Her eyes widened. "Why are you getting undressed?"

"We need to finish the challenge. Sit still and give me your foot." He could feel her eyes on his body as he worked to wrap the "injured" ankle and secure the fabric with sap from a nearby tree.

She caught him noticing her stare and instead turned her attention to his handiwork. "Did you learn that from a first aid course?"

"No. I'm just quick-thinking and logical," he said with a grin.

"I refuse to be impressed by you," she said. "And for the record, if this was a real injury, I could have taken care of it myself."

His grin vanished as he released her foot and stood. "Don't worry, you made it quite clear that you definitely do not need me," he said and walked away before he could say anything more.

CHAPTER FOUR

THE ALASKAN WILD after sunset was no joke. As the sun disappeared over the mountains, it took the day's heat with it, and the cool chill in the air mirrored the cold shoulder Kendra had gotten from Nolan for the rest of the afternoon after completing the simulated emergency challenge. They'd rejoined the other groups to gather berries and refill their water bottles in the designated stream, and had the option to take a hike or just relax around the central campsite fire—the guides had made one to help them all get their own started. All the while, Nolan had made sure they weren't together, instead chatting with Roger or the other team members.

It was important for him to get to know everyone… He already knew her far too well, but Kendra couldn't help feeling jealous as he continued to avoid her. She wanted to avoid him, obviously, but it annoyed her that he, too, was pulling this attitude.

What the hell had she ever done to him?

"Okay, everyone, time to get a good night's rest, because tomorrow we have another full day," Mike said, standing up from a log near the fire.

The others all stood and dispersed toward their shelters. Kendra's anxiety rose.

Sleep. Right. Next to the man she found both insanely attractive and intensely infuriating. Sleep wouldn't be happening unless the shelter collapsed on top of her and knocked her out cold. She groaned inwardly. Passing out on the trail that day had been humiliating, but the worst part was waking up in a dreamlike state, seeing Nolan's face above her illuminated by the sunlight filtering through the trees. She'd reacted to the sight of him as though it were a fantasy, like all the others she'd had…and for a split second she'd let her guard slip. What if she couldn't keep up the pretense of not caring that he just wasn't into her, that he hadn't hurt her?

She looked around. Everyone had disappeared inside their shelters. Including Nolan. She stared at the debris hut. Could she really climb in there with him? Maybe she could sleep outside. As long as she survived the night against the weather, the bugs, the bears…that was all that mattered, right? Technically, the debris hut was *more* comfort and they were supposed to be surviving on none.

A large dragonfly buzzed straight at her face and she quickly dove into the shelter on her side of the divider. Suddenly, taking her chances with the man who'd broken her heart seemed like a better choice. Slightly.

She lay on her back on the moss and branch bed and stared upward toward the sky. All was quiet on Nolan's side. Could he actually be asleep already? Unbelievable. He really didn't care about her or this crazy, awkward situation at all.

Don't worry, you've made it quite clear that you do not need me.

His words had replayed in her mind all afternoon. What the hell did he mean by that? Should she ask?

She sighed. Nothing good would come from starting an argument.

Just go to sleep, Kendra.

WITH THE DIVIDER in place between them, Nolan lay on his bed of brush and tried to get comfortable. Twigs dug into his neck, so he sat and removed what remained of his ripped shirt to make a pillow. He positioned it behind his head and was immediately more comfortable. Crazy how when stripped of the everyday things he took for granted, the littlest "luxury" made a difference. Damn, maybe he should offer the shirt to Kendra.

Right, and risk another snippy comment about how she could take care of herself? No, thanks.

He placed one hand behind his head and took several deep breaths. Gaps in the branches above him provided a spectacular view of the starry night sky, but they didn't provide a source of heat...

Was she cold? He really had nothing to give her, but he could add more wood to their little, contained fire...

Nope. If she was cold, she'd do it herself.

He closed his eyes and forced his body to relax.

Was she thirsty? She might still be dehydrated from that day. He might be annoyed with her, but he was still a gentleman. He cleared his throat and aimed for casual. "Hey, you okay over there?"

"Fantastic," she said.

"Not too cold? I have extra brush..."

"I'm toasty."

"I still have water if you need some."

"I'm good."

She was lying. Clearly she was out to prove that she didn't need or want anything to do with him, but that message had already been sent loud and clear.

He shifted to his side, facing the divider, catching sight of her hand lying at her side. A hand he'd held and kissed and stroked...just one part of her that he'd explored that week they were together.

Damn, this was going to drive him insane. He had to know what the hell happened. What made her change her mind? Or had it always just been a fling for her? If so, why had she acted like she'd wanted more?

He cleared his throat again and opened his mouth to ask, but he couldn't find the words. How could he ask her without sounding pathetic and desperate?

Best to let her believe he didn't care. That he hadn't been tempted to email her at the address on the business card she'd given him…or stop by her office that day a month ago when he'd been there for an interview.

He had his pride.

Still, this silence was torture. He deserved an answer. If they had any chance at a healthy working relationship, they needed to clear the air eventually.

"So, uh, how've you been?" he asked.

"Are we seriously doing this?" she asked, her tone cold.

Guess not. Why the hell was she so annoyed with him? He was the one who'd been made out to be a fool. Was she really that upset that she hadn't successfully skirted him for the rest of her life? That he'd applied for and gotten a job at her workplace? It was the position she wanted—he did feel bad about that. It would explain her coldness toward him now, if not the three months of silence.

"Hey, if you're upset about me getting this senior sales position… I am sorry that the promotion didn't go your way."

She scoffed. "You're a man. Of course you were given the opportunity without having to prove yourself."

Was that what she thought? "Actually, I've been busting my ass for this for a long time." The edge that crept into his voice couldn't be helped. He'd explained all of this to her in Seattle. How he'd worked three jobs while finishing school and how he'd had to support his single mother when she was sick. How he'd go into the office before 7:00 a.m. every morning and was the last one to leave. He'd also expressed his interest in working for a bigger company with opportunities for advancement, and she'd supported that ambition.

"I'm sure you did," she said now. "But so did I, and look which one of us got the position."

"So that's why you're annoyed with me? That's why you've tried to avoid me since I arrived?" And before?

"Oh my God, really?" She huffed her impatience. "Good night, Nolan."

If that wasn't it, then what the hell was wrong with her? Enough was enough.

Sitting up, he yanked down the divider. "Hey, I think we should clear the air about what happened in Seattle since we are going to be working together."

She sat up and turned to face him. Her eyes clocked his shirtless state and her cheeks flushed slightly in the glow of the fire outside the hut, but her expression was challenging as she nodded. "Okay. You start."

Shit.

He took a deep breath. "Look, what happened three months ago is in the past and I'm mature enough to move on and keep things professional in the office." Not that he wanted to, but what choice did he have? She'd made it clear she had no interest in pursuing things anymore.

"Great. Me, too," she said, folding her arms across her body.

He waited. No apology. No embarrassment. Just still annoyed.

"I mean it would help if there had been some sort of closure."

She nodded. "Yes, that would have been nice."

So why the hell hadn't she made her intentions clear back then? "An explanation of some sort…" Did she need him to spell it out?

"I could use one… I mean, just for closure's sake."

He frowned. "*You* could use one? For what?"

Daggers from her eyes. "For ghosting me."

Ghosting her? What the hell was she talking about? "What the hell are you talking about?"

She shivered slightly, but her voice never wavered as she said, "*You* never called."

Was she for real? "*You* gave me the wrong phone number."

She scoffed. "Nice try."

"It's true." Was she fucking with him right now, replacing the blame because she didn't want to admit she was in the wrong? Or did she really believe that he purposely hadn't called?

No way. He'd been so transparent about his feelings.

"I think you're full of shit and are making excuses now because you don't want to appear like an ass when you are my new boss," she said.

"Nope."

She frowned, her confidence in her accusation clearly diminishing. "So you didn't just lead me on and vanish?"

"Why the hell would I do that? We had an amazing week together."

"I know!"

"Like mind-blowingly amazing."

"I know!"

His heart raced. "And I thought we'd…connected. Beyond the physical, you know?"

"Yes! But then I didn't hear from you," she said, her annoyance returning.

He took a deep breath. "So you thought I was ghosting you and I thought you'd tried to ditch me with a fake number?" Oh no… All this time. Months of second-guessing his feelings, conflicted and tortured… It had all been a misunderstanding?

"Looks that way," she said, sheepishly.

He stared at her and his mind reeled.

Then her challenging stare returned. "Okay, but if you had the wrong number, why didn't you email or stop by when you were interviewing at the office?"

He'd definitely wanted to. Now he wished he had. "I didn't want to seem like a stalker. I can take a hint."

"One I wasn't giving," she said.

He ran a hand over his head. He knew that now, but was it a little too late? "Wow." He really wasn't sure what else to say.

"Yeah" was all she said.

He stared across the dimly lit hut at her for a long moment as he decided what to do next. So he hadn't been wrong about their connection. She'd felt it, too. It was all just a misunderstanding. "And now we...work together."

"Technically, you're my boss."

Pained, uncertain and confused, he was desperate to take her in his arms and kiss her, erase the last three months of torture and pick up where they'd left off...but he couldn't read her. Was it too late? Had she built a wall up to keep him away since she thought he'd purposely hurt her? What did she want? He was more than willing to put the mistake behind them and move forward. He was ready to reopen himself up to the possibility of a relationship, but was it really even up to them anymore? Being boss and employee certainly changed things. "So...what now?"

She looked disappointed as she lowered her head. When she looked at him again, her expression matched his hopeless one. "I think there's only one thing we can do." She replaced the divider between them. "Get a good sleep, Nolan. We still need to win tomorrow."

CHAPTER FIVE

As DIFFICULT AS being around Nolan was before, it was even more excruciating now.

The guy hadn't ghosted her, he'd just copied her number down incorrectly. Unbelievable. Three months of suffering, second thoughts, doubts, resisting temptation to reach out, countless tubs of ice cream and more tears than she'd ever admit to were all the fault of a misunderstanding.

All night she'd tossed and turned in their uncomfortable shelter, fighting the urge to bring down the divider and snuggle up with him. She needed to talk to him. There was so much she wanted to say, but how could they move forward until they knew the answer to the biggest question of all—was an office relationship possible now?

That morning, Kendra knew Nolan hadn't slept either—he looked adorably sexy-sleepy as they ate a breakfast of wild berries he'd tracked down nearby. The same irresistible way he'd looked the morning after their night together when they'd reluctantly parted ways in the hotel lobby.

Her stomach flip-flopped when he glanced at her across the fire and gave her a small smile. She couldn't stop looking at him. Being angry had helped her resist him. What could she cling to now?

"Hi," he mouthed.

"Hi," she mouthed back.

Oh God, she was in trouble. Her boss had her heart.

"Good morning!" Mike said, approaching the group with that damn clipboard.

Kendra nodded in greeting. All around her, mumbles about it not in fact being a good morning made Mike smile as though he derived great pleasure from their suffering.

"Hope everyone slept well," he joked. "If you're wondering where your boss is, Roger and his partner tapped out around two a.m. and Cassie took them back to town. They are sleeping comfortably in a hotel room."

For real? This was bullshit. If Roger could quit, they should all be able to.

"So before we start the day—anyone else want to give up?" Mike asked as Cassie returned and joined them.

Yes! She desperately did. She was exhausted and hungry and dirty. She craved a comfortable bed and hot shower, but Nolan was sending her a look from across the fire that said they needed to stick it out... She couldn't decide if it was for his competitive spirit or another reason.

Either way, looked like she was staying.

"Great!" Mike said when no one bailed. "Well, today's first challenge is our orienteering race. Each team will be headed to the same finish line checkpoint, but taking different equal-distance, equal-challenge routes to get there." He walked around, handing out their maps.

Nolan stood and approached her as Mike came toward them.

"Either one of you good with a map?" the guide asked.

The day before she'd have lied and claimed to be an expert, but truthfully, she'd get lost driving to work if it weren't for her GPS, so she glanced at Nolan. Hopefully he was better at reading a map than he was at copying a phone number. "Not really," she said.

Nolan nodded. "Yeah, I can figure one out." He stood and accepted their map from Mike.

"Great. The race starts in five minutes."

Mike headed off to hand out the other maps and Kendra watched as Nolan studied the map. "You do know how to read that, right?"

He nodded, but when his eyes met hers, they were full of conflicted passion. "Though I wouldn't mind getting lost…"

Her heart raced. She no longer cared who was at fault for the torturous time apart. She just didn't want to waste even more time feeling miserable and hiding her feelings. The look in his eyes told her Nolan was feeling the same way.

"You two learning to communicate better?" Cassie asked, joining them with a conspiratorial wink.

Shit. The guides' hut was next to theirs. Had Cassie heard them talking the night before, or was their attraction to one another obvious?

Kendra's cheeks flushed as Nolan said, "Getting there."

Cassie smiled. "There's nothing that unplugging in the wild outdoors can't fix. Helps to give you a new perspective on things," she said, before heading to the front of the group. "Okay, everyone—on your marks, get set, go!"

Nolan turned to her. "Ready?"

"Sure. Lead the way," Kendra said, falling into step behind him as he took the path indicated on their map.

What should she say? Did they even need to discuss things again? It was clear where they both stood, where their hearts were, but how could they make things work now?

Luckily, once they were out of earshot of the other groups, he spoke first. "So… I guess three months was enough time to move on…forget about our connection, huh?"

Was he asking her or letting her know? "I don't know," she said carefully, not wanting to reveal all her cards if he wasn't. "I mean, it was a long time ago and I thought you just weren't interested."

"I was... Still am." He stopped on the trail and grabbed her hand, pulling her closer. "Are you?" His questioning gaze only made her more conflicted.

She was, but... "Does it matter now?"

"Of course it matters." He stepped closer and took her face between his hands. "Since saying goodbye to you in Seattle, you were constantly on my mind. I was going crazy trying to figure out what had gone wrong. I thought for sure we'd had something special."

"Me, too," she whispered. "But now things are complicated."

He nodded. "But not impossible, right?"

She sighed. "I don't know." What could they do? Hide their relationship from everyone at work? A secret office romance might be exciting for a while, but eventually they'd need to tell everyone or it would get more frustrating than exciting.

"That's not a complete shutdown, so I'll take it." He stepped toward her, his expression intense. "Maybe this might help for clarity," he said, tipping her chin upward to face him.

Her mind reeled. She wanted him to kiss her, give her all the answers, but she was falling hard and fast for him, the three months apart only amplifying and confirming her feelings.

She swallowed hard and said, "We're not going to win the challenge if we don't get moving."

"Yeah, I'm starting to not care so much about the challenges," he said, before kissing her.

His mouth was warm and inviting. The gesture was soft, tentative, unsure at first, but quickly deepened with the familiarity and longing of two people who'd been missing each other. His hand cupped the back of her head as his tongue slid between her lips, desperate and hungry for her. His fingers tangled in her messy hair and she moaned against his mouth.

She wrapped her arms around his neck, pressing her body into his, closing her eyes and savoring the taste of him. Even dirty, sweaty and wearing yesterday's clothes, he was sexy as hell. She clung to him, never wanting to let go.

He pulled away slowly, scanning her face for any sign of remorse. "Is it okay that I did that?"

Breathless, she couldn't decide. Maybe it wasn't okay but it sure was amazing. "I don't know," she said. "Try it again."

He did and, an hour and a half later, long after everyone else, the two of them reached the finish line checkpoint blissfully in last place.

INCREDIBLE HOW TWENTY-FOUR hours could change so much. A conversation and a few kisses had certainly helped, as well. Nolan couldn't keep the smile off his face or his eyes off Kendra as they gathered around the campsite to get the instructions for their next challenge. At that point, Nolan felt like he could conquer anything, and he was desperate to figure out a way they could make things work.

"Next up is our final challenge," Cassie told the group. "The isolation challenge. This one is by far the hardest—it will test you mentally as you take on the wilderness alone without your cell phone or anything to keep you busy... Completely alone with just your thoughts."

He frowned. Alone? "You mean alone with our partners, right?" That wouldn't be a challenge at all. He could think of ways to pass the time with Kendra. Was looking forward to it, actually.

"Unfortunately not. This one is a solitary challenge," Cassie said.

"But we're supposed to work as a team," Kendra said.

His heart soared, knowing she, too, had been looking forward to being isolated with him for hours.

"Your points system will still depend on how well you both individually complete the challenge," Mike explained.

Damn it. Looked like he wouldn't get that alone time with her after all.

"Let's get everyone numbered off. We'll stagger everyone at different places in the forest, just slightly off the trail, about half a mile from camp." Mike made his way around the group, showing no signs of guilt as he split up Nolan and Kendra. "Ones follow me, twos follow Cassie. After we lead everyone to their respective stations, Cassie and I will return to base camp. If you can't outlast the full challenge, you can forfeit and make your way back to us. When your six hours are up, we'll come get everyone and bring you back to camp."

Nolan looked at Kendra as she followed Cassie and the others off into the woods to their isolation points. Her look of disappointment made his heart feel just a little bit better.

At his own location a little later, Nolan forced himself to relax. He had to sit there for six hours. Six hours without a phone, anything to read, anything to do… *Just be present with nature and tap into a different part of yourself,* Mike had said.

He could do this.

But fifty burpees, fifty push-ups and fifty crunches later, he realized physical exercise after no sleep and barely any food was not a great idea. His stomach rumbled and he felt light-headed.

Nolan lay on his back on a grassy patch of ground and closed his eyes. A nap would pass the time quicker.

Unfortunately, only images of Kendra appeared behind his closed lids, and the thoughts running through his mind and emotions running through his body prevented anything even close to sleep from taking over.

Her kisses earlier that day had confirmed that the connection between them was still very real and very much alive.

But what would it mean to move forward with her now?

He was excited about this new opportunity at Webber Pharmaceuticals, but if his new career meant not being with her, would it really make him happy?

He'd always known what he'd wanted out of his professional life, but until Kendra, his love life had never felt certain. He'd never had feelings like this for anyone.

But he knew that no matter what it meant, he'd find a way to make this work…even if he had to sacrifice his dream job.

DUSK WAS STARTING to settle over the forest and thick clouds made the sky gray and overcast. The large mountain range around them was now a breathtaking-yet-ominous-looking dark image in the distance. The air smelled like rain was coming and the breeze picked up, blowing Kendra's hair across her face.

Kendra wasn't exactly loving being out in the middle of the woods alone. After almost six excruciatingly long hours, she understood why this challenge was the hardest. In a world where technology and social media consumed so much time and attention, it was almost impossible to figure out what to do without those crutches to help pass the time.

Her short nap had been filled with images of Nolan and, now awake, she was struggling with an unsettled feeling in the pit of her stomach.

In such a short period of time, she'd gone from being disappointed and heartbroken to relieved and hopeful…but still just as conflicted.

Maybe they could talk to Roger, let him know what was happening between them, explain that they'd met and connected before Nolan had accepted the job there. See if there was some way company policy wouldn't stand in the way of a relationship. She didn't love the fact that Nolan was her boss, but she cared about him enough to get over it…eventually.

The sky above her opened and big raindrops fell, drenching her hair and clothing within minutes. She huddled under a large tree, hugging her knees to her chest and hoping there wouldn't be a thunder and lightning storm.

It was almost over.

It would be easy to give up at this point. She was hungry and tired and soaked to the bone, but she knew if she could make it through this challenge, maybe the strength and clarity she needed to follow her heart awaited her on the other side.

CHAPTER SIX

ALL THE OTHER teams had quit.

Arriving back at base camp with Mike, Nolan wasn't completely shocked to discover that he and Kendra were the last team standing.

Which meant they'd won.

Nolan watched Kendra approach camp behind Cassie, soaked and looking as exhausted as he felt. Pride surged through him. He hadn't doubted her ability to stick it out, not for a second. It had actually kept him going. He didn't want to disappoint her.

"So, guys, what's it going to be?" Mike asked, standing near the fire that was almost out due to the torrential downpour that had now given way to a light rainfall. "Are we heading back to town?"

Nolan hesitated, glancing at Kendra. She was shivering and he fought hard to resist wrapping his arms around her. Damn, he just kept falling harder and harder for her. Her drive and spirit were attractive as fuck and her no-quit attitude only made him want to work harder, achieve more. He knew what he wanted to do that evening—stay out there with her. Finish this with her, or maybe start over with her…but he'd call it if that was what she wanted to do.

Instead, she shook her head. "No…nope," she said with chattering teeth. "We've made it this far. I want to finish the weekend."

Cassie shot them a knowing look. "Okay, then, let's see if you make it through the night."

She and Mike disappeared into their debris hut and suddenly the woods around them felt quiet and intimate. The only sound was Nolan's thumping heart as he looked at the woman he was in love with. "Should we get some sleep?"

"Sleep? Probably not, but we should definitely get inside the hut," she said, the look in her eyes reflecting exactly how he felt.

HER WET CLOTHES clinging to her body, Kendra shivered as she climbed into the shelter. The cool evening air had chilled her to the bone, and she wasn't sure she'd ever get warm again.

Nolan worked quickly to make a new fire outside their hut and then he joined her inside. "Can I take this down?" he asked from his side of the divider.

Her heart and mind were in conflict.

Their kiss had definitely revealed that things were still as hot as ever between them, and her attraction to him hadn't faded at all. But they still hadn't discussed what being together meant, or what they'd both be willing to risk. Was the chance at being together worth one of them losing their job?

"Kendra?" he asked.

She took a deep breath and removed the divider between them.

His arms were instantly wrapped around her and immediately she felt warmer. "Is this okay?" he asked, kissing the top of her head.

She nodded eagerly, moving as close to him as she could.

"Man, this survival training is no joke. Sure you don't want to call it quits? We already won…"

She shook her head. "No w-way…" she said through chattering teeth. "I refuse to give up this close to the end."

In truth, as much as the situation sucked, she also didn't want to call an end to the weekend.

She wasn't sure where they went from here. Right now his arms were around her—if only for body heat—and she never wanted that to end.

"You're so competitive," he said, hugging her even tighter.

She nodded, allowing him to believe that was her only motivation for staying.

"Truthfully, I'd have packed it in with the rest of them, but I don't want to leave you," he said. He wiped damp pieces of hair away from her face and kissed her softly.

Her body tingled and a warmness flowed through her. Maybe that was the key…maybe a make-out session would help to warm them up and distract them from the long night ahead.

They were on survival training after all. They were expected to do whatever was necessary to stay alive.

"You know, I hear body heat works best when two people are naked," Nolan murmured. "Just throwing it out there."

They were so much alike, so in sync it was almost scary.

She moved away from him, lifted her shirt over her head and tossed it aside. "Then I guess we should get naked."

The intense attraction in Nolan's eyes made her pulse pound even harder as she removed the rest of her clothing and watched him do the same. Tanned skin, muscular chest and shoulders and abs…he was so hot.

He lay on the moss bed and his eyes scanned her body. "I have missed this view," he said, his voice slightly gruff.

Yep. Definitely not as cold anymore. Damn, he was sexy. She knew she couldn't have him right now the way she desperately wanted him…but there was no question that once this was over, they needed to find a way to be together.

He opened his arms to her and she lay next to him and

snuggled close. He was so warm and his body was unbelievable. She tangled her legs with his and rested her head on his chest, breathing him in. He smelled of summer rain and the outdoors, and when she placed a soft kiss on his chest, she tasted the salt on his skin. It didn't matter that they were both wet from the rain and hadn't showered in days—being so close together was all that mattered.

This weekend had challenged her in so many ways, but right now it all felt worth it.

He held her tight, stroking his fingers gently over her body, but there was still a hint of hesitation in his voice as he asked, "You sure about this?"

Honestly? "No. But I'll worry about that later," she said, reaching up to pull his head down to hers.

For that night, she would do what she had to do…in the name of survival.

A ROUND OF applause from their coworkers greeted them early the next day as they entered The Drunk Tank—a favorite local watering hole owned by Cassie's boyfriend on Main Street. It was just before noon. Kendra and Nolan packed it in at sunrise and showered and changed into their other clothing at the shower facilities near their campsite before returning to town.

The only team to "survive" the weekend, they were the official winners.

But Nolan had his heart set on another prize—one he was determined to figure out how to win. He'd lost the chance of something real with Kendra once before because of a misunderstanding, he didn't want to lose it again. There had to be a way to make this work.

Could he really have the career *and* the woman of his dreams?

Torn between handing in his resignation or convincing

Kendra that a secret relationship could be kind of fun, he took a seat next to her at a table reserved for their group in the bar.

His hand rested on the wooden bench and immediately she privately slid hers into it.

Thank God they were still on the same page. But if they had to live in a debris hut in the woods forever just to be together, just so he could hold her, he'd be willing to do it.

Roger—who looked well rested after his weekend in the hotel—smiled at them as he stood. He raised his pint of beer and Nolan and Kendra joined him in the toast. "Congratulations to Kendra and Nolan for completing this weekend's survival training. You two have definitely proved that you are the competitors I've known you to be. Driven by success…"

More like driven by attraction for one another.

"This weekend only confirmed my initial feelings that you will make a great leader for the team, Nolan," Roger continued.

Nolan nodded in thanks, but he felt Kendra shift in the seat next to him. It was tough knowing this new opportunity could potentially mean that she wouldn't get one. Would she be okay with the dynamic between them?

"And Kendra—your competitive nature was never in question." He paused. "However, you surprised me."

Nolan glanced at her and saw her surprised expression as Roger continued.

"I wasn't sure how well you'd take to having someone else on the team who matched your drive and determination…"

"I'm not sure I'd say matched," she said under her breath, but there was a note of teasing in her voice and Nolan hid a grin.

"But you were able to defer to someone else when the

time came, and I think the two of you really complement one another."

If only his boss knew just how well.

"Therefore, I'm happy to announce that I'd love to offer you, Kendra, the other senior sales exec position. The two of you will be our new senior sales team," Roger concluded.

The others clapped. Nolan's relief had to be written all over his face.

Kendra sputtered and coughed on her drink next to him. "I'm sorry, what?"

Roger smiled. "Did you honestly not expect to get the promotion after all the success you've had all year?"

"Well..." Obviously she had.

"I wanted to see how well you two could work together, and this weekend your combined competitive spirit knocked my expectations out of the park. You'll both lead your own team of reps, but essentially you'll work together to reach the company's sales targets," Roger said.

"Thank you, Roger. I'm very pleased to accept!" Kendra said.

"Everyone, this is your new senior sales team."

Another round of applause and everyone drank.

Kendra smiled as she turned toward him and whispered, "So, colleagues...that changes things." The sparkle in her dark brown eyes had his pulse racing.

"That's not as complicated," he said, squeezing her hand.

Her smile faded slightly. "Yeah...but what if things don't work out between us? It will be awkward working together."

"No more awkward than having to fight these feelings for you every single day," he said quietly, staring at her apprehensive expression. "Deep, real feelings." He knew he was falling for her. He had, the moment he'd seen her in Seattle. And now he'd be able to prove it to her.

Her smile was bright and hopeful as she said teasingly, "So maybe you'll call now?"

He shook his head and laughed. "And maybe you'll give me the right phone number this time?"

* * * * *

Get 4 FREE REWARDS!

We'll send you 2 FREE Books plus 2 FREE Mystery Gifts.

Both the **Romance** and **Suspense** collections feature compelling novels written by many of today's bestselling authors.